# FOR THE SHOW

All for Love: Book 2

KATIE VAN BRUNT

Copyright © 2025 by Katie Van Brunt

All rights reserved.

No part of this book may be reproduced in any form or by any electronic or mechanical means, including information storage and retrieval systems, without written permission from the author, except for the use of brief quotations in a book review.

This is a work of fiction. Any names, characters, organizations, events, or incidents are products of the author's imagination and used in a fictitious manner. Any resemblance to actual people or events is purely coincidental or fictional.

No generative artificial intelligence (AI) was used in the writing of this work.

Cover Design & Illustrations by Lauren Gnapi at Elemental Opal LLC

Editing by Beth at VB Edits

Proofreading by Brooklyn Marie at Brazen Hearts Author Services

ASIN: B0DKL1BSN4

ISBN: 979-8-89660-905-6

katievanbrunt.com

*To anyone who has ever felt uncomfortable in their body and wanted to crawl out of their skin, you're beautiful just the way you are. (It's okay if you don't believe me. I'll believe enough for the both of us.)*

*To those who round up half-star reviews. I wish you a lifetime supply of forehead kisses and orgasms.*

# Author's Note

I had a blast writing Ezra and Millie, and I hope you have just as much fun reading.

For the Show is an open-door romance intended for mature audiences. The characters are consenting adults, and there is explicit, on-page sexual content, explicit language, and adult situations. Not eighteen? Please come back later!

If you're someone who never reads the epilogue or bonus scenes, trust me—you don't want to miss out.

Please note that there are multiple ways to experience real-life events and I have done my best, alongside sensitivity readers, to do it justice. Though you may not relate, it doesn't make it untrue.

Your mental health matters to me. For a full list of trigger and content warnings, please visit: www.katievanbrunt.com

For the Show is the second book in the All For Love series, but can be read on its own.

# FOR THE Show

an
All For Love
novel

## KATIE VAN BRUNT

# Playlist

Available on Spotify

- **Numb Little Bug** by Em Beihold
- **Disgusted** by Song House, Wé Ani
- **RAIN** by Ben Platt
- **Harleys in Hawaii** by Katy Perry
- **The Man** by Taylor Swift
- **Stay With Me** by Sam Smith
- **Bed Chem** by Sabrina Carpenter
- **Just the Way You Are** by Bruno Mars
- **Cool for the Summer** by Demi Lovato
- **What Makes You Beautiful** from One Direction
- **Unwritten** by Natasha Bedingfield
- **Go Crazy** by Leslie Odom Jr.
- **Man! I Feel Like A Woman!** by Shania Twain
- **(You Make Me Feel Like) A Natural Woman** by Aretha Franklin
- **Untitled (How Does It Feel)** by D'Angelo

- **Summer Baby** by Jonas Brothers
- **Shape of You** by Ed Sheeran
- **Whatta Man** by Salt-N-Pepa, En Vogue
- **Green Light** by John Legend, André 3000
- **Naked in Manhattan** by Chappell Roan
- **Girlfriend** by Charlie Puth
- **While You Were Sleeping** by Laufey
- **Beyond** by Leon Bridges
- **Until I Found You** by Stephen Sanchez, Em Beihold
- **One Call Away** by Charlie Puth
- **mirrorball** by Taylor Swift
- **All That Really Matters** by ILLENIUM, Teddy Swims
- **Marry You** by Bruno Mars
- **Dreams** by The Cranberries
- **You're Still the One** by Teddy Swims

*Matilda:* You're very brave, Miss Honey.

*Miss Honey:* Not as brave as you.

*Matilda:* I thought grown-ups weren't afraid of anything.

*Miss Honey:* Quite the contrary. All grown-ups get scared, just like children.

# Chapter 1
## Millie

IF I WERE A VIBRATOR, I'd be *this* one.

"Aren't you going to put it back in the box?" the salesperson asks.

"Nobody puts Baby in a box." Winking, I carefully place the curved silicone vibrator directly into my purse. *Designed for internal A-spot stimulation?* Sold.

It's not until I get home that I discover it has eleven vibration speeds.

Unable to keep this beauty to myself, I FaceTime Joey. When my cousin spies the rose-gold disco ball on one end, she gasps. "That vibe is your doppelgänger. It's sparkly and complex, but it looks eager to please."

"You bitch." I throw my head back and cackle. "You're not wrong." When we've both calmed ourselves, I wipe the tears from my eyes and take in a cleansing breath. "Are you coming home soon? I washed your sheets."

"For someone who doesn't like to be domesticated, you sure enjoy doing laundry."

"Do not confuse liking clean things with domestication, darling." I preen, pulling my shoulders back.

Joey rolls her eyes, but there's no hiding her smile. "I'm just waiting for Cam to get out of the shower, then I'll head over."

Three hours later, she waltzes in the front door.

"That was one long shower," I call from my bedroom.

She plops herself onto my bed, cheeks flushed. "I doubt there's any hot water left on this side of Manhattan."

With a chuckle, I pull a plum sweater dress from my closet, then shuffle over to the floor-length mirror and hold it up to my body.

"Is that what you're wearing on your date with Sam?" she asks.

Sucking my lips in to keep myself from grinning, I nod. The date is a ruse, my alibi. While Joey thinks I'm out with Sam, I'll actually be setting up for a surprise party being held in her honor. Her boyfriend and I have been planning a private get-together to celebrate the publication of her debut novel.

By the way she's acting, she doesn't suspect a thing.

"That color looks amazing on you. It makes your green eyes pop."

"Thanks, boo," I reply, hanging it on the back of my door.

She sticks her lower lip out in a mock pout. "How come you got all the great features in the family while I'm stuck with these poop-brown eyes?"

"What are you talking about? I'd kill to have your thick, dark hair. And those eyebrows? You could stop traffic with those puppies."

She giggles. "You're right about that. Cam said they were one of the features that drew him in."

"Of course they were."

Joey scoots up to the top of my bed and makes herself

comfortable with my two hundred throw pillows. "How are things going with you and Sam, anyway?"

My chest pangs at the question, but I collapse onto the mattress and go with the truth. "Not much better than the last time we talked."

Early on, I wasn't sure Sam was into me. Then she was *totally* into me. Then she wasn't so sure. I backed off and let things cool down for a while, but when she flew out to Vegas to see me on tour in *Funny Girl*, I couldn't help but read into it.

"I thought things would come together now that I'm back in the city, but she's been distant lately, and I don't know what to make of it."

Joey loops an arm around me and kisses the top of my head. "Hopefully your date tonight will give you clarity."

My chest tightens at the sincerity in her tone. "Since when are you the one doing the comforting in this relationship?"

"You must have rubbed off on me."

Not so long ago, she wasn't sure about committing to Cam. But she's come so far since then.

"I'm proud of you, Jo."

When she pulls me in for a real hug, her stomach growls.

"Want me to make something to eat?" I ask.

We burst into laughter because cooking is not my forte. Nor is it Joey's. Unless Bagel Bites and Pillsbury cinnamon rolls count.

"Bubbe's Nosh Pit?"

I fling my hand out, smacking her in the stomach. "Gimme my phone."

Thirty minutes later, the owner of our favorite Jewish deli—who also happens to live in our building—hand delivers our takeout.

"I'm sure going to miss you," Mark cries for the umpteenth time this week.

Joey hugs the teddy bear of a man. "You act like I'm dying. I'm just moving."

"Can't Cam move in here?" he teases.

*Right.* This is a one-bedroom, and our landlord has been generous enough to let Joey live here without a sublease. I doubt we could convince him to add one more, even if we had the space. And I really don't want to be the third wheel in their lovefest.

"All right, I'm starving," I announce, breaking up their sappy moment.

While we eat, Joey and I veg out on the sofa, which doubles as her bed, and listen to my latest audio recording before I submit it to LULU.

For the last few years, I've worked as a voice actor for *Let Ur Love Unleash*, an erotic stories audio app. Working for the female-owned company means I can record from home—or anywhere, really—and the hours are flexible. It's ideal when I'm touring in a musical production. Plus, it's like getting free sex advice. The things I've learned while recording would make my grandmother Ruth blush from her grave. *May her memory be a blessing.*

I click submit, then close the lid of my laptop. "If you and Cam can't find a place right away, you can stay here while I'm gone."

"When do you leave for rehearsals?" Joey asks.

"Next week. I head up to Syracuse right after Thanksgiving."

"I can't believe you landed the lead in *Mamma Mia*. You're a badass bitch."

I don't even try to fight the smile that spreads across my face. While I usually keep my strawberry-blond hair at shoulder length, I grew it out months prior to my audition and box-dyed it platinum the night before, which, in hindsight, could have been an epic disaster.

*For the Show*

The casting director was a real stickler about appearances and made everyone cover their tattoos. Thankfully, I only have a small cluster of birds on the back of my arm, just above my tricep. Joey has them too.

After cleaning up and getting dressed, I leave to meet Sam for a quick drink before I'm due to help set up for the surprise. As I head for the pub, I shoot Cam a message to let him know that the coast is clear. He's been texting me so incessantly that I had to silence my phone so Joey wouldn't ask questions.

"How've you been?" I ask Sam as I approach the booth she's chosen in the corner. I invited her to join us for the party, but she already had plans, so we agreed to meet beforehand instead.

She stands to greet me, planting a chaste kiss on one cheek. "Busy."

"Yeah?"

Two drinks with cherry garnishes sit on the table. I don't like when people assume my drink order. In fact, it's a pet peeve of mine. Some nights, I want the strong buzz of a gin and tonic; others, I want the comfort of a full-bodied cab.

I swallow back my annoyance and focus on Sam. "What's going on?"

Her cropped blond hair really makes her brown eyes shine. Tonight, she's wearing a killer black corset top that lifts her small tits deliciously. A black leather skirt hugs her hips, and her toned legs are covered by tights and ankle boots. With a shrug, she slips back into her seat. "Not much. Just working a lot."

This girl gives me whiplash. For the last six months, it's been nothing but ups and downs with her. When I met her last spring at FrenchSHEs, the drag and cabaret club where I occasionally bartend, she was super flirty with me. I discovered quickly that she's flirty with everyone, so I didn't think much of it. Then, once she found out I'm bi, she'd come in with question after question for me. *How did you know you were bi? How many girls have you been with?*

It wasn't until I crashed at her apartment for a week while my building was undergoing structural repairs that she admitted she'd never been with a woman but had a crush on me. I almost never let girls "test drive" me, but she was so damn endearing and, well, *hot,* so I asked if she wanted to kiss me.

"That was your first girl-on-girl kiss?" I gasp when we finally break away. *That kiss felt seasoned. It was kneaded and smooth and moist, like baking bread. (Or what I imagine baking bread would be like; I wouldn't actually know.)*

*That kiss felt like it was made* on purpose.

*She studies my face, her eyes alight, like she's found the missing puzzle piece that's been hidden under the sofa for years. She looks like she never wants to stop kissing me. Like she wants to* devour *me. Eat the entire loaf.*

*So she does. I follow her lead, which rapidly turns into ripping each other's clothes off.*

*With my back against the pillows on her bed, she insists on going down on me first. But once she's settled between my legs, she hesitates, her brow furrowed.* "I thought, you know, because I have the same parts, I would know what to do, but..." *She buries her face in my thigh adorably.*

*I sit up and pull her on top of me, kissing the tip of her nose.* "It's a lot like putting makeup on someone else, huh?"

"Exactly." *She giggles.*

"We can slow down." *I give her an easy smile, hoping to take away some of her discomfort.*

*Rather than back off, she slips right back down until she's between my legs again.* "No. I don't want to. Will you talk me through it?"

*Though Sam's movements are tentative, she takes my instructions with humility, and soon, she finds her own technique, letting my moans guide her. And when she slides a third delicate finger inside me and curls it just so, I lose it.*

We were inseparable for months after that. After I left for rehearsals for *Funny Girl*, we talked often, so when I returned to the city, I expected to pick up where we left off. Instead, I've found that sometimes she's available and eager to hang out, and other times she's aloof and ghosty.

Now, tucked into this corner booth, I'm not sure where we're headed.

After one drink, Sam's much more relaxed, and when she slides her hand onto my leg and leaves it there for more than a beat, I take it as an opportunity to touch her back.

"Where've you been?" I ask, mindlessly twisting the rings on her fingers. Her usually short nails are long and manicured.

"What do you mean?" When she shifts in her seat, I can't help but peek at the apex of her thighs, but black tights block what I really want to see.

"You seem distant," I say as our server brings Sam another dirty Shirley. "You didn't answer my texts about getting together last week."

She takes another swig of her drink, nearly sucking it dry. "Oh, gosh, I'm so sorry. Life has been so busy. My mom was in town."

"She was? I would have loved to have met her." Moms love me.

Head lowered, she says, "Yeah, but I'm not out to my family yet."

"Oh?" I could have sworn she planned to tell them a while back. "Maybe someday soon, then." I shrug. The last thing I want is to push her. I understand how hard it is to have one foot out of the closet, and I'd never want to rush anyone's coming-out process.

"Totally." She grabs me by the inner thigh and pulls me in

close. "When do you leave for your show? Let's do something before. Maybe get out of the city? Think your brother will let us use one of his cabins?" Her breath skates across my neck, and she nips at my ear. "I got a new toy."

Chills erupt beneath my dress. "Yeah? How is it?"

"Dunno," she whispers. "I was saving it for you."

Now my goose bumps have goose bumps.

"You're so generous." I steal a kiss, testing to see if she's into it.

Why is it so hard to tell whether this girl is into me? I never have that problem with guys.

Her mouth covers mine hungrily, and the chatter in my head is forced to shut up. She tastes like cherries. It's a real Katy Perry cliché, but it's true. When she pulls back a fraction of an inch, I trace the soft fullness of her lips with my tongue.

She releases a moan only I can hear before recapturing my lips and demanding more.

The alarm on my phone goes off, reminding me I have other obligations, and we finally break apart. Sam insists on paying, and with one more kiss laced with the kind of passion that should be illegal, she promises to call me tomorrow.

# Chapter 2
## Ezra

"Did you take your meds, hun?"

"Yes, Mom." I have no doubt my eye roll can be heard across the country. "Stop being so codependent."

"You're my favorite child," she says from where she's stationed in front of the stove. "It's my duty to worry."

"I'm your *only* child. And a grown man. I can remember to take my happy pills."

"I don't know why you insist on calling them that. You know you don't have to be happy all the time, right? It's okay to feel down, just not..." She trails off, no doubt remembering just how low I was not long ago.

Exhaling, I round the island so I'm at her side. Grasping her by the backs of her arms, I force her to lock eyes with me. "The medicine is working, and I'm seeing that therapist you recommended. I'm doing really well. I promise."

With a pat to my cheek, she turns back to the stove. "Good. Now help me with breakfast, then get out of here."

"Why are you kicking me out so fast? Got a hot date or something?" I tease.

My mom sighs dramatically, puffing air into her hair. The bright white color is so different from the dark hair I inherited from my father. She went gray in her thirties but has never dyed it. She has no interest in abiding by patriarchal pressures.

"Yes," she chirps. "Your new daddy will be here any minute. And he's about your age, so it'll be super awkward if you're still here."

Stomach lurching, I go ramrod straight. "What the—"

She bursts into laughter, bracing her hands on her knees and wheezing.

"You little sh—"

"Shh. Don't curse in front of your mother." She waves an oven mitt at me. "You should have seen your face."

Shoulders relaxing, I lean a hip against the counter. "Not funny." Even as I tell her this, I can't help the smirk that escapes.

"It's nine a.m.," she says, handing me a plate. "Of course I don't have a hot date."

"But you're not denying *dating*." I scan her face for answers. "Are you dating someone?"

Her silence speaks loud and clear.

"*Mom.*"

"What, Ezra? Do you seriously want to hear about your mother's sex life?"

Slamming my eyes shut, I cup my hands over my ears. "I didn't say anything about sex. I'm talking about dating."

"Oh, what's the difference these days?"

Cringing, I grab my overnight bag from where I dropped it by the front door and sling it over my shoulder. "That's it, I'm out of here." I try to stay overnight once a month. It's always been just the two of us, and it's sort of a tradition.

As I grasp the doorknob, she calls out. "Sit."

With a huff, I let the bag fall down my arm. Then I shuffle back to the kitchen island.

*For the Show*

"You will stay and have breakfast with your mother." She smiles.

"Only if you promise to cool it with the sex talk."

My mom may be progressive, but a guy's still got his limits.

"Speaking of *dating*... Are you still seeing that young lady?"

A groan escapes me before I can stop it. "I thought we weren't talking about sex."

"Who said anything about sex?" Her smirk stretches into a full-on mischievous grin.

I roll my eyes at the ridiculous woman. Didn't she just say *dating* and *having sex* are one and the same? *They're not.* It's possible to have sex with someone without committing to dating. Which is often the case with me. I have terrible luck with women, and after what happened last year—when I discovered the woman I was seeing and had invested a lot of effort in was sleeping with me behind her husband's back—I took a break from dating.

I'll never forget the look on the poor schmuck's face when he walked in on me balls deep inside his wife. She told me they were divorcing. It made sense. The walls were bare, and the house was littered with moving boxes. It turns out they were *moving in* and definitely *not* divorcing, though that may have changed since I hightailed it out of there with my pants around my ankles.

The worst part was that she had a baby. For weeks, I couldn't stop thinking about it. Especially since I have firsthand knowledge of what it's like to be the child of a cheating parent.

When she was young, my mom and her friend Valerie, burned out from college and looking for a change of pace, relocated to Oahu. They supported themselves with random freelance jobs while earning their cosmetology licenses. My mother met my father at a party and got pregnant. They moved in together and started a life, but when she was nine months pregnant, she discovered he was sleeping with other women. Without the support of family—and with a newborn—she tried to make things work with him. However, when the verbal and emotional abuse began around the time I started walking, she bought a one-way ticket back to New York City.

My father never missed a child support payment, and though he never traveled to Brooklyn, I visited him every other year. Those were confusing times. I couldn't tell whether he enjoyed having me around. He'd show me off to his friends and brag about my academic and athletic accolades, but he'd practically ignore me around the house. I was thirteen when he started dragging me to bars and using me as a pawn to pick up women. He "taught" me how to make a woman feel like the center of the universe before discarding her like garbage the next day. "Charm your way in, then charge your way out," he'd say.

I didn't stay long after breakfast, mainly because I couldn't tell whether my mom was actually joking about having a date. She's never been married. Likely because of the damage my father inflicted on her.

She raised me to believe that a woman doesn't need a man—something she's proven time and again my whole life. Even so, I can't help but want a marriage of my own, a person to share the highs and the lows of life with. More and more, though, I worry it'll never happen. My track record is embarrassingly pathetic. I keep falling for women who either screw me over or are just looking for a fling.

The commute from Brooklyn to Washington Heights, where my roommate, Cam, and I live, is an easy one this morning. Thank goodness, because he's wound up like a tightly twisted knot. He texted me three times while I was on the train to make sure I wouldn't be late for the surprise party he's throwing for his girlfriend tonight.

He has been my best buddy since high school, when we were thrown together for a mentor program. I was a senior and Cam was a freshman, so I took the newbie under my wing and never looked back. He moved in with me a year or so ago, after he quit his job and broke up with his then girlfriend. The guy is a romantic, and he fell head over heels for Joey fast. Now the two of them are looking for an apartment. Even though I'm used to having my own space, I like living with someone. It'll be too quiet without him around.

I greet my doorman, then take the elevator up to my apartment, where I find Cam pacing back and forth in his bedroom.

"There you are. It's about damn time," he huffs.

"Dude." I lean against his doorframe. "You okay? What can I do to help?"

His eyes are wide and his hair is a mess, like he's been running his fingers through it. "You don't think Joey suspects anything, do you?"

"Absolutely not." I shake my head. From what I can tell, she doesn't have the slightest idea anything is happening tonight. "It's going to be great. We've got lots of time to kill. Let's go play some pickup."

It takes some convincing, but eventually, he agrees. There's an outdoor court around the corner from our apartment, so we head that way and get in a few games. The endorphins help, and when we return a couple of hours later, he's like a new man.

After he makes me swear that I won't be late to the Black Hole, the coffee shop where the party is being held, he leaves to take care of last-minute arrangements.

When my phone chirps, I swipe it from the counter, and at the name on the screen, my chest tightens with anticipation. It's a text from the girl I'm seeing. I like her a lot, and for the first time in a long time, I think I can see a future with someone. I invited her to the celebration this evening, but she was worried it would be too weird to meet my friends for the first time at a private event. Instead, she promises to meet me at the Black Hole after so we can go out for a nightcap.

Though she's spent the night a couple of times when Cam's been away on business, I mainly stay at her place. Early on, I asked if she was hiding a husband in a closet in her tiny one-bedroom loft. She laughed like I was joking. I wasn't.

I fire off a text to confirm a meetup time, then head out the door.

I'd ask Cam and Joey to join us for celebratory drinks, but I have no doubt that Millie will be at the party, too, and if I invite Joey, it would be rude not to invite her cousin-slash-best friend, and that is not happening.

Millie and I met at a bar on the island of Crete in Greece, where we had a lengthy debate about karaoke before she mesmerized me with her outstanding performance. I must have made an impression with my own, because later that night, she dragged me into a closet labeled *Staff Only* for a hot-as-hell hookup.

We got together once more that week, but the electric current coursing between us fizzled prematurely. The second I mentioned meeting up when we returned to the city, she pulled back.

Initially, Joey did the same to Cam, but he eventually wore her down with his charm, and she couldn't stay away.

I didn't try with Millie. I respected her wishes and parted ways. Tonight will be the first time I've seen her since.

*Is she seeing anyone?* I shake off the thought. It doesn't matter now, anyway.

# Chapter 3
## Millie

It's chilly tonight, though not as cold as I expected it to be this close to Thanksgiving. When I step into the Black Hole, I'm greeted by Aunt Elin, Joey's mom, who immediately pulls me into a hug.

Her warmth and happiness soak into me as she rocks me from side to side. "Amelia, sweetheart."

She's a few months sober and looks the best she has since my Uncle Noah died thirteen years ago. When planning this surprise for my cousin, Cam and I agreed that a dry function—offering mocktails, coffee, and tea only—was the best way to go.

"Oh my gosh, hi. I'm so glad you could make it."

Aunt Elin flew in this afternoon from California and came straight to the coffee shop so she wouldn't ruin the surprise for her daughter.

"I wouldn't miss Josefine's book launch for the world. Such a shame your folks couldn't make it. Your mom said they caught the flu from Asher and Bea?"

I mirror her frown. Not only are my brother and his daughter unable to make it, but now that my parents are sick as well, I'm the sole member of my family here supporting Joey. "Yeah, they're super bummed."

I promised I'd help Mark and his wife lay out the food they've so generously catered, so I introduce my aunt to my next-door neighbors, Peg and Fran, who have been surrogate mothers to Joey and me, then I take off, ready to help set up.

A gold banner that reads *I did it... for the plot* falls from one side, and I scurry over to tack it back to the wall. I hoist myself onto a wooden chair and crouch to grab the end of the banner. As I straighten, my balance falters, but just before I go down, a strong hand steadies the outside of my thigh.

"Careful," the deep voice warns.

My breath catches, and I pivot on the ball of my foot so I can face my savior. It's a terrible idea, spinning around like this, because the sturdy fingers have now shifted dangerously close to the *inside* of my thigh.

The man hovering below me pulls his tan hand back like I've shocked him.

"Oh, you. Um, hi," I stutter. Though I should have expected to see him here, I'm startled by our reunion.

Ezra may be Cam's closest friend, but he's also the man I hooked up with in Greece several months ago and haven't spoken to since. After two ridiculously hot encounters, the guy was giving off major family-man vibes, and that's just not my thing. I'm looking for a family *woman*, to be honest. Though I love a pretty cock, I've always imagined myself marrying a woman. Not that I'll be ready for that anytime soon. I'm only twenty-seven.

It wasn't my intention to avoid him when we returned to the city—I just didn't go out of my way to see him. As busy as I've been, it's been ridiculously easy to *not* bump into him. For months I've had my hands full, traveling with the theater, voice acting, hanging out with Sam, and bartending at the club.

For a moment, I give myself permission to reexamine the man

with eyes like melted chocolate. *And a man he is.* His dark, unruly curls are pulled back into a bun, and his beard is perfectly groomed, as always.

I accept his hand and follow the line of corded veins that peeks out from the black button-down he's got rolled to his elbow. "Thanks," I croak. "How are you?"

He crosses his arms over his chest, making it a challenge not to take in the definition there as well. "Really good. And you? It's been a while."

If there's more to that statement, I can't tell.

"Really good, yeah. Thanks."

Oh god, this is the lamest reintroduction ever. He'd have more success talking to a monkey.

I clear my throat and put in a little more effort. "What have you been up to?"

He scratches his beard, instantly throwing me back to the feeling of it against my neck.

"Work keeps me busy."

"Teacher, right?" I vaguely remember him telling me how much he loves the youth. I could practically taste the "settling down" vibes oozing from his pores as he went on about his job.

"Yes. I teach middle school social studies. And you? Joey mentioned you're in a show?"

"I am. *Was*," I fumble. This man is so damn handsome, it hurts to look at him. "I was in a production, and I'm getting ready for rehearsals for another one, actually."

His brows lift, along with one side of his mouth. "Love to hear it." He sounds genuine too.

As I search for another appropriate topic to keep the conversation from turning awkward, my breasts buzz, startling me. With a quiet gasp, I yank my phone from my bra—this damn dress doesn't have pockets (Big mistake. Big. *Huge.*)—catching the way Ezra's eyes widen, then quickly flit away.

The text from Cam is a single random emoji—our signal that they're on their way.

"Oh shit." I shuffle to the center of the room and announce to the crowd that we have about ten minutes before Joey arrives.

Without hesitation, every person here gets to work with the final tasks we need to complete. The blinds are closed, which means that she won't be able to see us from the sidewalk. The barista, Iris, fiddles with the music on the speakers, Aunt Elin straightens the food platters, and Peg and Fran pass out Sharpies and copies of my cousin's book. Cam's family and Joey's writing buddies are here too. I can't wait to see the look on her face when she walks through the door. She'll appear mortified, though secretly, she'll be ecstatic.

I stand guard, watching for them, and when I spot them at the end of the block, I wave my hands in the air. "Shh. Shh. Everyone, it's go time."

Legs crossed, I will my bladder to get her shit together. Anticipation always makes me have to pee. As a kid, the only way I could play hide-and-seek was if I hid in the bathroom.

When Cam swings the door open and we all shout "surprise!" Joey's instinct is to spin around and bury her head in his chest. After a moment, though, he twists her around, and we all take turns hugging her.

I couldn't be prouder of my best friend. She did the damn thing. She wrote a motherfucking book.

The party is off to a great start, and when it looks like all the guests are enjoying themselves, I grab myself another mocktail and take a moment to breathe. From my spot against the wall, I survey the crowd, taking it all in.

Cam's sister, Claire, is deep in conversation with Ezra, their familiarity making me wonder if they're an item. When he shoves her in the shoulder in the playful way my brother does to me, I decide that's probably not the case. Though I can't help but wonder if they've ever hooked up. Not that it's any of my business.

Several folks give speeches, including me, each of us gushing about how proud we are of Joey for going after her dreams. And when Aunt Elin dotes on her only child, there's not a dry eye in the room.

I'm moderating Peg and Fran's heated debate over their favorite Campbell's soup flavor when I spot my aunt tearing up halfway across the room. Concerned, I follow her line of sight and—"Oh my god."

"What?" Ezra sidles up next to me. "What's wrong?"

Heart pounding, I turn to him, then back again. "Did you—did you know?"

"Know what?" he asks, searching for what I'm homing in on.

"Did he just—*ahh!*" I rush over to Joey, who's wrapped up tight in her mom's arms, and Cam, who's hovering a step away. I punch him in the bicep. "Jerk. Why didn't you tell me?"

With a squeal, Joey embraces me.

As she breaks away, I snag her left hand and bring it up to my face.

"Holy shit."

Resting on my cousin's hand is the most stunning engagement ring.

I can barely see her through the tears in my eyes as I enthusiastically yank her in for another hug.

She's speechless and sobbing into my neck.

No words are needed between us. I know her as well as I know myself. For her, the emotions of this moment are overpowering in all the best ways.

Stepping away so others can offer their congratulations, I help Mark switch out the appetizers for dessert. I'm reeling as I work. My cousin is *engaged*. She has never been one to dream about marriage the way little girls stereotypically do, but by her endearing smile and the elation radiating off her, it's clear that she's thrilled.

A double surprise party. Wow, what a night it's turning out to be.

I'm grabbing a black-and-white cookie from the spread on the table when I overhear my aunt speaking to Ezra. "Are you seeing anyone?"

Intrigued, I pretend to be engrossed in the desserts and keep my ear open for his response.

"I am," he replies.

"Is she here?"

"No," he says. "She thought it would be awkward since she hasn't met my friends yet." In my periphery, he pauses to look at his watch. "But she's meeting me here in a bit before we head out for the night."

"Oh, Millie, there you are." My aunt waves me over to join them as I move down the dessert table. "What about you, hun? Are you still seeing that young lady? Joey mentioned she's dying to meet her."

Ezra's eyes go wide. I'm not sure whether it's because he's surprised I'm seeing someone or because that person is a *woman*. It's possible he doesn't know I'm bi. My sexuality hasn't been a secret for about a decade, but I'm not in the habit of introducing myself as bi. Straight people don't have to "come out" every time they date someone new, so why do queer people?

"I am," I say, because drinks with Sam earlier went really well.

"That's wonderful." Aunt Elin rubs my shoulder. "I'm happy for you."

Ezra catches my eye and smiles warmly. When my aunt yawns, I offer to call her an Uber so she can head back to her hotel, and several minutes later, Joey and I hug her goodbye. I let

## For the Show

go of the door once she's stepped out, but when it doesn't snick shut, I turn, assuming she's stepped back in.

Instead, the third surprise of the night appears.

"Sam?"

I don't have time to decipher the odd look on her face before Ezra pulls her in for a hug and presses a kiss to her cheek.

My stomach sinks. *What the hell?*

"Hey, babe," he sings.

*Babe?* With that, my stomach plummets straight to the floor.

Her astonished face says it all, but in the next heartbeat, the deer-in-the-headlights look shifts to one fitting of a doting girlfriend. Damn. I'm the trained actress, but I may have some competition here.

Completely oblivious, Ezra turns to me. "Millie, this is Samantha, my girlfriend."

Sam—er, *Samantha*—flinches, though Ezra doesn't notice.

"Samantha, this is Millie, Joey's cousin."

The urge to shed my skin like a snake is almost impossible to ignore. Never have I been so humiliated. And there's literally nothing I can do about it. Not here. We're celebrating my best friend's biggest accomplishment. I absolutely cannot make a scene. So I do what I've been doing most of my life—I pretend.

While a handshake feels like overkill, I force a smile and politely offer a "nice to meet you."

Convincing enough.

Ezra guides Sam by her lower back to the newly engaged couple, where introductions are made.

We're gathered in a circle later—Sam included—when Joey nudges my side. "What's with you?"

Guess I'm not so convincing, after all.

"Nothing." I force a smile, praying she's distracted enough not to see right through me.

"Cam and I are going to head out soon, have a little private celebration of our own." She waggles those money-making brows.

"Go," I tell her, grin still in place. "I've got cleanup duty."

"Oh, shoot. I didn't even think about that." A frown mars her face for the first time tonight. "We can stick around to help."

"Don't be ridiculous," Ezra pipes in. "There's no way you're cleaning up after your own party. We'll hang back and help. Right, babe?" He turns to Sam.

Great.

Shortly after Cam and Joey leave, the remaining guests follow. I'd sneak out the door along with them if I hadn't promised Iris I'd lock up for her. She's been at the café for over twelve hours; I couldn't possibly let her stay a minute longer.

*And then there were three.*

The tension in here is so thick I couldn't cut it with a jackhammer if I tried. I haven't yet decided what bothers me more. The discovery that Sam is a lying little cheater or finding out that she's been cheating on me with a man I once hooked up with.

My stomach twists in a painful knot. This is so fucked up.

As I go through the motions of cleaning, I pray silently that I can make it out of here unscathed. But when I accidentally stare—or maybe it's a glare?—at Sam across the table for a little too long, Ezra notices.

Clearing his throat, he frowns at me. "Am I missing something here? Why do I feel weird energy radiating from you?"

I quickly look away, though I realize there's no reason to play this off. Now that Cam and Joey have left and their night has gone off without a hitch, I don't have to be polite.

"Why don't you ask Sam?"

"Sam?" His voice pitches in confusion, making it clear he doesn't know her by that name. "Samantha?"

Good thing she's already handling the trash can. The girl

looks like she's about to vomit. "Uh, I, um..." She doesn't have the ovaries to woman up and own her shit.

As mad as I am, Ezra's furrowed brows inject a serum of empathy into my veins, so I tread lightly. "I'm sorry, but your girlfriend hasn't been honest with you."

Eyes widening, he homes in on Sam. "What is she talking about?"

When she averts her gaze rather than owning up, he turns back to me, his face etched in confusion.

"God, this is awkward," I sigh. I tug on the collar of my dress, which feels way too tight and scratchy all of a sudden. "We're both dating Sam. Or Samantha."

"The fuck?" He steps back, swiping a hand down his beard, and whirls on Sam. "Is that true?"

Finally, she looks up, this time with tears welling in her eyes, and nods.

Rage flares to life under my skin. Oh, hell no. She doesn't get to play victim.

"Why—what—why would you..." He trails off.

Poor guy looks broken, and it's too painful to watch. I almost wish I'd kept my mouth shut. But he deserves to know what kind of woman he's with.

I set the trays I've been wiping off on the counter and straighten, chin lifted. "I'd like to know why too."

Sam sweeps her fingers through her short strands, the move making her look a lot like Kristen Stewart. Now that I've discovered she's a two-timer, her sexiness has melted away.

She takes a step forward, creating an equilateral triangle between the three of us. "Millie, I really have had fun these last several months."

"*Several?*" Ezra staggers back a step.

"But I, uh, you know I've been confused about my sexuality,

and I thought dating both a man and a woman would help me figure out what I really wanted."

"So, what, we were some sort of experiment to you?" I seethe. "Play with Ken and Barbie and see which you like best?" My vision goes red around the edges. I'm not just upset with Sam, I'm furious with myself. I should have seen this coming. Clearly, I was blinded by fresh pussy.

"No, it's not like that. I—"

"That's exactly what it seems like," Ezra interjects. He drops his head and laces his fingers at the back of his neck. "I'm such a fucking idiot."

My heart pangs for him. Why is he an idiot? He didn't do anything wrong.

"I should go." Sam heads for the door.

"You think?" Ezra barks, not even watching her walk away.

I take a step toward him, but when he whips his head around and narrows his eyes on me, I stop. "Don't," he says so quietly I nearly miss it.

"I'm so sor—" I snap my mouth shut before I can apologize. I'm not in the wrong here. If only there were an alternative version of "I'm sorry" that fit this type of situation appropriately. A moment where I'm not in the wrong, yet I still want to offer sympathy.

"Just—" He stops short, takes one look at me with the saddest fucking expression on his face, and strides out the door, leaving me alone.

# Chapter 4
# *Ezra*
## Six Months Later

> **MOM**
> Are you sure you're ready?

> **ME**
> It's one date. I'll be fine

> **MOM**
> It just seems too soon. I'm worried about you

> **ME**
> Mom, it's been six months. I promise I'm good

I CAN'T REALLY BLAME her for worrying about me, I suppose. It may have been six months since my girlfriend screwed me over, but it's only been three months since I haven't felt depressed. Finding out the girl I was dating was *also* dating a girl I'd hooked up with in the past really fucked me up. Like kick-started a full-on depression. The second bout in a year. Before that, I hadn't experienced an episode in a solid decade. I hadn't felt that awful since I visited my father for the last time.

Agitated, I yank my shirt off, cursing the tag that's irritating my neck. My sensory issues have really ramped up these last few months. Though my depression is under control, I've yet to rein in these sensations. Reactively, I rip the tag off, and when I put a hole in the seam, I let out a string of curses. I toss it onto the floor and throw on another.

I have an hour until I meet... uh, what's her name again? Ronnie? Robyn? I open the dating app on my phone. Robyn, but goes by Ronnie. Got it.

In front of the mirror, I take a moment to breathe deeply, evenly. These days, I once again recognize the face staring back at me. After finding out the truth about Sam, I flew out of the Black Hole and stumbled back to my apartment where I took kitchen shears to my hair. It was a terrible mistake. I looked like the before picture of a dog in an animal shelter. I thought that if I shaved my beard, I'd look better; instead, I could have been mistaken for one of those starved animals in a Sarah McLachlan commercial.

That night, I felt unclean. I'd been used and was hit with a visceral urge to shed myself. In that state of mind, chopping off my hair seemed like the only way to make that happen.

In reality, what I needed was a dosage change and a therapy session ASAP. At the time, though, I wasn't thinking clearly. Instead, I called in sick that Monday. Then again on Tuesday. When I called on Wednesday, my boss urged me to take the rest of the week off.

By Thursday, Cam, who'd been unable to break through the haze I'd gotten lost in, had called my mother.

Even then, no amount of matzo ball soup could flush the sad feelings out of me.

My dad was the first person to show me I wasn't worthy.

While my mom couldn't live with—or even near—the man, she never kept me from having a relationship with him. It pained her to watch me fight for his approval, but she never tried to tell me how to feel, and I was grateful for that. She was always there when he let me down, and she never judged me.

Lennon—the woman who told me she was separated from her husband—was the next person to show me how unimportant I was.

And the third was Samantha. Or Sam. Or whoever the fuck she is.

This time around, my mom let me wallow for a few days, then dragged my ass to therapy. It wasn't my first rodeo, so I knew I'd have to talk if I wanted to improve.

"Why am I not good enough?" Tears roll down my stubbled cheeks as I plead with my therapist. "Why, when I'm screwed over by someone, does my brain say 'maybe we should be depressed'? I'm so sick and tired of feeling sick and tired. I wish I had more control."

Monty didn't "cure" me that day like I begged him to, but therapy twice a week for a month kept me accountable for making good choices in my life.

"When you do good, you feel good. Continue doing the things you would normally do when you aren't depressed, and I promise your brain will catch up."

My mom added to that sentiment later by reminding me that I'd overcome my depression before, so there was no reason I couldn't do it again.

Taking care of myself was the last thing I wanted to do, but both Monty and my mom were right. I had to push through, even if my brain felt like it was in quicksand.

With Monty's encouraging words written on a sticky note on my mirror as a reminder, I tap into the excitement I used to feel when getting ready for a first date and focus on the endless possibilities. Today could be the first day of the rest of my life. And if it's not? It'll make for a good story over drinks with friends. Either way, I'm feeling optimistic.

I still have a good half hour before I meet Ronnie, so I park myself on the sofa next to Cam. Though he moved out months ago, he's hanging out here while Joey visits with her cousin.

*Millie.* My chest tightens painfully at the thought of her. We haven't spoken since *that night*. Too stunned to think, I ran out on her at the Black Hole and didn't look back. I absolutely need to apologize but haven't had the opportunity. Shortly after the incident, she left to tour with the musical she was performing in. Then I was too depressed. Now I'm embarrassed about how much time I've let pass by.

"You ready?" Cam asks, setting his laptop on the coffee table in front of us.

"Not you too," I scoff. I do not need every person I know walking on eggshells around me. I'm fucking fine.

"Hey, no, I didn't mean it that way. I just wanted to know if you're excited."

Relieved that I don't have to defend myself again, I sag against the cushions. "Yeah." Though *excited* isn't the descriptor I'd used. I haven't so much as touched a woman since Samantha. My sex drive took a huge hit during this bout of depression.

So, naturally, I'm afraid of getting hurt again, of being lied to.

My father's voice worms its way into my brain. *You're just like me, son. Meant to be single.*

Before it can take root, I will the intrusive thought away. I don't want to be a lonely old bastard like him.

"I can cancel my date," I say to Cam. "I feel bad ditching your ass."

*For the Show*

"No, it's cool. That's on me for dropping by unannounced. I'm perfectly fine kicking up my feet. I've got a bunch of photos to edit for that resort in Italy."

As I'm finalizing my Uber reservation, a notification banner pops up on my screen.

*@islandboykane wants to send you a message*

Opening Instagram, I click on Requests and—

My heart lurches. "What the fuck?"

Cam scoots closer, peering over my shoulder. "What is it?"

I read the words again, shock and nausea battling for top billing.

*@islandboykane: hi. yea so this is random and weird, but is rob masters your dad? i found your name and picture in his house and i think you might be my brother.*

# Chapter 5
## Ezra

In a matter of minutes, I've canceled my date. People get scammed online all the time, but deep in my marrow, I feel it. This is real. I respond to *@islandboykane*—a.k.a. Kane Adams—right away, and within a minute, we switch to video.

A teen with a mop of blond hair pops up on the screen, and behind him, a wooden sea turtle hangs on the wall of the bedroom I would stay in when I visited my father as a kid.

"Uh, hi," he says, his expression etched with apprehension.

"Hey."

Silence.

My heart is racing and my mind is swirling too quickly to form coherent thoughts.

Cam knocks the side of my leg, urging me to carry on.

I inhale deeply and hold it for five counts before letting the breath out slowly. "I don't even know where to begin. How am I just now hearing about you? Rob never mentioned another kid."

"Probably because he didn't know about me." He scoffs. "And I didn't know about him either."

Bewildered, I blink at the kid. "*Okay?*"

Kane goes on to explain that his mother recently passed away from an aggressive form of cancer. Shortly before she died, she contacted Rob, and with a blood test, they confirmed paternity. Kane's mother, Wren, lost both her parents in a car accident when she was eighteen, which leaves my dad as the kid's next of kin.

I try holding back the tears in front of him, knowing this has got to be a difficult subject, but I can't help it. "How old are you?" I choke out.

"Fifteen."

"Fuck." *So young.* "Does Rob know you've contacted me?"

He heaves out a breath and shakes his head.

"How did he take the news when he found out about you?"

Kane curls his lips inward. "He was shocked, maybe?" He lifts one shoulder and lets it fall. "I don't know. He doesn't say much. It's weird, you know? And this is even weirder. Talking to you. I found some information about you in a drawer here and, I don't know, I thought maybe you'd want to meet me?" He gnaws on his lip, his attention dipping to his lap. "It's stupid. I'm sorry. I should go."

Heart lodged in my throat, I clutch my phone tighter. "Wait."

This kid has been through hell. First losing his mom and now living with a total stranger. That's got to be scary.

"I do."

Kane stares into the screen. I can't quite decipher the color of his irises, but his eyes glisten with hope.

"I do want to meet you. I-I'll figure it out. I'm a teacher, and summer break starts soon. I could come to Oahu then." This kid deserves to have someone in his life who'll show up for him. Lord knows my—*our*—father won't.

"Really?" He perks up, his face brightening.

"Really. Let me call Rob and sort some things out, then we can make plans, yeah?"

His jaw is clenched tight as he nods, like maybe he's holding back emotion the way I'm trying to.

"It was great meeting you, Kane. Hang in there, okay?"

"Yeah, okay." He blinks rapidly. "Thanks, Ezra."

After hanging up, I sit in silence for I don't know how long. Cam, being the kind of friend he's always been, sits quietly by my side.

Eventually I call my dad. According to him, Wren was a one-night stand years ago, and he doesn't even remember her. *Repulsive.*

"You know what it's like for bachelors like us. I could have a million kids running around this island for all I know." He laughs, the tone laced with a kind of pride that makes my stomach turn over.

"I'm nothing like you," I grit through clenched teeth.

"Oh yeah? You're single, aren't you? Approaching forty and free just like your old man."

Biting back a growl, I bolt up straight, my spine rigid. "I'm married now."

Clearly, I've lost my mind, but the word vomit doesn't even faze me. I couldn't care less about lying to my dad. I'd say just about anything to get him to shut the fuck up about how he thinks I'm just like him. Especially when the only things we have in common are our dark hair and our single status. We don't even share the same last name. I said I have a wife, so what? It's not like he follows me on social media or ever comes to New York. We barely talk; he'll forget all about this conversation in five minutes.

"Since when?" he asks.

"We eloped last month." The lie rolls off my tongue seamlessly. I'm fully committed to the act now. And completely ignoring the way Cam nudges my leg.

*For the Show*

From there, I quickly divert the conversation, mentioning that I want to meet Kane, and he drops the subject.

Just as I'm itching to end the call, sick of the sound of his voice, he says, "When you come this summer, bring that wife of yours, yeah? I want to meet her."

My heart sinks. *Shit.*

"I, uh—"

"Unless she doesn't exist?"

Dammit. The man is seriously calling my bluff?

"Remember that time you had an imaginary girlfriend?" He laughs down the line.

Irritation flares in my gut. "I was six."

"What about that chick in high school? I told you to bring her, and you never did."

"Dad." I huff. "There was no way her parents were going to let her hop on a plane to Hawaii with her seventeen-year-old boyfriend."

Fuck, the man doesn't have the first clue how to be a parent, clearly.

"It's okay. No need to lie. People like you and me don't need an ole ball and chain."

"I'm not—"

"We can teach your new brother how it's done."

I don't even bother to ask what he means by that. He's delusional if he thinks I'll let him bring a fifteen-year-old kid to a bar like he used to do with me. History will *not* repeat itself.

Refusing to add fuel to the fire, I take slow, deep breaths to regulate myself.

"Fine, I'll bring her."

After I've ended the call, Cam asks, "What the hell was that?"

My chest pinches painfully. "I panicked, man. I can't stand

the idea of him thinking I'm anything like him. It fucking pisses me off."

"But *a wife?*" His eyes bulge. "You couldn't have said girlfriend instead?"

"I told you, I panicked. You know he makes me lose it sometimes."

Sighing, he nods once. "What are you going to do?"

"Fuck if I know."

*Where am I going to find a wife?*

# Chapter 6
## Millie

"I wish you'd told me the tour ended early. I would have come home sooner," Joey says the instant she bursts into our apartment. *My* apartment, I suppose, now that she's been traveling—and writing another book—while her fiancé photographs some of the most elite destinations in the world.

I pull her in for a tight embrace, relishing the connection. "You were busy. It's no big deal."

"Why'd it end early anyway?" She kicks off her sandals by the door.

"Hey." I frown. "Are those my Birks?"

Joey scrunches her face. "No?"

"You thief." I laugh. "I've been looking for them everywhere."

Winking, she plops onto the sofa and tucks her feet under. "So... the show?"

Damn. I was hoping I could avoid this conversation. I should have known better. "Um." I gulp. The show *did* end early. Kinda. But I'm not ready to open up about the real reason I came home, so I say, "Something about the budget? I don't really know."

Though she eyes me a beat, she doesn't push. "I'm happy to see you. What have you been up to for the past month?"

I curl up next to her on the sofa. There's no way she hasn't noticed how much weight I've gained, even if I'm hiding beneath an oversized shirt. Why hasn't she said anything?

"I've been working for LULU a lot."

"What about FrenchSHEs?"

I shake my head. Since gaining all this weight, I've been too embarrassed to show my face there. I really miss karaoke nights, though. I've made enough putting in extra hours with LULU—and even dabbling in the audiobook industry recently—to keep myself afloat. Thank goodness my apartment is rent-controlled.

"Are you okay?"

With a sigh, I close my eyes for a long moment. I might as well get it over with. "How come you haven't asked about my weight?"

Brows furrowed, she tilts her head and studies my face. "Why would I ask about your weight?"

I look down at the dimples in my thick thighs. The new, albeit faint, stretch marks peeping out from my cutoffs. My curves stand out in stark contrast to her toned and petite frame. We used to share clothes. Clearly, that won't be happening any time soon.

"If you want to tell me about your body," she says, "that's your prerogative. I'm here to support you, no matter what." She squeezes my hand three times, our unspoken way to say "I love you."

I squeeze back four times—*I love you too*—and push back the tears. My cousin is so damn sweet.

Inhaling deeply, I ground myself. "The tour was so stressful, Jo. The director was an assho—really demanding. The castmates I lived with were big partiers. They'd be up late blasting music, and I could never get enough sleep. I wasn't eating well either. I

*For the Show*

didn't love the people I worked with and... it was so stressful." Tears crest my lashes, and though I wipe at them quickly, more fall behind them. "I don't even know how it got this bad. It just happened. I used food to cope, and now I can't get the weight off."

"Shh. It's okay." Joey hugs me.

I sob into her neck, and when she pulls back, I tug at the hem of my shirt to pull it away from my body. "I feel so stupid. And gross."

"Stop it. Don't talk about my best friend like that," she scolds.

"It's true," I whisper, forcing myself to maintain eye contact. "I don't even know who I am anymore. I don't recognize myself in the mirror. I don't know if I want to keep doing this."

Joey's eyes widen. "Doing what?"

"Performing."

"But that's your dream."

I sniffle, chest aching at the thought.

I've been performing for as long as I can remember. School plays, theater camp, vocal lessons, dance classes. I've dreamed of being on Broadway my entire life. I memorized every word of *Annie* by the time I was five.

"It was fun in the beginning, but I don't know. There's so much pressure and..." I trail off. That's all she needs to know.

She gives me a sympathetic smile. "So what's next?"

"To be honest, I think I'm going to take a break from acting for a bit. Live theater, at least. I love working for LULU, and if I visit Asher this summer, I can bring my equipment and work from there."

"Uh." She cringes. "Do you really think it's a good idea to record erotic stories at your brother's house? And around his daughter?"

"Fair point." I laugh, a hint of lightness threading through me.

"That would be humiliating. But there are other cabins on the property. I could have my own space."

My brother owns a retreat center on a lake that doubles as a summer camp for families an hour and a half north of Manhattan.

"Ugh," I groan. "What I really need is a fucking vacation."

Joey's phone rings, interrupting my mini meltdown.

She eyes me, worrying her lip. "It's Cam."

Lord, that man cannot go two hours without her.

With a wave of my hand, I scoff. "Answer it."

"Hey, babe," she sings. "Yeah, she's right here. Why?" Nose scrunched, she eyes me. "Cam wants to know if we're doing anything tonight."

I shrug. I'm too emotionally exhausted to make any kind of decision about my life, even if it's nothing more than dinner plans.

"We're free," she says into the phone. "What's up?"

For a moment, she's silent. Cam is speaking quickly, but I can't make out his words.

Joey's jaw drops, and she blinks at me. "Wait, slow down. He found out what?"

He? Who? And what has he discovered?

"Damn, that's wild. Is he okay?"

I'm at the edge of my seat. Literally. I haven't the slightest idea what's happening on the other end of that line, and I'm itching for the details.

"Okay, but what does that have to do with Millie?" More murmuring from Cam. Then my cousin turns and looks me dead in the eye. "How badly do you want that vacation?"

# Chapter 7
## Millie

"Josefine Noa Beckham, why the hell would you tell Cameron I'd come to dinner when Ezra will be there too?" I shoot off the couch and into my room, where I throw myself onto the bed. Yes, I'm being dramatic. I am an actor, after all.

My cousin follows me into my bedroom. "What's the big deal?"

"The big deal?" I flop over onto my back. "Jo, I haven't seen him since your engagement."

"So?" She fists her hands on her hips, looming over me.

Pain lances my chest as I cover my face with both hands. "I was skinny then. Like NYC Pilates-toned skinny. And now I'm... this."

"Oh, Millie." Voice gentle, she sits on the bed next to me. "I can't pretend to know how you feel, but you still look hot as fuck. And you've got to know that your worth has nothing to do with your clothing size."

"I know," I sigh. But emotionally...

"Listen." She shakes my shoulder. "Thick thighs are in. Just look at Reneé Rapp."

I can't help but laugh. Joey knows she's my celebrity crush. The amusement fades quickly, though.

"What about the shit that went down with Sam? We were dating the same freaking girl. Don't you think that's weird?" With a groan, I throw my arm over my face. "Why do I even need to come to dinner?"

"You need to hear that from him in person."

Interest piqued, I heave myself up. "At least help me find something to wear."

Standing in the doorway of my walk-in closet, I scan my inventory. It might as well be a pop-up shop for Zara—I have jeans in every size under the sun.

Joey snags a cream-colored strappy top from the rack as I pick out a pair of ripped black skinny jeans, and once she shuffles out to the living room so I can change, I pull the top over my head. It only takes an instant to realize it's too small. *Dammit*. Rather than trying to force it over my breasts, I retrace my steps to take it off. Only, as I do, it gets stuck.

*Fuck.* This is a sensory nightmare.

My mouth is covered by the fabric, causing a sense of panic to wash over me. Tight spaces like elevators or the subway during rush hour don't bother me, but getting caught in my clothes sends my heart racing. It's why I must sleep naked.

"*Joey,*" I call, my voice pitchy and trembling. "Help me."

"Just breathe," she says when she approaches me, her tone calm. "Don't move. I've got this."

I'm surprised she isn't laughing like she did the time I begged her to cut me out of a shirt in a changing room when we were teenagers. I swore I'd be suffocated by polyester that day.

After what feels like an hour—though is probably closer to a minute—I'm freed from the shirt and am panting for air.

"You good?" she asks.

"Fuck." I double over, my hands on my knees. "I hate when that happens."

Cursing the shirt, I settle on a flowy black V-neck instead.

"Damn." Joey's eyes are glued to my chest. "I hope this isn't offensive, but your new boobs are a huge perk. Pun intended."

"You're right. My tits are a fucking smoke show now." Laughing, I give them a squeeze for emphasis.

Once I'm fully dressed, she insists on curling my hair, so I let her pamper me.

An hour later, with spiked boots sharp enough to kill a man, we climb into an Uber.

At the restaurant, Ezra's eyes scorch my body the instant I step through the door. Heat creeps up my neck as I force my shoulders back and keep my chin high. I'm so self-conscious right now.

When we approach the table, Cam tugs me into a tight hug, shaking me back and forth with so much vigor I feel like a bobblehead.

When he releases me, Ezra steps forward.

The sight of him up close makes my knees wobble. He's also in ripped black jeans, accompanied by a fitted white tee. His beard is trimmed nicely, and his unruly curls rest just above his shoulders. He looks... different.

"Millie." It's quick, but he looks me up and down, probably assessing how much I've changed too.

"Ezra." I nod.

"You look—"

"Can I get you drinks to start off?" A petite young woman appears beside the table.

Thank god too. Whatever he was about to say regarding my looks, he can shove it up his stupidly tattooed ass. Yeah, I might have been intoxicated when we hooked up in Greece, but I remember that infamous peach well, along with the inked *Your Name* at the top of one cheek. Apparently he got it right after high school so that when he was with a girl, he could say "I got *your name* tattooed on my ass."

I should have thrown him out of my hotel room right that instant for being so corny, but the way he told the story strangely endeared him to me. Don't we all do stupid shit when we're eighteen? He has to live with that tattoo for the rest of his life, so I'd say the guy has suffered enough.

The server sets four glasses of water on the table, then stands obnoxiously close to Ezra as she waits for our beverage order. She's hot and moody-looking (totally my type), but I can't peel my eyes from the man sitting across from me.

"A round of tequila shots," he orders, head tipped back.

"Actually, I'll have a vodka tonic with lime." I zero in on him. "I hate when people order my drink."

"Noted." With a thick swallow, he props his elbows on the table and cracks his knuckles.

Why does he look so nervous?

"So, Millie, any cool auditions lately?" Cam asks.

Before I can answer, there's a *thunk* under the table, and he frowns at Joey.

"Can we just cut to the chase?" Picking up my glass, I lock eyes with Ezra. "What are we doing here?"

"Fine." He pulls his hair into a knot with an elastic tie, looking anywhere but at me, then lets out a sigh so big his whole body deflates. "I need you to be my wife."

I choke on the sip of water I've just taken and spit it onto the table. "Come again?" I scramble for a napkin and dab my lips. "They must have put crack in this, because I could have sworn you asked me to be your wife. No, wait. There was no proposal. It was more of a demand. What the fuck?"

Joey lays a hand on my forearm, steadying me.

"Shit," Ezra says, pulling at the front of his shirt like he's fanning himself. "That's not what I meant to say. I got nervous."

The confident man I met a year ago is sweating now, so I give him the benefit of the doubt and remain silent so he can explain.

"I just found out that I have a brother."

Eyes narrowed, I glance at Cam, but he's staring at his buddy.

"He didn't know that my father is also his father until recently. His mom died and, well, my dad, Rob, is the only family he has now. And me, I guess."

My heart pangs at the thought of a kid losing his mom. "Oh, I'm so sorry." Lips pressed together, I study him. "But what's that have to do with—"

"My dad's a dick," he interrupts. "He cheated on my mom when she was pregnant."

There's no stopping my grimace.

"Yeah. Kane—that's my, uh, brother—found me on Instagram. We got to talking, and he wants to meet me."

I turn to my cousin, then back to Ezra. "*Okay*. Again, what does that have to do with me?"

He takes a swig of his drink, his eyes darting back and forth. "I may have let it slip to Rob that I'm married now."

"I'm still not following."

"My whole life, my dad has tried to convince me that I'm just like him. But he's a misogynistic, cheating womanizer and I..." He huffs, falling against the back of his seat, his brows furrowed. "I'm nothing like him. But he continues to make comments about me being a 'chronic bachelor' and how it's my 'destiny to be single' like him. I'm just so fucking sick of it."

"I'm so—"

"So." He cuts off my apology. "I panicked and told him I eloped last month. I figured it would get him to shut up and drop the topic. Instead, he asked me to bring *my wife* when I meet Kane this summer."

I nod slowly. His reason for lying makes sense, but—

Gasping, I slap a hand to my chest. Shit. I know exactly what's coming next.

"No." I shake my head. "No, no, no."

"Millie," Joey hedges. "You just said you need a vacation."

"I didn't mean like this." I push off the table, the chair screeching against the sticky floor, and turn to Cam and Joey. "I can't believe you set me up."

I'm out of the restaurant and striding down the city sidewalk faster than a bullet train. I'm halfway down the block, moving as quickly as my stilettos will allow, when I hear my name.

"Millie."

*Click-clack.*

Hands balled into fists and vision tunneled, I continue on.

*Click-clack.*

"Millie."

*Click-clack.*

"Amelia." Ezra darts in front of me, blocking the path.

I have no choice but to come to an abrupt halt. The sudden stop causes a pedestrian to bump into me, which, in turn, forces me to fall like a domino into Ezra's chest.

Hands splayed across his shirt, I steady myself. *Damn, his muscles are hard.*

"What?" Without making eye contact, I sidestep him.

He grasps my wrist and leads me under an awning. "Can we talk?"

"No, we can't fucking talk. Have you lost all good sense? I'm not going to be your wife."

"*Fake* wife."

Mouth agape, I stare at his stupidly handsome face. "Do you hear yourself right now?"

"Millie," he exhales. He's close enough that his breath causes the hair at my temples to flutter. "I wouldn't ask you if I wasn't desperate."

I glower at him. "Oh, that makes me feel *so* much better."

"That's not what I meant. *Ugh.* I'm fucking this up." He drags a hand down his face. "Please, can we go somewhere to talk, just the two of us?"

An exasperated groan escapes my lips. I really don't want to, but obviously, he's not going to give this up until I hear him out. Plus, my feet really hurt from hightailing it in these shoes.

"Fine."

"Would you mind coming back to my apartment?" Head lowered, he stuffs his hands into his pockets. "Only so it's quiet and you can say whatever the hell you want."

Lips pressed together, I harrumph. It's like he knows I need space to be dramatic.

Neither of us speaks the entire ride to his place, but when his doorman greets us, I'm forced to dig deep for genuine politeness. The second the elevator doors close, though, I'm back to stoic. There's no way he can convince me to follow through with this scheme of his.

"Do you want something to drink?" he asks, toeing off his shoes at the door.

I follow suit and hang my purse on a hook, then follow him to the left into the main living space. Only when I've parked myself on one of two leather captain's chairs do I respond. "Something strong."

While he moves into the kitchen, I observe the collage of pictures on the wall, all of which I assume Cam took.

Ezra returns with a glass tumbler filled with an amber liquid. One quick sniff confirms it's straight-up whiskey.

"Would you prefer something—"

"This is good, thanks." I take a swig, welcoming the burn in my chest, then quickly gulp down another before setting the glass on the table beside me.

He sinks into the sofa adjacent to me, and for a long moment, we're both silent.

"Look," he eventually says, "I realize this is a lot to ask—"

"No shit."

He eyes me, his jaw clenched.

"Sorry." I take another sip of my drink. "It's just that... the two of us have slept with the same person. Don't you think that's weird as fuck?"

With a long exhale, he leans back, knees wide in that manspreading position I secretly find so hot. He's got one arm draped across the top of the sofa and his other hand wrapped tightly around his whiskey, which he rests on his thick thigh. "It's not ideal."

A sardonic laugh escapes me. Honestly, our situation is ridiculous. "How did this even happen?"

"I met Samantha at karaoke night at—"

"FrenchSHEs?"

He dips his chin. "Mm-hmm. Cam and Joey dragged me there one night."

Head tilted, I consider his words. "Do you think there were others?"

"Honestly, I hadn't given it much thought."

"I feel like such a fool."

He angles forward and sets his drink on the table between us. "You're not a fool. I've had a lot of time to think about it and a whole hell of a lot of therapy. It was not my fault or yours. Sure, it's a little weird that we've slept with the same person, I'll give you that, but it's not like you and I haven't..."

My face heats, and not because of the whiskey.

"Listen," he continues. "We can't change any of that, and I'm willing to get past this whole Samantha thing if you are." His deep brown eyes penetrate mine.

What are the odds that in a city of over eight million people, the two of us have shared the same woman?

"Did you get tested?" I blurt.

He barks out a laugh. Probably at my word vomit. "Of course. You?"

I nod.

Another round of silence passes between us.

"You walked out on me, though," I say, picking at a loose thread, gaze averted. "That night. At the party. You left me there after Sam dropped the bomb."

"Fuck."

The single word, spoken with so much pain, snags my attention.

He dips his chin to his chest. "I know. I was in utter disbelief, and I'm not proud of the way I handled the situation." His eyes find mine. "I'm so sorry."

He pissed me off that night, abandoning me the way he did. But I was shocked, too, so I guess I can understand.

"So, about that crazy idea of yours..."

"Right." He scoots to the edge of the couch. "I realize it's a huge ask. But I can't show up at my dad's doorstep single. I just—I just can't."

My stomach twists at the emotion in his voice. My parents are practically perfect, the spitting image of support, so I can't imagine what it must feel like to grow up with a parent like Ezra's dad.

"All my life, he's told me I'm just like him. He acts like bachelorhood is some sort of club that gives men permission to be assholes. And I'm fucking sick of it. I don't expect you to understand, but I need this." He gazes down, like the words he's searching for are written on the floor beneath his feet, and eventually homes in on me again. "Has Cam ever mentioned my depression?"

Lips pressed in a straight line, I shake my head.

He clears his throat. "It's under control, and I'm on medication, but..."

My heart pinches inside my chest at his pained expression.

"That's why I never contacted you after *that night*. I was in a really dark..." He shakes his head. "For a long time, I wasn't myself. My breakup with Samantha brought up a lot of childhood trauma and other shit." He straightens again and picks up his glass. "The truth is, I worry that if I go to Hawaii, spending time with my dad will trigger my depression. If I show up alone and am forced to hear him compare us over and over, I'm afraid I'll eventually believe it."

Emotion clogging my throat, I croak, "Ezra..."

He holds up a hand, but there's nothing rude about it.

"Again, I don't expect you to understand, and I realize this is a huge ask, but—"

"Fine."

His eyes nearly bulge out of their sockets. "What?"

"I'll do it." I shrug, feigning nonchalance, despite the apprehension coursing through me. "How hard can it be? I am an actress, after all." I flip my hair over my shoulder for dramatic effect.

Across from me, he cracks a grin that makes my heart thump against my breastbone.

It feels good to make him smile. I may not always know the right things to say during intense moments like this one, but I'm pretty damn good at making people smile, so I focus on that for the time being.

# Chapter 8
## Millie

BESIDES NEEDING information from me to book our flight to Honolulu, Ezra and I haven't spoken in a month. I'm supposed to convince his family I'm his wife, yet I know very little about the man.

Okay, I *did* hook up with him, so "little" is not quite accurate. Even so, when it comes to him, all I know is that he's super competitive, he can sing the fuck out of a Freddie Mercury song, he has one tattoo (that I've seen), and he takes medication for depression. Oh, and, apparently, we have the same taste in women.

Other than that? I'm clueless.

When I'm hired for a role, I spend time researching the character—their motivations and what makes them tick. Even as my LULU persona, Jules, I'm given a small backstory to get into character.

Determined to change the situation, I swipe my phone off the kitchen counter and open our text thread.

> **ME**
> I think we should get to know each other better before Hawaii

I've finished my coffee by the time he texts back.

> **EZRA**
> What do you mean?

> **ME**
> I'm supposed to be your wife starting next week, but I don't know anything about you. How do you take your coffee? Do you even drink coffee? Do you snore? How did we meet?

> **ME**
> How did you propose?

> **ME**
> Do you have any weird quirks?

> **ME**
> Kinks?

> **EZRA**
> Why don't you come over for breakfast tomorrow? We can talk then

> **ME**
> Fine. What should I bring?

> **EZRA**
> Nothing. I'll cook

> **ME**
> *Can* you cook? See, these are things I need to know

> **EZRA**
> You can find out tomorrow
>
> Do you have any allergies?

> **ME**
> Look at you being a good hubby already

> **ME**
> Cashews

*For the Show*

EZRA
Got it. See you tomorrow, honey

ME
Honey?

EZRA
Yeah. It's your wife nickname

*Honey?* That's what he's chosen?

A memory pops into my mind unbidden. It's from a night at the bar in Greece when he thought he could do a better job at karaoke than me.

*Watch and learn how it's really done,* honey.

The nerve of that motherfucker. He'd pissed me off. Mostly because he *was* better than me.

ME
Hmm, we may need to work on it...

What's my nickname for you?

Pumpkin?

EZRA
No

ME
Sugar lips?

EZRA
Absolutely not

ME
Sweet cheeks?

EZRA
Try again

ME
Daddy?

When he doesn't reply right away, I worry he's ghosted me. But…

> ME
>
> OMG
>
> Did we find *the one*?

Three little dots appear, then disappear, only to dance on the screen again a few seconds later.

> EZRA
>
> You're a menace. See you tomorrow

---

The music playing in Ezra's apartment is so loud I can make out every word from the hall. It's a Frank Sinatra song, though Ol' Blue Eyes isn't the one singing. This voice is much more raspy. Ezra, maybe?

I knock and quickly adjust my bra straps beneath my white linen maxi dress while I wait. The bra is new, and so far, I hate it. What I'd give to take it off. *Free the nips* and all that jazz.

The door swings open, but instead of a very large man, I'm met by a middle-aged woman with white hair and hazel eyes.

"You must be my daughter-in-law."

My heart lurches right out of my chest. *Come again?*

"*Mom.*" Ezra flies around the corner, his beard dusted white. Either it's powdered sugar, or my fake husband is doing cocaine at ten a.m.

"Hi," I say as I'm ushered into the apartment by my, uh, *mother-in-law?*

*For the Show*

As I slide off my sandals, Ezra takes my purse and hangs it by the door.

A whiff of almond and orange passes in the air between us as he eyes me. "You look shocked. Didn't you get my text?"

Shaking my head, I pull my phone from my purse. Sure enough, I have an unread text.

> **EZRA**
> Sorry it's last minute, but my mom is here. I hope you don't mind, but she's staying for breakfast.

"She comes over once a month for breakfast, and I forgot to cancel." He frowns.

"It's okay," I reply, though I'm not sure it is. Typically, I'm great with moms, but in a circumstance like this? I don't have the first clue how to play things. "Does she know—"

"About your fake nuptials? Yes," she answers.

"Oh." Relief floods my system. I'd hate to lie to more people than necessary.

"I'm Dawn Miller, by the way." She envelops me in a hug. "You smell good."

"Thanks." I return the embrace, surprisingly comfortable in such close proximity to this woman. "I'm Millie."

"Nice to meet you, Millie." She pulls back. "Is that short for anything?"

"Amelia."

"Beautiful. Just like you." Her smile is bright, and she looks like she wants to pinch my cheeks the way a stereotypical Jewish mother would.

I love this woman already.

"Come, let's sit and get to know each other," she says.

I look over my shoulder to her son first. "Do you need any help?"

"I'm almost done here, but do you want to fix your coffee the way you like before you get settled?"

While Ezra fills a mug, I open the refrigerator and find only vanilla oat milk in the way of coffee additives. I suppose beggars can't be choosers, so I pull it out and turn. "Do you have sugar?"

With the glass jar he offers me in hand, I shake a generous amount into my mug, followed by the oat milk.

With an exaggerated gasp, he teases me. "Need any coffee to go with that sugar?"

"Oh, hush. I like my coffee sweet."

"That's not coffee, honey. That's a sugar rush in a cup."

I scowl. I never used to be self-conscious about my sweet coffee fix, but since my last director shamed me about my weight gain in front of the cast and demanded I cut back on calories, I've been acutely aware of it.

"Look at you two—a bickering old married couple already." Dawn leans into me, her lips quirked up on one side. "Don't let his comment get to you. This big guy's got a giant sweet tooth."

The way his mom calls him "big guy" makes me chuckle.

"She's right," he says. "But I don't drink coffee."

I rear back and slap a hand to my chest. "Excuse me, what? I think we need a divorce."

With a huff, he rolls his eyes. "*Ha ha.*"

"No, seriously. You're a teacher. How do you wake up so early, then have the energy to deal with children all day?"

"I prefer black tea."

"Oh, so you still have caffeine. Not a total psychopath. Got it." I grin over the top of my mug. "But wait. I've seen you drink coffee before. In Greece."

Tentatively, he studies me. "During my last depressive episode, I developed an aversion to it." He shrugs.

Dawn pours herself a cup of coffee with a splash of oat milk, then ushers me over to the table already set for three.

From my seat, I have the perfect view of Ezra when he slides on oven mitts and pulls a casserole dish from the oven. Instantly, the hints of orange and almond compound until the apartment is thick with the saccharine scent.

"It smells delicious. What is it?"

"French toast casserole. Made with challah bread." He sets the dish on a hot plate in the center of the table.

Color me impressed.

When the three of us are served, I'm the first to speak. "So, Dawn, are you cool with this thing we're doing?"

"You mean lying to my ex?" Her eyes light up. "Yes, darling, I'm more than okay with it. I wish my son would tell him to stick it where the Hawaiian sun don't shine, but I understand why he wants you there."

"And why is that?" I turn to Ezra. "Why *me*?"

The man beside me could have any woman in New York City, yet he's asked me.

"Because you're a talented actress."

A hint of something that feels like disappointment scratches at the back of my mind, but I ignore the sensation. "How would you know?"

He side-eyes his mom, then sheepishly lowers his focus to the table. "I may have seen you in action."

"What?"

His expression is earnest when he meets my eye. "When you were in *Mamma Mia*."

"You saw that?"

"We both did," Dawn pipes in. "You were fabulous. Absolutely fabulous."

I'm stunned into silence. And extremely flattered. Ezra's mom is delightful. "Thank you," I beam. "So, Dawn, what do I need to know about my husband?"

On my way home, I pop in my AirPods and call my parents, figuring I should give them a heads-up before I leave the continent.

"Amelia," my dad answers. "Can you switch to FaceTime? Bea wants to say hi."

I flip to video, and my newly four-year-old niece's chubby cheeks fill the screen.

"Hi." Gosh, I love her mousy little voice.

"Hi, Dolly," I say, using the nickname I gave her the day she was born. All swaddled up with a pink hat on her head, she looked just like the baby dolls I had growing up. "How are you? I miss you."

"Miss you," she squeaks. And with that, she drops the phone.

My mom comes into view then, wearing an indulgent smile. "She's off. You know how active she is. Never sits still."

"That's okay. How is she? Are you at Asher's?"

"Yes. Why don't you come up?"

"I wish I could, but I'm actually leaving for Hawaii."

"Hawaii?" My dad appears next to my mom, his brows lifted in question.

"Yeah," I sigh. "I need to get out of the city for a bit."

In unison, my parents nod.

"You deserve a break, sweetheart," Dad says. "We know how stressed you've been."

"Who are you going with?" Mom chimes in.

"Just a friend from work." It's not really a lie. This *is* work, even if I'm not getting paid for it.

If I tell them the "friend" is Ezra, they might try to talk me out of it. They know all about Sam and the fucked-up threesome (as opposed to the sexy variety).

Truthfully, if she had been genuine from the beginning and explained that she was exploring *and also* dating a man, I think I would have been okay with it. And the three of us together? That could have been a really fucking hot threesome. Not that I think Ezra is anywhere close to the nonmonogamous type. He's using me to prove to his dad that he's a one-woman man, after all. Though, to be fair, I'm not going to Hawaii against my will. While the circumstances are wild, this trip is coming at the perfect time. Showbiz is burning me out, and I desperately need a change of scenery. I'd be nuts to turn down a free trip to a tropical island in exchange for kissing an attractive man on the cheek a few times and holding hands.

"You still there?" my dad asks. "You're frozen."

"Still here. Can you hear me?"

"The connect... not... ood. Okay? We'll... late... have fun."

"Fun," Bea echoes in the background the instant before the call drops.

## Chapter 9

# Ezra

"Millie, where are you?" I whisper, praying she can hear me telepathically.

Our flight boards in half an hour, and while it's not international, it *is* off the continent, and I told her to be here two hours before our departure time. All my phone calls have gone straight to voicemail and my texts have gone unanswered.

I tug at the collar of my shirt, really wishing my deodorant wasn't at the bottom of my bag.

Seated at the gate for our flight to Honolulu, sweating like I'm in a sauna, knee bouncing, I can only imagine how suspicious I look. Oh god, did she change her mind? Is she not coming? What the fuck am I going to do if she doesn't show? If I arrive solo, I'll never hear the end of it from my dad.

I'm standing in front of my chair, scanning the long hallway of the terminal, when she finally appears. She's walking quickly, dodging families with strollers and nearly taking out a toddler with her rolling suitcase. In her other hand, she's holding a coffee and a phone charger.

"There you are."

"I'm so sorry." She tips her coffee back, then tosses the cup into a bin nearby.

"I told you to be here two hours before takeoff."

She huffs. "Yeah, that's ridiculous." Grumbling, she pulls her phone from her black leggings and plugs it into an outlet. "Who shows up two hours before a flight?"

I jab a thumb into my chest. "Me."

With a roll of her eyes, she waves dismissively. "My phone died on the way over, and I must have forgotten to pack my charger. Had to stop to buy a new one, so that's my bad."

I release a long exhale and shake off my agitation. No sense in giving her grief over it. She's here, and that's all that matters.

"Would Mr. Ezra Miller please come to gate twenty-four. Mr. Ezra Miller to gate twenty-four."

With a confused look, Millie unplugs her phone and lifts the handle of her suitcase. Then she trails behind me to the counter, where we're greeted by an older woman.

"Mr. and Mrs. Miller? It looks like you've been upgraded to first class." With a practiced smile, she hands Millie two tickets. "You will be boarding in a few minutes. Feel free to go ahead and get in line."

"First class? What for?" I ask.

The woman's face brightens. "Because it's your honeymoon, of course. Let's see that ring, sweetheart."

Millie pulls her hand back from the counter like it's burned her. "Oh, I uh—"

In a flash, I dig into my pocket. "She left them on the counter this morning," I announce, presenting a thin white-gold band and a matching ring with a circular diamond surrounded by smaller diamonds.

I don't know which sparkles more, the rock or Millie's eyes.

"Here, honey." I slide the rings onto her finger.

Thank goodness Joey gave me her ring size.

I turn to the woman behind the desk. "I guess she's not used to wearing them yet." Forcing a chuckle, I silently pray the woman doesn't see through our little facade and rescind the offer for the upgraded tickets.

Instead, she laughs along with me. "I remember those early days of marriage."

Millie's hand is frozen in midair, her attention fixed on her hand.

Interlacing my fingers with hers, I thank the woman. Then I lead my fake wife toward the front of the line.

It isn't until we reach the third aisle that I release her. When I do, I flex my fingers, already missing the way her hand fits in mine.

*Hmm, weird.*

We ended up on the same flight home from Greece last year, where I learned that Millie prefers the aisle seat over the window, so I slide in first. As I'm settling in, the elderly man who boarded behind us struggles to lift his carry-on into the overhead bin, so Millie offers assistance. When she raises her arms, her shirt lifts, and I'm gifted with a sliver of her perfectly creamy abdomen.

She catches me staring and immediately tugs on her shirt, then slides into her seat. *Okay.* It's becoming clear that my attention makes her uncomfortable; I'm not sure why—her new curves are incredible.

Turning to me, her lip caught between her teeth, she flashes her left hand between us. "These are fake, right?"

"Nope." I flash her my matching band.

"*What?*" she gasps. "I can't. No." She twists the rings with shaky fingers. "Obviously I'll give them back after all this."

"Yeah, that's fine," I say, my attention catching on a cuff around her wrist. "What's that?"

"Oh, a motion sickness band." She sighs. "I didn't use to get queasy on flights, but for some reason, I do now." As she plugs her

*For the Show*

phone into the complimentary outlet, it buzzes. "Look," she laughs, angling the screen in my direction.

> JOEY
> Enjoy first class, bitches 🥂

On the eleven-hour flight, we had more than enough time to solidify our story about how we met, got engaged, and ultimately eloped. And her long nap during the last part of the flight gave me ample opportunity to admire her. Her fair lashes fluttering, mouth ajar. Her beautiful chest rising and falling in a meditative rhythm.

With the six-hour time difference, it's eight p.m. in Honolulu when we land, but I'm wiped. Jet lag is the absolute worst; our sleep is going to be all sorts of fucked up tonight.

Valerie, my mom's oldest friend, picked us up from the airport and gives us a quick tour of the apartment above her garage, where we'll be staying for the next couple of weeks.

At the top of the landing, we abandon our suitcases so Val can show us around. On the covered lanai off the main living space, the ocean is visible, even in the dark. Behind the living room is a small kitchen with a table and four chairs off to the side. Beyond that is a bedroom and en suite bathroom with a shower and separate soaking tub.

"I'm sure you two are exhausted," Val says. "I'll leave you to it. I'm not working tomorrow, so when you're up and around, let me know, and I'll take you over to the car rental place."

"Thanks, Val."

"I'm just so glad to have you back. And happy to meet your wife." She winks.

After she lets herself out, I bring our luggage to the bedroom.

"One bed, huh?" Millie states when I find her standing in the middle of the space.

"Yup."

She angles to one side and peers through the doorway. "You're not gonna offer to sleep on the sofa?"

"Nope." I make a point to pop the *p* this time. "This isn't one of those romance books Joey loves so much. I'm not going back and forth with you on this. We're adults, and I'm far too old—and big—to sleep on the sofa. But if you'd feel more comfortable out there, be my guest."

"Fine." She leaves the room and returns a few seconds later, her arms loaded with throw pillows.

"What are you doing?"

With a grunt, she heaves them onto the bed. "They're for the pillow wall."

"What the fuck is a pillow wall?"

"A barrier. So don't try anything funny."

Amusement washes over me. "Honey, if I tried anything with you, you'd be too busy moaning to think it was funny."

Lowering her head, she clears her throat and busies herself with her suitcase. "We should probably force ourselves to stay up a bit, yeah? It'll help us adjust to the time zone."

"You're right." Following suit, I unpack my toiletries and stash them in the bathroom.

"Are you hungry?" I ask once we've unpacked and have wandered out to the kitchen.

"Not really." But she opens the fridge anyway and pulls out a container. "Look. Poke bowls."

I open the plastic lid and am instantly hit with the tangy aroma of ginger and green onions. The poke bowls in Manhattan are nothing like the kind here in Hawaii. "Val must have gone shopping. That was nice of her."

Millie opens drawers and cabinets, revealing a fully stocked kitchen. Val picked up fresh fruit and vegetables, as well as milk, juice, and bread. As I peruse the snacks, I spot a variety of nuts—

cashews included—so I toss those out immediately. We do *not* need a visit to the hospital.

After we've yawned at least a dozen times each, I suggest we call it a night.

"Check out the cuck chair," Millie says as we shuffle around the bedroom.

I nearly choke at the words coming out of her mouth. "Come again?"

She points to the upholstered chair in the corner of the room. "You know, the chair in por—"

"I know what a cuck chair is."

She raises a brow, her lips twitching.

"Not like that," I laugh.

"Well, it's officially the laundry chair now," she announces, tossing a sweatshirt onto it.

While she shuts herself in the bathroom, I climb under the covers and situate the damn pillow wall she's created.

"Hey," she says as she appears again. "Who says you get the left side of the bed?"

Frowning, I sit upright on the mattress. "What are you talking about? This is the right side."

She looks at me like I've just told her the Earth is flat.

"I'm in the bed, and I'm on the *right* side."

For a second, I catch her checking out my bare chest, but she gives her head a tiny shake and focuses on my face again. "That's not how you determine which side of the bed it is."

"Enlighten me." I wave a hand.

"If I'm looking at the bed," she says, hands on her hips at the foot of the mattress, "you're on the left side."

"Okay, but you sleep in a bed, so sides have to be determined once you're *in the bed*."

She lifts her chin, scoffing. "That makes absolutely no sense."

"*You* make absolutely no sense." I laugh out loud. This is

literally the most ridiculous debate I think I've ever been involved in—and that's saying a lot, since I teach middle school.

"Whatever." She rolls her eyes. "Agree to disagree. But do you mind if I have that side?"

It makes no difference to me which side I sleep on, so I scoot —to my left—at her request. Only the wall of pillows stops me. Clumsily, I shimmy beneath them, staying under the covers, then rearrange them once I'm settled. "Are you getting in?"

"Um, can you turn around?"

I sit up and grin. "Why? Do you turn into an ogre at night?"

"*Ha ha*, very funny. At least I don't look like one all the time."

With a mock gasp, I toss a pillow at her, which she easily dodges.

As she straightens, she sobers, her expression going pensive. "Actually, I, uh, kinda don't sleep in clothes, so I need you to face the other way."

Heart stuttering, I gape. "That makes two of us."

With a brow arched, she crosses her arms over her chest. "Excuse me? You can't sleep in the nude if I'm sleeping in the nude."

I match her stance, crossing my arms. "Why not?"

"Because..." She trails off, as if she doesn't have a valid reason. "This is absurd. Just put some clothes on."

"Why me? If you're so uncomfortable, then you should be the one to keep your clothes on."

"I can't sleep in pajamas. I have..." Eyes darting around the room, she worries her lip. "Sensory issues."

This time I swear my heart stumbles over itself. "That makes two of us. *Again*. Being restricted in clothes while I sleep is a nightmare."

"Me too," she whispers, her eyes widening. "Shit. This is awkward. What are we going to do?" She peers over her shoulder and out the open door, like she's considering sleeping on the sofa after all.

"We have this heavy-duty pillow thing. It'll be like we're sleeping in separate beds. It's fine."

Shoulders slumping, she sighs. "I guess you're right."

"What's that?"

"I guess you're—" Eyes narrowing, she picks up a pillow and throws it at my face. "Jerk." She breaks into a smirk and plugs her phone into its charger. Then she commands me to look away.

As the bed dips from her weight, I close my eyes, even though my back remains toward her. "Get some rest."

"Yeah, you too."

For several minutes, we're enveloped in the quiet of the night, the only sound the humming of the ceiling fan and the wind singing outside. Despite how exhausted I am, my mind races with thoughts of my dad and Kane.

"Hey, Millie?"

"Yeah?"

I swallow past the lump that's formed in my throat. "Thanks for coming."

"Good night, Ezra."

## Chapter 10

# Ezra

I find Millie on the lanai the next morning, barefoot and resting her elbows on the railing. Before she notices me, I steal an opportunity to ogle her plump ass, and when I finally join her, I'm met with a double rainbow arched over the ocean. The gorgeous sight hits me in the solar plexus, stealing the air from my lungs.

"Morning," I say once I've regained the ability to breathe.

Millie startles, sloshing hot coffee over the side of her mug and onto her hand. "Shit. Ouch." Shaking her hand out, she glares. "You scared me."

Teeth gritted, I drag her by the wrist into the kitchen and flip on the faucet, letting the cold water soothe the sting. "Are you all right?" On instinct, I rub light circles over her soft flesh.

"I'm fine." She yanks her hand back, as if my touch is hotter than the coffee, and wipes it on her white sundress. It's linen and similar to the one she wore to my apartment, but this one hits mid-thigh and dips into a V in the middle, making it hard for me not to overtly ogle her again.

I take a step back and stuff my hands into my pockets. "If

we're going to convince my dad we're married, you can't pull away when I touch you."

"I wasn't. I—" The words die on her lips, and she gives me a one-shoulder shrug.

"You look really nice, by the way."

She adjusts the top of her dress, and her breasts rise and fall. Her tits are much bigger than they were in Greece. I was hoping the stupid pillow dam would self-destruct and I'd get a glimpse of them in the middle of the night, but no such luck.

Dammit, she's talking to me, but I'm halfway to a hard-on and haven't heard a word. "What's that?"

"I said that I wore white, hoping it sends a subliminal message of matrimony. Newly wedded women love to wear white, don't they? Or is that just a reality TV thing? Plus," she says, holding out a tin of tea bags, "didn't you tell your dad that this trip is a sort of honeymoon for us?"

"Right. Yes. Honeymoon." I select a black tea and fill a mug with hot water from the kettle. The water instantly turns an oily reddish-brown. I hold back a sigh and make a mental note to pick up better quality tea while we're out today. "You look very pretty."

*Shit, didn't I already compliment her?*

Her lips tip up on one side. "Look at you. Nailing this husband thing already."

My chest goes tight at her assumption that I'm acting. "I—that wasn't—"

She spins away and pours herself another cup of coffee.

Giving up on my explanation, I pull a bowl of fruit from the refrigerator and set it on the counter.

Millie sidles up beside me, sipping her coffee, and plucks a piece from the pile, examining its dark purple skin. "Is this a plum?"

"No, it's a passion fruit."

"Hmm. What's it taste like?"

I take the fruit from her, our fingers brushing in the process. "I'll cut it open, and you can try it."

After slicing it in half, I scoop the goopy seeds with a spoon and hold the utensil out.

When she slurps it into her mouth, her face puckers. "Too sour."

I disagree, but then again, this woman takes a splash of coffee with her cream and sugar.

"Here." With a thumb, I swipe at the juice running down her chin and on instinct lick the sweetness from it.

As I pull my hand away, the air grows heavy, and her eyes narrow on my mouth.

Stomach dipping, I clear my throat and take a step back. "We better get going."

---

When my dad's bungalow comes into view, I'm hit with a wave of nausea.

"You okay?" Millie rubs a hand on my thigh, keeping the touch close to my knee.

Still gripping the steering wheel, I focus on my breathing. *In for four, hold for seven, out for eight.* Just like my therapist taught me. "Mm-hmm." I turn to her. "I just need this to go well. My relationship with my dad is complicated. One minute he's kind of rude, the next minute he's spoiling me and praising me. He gives me whiplash. But he's my dad, you know? I shouldn't let his opinion affect me so much, but I can't help it. I'm still working on it.

"Not only that," I say as another thought hits me like a smack to the face, "but I'm meeting my *brother* for the first time." The word feels foreign on my tongue. "What if he doesn't like me?" My chest tightens, making my button-down feel restricting. Instinctively, I go to roll the sleeves, only they're already cut off at my biceps. I undo an extra button at the top instead.

With a hand on my chest, Millie draws circles against my exposed skin. "Breathe," she commands, her voice barely audible over the pounding in my ears. "He's going to like you."

For a moment, I focus on my breathing, and when it's mostly steady, I ask, "How do you know?"

"I don't," she admits. "He could hate your guts."

A laugh rumbles out of me. "Gee, thanks. You're really making me feel better."

She grins, her apple-green eyes alight. "Listen." She brings her hand to rest against my forearm, her fingers twitching. "If Kane doesn't like you, that's a *him* problem not a *you* problem, got it?"

"Mm-hmm." I wipe at the sweat around my temple, wishing I could pull my hair back with an elastic right now, but Millie encouraged me to keep it down.

She jostles my arm, then reaches for her door handle. "You ready? We've got all our stories straight, yeah?"

I dart a hand out to stop her. "Wait. We haven't kissed yet."

"Hmm?" She whips around, her eyes wide.

"We, uh..." I scratch at the back of my neck. "We haven't had a practice kiss. What if we have to kiss in front of my dad, and it's all awkward? We need to be convincing."

She huffs a laugh. "Unless your dad is a voyeur, I think we'll be fine. No one's going to expect us to kiss in front of them."

"I don't know. Wouldn't it be suspicious for a newlywed couple not to be all over each other?"

Humming, she scrutinizes me. "Fine. I'll sit on your lap and hold your hand. And the occasional quick kiss is okay. Happy?"

"What about an ass grab?" I tease.

"There will be no ass grabbing in front of your little brother."

"Oh, so you're saying there *will* be some ass grabbing when he's not around?"

With a groan, she shoves my shoulder. "C'mon, big guy."

My mom calls me that sometimes, but from her mouth, the term of endearment makes my dick twitch. Fuck, what is that about?

---

Before I even have a chance to knock, the door swings open. As if on cue, Millie grabs my left hand and threads her fingers through mine, the warmth of her palm instantly bringing me comfort. She's already nailing this fake marriage thing.

"Ezra, my man," my dad booms. His voice is as big as he is. He's about my height and strong, but with a hard extra layer packed around his muscles from years of drinking. He pulls me in for a hug, but I refuse to let go of Millie, so we end up locked in an awkward half embrace, with her being pulled alongside me.

"This must be your wife."

"Yes." I clear my throat. "This is Mil—"

"Come," he interrupts, guiding us into the house.

I'm gearing up to call him out for being rude, but the words are stolen the moment I catch sight of a tall, lanky blond boy standing in the middle of the living area.

"This is Kane," Dad says, his tone flat.

Fuck. I've seen him introduce his car with more spunk.

The urge to embrace Kane is pretty powerful, but worried I'll freak him out if I get too touchy-feely, I settle on offering my hand instead.

"Hey, I'm Ezra. It's really great to meet you."

As he reciprocates the gesture, a small yet genuine grin paints his adolescent face. "Yeah, hi. Nice to meet you."

We stare at one another, silent, until Millie tugs on my arm. "Oh, right. This is my wife..." I clear my throat. "Millie."

Releasing my grip, she steps forward and embraces Kane with zero hesitation.

"Your name's Millie *Miller*?" my dad guffaws beside us.

Millie pulls back from my brother, her wide, panicked eyes immediately locking on mine.

*Shit.* We went over so many details but clearly did not think through the last name part.

"She, uh," I stammer. "I, uh... I took her last name." *Shoot, what's Millie's last name again?* Oh, yeah. "Greer."

My dad shakes his head, his lip curled up on one side. "The woman's supposed to take the man's last name, son."

My gut twists. Fuck. We've been here three minutes, and he's already acting like a chauvinistic asshole. I don't know why I'm surprised.

"Why?" Millie challenges, chin lifted high.

Normally a woman who speaks up is a total turn-on, but dread coils in my chest as I assess her because I'm worried about what may come out of my dad's mouth next.

"Why? Because he's *the man*, that's why." His tone isn't rude when he says this; he really believes it.

But judging by Millie's expression, she's about to belt out Taylor Swift's "The Man" in the middle of this living room.

"That makes absolutely no sense." She huffs. "What if two men—or two women—married each other? What then?"

"That's funny. You're funny." He turns to me, absolutely not catching on that this is no laughing matter. "Your wife's funny."

Millie's jaw drops, and she takes a step forward, but I wrap an arm around her waist and sweep her in close before she can lose it on him. It's a total man move, but Kane looks wildly uncomfortable, and this is not how I want introductions to go.

"Let's talk later," I whisper in her ear.

She sighs but otherwise stays quiet.

When she doesn't fight to be released, I turn to Kane. "How do you like Oahu?"

"S'fine, I guess." He shrugs. "Different from Maui."

"Food's on the grill," my dad announces before I can dig deeper into his short answer.

One by one, we file out the glass doors and onto the deck, where he pops the top of a local beer and hands it to Millie.

She grimaces at the can as she takes it.

Biting back my own disdainful look at my dad, I take the can from her. "What can I get you?"

"There's sparkling water in the fridge," Kane pipes up. "Lime flavored."

With a shake of his head, Dad scoffs. "I don't know why he drinks that fluffy stuff. I told him he's welcome to a beer."

"Dad." My hackles raise in irritation. "He's fifteen. He can't drink."

He lets out a derisive chuckle. "Take the stick out of your ass and live a little."

Millie catches my eye, her lower jaw nearly detached from her head. Rather than refute the statement, she turns to Kane. "Sparkling water would be great, thank you. Lime's my favorite."

"Me too." With that, he slips inside. When he returns with two cans, my fake wife and my new brother tap their drinks together in a toast.

Though my dad frowns at them, I ignore his ire and spend the next hour focused on getting to know Kane.

*For the Show*

Millie and I offer to clean up after lunch, leaving my dad and brother behind on the deck.

"He's the absolute worst." She shoves paper plates into the trash can with so much force the whole thing nearly topples over. "I don't think I can do this. We've been here for barely an hour, and I already want to toss him into the Pacific." She strikes a hand through the air. "Tied to a thousand-pound anchor."

I turn to the closed sliding glass door to make sure we're still alone, then clasp my hands over my chest. "Please don't leave," I whisper. "I don't know how I'll make it up to you, but I promise I will. If not for me, then for Kane. He just lost his mom, and this is who he has to live with now. Please, Mills."

I'd get on my knees right now if it meant she'd stay. Not that I'd mind the view.

She exhales in response, cutting into the visual forming in my mind. I shake that image off faster than a dog after a bath.

Stepping so close I'm practically looming over her, I unleash my best pleading face, hoping like hell the expression and my comment about Kane and his mom tug at her heartstrings.

"Fine," she grunts.

Instantly, my shoulders sag.

"*But.*" She jabs a finger into my chest. "I will take payment in foot rubs and tacos, thank you very much."

"Feet and tacos. Got it." I salute.

"Not *feet*, you goof." Head tipped back, she laughs. "Unless you have a foot fetish?" She quirks a brow.

## Chapter 11
# Millie

KANE LEAVES to hang out with friends, and Rob excuses himself to do who knows what. Thank the fucking gods, too, because I don't know what I'd do if I had to endure one more minute in that awful man's presence.

Thirty seconds with him nearly caused an aneurysm. How am I supposed to last two weeks?

*Free vacation to Hawaii.*
*Free vacation to Hawaii.*
*Free vacation to Hawaii.*

I can do hard things.

Ezra puts the car in reverse. "Let's go to the beach."

My stomach sinks at the prospect. "Uh..."

"Oh my god, please don't tell me you're one of those girls who hates getting her hair wet or a little sand between her cheeks."

Despite the dread that's churning inside me now, I chuckle at the comment. I'm familiar with the type of girl he's talking about. High-maintenance girlies are so not my type. If you can't let your hair down—and get it wet—what kind of fun are you even having?

"No. I grew up in Southern California, remember? It's not that. I, uh..." I breathe deeply, ignoring the pain in my chest. "I actually didn't bring a bathing suit."

"What?" He jerks his head in my direction. "How could you come to Hawaii and not pack a bathing suit?"

"Um..." Because my old suits resemble dental floss now. When I tried them on, I looked like a tightly wrapped burrito ready to burst. Not that I'd tell him that. I planned to buy one or two before the trip, but I dreaded standing under horrible fluorescent lighting in a dressing room and kept putting it off until... well, I never got around to it, clearly.

Ezra passes the street that would take us to Val's without even a glance that way.

"Where are we going?"

His lips quirk, though he doesn't look away from the road. "To a nude beach."

All the air is sucked from my lungs. Hell, the entire car, I think. "Wh-what?"

"You said you don't have a bathing suit." With a grin, he squeezes above my knee quickly before planting his hand on the steering wheel again. "Relax. We're going to get a suit for you."

I absolutely do not want to go shopping with this man and his book-boyfriend body, but I have no interest in explaining my reasons. Plus, he's right. What was I thinking, showing up in Hawaii without a bathing suit?

Inside the store, we go our separate ways—me to the swimsuit section and him to the surfboards. It's a small shop with a minimal selection of boards, so before I can even make it to the dressing room, Ezra is following me.

"What are you doing?" I ask, hanging suits in a variety of sizes and styles on a rack.

"Sitting." He plops his large frame onto a small stool and laces his fingers.

Eyes narrowed, I close the curtain with more gusto than necessary. Then I force myself to face the mirror.

Fuck. I don't want to be here. There was a section of full-body wetsuits out there. Maybe I could get away with wearing one of those. But the thought of stuffing my body like a sausage into neoprene creates a tightness in my chest.

*I can do hard things.*

Repeating that mantra, I strip down to my thong and quickly throw on the first bathing suit, avoiding the mirror until it's in place. It's a one-piece, which will solve the problem of hating my midsection, but future me will probably despise how pale my stomach will be in comparison to the rest of my body. So I peel it off and replace it with a basic black bikini.

"You okay?" Ezra calls, his voice gruff.

"Yeah, just... why do they make the lighting so awful in these things?"

"Come out here and look. There's a mirror, and the lighting looks pretty good."

Slipping my feet into my Birks, I pull back the curtain. As I step out into the tiny hallway, I nearly bump into Ezra's knees.

He straightens his spine, his eyes level with my—

Cheeks heating, I cross my arms in front of my breasts, but that only pushes them up.

He swipes a hand down his face and clears his throat, shifting his long legs to the side to make room for me to pass by. At the mirror, I can see him, which means he can see me. *All of me.*

Fuck, why am I like this? I never used to be this insecure about my body.

The lighting really is better out here, giving the illusion of less cellulite and fewer stretch marks. A hint of relief travels through me as I take myself in. The bikini keeps all my lady bits secured properly, so rather than torture myself and try on any other suits, I dart back into the changing room and put my clothes back on. Then I grab the same suit in two other colors and snag a large, flowy cover-up before heading to the checkout counter.

Ezra tosses a bottle of sunscreen, two towels, swim trunks, and a white bikini onto the counter, then pulls out his credit card.

"What? No, you—"

"I've got it." He winks at the salesclerk. And because I've exhausted all my energy arguing with myself over my swimsuit choices, I keep my mouth shut.

When we get outside, I snag the keys from him and hop into the driver's seat. Blessedly, he doesn't argue. He just rounds the car and climbs in, bag in hand.

"What was that back there?" I jam the key into the ignition.

"What?"

I purse my lips and shoot him a glare. "Don't act dumb. It doesn't suit you."

"We're on our honeymoon, remember? I can't have people thinking I don't take care of my wife."

With a slow blink, I cock my head. "Ah, yes. The wife whose last name you took. Makes total sense."

Ezra is silent a beat, then exhales loudly. "You're right."

"Sorry, what?"

"You're ri—oh, fuck off." He chuckles.

After changing in a wooden stall at the beach, I join Ezra, where he's laid the towels out side by side. He's wearing pale pink trunks that hug his upper thighs immaculately.

"Wow, it's stunning here." Digging my toes into the brown sugar–like sand, I take in the lush, green mountains. They're extravagant, straight out of a movie.

"This side of the island is windier, but it's definitely the prettiest."

Waves a palette of blues and greens gently crash onto the shore, providing the perfect ambience for our silence. The faintly floral scent of the tropical breeze is mixed with the rich, smoky aroma of a nearby barbecue, as well as Ezra's sunscreen. The coconut smell sends me straight to the summers I spent at theater camp. Spider webs nestled between bunk beds, sopping-wet underwear abandoned in shower stalls, and potato chips stuffed in turkey bacon sandwiches. Quirky memories like those always hit me first. The innocent and goofy ones. Sure, I experienced moments with the stereotypical cliques and backstabbers clawing their way to the top, but overall, it was the most fun I had as a kid. A place where I felt truly alive and welcome.

Ezra clears his throat beside me, breaking through the haze of nostalgia. "Can I say something without the risk of sounding like a total ass and offending you?"

I huff a loud breath and cock a brow. "Can you?"

"I don't know how to say—"

"Then don't." I sense in my veins what's next. Something along the lines of "you've gained weight." Though I doubt he'd be that blunt, it doesn't make the question any more appropriate.

He scans my body, top to bottom, then zeroes in on my legs below the hem of my cover-up.

This is it. Annoyance flares to life in my every cell. This is where another man has an opinion about my body.

Head tilted, he says, "I don't know why you're covering up."

Without missing a beat, I feign laughter. "Have you seen how pale I am? I'm like Casper the Friendly Ghost next to you." I nudge his naked arm with my elbow.

"What's wrong with fair skin? Just make sure to use sunscreen so you don't burn." He tosses the bottle to me. "Plus, you've gotta get in the water sometime."

"I'm waiting until I'm hot enough."

"Oh, you're plenty hot, honey." He winks.

I blink in astonishment, my mind going blank.

"If you don't take that damn muumuu off right now, I'm tossing you in the water with it on."

"You wouldn't dare."

Luscious brow quirked, Ezra hauls me off the ground and throws me over his shoulder in a fireman's carry. Then he takes off toward the water, his shoulder digging into my hip as he runs.

Boobs bouncing against his back, I squeal and smack his ass. (Instant regret. It's a nice fucking ass.)

As salt water splashes in my face, I close my eyes and sputter. "Put me down." I smack his backside again, though a little higher this time. "I didn't think you were serious, you jerk."

Ezra sinks until we're fully submerged, and when we come up for air, he sets me on my feet in the water, causing a cool sensation to sweep against my skin at the break in contact.

"I was seriously getting sick of you covering up that smoking-hot body."

I splay both hands over my chest where the wet fabric of my cover-up is plastered against my skin. "What. No, it's not—I'm not—"

"Millie, stop."

Flabbergasted, I search his dark eyes for humor; it's not the comment I was expecting.

"Don't think I haven't noticed the way you've been hiding your body. That's not like you."

My stomach twists painfully. "You don't even know me."

He breaks into a knowing smile, backlit by the sun. "I wouldn't say *that*." He flicks water at my face. "I know you're not shy about your body."

"That was before..." I let what I really want to say float away on the horizon.

"Before what?"

I shake my head. Are we really having this conversation right now? "I've gained weight," I whisper. "Haven't you noticed?"

His lips turn down in a frown. "This feels like a trick question."

A shallow wave crashes, splashing our faces, and in unison, we wipe our eyes.

"Can I be completely honest?" he asks, though he doesn't wait for me to respond before going ahead with the statement. "When we met in Greece last year, you looked... great. Wonderful. But now? You're *stunning*. So fucking sexy I can't keep my eyes off you."

My heart trips over itself just as another sapphire swell crashes. It forces my feet off the ocean floor and shifts me closer to Ezra before setting me back down. "Really?"

"Really. Every new curve..." He raises a hand like he's going to touch me but submerges it again quickly. "Fuck. Let's just say I'm glad the water's covering me right now."

I'm grinning when another wave crashes over us, this one with more force, and I'm tossed against Ezra. He catches me by the waist, and I feel just what he's talking about.

---

"I felt his thingy, Jo," I whisper-shout at my cousin over FaceTime.

She cackles, her voice tinny through the speaker of my phone. "You did not just call Ezra's dick his 'thingy.' Please tell me that's not what the cool kids are calling it these days."

"Ugh." With a groan, I peek out the door one more time. Ezra left for a run a few minutes ago, and I absolutely do not need him to know I'm talking about his package. His *packing* package.

"What did you do?" Joey asks.

I settle on the sofa, basking in the late afternoon breeze coming in from the open window. "Nothing. I schlepped my ass back to the car. I didn't even fully dry off. It was awkward as hell."

Rather than respond, she tilts her head and assesses me quietly.

"What?"

She shrugs. "I didn't say anything."

"Yeah, but you're giving me a look."

"Fine. Did you like his *thingy*?" She can't help but giggle.

"Don't call it a thingy," I shout.

"Hey, you started it." She grins. "But seriously. Did you?"

I'm forced to confront what I've been avoiding for the last half hour. Did I like the feel of his semihard cock against my pelvis?

Is the sky blue?

Are otters cute?

"It doesn't matter." Desperate to change the subject, I scan the room behind her and quickly come up with the perfect distraction. "Speaking of *thingies*, what is that behind you?"

Her eyes widen, and she lets out an audible gasp.

"Is that your strap-on?" I squeal.

"*Maybe...*" She snatches it from her nightstand and tosses it out of view.

"Oh. I've got a serious question." I waggle my brows, eager to continue the deflection. "Obviously you and Cam would never break up, but hypothetically speaking, if you did, who would take ownership of the strap-on?"

She barks out a laugh. "You act like it's a dog."

"I *have* heard you call Cam a good boy."

"Oh my god."

"It's not my fault the apartment walls are thin."

"Anyway," she yawns. "It's getting late, and we have an early flight in the morning. I should go, but don't think this conversation about Ezra's—"

"*Don't* say it." I laugh, nearly dropping the phone.

"Monster cock."

My heart stutters, and I sober. "Wait. How do you know that?"

"In Greece. I walked in on you two in bed the next morning, remember?"

"Barely," I sigh. "I'd been drinking that night, and he refused to have sex with me."

A Cheshire smile spreads across Joey's face. "Sounds like Ezra's a good boy too."

"You're ridiculous. Say hi to your mom for me when you see her, and have a safe flight, 'kay?"

"Will do. I love you."

"Love you more."

# Chapter 12
# Ezra

"Are you awake?" A quiet voice cuts through the air.

"Mm-hmm." I've been staring at the ceiling for over an hour now. *Damn jet lag.*

Millie snags her phone from the nightstand, its screen illuminating the room. "Ugh, it's four a.m. I'm starving. I'm never going to fall back to sleep."

"Alrighty then." Tossing the sheets off, I hop out of bed. Only when the cool air hits my bare ass do I remember that I'm not wearing a stitch of clothing. Fuck it. I have no problem being nude. Maybe I was European in a past life.

"Pants," she shouts, hurtling a pillow at my backside.

Chuckling, I strut to the bathroom, and when I return a few minutes later, she's in the kitchen. She's dressed in one of those attached shirt and shorts things, pouring sugar into her coffee. When she turns around, I'm greeted by a cup of hot water for my tea and... *fuck*, she's not wearing a bra.

It's too early for this. Waking up thinking about my half-hard cock against her bare stomach in the ocean was bad enough.

"Thanks." My fingers brush over hers in the exchange.

"That better not be Viagra," she says, nodding at the little blue pill I set on the counter.

"Very funny. It's an antidepressant."

I leave it at that. Talking about mental health makes people squirrelly; they either change the subject because of their own discomfort or they inject toxic positivity into the conversation.

"It's great that you're taking care of yourself. How do you feel?"

My heart clenches at the genuine question. Damn, her response is refreshing. I pop the pill into my mouth. "Good. I feel good. Thanks." While I steep my tea, I say, "We should probably go to the store. Pick up some food."

"Agree. At least Val provided eggs and toast. Is that all right with you for now?"

I nod, pulling out a pan from the cabinet.

Between cooking and eating breakfast together, dozing in front of the TV (because jet lag), and grocery shopping, we talk about everything and nothing. We touch briefly on my first impression of Kane—reserved yet open—and how we're looking forward to getting to know him better. We talk about things we can do without overwhelming him, like renting a boat or going on a hike.

Millie mentions using the walk-in closet to record for the audio app because it has the best acoustics.

I can't imagine listening to her perform. I especially can't tell her I have a membership.

When the last of our groceries has been put away, I ask, "Do you want to go for a run with me?"

"Do you want a divorce?" she says without missing a beat.

A smile takes over unbidden. "C'mon, it'll be fun."

"I think you and I have completely different definitions of fun, *pumpkin*."

I bark out a laugh. She's cute when she's snarky.

*For the Show*

The rhythmic pounding of shoes on pavement does little to drown out my thoughts of Millie. At the beach yesterday, she was so hard on her body. It doesn't make sense. A year ago, she was obviously comfortable in her skin. What happened? If my mom taught me anything about feminism, it's that a person should never comment on a woman's body. Though I think telling them they look stunning is the exception. Sure, we aren't really married, but that doesn't mean I can't make her feel good about herself. The question is how.

I mapped out my run ahead of time, creating a loop around Val's neighborhood so I'd end up at the food trucks set up nearby. Google Maps advertised tacos, which will be the perfect way to reward Millie for putting up with my dad.

As I close in on the trucks, I slow my pace and watch for traffic. Once I've crossed the street, though, I halt completely. Ahead, my dad is there, facing away from me and gesticulating wildly to a couple of kids.

On further inspection, I realize he's berating Kane and another boy about his age.

I take a tentative step forward to get a better listen, but not close enough to interrupt.

"This is who you've been spending time with?" my dad barks. "No wonder your grades are shit. You have no brain cells if you're hanging out with this fucking fag."

Kane flinches at my dad's words.

"Are you a—"

In two giant, swift strides, I step into the conversation and put myself between my dad and the boys. "What's going on?"

In unison, both kids turn to me. Kane's expression is... terrified? Sad? Both?

"Dad?" I press for a response. He can be an ass, but I've never heard him spew hate in a person's face like that. My stomach tightens in a knot, but I don't dare pull my focus from him.

He stabs a finger at my brother. "I want him out. There's no way I'm letting a fucking—"

"Do *not* finish that goddamn sentence." Lowering my voice, I command, "Walk away. *Right. Now.* I've got this."

"Fine," he spits, the faint smell of alcohol on his breath. "He's your problem now." He throws his hands in the air and kicks up dirt when he stomps away.

"The only problem is you," I snarl.

He doesn't hear me, or maybe he's chosen to ignore me. Either way, he doesn't turn or respond.

With a heavy sigh, I focus on the boys, and instantly, my heart sinks. There's no mistaking the tears in Kane's eyes.

His friend rests a sympathetic hand to his shoulder, but he pulls away.

"Forget him, dude," the kid declares. "He's a douche."

"Hey," I say, extending my hand. "I'm Ezra. Kane's—"

"Brother," the friend finishes. "Yeah, I heard about you. I'm Mano."

"Nice to meet you, Mano. I'm sorry about that. It was a dick move." I refuse to apologize on *behalf of* my father, but the kid deserves some empathy.

"S'fine." He shrugs. He's tall like my brother but much leaner. Cut from years on a surfboard, if I had to guess. His frizzy dark hair falls past his shoulders. To be honest, he looks more like me than Kane does.

Kane sniffs and wipes his eyes. "What the fu—" He huffs. "What am I supposed to do now?"

"You'll stay with me," I say without hesitation.

"But—"

"No buts." I wave a hand in the air and step up to the line for the food truck. "We'll figure it out later."

"What are you doing?" Kane peers around at the people still gawking at us.

"Getting tacos for Millie. Want any?"

Both boys shake their heads, and Mano leans in to whisper to Kane. I keep my focus fixed on the line ahead of me to give them some privacy as they quickly hug.

"What'll it be?" a spritely woman calls from the truck after Mano says goodbye and takes off.

"Hmm, what does Millie like?" I mutter, scanning the chalkboard menu.

Kane side-eyes me. "You don't know what kind of tacos your wife likes?"

Shit. "No—I—of course I do," I fumble. "I'm just not sure what she'll be in the mood for. Women. They're complicated," I add for effect.

The woman poised to take my order rolls her eyes and motions for the customer behind me.

Yeah, that's fair.

"I wouldn't know." Smirking, Kane shrugs.

"Oh my god, did you just crack a joke?" I elbow him. "Listen. You don't have to share anything you're not ready to share, but Millie is…" Fuck, I can't out my own wife—*fake wife*—that's her story to share. I clear my throat. "Millie and I are allies. So we're cool."

"You're *cool*?" He says it like he's mocking a fifty-five-year-old man trying to hang with "the youths."

"Hey, don't make this weird." I grin, and I'll be damned if he doesn't flash the quickest of smiles.

Kane trails behind me as I unlock the gate that leads to the garage apartment. We kick off our shoes, and as I ascend the stairs, I call out, "Honey, I'm home. Are you decent?"

Behind me, Kane gags, making me chuckle.

"Of course I'm decent. Why would I be naked in front of—Oh." Millie gasps as she spots us at the top of the stairs. "Right. Because we're newlyweds and we've been doing nothing but having all the naked sex."

I narrow my eyes, silently scolding her acting skills.

"Hi, Kane." She tilts to the side and smiles at my brother, who has stopped behind me. "You're lucky I'm completely covered up. I—"

He barks out a laugh behind me. "Don't worry, you're not my type."

"*Ouch*."

"I'm into dudes." He shuffles to my side.

"Oh. That's better, then." She tackles him in a cool aunt-like hug and ruffles his scruffy hair.

By the way his eyes sparkle as he playfully bats her away, it's obvious he enjoys her attention. My heart aches for this kid. I can only imagine how much he misses his mom's affection.

With a chuckle, he throws a thumb my way. "He said you two are cool."

"*He* thinks he's cool?" She points to me.

"Hey. Take that back. Or I'll eat your taco."

Millie snorts, her brows jumping to her hairline at my accidental euphemism. "You wouldn't dare."

I waggle my brows in a challenge. "Try me."

I hold the bag above her head, and when she reaches for it, I tickle under her arm.

Kane and Millie get settled at the table while I head to the kitchen for drinks. When I come back, Kane has already inhaled a pork taco. Good thing I got extra.

*For the Show*

"Want one?" he asks Millie, who's sitting on his other side.

"No, thank you. I don't eat pork."

"What?" Kane says, like it's sacrilege.

Honestly, in Hawaii, it sort of is.

"Yeah, I keep kosher," she replies.

"You do?" I choke on my food, quickly eyeing Kane. Dammit. This is the second time I've let it slip that I don't know my wife very well. "But you ate shrimp in Greece."

"Ah, yes. Kosher except for shellfish because, *gah*"—she tosses her head back—"I love shrimp."

"A cherry-picking Jew like me." I laugh.

"You're Jewish? That's cool," Kane says around a mouthful of his third taco.

I huff out a laugh. "Oh, so you can say 'cool,' but I can't?"

Though the meal started out lively, we quickly fall into an awkward silence. I'm racking my brain for ways to break the tension when Millie grabs a chicken taco and adds an extra dollop of guacamole to it.

"I'm picking up weird vibes. Does anyone want to fill me in on what's going on?"

I study Kane, then Millie. When I turn back to Kane, I give him an encouraging nod, hoping he'll open up to us.

He wipes his mouth with the back of his hand and lets out a long exhale. "So, it's not like I was in the closet…"

*Oh, we're jumping right in. Okay, then.*

"But I haven't totally come out, you know? I never talked about it with my mom." He takes a long sip of his water while we patiently wait. "I'm sure she suspected… I dunno, maybe not. She was so sick at the end." Kane lowers his head and picks at a fleck of dust on the tabletop. "Probably too drugged up."

Millie and I instinctively squeeze his shoulders, but neither of us speaks.

"I definitely didn't feel comfortable telling Rob. Mano and I haven't labeled our relationship or anything, but he's been out for a while, and I guess we weren't being as careful as we should have been."

Millie frowns, her face a mask of confusion, so I quickly fill her in on the confrontation with my dad.

"Kane." Though her jaw is tense and her breaths are harsh, her voice is controlled. "You shouldn't have to be careful, and you shouldn't have to hide who you are. But I understand being sort of in and sort of out of the closet."

My brother blinks rapidly. "You do?"

"Yeah. I'm bi." She straightens, her shoulders pulled back. "Married to a guy."

"Who, me?" I scan the room in faux innocence.

With a genuine smile, she squeezes Kane's arm. "My parents never gave me any reason to believe they wouldn't be supportive, but it was still a confusing time. If I had a girlfriend, people assumed I was a lesbian, and if I was dating a guy, then they'd say, 'Oh, it must have been a phase.'"

Kane huffs. "Yeah, bi erasure is real."

"Totally." Millie takes a bite of her taco, then, through a mouthful of food, asks, "Are you using condoms?"

"*Amelia.*" Heart lurching, I look at Kane, who's covering his face.

"What? Don't you remember being a teenager?"

"Yes, but—"

"But what? Safe sex is important. Oh, and clean fingernails." She grabs Kane's hand and inspects his nails with a hum. "Nice and trimmed too. Good job." She rises and refills her water at the sink as if she didn't just hand out sex advice like popcorn to my younger brother, whom we've both known for a whopping twenty-four hours. She really has no filter sometimes.

*Why am I into it?*

Not long after we clean up, Kane stands and heads to the top of the stairs, phone in his hand. "So, uh, thanks for dinner, but Mano's here. His mom says I can stay with them for a little while."

"Wait," I call. "What about—I mean, I thought you'd stay here."

He scans the living space, pausing on the small sofa. "Nah, man. I don't want to get in the way of all *the sex*." He puts up air quotes, accompanied by a smirk.

Millie snorts beside me.

"But—"

She rests a hand on my forearm. "If that's what makes you the most comfortable. We're here for you."

He gives her a sincere smile in return.

"I meant what I said." I take a step forward and pull him into a hug. If Millie can do it, then so can I. "I'll figure it out. *We'll* figure it out. I promise."

After he leaves, Millie slumps onto the sofa. "What are you going to do?"

"Fuck if I know." My stomach twists into a tight knot as I sink onto the cushion next to her. "But I've gotta do something. He can't go back there."

"And your dad?" she asks, worrying her lip.

"What about him? I never want to see him again."

"Seriously?"

I nod, determination growing alongside the dread that's plagued me since I saw him shouting at Kane. "How can I? He was pretty shitty to me when I was a kid, but not like this. The worst he did was forget to pick me up from the beach or go an entire day without speaking to me because I didn't take out the trash. He always made sure I had a bed to sleep in. Yet he's throwing Kane out on the goddamn street. A kid who already doesn't have a mother. What kind of monster does that?"

For a long moment, I'm swamped with one thought after another, my brain a chaotic mess.

Beside me, Millie sighs, pulling me back to reality. "I guess we can call the whole fake marriage off."

My body stiffens in response to that suggestion. "No."

"No?" She frowns, searching my face. "Why? You don't have anything to prove to your dad now."

"Yeah, but I can't very well admit to Kane that I straight-up lied to him the moment I met him."

"You should have thought about that *before* you flew me out here." She propels herself off the sofa.

"Look, I don't know what the hell I'm doing, okay?" I rise to meet her and rough a hand down my face. "I'm in my thirties with a terrible dating record. This isn't what you signed up for, but can you please not say anything to Kane until I figure out what to do next?"

Her eyes swim with anger. Shit. Is she mad at *me*? Does she want to leave?

Holding my gaze, she sighs. "Fine. I'll continue to play my role. But it'll cost you double the foot rubs." She pokes a finger into my chest. "This just went way past complicated," she mumbles.

"I'm sorry." Lips pressed together, I take her hand in mine. "I never expected this to happen. I figured I'd come out here, meet my long-lost half brother, catch a few waves and bond, then go home. Maybe stay in touch through stupid memes and the occasional FaceTime." I release her hand with a sigh. "I'm going to shower."

"Phew." Her lips quirk, her exasperation evaporating. "I wasn't going to say anything, but..."

*For the Show*

"Hey, watch it. I know where you sleep at night," I tease. "I can't believe we've only been here for two days. I'm exhausted."

While the warm water does not wash away my worries, it does clear my head a bit. I'll call my mom in the morning and ask for her advice. In the meantime, I've gotta up my game when it comes to knowing my wife better, or else Kane will figure out that we're pretending.

# Chapter 13
# Millie

"I'm kicking you out."

"Excuse me?" Ezra sputters from behind his toothbrush.

Averting my attention, I hand him a towel. The man hasn't put a shirt on yet this morning, making it far too easy to drool over him. I both love and hate that he's comfortable in his skin. But mostly, I miss feeling that way.

"Let me rephrase that." I prop a hip on the bathroom counter. "I have to record for the app today, so I really need you out of the apartment, please."

"Why?" He spits toothpaste into the sink.

Shit. Why was that so hot?

"I am not recording erotic stories in front of you." I cross my arms over my chest and arch a brow.

Ezra follows the movement. "I can be in the next room... with my ear pressed against the wall." He laughs.

With a huff, I wind up and punch his bicep.

"Ouch," he whines, rubbing at his arm. "You've got a mean jab."

"Looks like my older brother was good for something."

"Is he protective? Asher, right?"

"Yeah." I pull my hair into a topknot with one of Ezra's hair ties. "He always has my back. And since he has a little girl of his own now, he's extra protective."

"I imagine that's how I'll be when I have kids. *If* I have kids."

My heart clenches at the defeat in his tone. "Why do you say 'if'?"

He rolls his shoulders, looking away from me. "I dunno. I'm almost forty, and it hasn't happened yet."

"Thirty-five is not *almost forty*."

He swallows audibly and forces his attention back to my face. "Thirty-six."

"Huh?"

"I'm thirty-six."

Confused, I prop my hands on my hips. "But I thought..."

"Today's my birthday."

"Why didn't you say anything?" I punch him in the bicep again.

With a shrug, he plucks an elastic from the counter and pulls his hair into a knot too. "Thirty-six feels like *late thirties* and... I don't know, I didn't want to be reminded that I thought I'd be married with a kid by now."

I study him, deciding to circle back to celebrating his birthday later. "Is that something you've always wanted? A family?"

"Yes. Casually dating was fun when I was in my twenties, but even then, I didn't want to be a chronic bachelor like my dad. Nor do I want to swing the opposite direction and be alone like my mom."

"Do you think she's lonely?"

His lips turn down in a solemn frown. "I don't think she's unhappy, but yeah, I do think she's lonely."

"She never found anyone else?"

"Not really. She told me recently that she's dating, but I kind of think she was kidding. Anyway, what about you? Do you want kids?"

*Oof.* Now there's a loaded question. "Eventually. Though I'd rather marry a woman so *she* can carry the baby. Being pregnant sounds terrifying."

He cocks his head. "How so?"

"Carrying a tiny human in my body for nine months?" I look down at my stomach, hating that it's already bigger than I'm used to. "I don't know about that."

"I bet you'd be gorgeous while pregnant."

With an exaggerated gasp, I swat at his arm, but he dodges me just in time. "Do you have a breeding kink? If you do, I need to know."

"Why? Does that turn you on?"

I'm not into cold plunging, but someone needs to shove me under the showerhead right now. "No." *Maybe.* "But if you're my *husband*," I put up air quotes, "then that's probably something I should know."

"It's not like we're sleeping together. Unless…" He arches a brow.

"You perv." With a laugh, I turn away and snag my toothbrush.

"How am I a perv? You're hot." He points at me. "*I'm* hot." He points at himself. "We could be two consenting adults. Plus, I've gotten you off before, remember?"

*Do I remember?*

Greece.

Storage closet.

I rode his fingers like a buckle bunny in those cowboy romances I love to read.

Heart racing, I hop off the counter and get to work washing

my face, hoping the cool water will reduce the redness in my cheeks.

"*Anyway...*" I change the subject before my mind gets totally lost in the gutter. "What's next? What are you going to do about Kane?"

"I'm going to pack up his stuff at my d—*Rob's*. Val said I can store it in the garage for now."

I nod. "Are you okay with him staying with Mano?"

His chest rises and falls as he pulls in a deep breath, holds it, and lets it out again. "It's not ideal, but I'm not his dad, or even his guardian. Not yet, at least. So I can't tell him what to do, but I don't love it."

"Not yet?"

He presses his teeth into his bottom lip, focus averted. "I'm going to discuss it with my mom today, but I think it's what I need to do."

"You're going to adopt him?"

"I don't know how it all works, to be honest, but I can't imagine Rob will put up a fight. It's not like he made much of an effort to raise me."

My heart pinches at the sadness in his tone. "I'm sorry."

"Me too."

After triple-checking that Ezra has left, I set up my recording equipment in the walk-in closet. I opted for tea instead of coffee this morning since cream and sugar affect my vocals, and I loaded up on green apples at the store yesterday, which help minimize mucus. Once I'm settled, I read over the script, then go through my vocal warm-ups. Today, my alter ego, Jules, is going on a steamy camping trip with her lover. *Lucky lady.*

During our last virtual meeting, my boss told me subscribers love Jules—that she's so believable they forget they're listening to an app. I take pride in that feedback. I never want my work to feel scripted or overacted.

It takes me about an hour to record thirty minutes of audio, and since Ezra still isn't back yet, I search for a mat Pilates exercise on YouTube. After spilling my insecurities to Joey, I asked her to keep me accountable to move my body for at least ten minutes a day. After the workout, I fire off a selfie to her as proof. It may be silly, but the gold star emoji or "good girl" GIFs she sends really are good motivation. I'm sitting on the sofa doomscrolling when Ezra appears at the top of the stairs, his eyes roaming over my body.

"Hey," I squeak, pulling my knees into my chest to hide the stomach rolls hanging out between my hot pink sports bra and my high-waisted black leggings.

"Hey." He collapses beside me, sitting close enough that my toes touch his thigh.

"How'd it go?"

"As well as it could, I guess. I picked up boxes from U-Haul and called my mom from the parking lot before going over to Rob's."

"Was he home?"

"Yeah," he sighs, closing his eyes.

"And?"

Straightening, he frowns. "I told him I want nothing to do with him and demanded he relinquish his rights as Kane's guardian."

I gasp. Even though that was the plan, what he did today took a lot of guts. "What did he say?"

Ezra pulls my feet into his lap, face lowered. "He said yes. Just like that. Gave him up without a moment's hesitation. He's such an asshole. He didn't even help me pack up. I can't believe I wasted so many years trying to impress him. And for what?"

"That's awful." I grasp his forearm and wait for him to look at me. "You should have called me; I would have helped."

"No, no. I've dragged you too far into this mess already. I'm sorry. It was supposed to be a vacation for you." He forces a smile, but there's no hiding the sorrow behind it. "I'm going to make it up to you."

I wiggle my toes and grin. "I believe you owe me a foot rub. You can start there."

Gripping one ankle, he digs his thumb into the arch.

Immediately, an unexpected moan escapes my lips. *Lock that shit down, Millie. You should have gotten out all your moans during recording.*

I clear my throat and tamp down on the relief running through me at his touch. "What about Kane?"

Ezra switches to my other foot. "I went to Mano's and talked to his mom. Kane's grades really are pretty bad, but honestly, I'm not surprised. He lost his mom, then he had to pick up and move to a place where he knew no one. The issue isn't that he's been slacking off. I put in a call to the school to get him enrolled in the summer program, and Mano's mother said he's welcome for as long as needed."

"Are you okay with that?"

"I think I am." Wearing a thoughtful expression, he twists his mouth to one side. "For now, at least."

I stare at his profile, his loose hair brushing his shoulders.

An urge to tuck it behind his ear hits me hard, so I give in and do just that.

Squeezing my foot, he zeroes in on me, a grin tugging at his lips. "Would you mind sitting with me while I watch TV for a bit? I just need to shut my brain off."

"Not at all." I scoop the remote up off the coffee table and hand it to him.

Ezra takes it, then pulls me in closer. Though I should probably push back, I sink into his touch instead. I'm instantly engulfed in the spicy scent of his beard oil and the warmth of his body. We're too close. But it's clear that this is what he needs right now.

Plus, it's just cuddling.

# Chapter 14
## Ezra

I ASKED Millie to sit with me so I could give my brain a break, but that plan went to shit as soon as I started petting her. I didn't mean to, but the second she pulled *my* elastic from *her* hair, instinct took over, and my fingers acted of their own volition. At first, I rolled the ends of her silky strands between my fingertips, but eventually I was fully massaging her scalp and neck. I don't even fucking know how long I'd been doing it before she groaned "that feels nice."

I could have stopped.

I should have.

But her soft, throaty voice was like a drug, and I needed another hit.

Now, three episodes of *New Girl* later, her legs are draped over my lap and my arm is wrapped around her waist.

"All right, birthday boy." She claps, her eyes sparkling with anticipation. "As much as I love watching Nick and Schmidt's bromance continue to blossom, we're celebrating. What do you want to do?"

A lump lodges itself in my throat. "I don't like celebrating my birthday."

"What?" She gasps, her lightness dimming. "I will not accept that answer. Try again."

Knowing her, there's no use arguing. "Ugh, fine. What did you have in mind?"

That green-eyed sparkle returns. "Prepare to have the *time of your life*, honey."

"Are you suggesting karaoke?" I'm catapulted to the last time she sang those words. I could have sworn she was going to perform the infamous *Dirty Dancing* song in Greece. Instead, she impressed the pants off the entire crowd when she sang "Dancing Queen."

Months later, my mom and I saw her perform as Sophie in the traveling production of *Mamma Mia*, though I much preferred her karaoke version. Zero inhibition. Pure joy.

"Did you have fun at dinner?" Millie asks as we stroll along the boardwalk to the bar.

"I did, thank you."

Val met us at the restaurant, along with Kane and Mano. Millie also arranged for my mom and Cam and Joey to join us via FaceTime when the servers brought out a dark chocolate cake lit with an obnoxious number of candles.

After the entire restaurant sang and my blood pressure and body temperature spiked, I leaned into Millie so only she could hear. "You'll pay for that."

I've disliked celebrating my birthday for as long as I can remember. Most of the time, I spent it in Brooklyn, longing for a dad to light my birthday candles and sing loudly and embarrassingly like all my other friends' fathers. Occasionally, I was here in Hawaii, wishing my father *was absent* because he'd use my birthday to score women and free drinks. In either scenario, I was miserable.

"Oh my god." Jumping, Millie points at a wild rooster and a hen with chicks.

They're so common on the island that I barely notice them anymore, but it's clearly a novelty to her.

"That's the biggest cock I've ever seen."

"Hey, I'm offended." I poke her in the side.

She sticks her tongue out. "I'm sorry, did I threaten your masculinity?"

When I puff up my chest, I revel in the way her gaze flickers to my pecs. "Not at all."

"I'm not a bird freak or anything," she assures me, her tone pure tease, "but that's a beautiful fucking cock."

I stumble over my own feet at her brazenness. Twice now, she's shouted *cock* in public without an ounce of shame.

At the door to the bar, she stops to fiddle with the straps of her white dress. It's the same one she wore the other day, and tonight, she's paired it with heels that make her calves look deadly.

"I don't think you've seen enough cocks to make that decision," I say. Not that I want her seeing a bunch of other cocks.

"Noted. I'll be sure to create flyers for the beautiful cock competition." With a wink, she tips her head back and surveys the flashing lights above the door. "The karaoke bar is called Melody's? How original," she deadpans.

"The owner's name is Melody."

"Aw." She chuckles. "That's clever. I love it. Come on, I'm going to smoke you. *Again.*"

"Is that what you think is gonna happen?"

Millie insisted on picking out my outfit this evening. She's taking this whole fake marriage thing a little too far, if you ask me. But I must admit, catching her checking me out as I pulled the fitted black tee over my head earlier was a boost to my ego. And the ripped black jeans are my favorite.

"If my memory serves me, you couldn't stand that *I* beat *you* in karaoke in Greece."

She whips around so fast I nearly bump into her. Eyes narrowed, she stabs a finger into my chest. "You absolutely did not win that night."

I raise my hands in defense. "Oh, my mistake." Looming over her, I bring my mouth to her ear. "Does that mean getting you to come all over my fingers in the storage closet was my consolation prize?"

Her cheeks are bright red as we walk inside, and it's not from the summer heat.

"What do you want to drink?" she asks when we reach the bar.

"Tequila?"

"Two shots of tequila," she calls to the bartender. "And keep 'em coming." With her forearms resting on the bar, she scans the space, nodding at a couple in a VIP booth. "How come they're getting special treatment?"

"Maybe because they're newlyweds?" I shrug.

"How can you tell?"

"She's wearing white. Didn't you say newly married women love to wear white? Plus, she keeps gesturing with her left hand. Watch."

Right on cue, the young woman picks up a fruity cocktail with her left hand and holds it out, nearly hitting the server in the face with her massive rock.

Teaching middle school for a decade has taught me a thing or two about reading body language. Adolescents think they're being stealthy, but I notice far more than they think—from passing notes, to cheating on tests, to ruses to get one's crush to notice them. I smell these things from a mile away.

"They were also singing 'Endless Love' when we walked in. Dead giveaway."

The bartender slides our shots to us, and we down them. When Millie slams her empty glass down, she grins at me, the expression screaming *I've got an idea.*

"Tonight, we're on the same team." She drags me to the karaoke sign-up and flips to the list of duets. "Pick one."

Oh, she wants to compete *together?* This I can get behind.

"What about 'A Whole New World'?" I ask.

"Nah. Too corny."

"Okay, *rude.* What about 'Senorita'?"

"Nuh-uh." She shakes her head sharply. "I'm still bitter about their breakup."

"How about you go stand over there and let me surprise you?"

"No way. You'll pick something cheesy."

"*Gasp.*" A laugh bubbles out of me. "I will not. C'mon, it's my birthday." I flip my bottom lip into a frown, determined not to let Millie be the dramatic one all the time.

"Fine." She rolls her eyes playfully. "I have a feeling I'm gonna need another shot for whatever you have up your sleeve."

After settling on a song I'm sure she'll hate, I meet her at the bar and toss back a shot of tequila. Then I lead her onto the dance floor while we wait to be called up on stage.

When I pull her in tight and sway to the beat, she arches back, eyes wide. "Um, excuse me, sir. How did I not know you could dance?"

"You never asked."

I'm certain a breathy "fuck" escapes her lip as she tucks in close so I can no longer see her face.

I grin into her hair. She smells soft and peachy, like the

plumeria flowers on the island. I slip a hand to her lower back, relishing the warmth of her against my palm. At first, she tenses, but before I can pull away, she presses in closer to me, her hard nipples glued to my chest. Soon enough, she relaxes, and I get a flash of the uninhibited Millie I met in Greece. When I spin and dip her, causing her hair to whip me in my face, her smile is brighter than the disco ball above us.

The song ends, and the DJ comes through the speaker. "Next up, we have a pair of newlyweds. Mr. and Mrs. Greer, come on down."

My heart stutters. *Mr. and Mrs. Greer.* Why do I like the sound of that?

Millie eyes me suspiciously as we take our places on stage, then forces her attention to the blank screen, bouncing on her toes in anticipation.

As "What Makes You Beautiful" by One Direction pops up, I prepare for impact.

I should know better, though; Millie's a professional. And she's the kind of woman who once dragged her brother to an improv class as an April Fools' joke.

"I'll take Harry's solo parts," I say, "and we'll split the rest, yeah? And don't forget..." I angle in close, my lips brushing the shell of her ear. "We're supposed to be newlyweds. Let's give the crowd a show."

Nodding, she brings her mic up in preparation.

I thought it was thrilling singing *to* Millie, but singing *with* her is one thousand times better. Being in such proximity to her talent does something to me I can't quite put a finger on.

The woman is captivating and magical.

Despite the heat from the overhead lights, her stunning voice sends chills through me. If Idina Menzel and Pink had a baby, she'd sound like Millie.

I picked this song because every lyric rings true. She doesn't know how beautiful she is. She's completely oblivious to the way people stare everywhere she goes. This song is an excuse to tell her she doesn't need to be so insecure.

Not with me.

As the music ends, the crowd goes wild. Who can blame them? We can fucking sing.

"Everyone's watching." I slide my hand to her nape, my fingers slick with her sweat.

Licking her bright red lips, she assesses me.

Fuck, I want to do indecent things to her. Stepping forward, I squeeze her neck, and without a second thought, I press my lips against hers.

When I pull away, her eyes widen in panic. "What was that for?"

"For the show." I jut my chin toward the sea of people hollering and chanting.

"Right." Cheeks flushed, she steals a look at the crowd. When she turns back to me, she yanks the elastic from my hair so it falls like a curtain around us and tugs me in close. "I think we can be more convincing."

She grips my shirt at my waist, and in the next second, her tongue grazes against mine.

I nearly lose it. My heart races, and not from the adrenaline of our performance. *It's this kiss.* Arms looped around her waist, I pull her flush against me. This kiss makes me forget where I am. It makes me feel alive. When I worry I'll pass out from lack of oxygen, I regretfully break the connection. But I rest my forehead against hers, our breaths mingling.

Her expression has morphed from wary to intense, like maybe she feels the same mixture of wonder and desire as I do.

The DJ breaks our trance when he calls, "Let's give it up for Mr. and Mrs. Greer. Wow. Someone get these two a bottle of bubbly and a VIP booth. On the house."

"Yes," Millie hisses. "See? I told you we could do it." She shimmies her shoulders with pride as we're escorted to a cozy U-shaped booth.

With one arm around her, I tap my champagne flute to hers. "Cheers."

"What was it they said in Greece?" she asks.

"Yia mas."

"That's right. Ugh, and that raki was deadly." Though she groans, a smile creeps across her face.

"Just about," I laugh, nudging her knee with mine. "That shit tasted like straight-up rubbing alcohol."

We listen to the house music and sip champagne, taking a breather. My body temperature has just returned to normal when she knocks back the last of her drink. "Wanna dance again?"

"For the show?"

She shakes her head. "For fun."

# Chapter 15
## Millie

IF THE THEORY that one can tell a lot about a person's performance in the bedroom by the way they dance is true, then holy fuck. Can Ezra and I consummate our fake marriage?

Would it be so bad if we fooled around?

Shit. *Yes.* Ezra has made it clear he's nothing like his father, so I can't see him being interested in a summer fling.

But...

Would he make an exception if I were the one to initiate it? Surely he'd appreciate a birthday blowie.

"Are you ready?" he rasps against my ear.

My back is plastered against his front and has been for the past several songs. I've been grinding my ass into those tight black jeans like a cat in heat.

If it weren't for the champagne, I might actually be embarrassed.

But probably not.

For once, I feel like my old self. Silly and carefree.

I turn in his arms. "Let's go home." His hands flex against my waist. "I mean—the apartment. Let's go—"

"Let's go home, Mrs. Greer." With a chuckle, he guides me off the dance floor.

We're hit with a warm breeze as we stumble out of the bar, and as we cut through a narrow trail back to the apartment, our hands brush, sending tingles through my extremities. Touching Ezra is like dipping my toes into a hot bath for the first time.

At the top of the stairs, he crouches and unstraps my shoes. "You good?"

"Mm-hmm," I hum, clasping his shoulders to steady myself. "Just thirsty."

Once I'm barefoot, I fill glasses of water for each of us, and we collapse on the sofa. The move causes my dress to slip up my thighs, but I quickly tug it down.

"I had fun tonight."

"Me too. It was nice to be back on stage without—" I snap my mouth shut before I say *without being judged by the way I look*. "It was nice to be back on stage."

Ezra assesses me, his eyes searching for answers, but he doesn't press. "What's the weirdest thing you've had to do for an audition?"

I bark out a laugh. "Fuck a chair."

He chokes in surprise, wiping his mouth with the back of his hand. "You're kidding."

"I swear."

"Can I see?"

"I destroyed the evidence after I didn't get a callback."

"I mean..." He clears his throat. "Right now."

I set my glass down and cross my arms. "You want me to fuck a chair? In front of you? Have you lost your damn mind?"

If he juts out that pouty lip again, I don't think I could resist. Fortunately, he changes the subject.

"Thanks for taking me out tonight." He pulls my feet onto his lap and rubs his thumbs along my arches.

I sink deeper into the sofa in response. God, he's good at that.

"You're welcome. Thanks for not fighting me on it. Everyone deserves to be celebrated on their birthday."

"Is that so?" he asks, his fingers venturing to my calves.

Static crawls across my skin. *That's nice.* The move is an unconscious one, but I soak in the sensation anyway.

I feel bad that I didn't get him a birthday gift, so with the ounce of liquid courage I have left, I swing my leg across his lap and straddle him.

He gasps, his hands gripping my thighs.

Without giving myself a moment to chicken out, I plant a kiss on his forehead. "One." I kiss against his temple. "Two."

"What are you doing?"

"Kissing the birthday boy. Thirty-six kisses, is it?" I kiss his entire face, particularly enjoying the softness of his beard, and stop at the corner of his mouth. "Thirty-six," I whisper against his skin before pressing my lips to his completely.

I'm just about to slip my tongue inside when he pulls back. "Fuck, Millie, I really want to do this. But we can't."

Stomach sinking, I pull back too. "Why not?"

"You've been drinking." His dark eyes are fathomless inky pools full of nothing but honesty and respect.

"So? You have too. If you're worried about whiskey dick, it's fine. I probably won't remember in the morning anyway."

Ezra pulls me to his body and pivots, then tosses me onto my back and pins me with his weight, locking my arms against my sides, engulfing me in his scent—those spicy notes mixed with sweat and champagne. "Honey, when I fuck you," he growls into my ear, "I want the memory so ingrained, you'll never get it out of your damn mind."

I groan, cursing the light coming through the blinds. I really miss my blackout curtains. It takes a moment to piece together why my head is pounding. I'm just coming to my senses and mentally taking note of each part of my body when something moves against my shoulder.

The sensation startles me, and that's when I notice the hand *cupping my boob.*

"Motherfucker." I yank the sheets up my body, jolting upright, and instantly, my head screams at me.

"What's wrong? Are you hurt?" Ezra asks, his voice thick and gravelly. He sits up, the sheets pooled around his waist, his perfectly tanned pecs on display.

"Worse," I gasp. "I'm a total cliché."

"What are you talking about?"

"It's the classic one-bed-wake-up-tangled-together trope. Did you do this on purpose?"

"Of course not." He swipes his fingers through his messy hair. "And what the fuck's a trope?"

"Right. I bet you woke up and thought *I'll rest my monster morning cock-wood between her ass cheeks and—*"

"Monster morning—you've got to be kidding me." Ezra laughs into his hands. Like full-on shoulders-shaking belly laugh.

"It's not funny." I shove him and scan the room. "Where is my pillow protection?"

"On the ground, you goof. Where *you* put them." One side of his mouth curls up in a smirk. "Do you not remember?"

I shake my head.

"This is exactly why I didn't want to have sex with you," he mumbles.

Heart lurching, I clutch the sheets to my chest tighter. "Excuse me?"

"You wanted to have sex, and when I told you it wasn't a good idea because you'd been drinking, you got mad, took off your clothes, threw the pillows onto the floor, and said..." He swallows thickly, a flicker of trepidation in his dark, delicious eyes. When he continues, his tone is gentle. "You said if I wasn't going to fuck you, the least I could do was hold you."

Heat creeps into my cheeks. I said that?

"And since we both sleep naked, well..." He motions between us. "Here we are."

"Ugh." I drop my head into my hand. I don't remember any of that.

"Hey." He nudges my shoulder. "Don't be embarrassed."

"I'm not embar—"

My mind registers a trickling sensation between my legs, and I suck in a breath. *Fuck.* Looks like I am embarrassed after all. But not because I drunkenly destroyed the pillow wall and forced Ezra to snuggle.

"Get up."

His brows pinch. "Huh?"

"Can you just please go in the other room so I can..." I sigh. "*Please.* Just go."

He stills, his face a mask of confusion. I can't blame him, but I also can't tell him I'm 99.9 percent positive I've started my period and 0 percent sure I haven't leaked onto the sheets.

Clamping my eyes as tight as I can, I beg the period demons to keep their destruction to a minimum. Only when Ezra exits the room, calling out from the hall that I'm alone, do I open my eyes. The door isn't quite shut, so I race to the bathroom.

After confirming I have indeed started my period, a cold shower sobers me up real quick.

Once I'm dried off and wrapped in a towel, I step into the bedroom and come face-to-face with a bare mattress. "Uh, excuse me?"

"Have you seen the spare linens?" Ezra asks from the hall, ignoring my panic. "Ah, never mind. Found them."

If I wasn't embarrassed before, I'm mortified now. Hawaii is known for its volcanoes, right? Because I need to jump in one immediately.

"You didn't have to do that." I groan. "Actually, I wish you hadn't. How bad was it?"

"It's fine." Ezra appears in the doorway, lifting one shoulder. "Your body's just doing body things. It's no big deal."

"My body's just doing *body things*? What, are you a—"

"Middle school teacher? Yes." Laughing, he tosses one side of the fitted sheet across the bed. "And part of my job is to teach sex education."

Together, we make up the bed with some of the softest linens I've ever felt. I want to trade my skin for these sheets.

"Thank you," I say when we place the last of the pillows on the bed.

"You're welcome."

After breakfast, my cramps hit me like a wrecking ball, so I retreat to the sofa with ginger ale.

Ezra eases onto the couch beside me, his brow furrowed in concern. "You okay?"

"I will be once the ibuprofen kicks in. I'll probably watch a movie and rest. The first two days of my period usually knock me on my ass." I laugh, though nothing about that is funny. "You don't have to sit here with me. I don't want to bore you."

"It's cool. I have a video call with my lawyer, but it's not until later. Then I promised Kane we'd grab a bite to eat."

With a wince, I curl my feet under my bottom and rest my elbow on the sofa. I've never been more thankful for period panties and sweats.

Remote in hand, I regard Ezra. "I know you were away for your birthday this year, but did you get everything you wanted?"

Focus averted, he tugs at the bottom of his black athletic shorts. "Not exactly."

I can't help but grin at him. "I told you I'd give you a birthday blowie."

"What?" He scoots in closer and rests an elbow over the back of the sofa. "No you didn't."

"I didn't?" I hold up a hand, smirking at the chipped pink polish. "Hmm, must have just thought it, then."

He licks his lips, his gaze intense. "That's not what I wanted."

I raise a brow in question, willing my heartbeat to remain steady.

"Not that I *wouldn't* want that." He clears his throat. "Maybe we can, uh, revisit that later. No, there was this moment yesterday, right before I blew out my candles, when I looked at you and wished..." His dark eyes scan me over from chest to core, stealing my breath and all rational thought. "I wished you'd feel comfortable in your body again."

I rear back in shock at his statement. "What? I feel—"

Brows lowered, he pins me in place, his expression so frigid I feel like Princess Anna, forced into a standoff with Elsa.

"*Okay*. Maybe I don't. It's just..." Inhaling past the lancing pain in my chest, I focus on the horizon over his shoulder and beyond the lanai, praying for courage from the universe.

"What happened? Who did this to you?" With my chin between his thumb and forefinger, he forces me to look at him. "I'm not trying to push you, Millie, but you can trust me."

I scan his face for any sign of insincerity but come up empty.

"I promise."

It's wild, how safe I feel with him when we really don't know each other well at all. So with a deep breath, I begin. "You know how I was on tour for *Mamma Mia*?"

He nods.

"The director was awful." I grimace. "It was grueling work, and he demanded long hours of rehearsal with minimum breaks. It was probably illegal, now that I think about it. Anyway, I was under so much pressure as the lead. I was stressed and wasn't taking very good care of my body. I slept like crap and ate like it too. I didn't realize how bad I let it get until my costumes were too tight. Ugh." My voice cracks. "Why couldn't I have channeled my stress into running instead?" I wipe my tears, forcing myself to meet his eye. "The director noticed and threatened to give my part to my understudy if I didn't get my shit together and *lose the rolls.*"

His eyes widen and his jaw drops in horror. "He said that?"

I wring my fingers in my lap. "Among other things."

"Son of a bitch. What did you do?"

"I tried to suck it up. The theater is my world. My life. My everything. But I couldn't get my weight down. And then I stopped trying. It wasn't hard to get out of my contract—the director didn't want a *fat actress*. So I handed over my costumes to my understudy and flew home. I've sort of been hiding out in my closet recording for LULU since."

I'm shocked I just spilled it *all* to Ezra, but damn, it feels good to finally get the whole truth out. The theater is supposed to be my safe, happy place, and that prick of a director ruined it.

"Fuck. I'm so sorry." He balls his hands into fists on his thighs. "I could kill that man."

"Easy tiger," I laugh. "Don't go all morally gray on me. That's only hot in romance novels."

He doesn't react to my joke, but after a moment, his pinched expression relaxes. "Do you know why I chose that song last night?"

"So we could beat that other couple?"

He shakes his head and inches closer. "Because it's how I feel about you. You're beautiful just the way you are. And it kills me that you don't know it."

My nose stings, and tears flood my eyes. With a deep breath

in, I fight back the emotion. I'm used to finding ways to make myself cry on stage—not the other way around.

Ezra lays a hand across my stomach, the sensation making me flinch.

"Don't do that," he commands. "I love your body."

"Yeah, right." I sniffle. "My old one, maybe." The one that carried me through every audition, that fit into every costume. I'm sure he wishes he could see that body again. I do too.

"No." His voice is gruff. "This one. Right fucking here. Right now. I love *this* body." He gently squeezes my thigh, sending an unexpected bolt of electricity shooting straight to my core. "I will tell you every damn day until you believe it, even if I have to remind you every day for the rest of your... for the rest of this trip."

# Chapter 16
## Ezra

It was difficult to pull myself away from Millie and leave her on the sofa looking pained and pitiful. She insisted she was fine, but her tone suggested she's used to feeling this way, and that didn't sit well with me.

But as much as I wanted to stay and rub her feet, I had to discuss my brother's future with my lawyer.

I don't know whether the meeting went better or worse than I expected. Custody by guardianship is fairly easy to obtain, and though I can petition for termination of parental rights, most courts won't allow a parent to relinquish their rights just because they no longer want their child. Typically, severe child abuse or neglect must be present. We can, however, push to prove that Rob is an unfit parent. It just may take a while to prove to the judge that Rob's parenting and involvement won't improve.

After that meeting, I had a telehealth appointment with my therapist. By the time I hung up, I was 100 percent confident I'm doing the right thing.

I've been dreaming of having a family for years now—I just

didn't envision I would have a fifteen-year-old kid before having a wife. A real wife, that is.

> MILLIE
> Are you almost done in there? I really need to pee

Cringing, I hop up off the bed and dart out into the living room. "Shit, why didn't you say anything?"

Millie leaps off the sofa and bumps my arm as she strides past me. "I didn't want to interrupt," she says as she disappears.

I'm brewing tea when she returns. "Want some?"

"Sure, thank you."

"You could have come in, you know." I hold out the tin of tea bags to her.

She picks a lemon and ginger blend. "You were on an important phone call. I didn't want to disrupt you."

"You can always disrupt me." The second the words are out, I wish I could suck them back in. They were way more intense than I meant for them to be. Even if they're true. Between the made-up marriage and the situation with Rob and Kane, my whole world has been disrupted.

Once upon a time, this would have caused me to spiral. Honestly, I still might, but this part right now—a new beginning with a brother I never knew I had and steeping tea in paradise with the most beautiful and interesting woman—feels right.

"How did it go?"

"Good, I think. Though, um, I don't know how long I'll have to be here." I tuck my hair behind my ear and peer at her over my mug.

"Oh?" She leans a luscious hip against the counter.

"I don't know how long the process will take or whether I'll be allowed to take Kane with me to Brooklyn before everything is settled. There are a lot of unanswered questions right now."

Millie's quiet, her expression open and thoughtful.

"I was wondering." I clear my throat, working up the nerve to get the words out. "Would you like to stay longer?"

Her shoulders sag. "I don't know if that's such a good idea."

"Why not?"

"Because..." She takes a sip from her mug, her throat bobbing as she swallows, then sets it down. "This is a family matter, and I'm not—"

"I know." Just like a movie reel, scenes of a life where Millie is really my wife flash before my eyes. Singing in the kitchen while I cook breakfast and she pours tea. Nude beaches in Greece. Picking out baby clothes in a stupidly expensive boutique on the Upper East Side. Her asleep on my shoulder after watching reruns of *Glee*. "But..." *I really want you by my side through this.* I don't say that. I can't. Instead, I go with "Do you have to be back in the city right away?"

"No." She shrugs. "Not really."

"Then stay. Val has offered the apartment for as long as we want." I search her eyes for clues about how she's taking this proposal, but her green irises are indifferent. "C'mon, what do you say?" *Please say yes.* "What else do you need here? I'll buy a second bed if that'll make you feel more comfortable."

She grins. "No. Our bed situation is fine."

My lungs constrict with tortured anticipation as she assesses me, still wearing an impossible-to-read mask.

"Okay," she finally says.

"Okay?" I don't even attempt to hide the smile that splits my face. Without a second thought, I scoop her into my arms, nearly knocking over her mug in the process. I press my lips into the soft skin at her neck and exhale my relief. "Thank you, Mills," I whisper. "Thank you."

While she doesn't quite sink into my embrace, she doesn't resist it either, so I count it as a win.

*For the Show*

"Are you hungry? Have you eaten?" I ask like a fussy Jewish mother.

"I've been too nauseous and tired to eat."

I release her and take a step back to study her. Her face is pale, though her cheeks are flushed, probably from the heat of the tea.

I grab the keys to the car off the counter and head toward the stairs. "I'll be back soon with food. Will you be okay?"

She nods, and I'm out the door.

# Chapter 17
## Millie

PERIOD CRAMPS ARE A BITCH. But this heavy flow is even worse. While Ezra is gone, I take another shower, this one as hot as I can stand. When I'm finished and dressed, I find the ibuprofen on the nightstand. Beside it, Ezra's phone buzzes. It's a text from Kane. The preview banner reads *Did you talk to the lawyer?*

I'm wringing my wet hair with the towel when another text comes through. *Sorry, I'm just really nervous. Text me back so I...*

Oh, poor kid. I wish I could reply, but I don't know Ezra's passcode.

*Can I call you?* pops up.

A moment later, Kane's name flashes on the screen, and without a second thought, I answer.

"Kane, hi. It's Millie."

"Oh, hi. Is Ezra there?"

"He stepped out and forgot his phone. Is everything okay?"

He doesn't respond, and he's silent for so long that I pull the phone back to make sure the call hasn't been disconnected.

"Yeah, just—did you talk to your lawyer today?"

An involuntary smile surfaces at the thought of Ezra and me sharing a lawyer, but I tuck that back in quickly.

"He—*we* did." It's only a small fib.

"And?"

"And I think it's best if you have this conversation with your brother. Why don't you come over? He should be home soon."

"Yeah, okay. Bye." Without waiting for me to respond, he's gone.

Fifteen minutes later, I welcome Kane into the apartment with a long embrace and guide him to the sofa. "What's going on, bud?"

He sits on the edge of the cushion, one knee bouncing. "Are you going to adopt me?"

I nearly choke on my saliva, and it takes everything in me to keep my eyeballs from popping out of my face. He thinks we—*Ezra and I*—are going to adopt him. I'm only ten years older than he is. Do people adopt kids who are only a decade younger? What am I even saying? *I'm* not adopting Kane. Ezra is. Or he's trying to. But Kane thinks we're married, so of course he'd think we both are. Now would be the time to come clean. Tell him we made the whole marriage up to save face in front of Rob.

I'm garnering the courage to admit the truth to him, but before I can, Kane hits me with the saddest look.

"It's just that..." He runs his hand through his shaggy blond hair just like Ezra does when he's nervous. "It's only ever been me and my mom. I only know what it's like to have a mom—not a dad—and well..." A small sob escapes him before he can choke it back.

I scoot in closer and rub his arm, doing my best to comfort him.

With a deep inhale, he continues. "I miss my mom every fucking day, and no one will ever replace her, but," he peers at me, his hazel eyes filled with so much anguish and desperation, "you seem cool, and it's obvious my brother loves you."

I stiffen at that remark but tell myself he's drawing a normal conclusion that a husband would love his wife—not that Ezra specifically loves me.

I really wish Ezra were here. He'd know what to do. Probably. I can't possibly tell this lost, devastated kid that our marriage is a sham. My heart breaks for him, losing a parent at such a young age.

"Are you going to adopt me?" It's the second time he's asked, and it punches my heart just as hard.

"Oh, Kane." I pull him in and sob right along with him.

At the sound of a crash nearby, Kane and I pull apart and turn, finding Ezra standing at the top of the stairs with grocery bags scattered around his feet and oranges and an onion rolling across the tile.

"What's wrong? Are you hurt?" He looks at me first, then to his brother, his eyes wide with panic.

I scoot over and motion for him to sit between us.

"We're fine," I confirm while Kane wipes his eyes and nose with his shirt.

Ezra sits and cups my jaw, tenderly thumbing my tears from my face. His eyes ask *Are you sure you're okay?*

I nod, leaning into his hand. *I'm okay.*

"He wants to know what happened with the lawyer. We were waiting for you." Diving into the rest of our conversation will have to wait until later.

Ezra goes into the details of his call with the lawyer, and though it's the first time I'm hearing them, I keep my face neutral so Kane doesn't catch on.

"Do I have to go back to Rob's?" Kane asks.

"Absolutely not," Ezra replies. "You can continue staying at

*For the Show*

Mano's for summer school, or you're welcome to the pull-out sofa here with us."

*Us.* There's that word again.

"And I eventually get to live with you for good?"

I dig my nails into Ezra's hip, silently signaling to him that we'll have to deal with *us* later. "Yes," I reply on his behalf.

He reaches over to interlace our fingers. His hand is strong and warm and brings a sense of comfort I haven't felt in a long time.

Kane lets out a huge sigh of relief. "Okay."

"Okay, what?" Ezra asks.

"Okay, I'll stay at Mano's until summer school is over, then I guess I'll go back to New York with you?" His voice cracks at the end.

"Is that what you want?" It's suddenly occurred to me that he probably hasn't been asked that question since his mother died.

He nods, his hazel eyes glossy with honesty.

"Good. It's settled. What's all this?" I ask, standing to collect the bags off the floor.

Ezra rises and takes the groceries from me. "I'm making matzo ball soup for you. You too, Kane. You're staying for dinner."

"What's matzo ball soup?" his brother asks.

"Only the soup that cures everything."

I'm kicked out of the kitchen—which is totally fine by me—so Kane and I observe Ezra from the barstools and include him in a game of would you rather.

"Would you rather," I begin, "dress up as a rabbit every day or eat rabbit food for the rest of your life?"

"What do rabbits eat?" Kane asks.

"Hay, grass, and vegetables."

Ezra quirks a brow at my reply.

"What? I had a rabbit growing up. Her name was Bunny."

Kane barks out a laugh. "Your bunny's name was Bunny?"

"Just answer the question." I pick a tiny seashell from the dish on the counter and fling it at him.

"I'd dress up like a rabbit," Kane says.

"Same," Ezra agrees.

He took his shirt off after he splattered oil on it, and now I'm forced to stare at the dark smattering of hair that starts just below his navel and travels down, down, *down*—

"I've got one." Kane's voice snaps me back to the present. "Would you rather get stung by a bee every day or pee every hour?"

"Gross," I laugh. "Get stung by a bee."

"What? No. Definitely pee," Ezra says, whipping around to look at me. "You'd want to get stung by a bee?"

"Of course you'd choose to pee. If I had a dick, I'd choose that too. But for a woman, peeing every hour would suck."

Kane nods solemnly. "That's fair."

"My turn." Ezra's voice is low. "And it's a serious one."

Kane and I lean in, elbows on the counter and ears turned his way.

"Would you rather go to school naked every day or have your most embarrassing moment go viral on social media?"

"Naked every day," I reply instantly.

"Really? Why?" Ezra asks.

"Because videos on the internet live forever."

"Yeah," Kane says, "but everyone has a camera phone, so if you showed up naked to school, *that* would also go viral."

"Mmm," I hum. "Good point."

"Both options suck." He roughs a hand through his messy blond hair. "I guess it would depend on what your most embarrassing moment is."

"True." I shrug. "What would you pick, Ezra?"

"Go to school naked. Let that shit go viral."

*For the Show*

We all cackle at his response.

When we finally sit down to eat, Ezra and I watch Kane, waiting for his reaction to the soup that cures everything. My grandparents and parents always made matzo ball soup when either Asher or I was sick. I don't know what kind of voodoo Jew-doo magic is in it, but it works every time.

Though Kane refers to the matzo balls as "squishy bread testicles," he declares it delicious.

Ezra sits back, sighing in relief, and we all dig in. While we eat, Kane shares a few stories about his mom, and in turn, Ezra and I share about our own childhoods. We play a few more rounds of would you rather, then I offer to clean the kitchen.

"Thanks, Millie," Kane says as he hugs me goodbye.

"What for?"

His lips tip up in a sheepish smile. "We just met, and you already make me feel like I'm a part of the family."

Ezra's hand flexes against my hip.

Stunned, and with my heart lodged in my throat, I can only stare at him.

"That's because *you are* family," Ezra answers for me.

---

"Tonight went really well." I roll to face Ezra, barely making out his features in the dark.

As soon as the kitchen was cleaned, I changed into my amazing period panties and collapsed into bed.

"It did," he says. "Thank you for being so great with my brother."

"You're welcome. He's a great kid."

"Yeah, he really is. How are you feeling?"

My answer is a moan, and not the sexy kind.

127

"That good, huh?"

"I'm fine." I wave a hand lazily. "I get really heavy periods. I'm sure that's not what you want to hear while you share a bed with me, especially after this morning, but I promise I'm not naked under here." I laugh nervously.

"I figured. Have your periods always been bad? Sorry if that's too personal."

"No, it's okay." I shift under the covers, searching for a more comfortable position. "They've always been pretty awful, but they've gotten a lot worse lately."

"Have you seen a doctor?"

"No, I haven't, *Daddy*," I quip.

Ezra sucks in a breath.

My heart stutters at that reaction. "What was that?"

"What was what?"

"You did a thing when I called you Daddy."

"What?" he says, his voice high-pitched. "I didn't do a *thing*."

"You totally did. Oh my god," I gasp. "Do you have a daddy kink?"

"I don't know what you're talking about." He's got his face half buried in the pillows, so his words are muffled.

During our text exchange prior to coming to Hawaii, he neither confirmed nor denied it. I'd forgotten about that until now. "Oh, you definitely have a daddy kink."

He pushes against the pillows between us. "Shut up and answer the question."

*Mmm, bossy too.*

I roll back a bit and huff a sigh. "I haven't had time."

"Millie."

"Ezra."

"*Amelia*," he reprimands.

My stomach flips. Damn, why does it sound so hot when he uses my government name?

*For the Show*

"I've been bouncing from rehearsals to tour to rehearsals for years. I barely stay in one spot long enough to find a doctor."

Voice low, he says, "Promise me when we get back to New York you'll see a doctor, yeah?"

"Yes, Daddy."

With a grunt, he smacks me with a pillow. "I was going to ask if there's anything I can do to help, but after that, forget it."

I laugh so hard it comes out as a wheeze. It's so fun to rile him up. "I'm sorry, but it was too easy." Wiping at my eyes, I take a deep breath. "Fine, I'll behave."

He narrows his eyes, the move barely visible in the light of the moon.

"You said something about helping me?"

"Yes. Is there anything I can do?" he asks. "Medicine, maybe? A heating pad?"

Warmth blooms in my chest at the sincerity in his voice. I've already taken ibuprofen, and using a heating pad in the summer in Hawaii would probably feel a lot like being in the ninth circle of hell. "When I was living with Joey, she would rub my lower back." I'd kill for one of her massages right now. "But you don't—"

"I can do that."

"No, really, it's fine. I—"

"Millie."

"Ezra."

"Oh my god, not this again," he groans. "You're in pain, Mills. Please just accept my help."

Relief and trepidation war for dominance inside me. "Okay."

"Permission to cross the pillow border?"

"Permission granted."

Chuckling, I help him toss them to the ground, then settle onto my right side with my back to him.

When his large hand wraps around my bare waist, a shiver shoots up my spine, and I startle.

"You okay?"

"Mm-hmm." I swallow hard, digging my nails into the mattress.

Beneath the sheets, Ezra kneads my lower back above the elastic of my underwear. I force myself to relax, and I absolutely do not think about how close his fingers are to my ass. Absolutely not.

I'm lost in his touch, the relief he's already bringing me, when his ministrations come to an abrupt stop.

I peer over my shoulder, finding him scrolling on his phone. Rude. "What are you doing?"

"It says here orgasms help with period pain."

"Great. Next time you get your period, you can jerk off."

"Don't be a brat." He pinches my side. "I'm trying to help."

"If you want to help so badly, why don't you—" Shit. I do *not* need to finish that sentence.

Neither of us speaks, the only sound a faint humming from the overhead fan.

Then, "I could, you know."

My breath catches. "Could what?"

"Help with the, um, orgasm."

I roll to my other side, dragging the sheet with me. "How the hell do you expect to do that? I've got the fucking Red Sea gushing out of my vagina."

"Wow, you sure know how to turn a guy on."

"I'm not trying to turn anyone on. I'm trying to bleed in peace," I wail.

*Why is being a woman so fucking painful sometimes?*

"I'm not trying to be an ass. I promise." He watches me, his expression filled with nothing but kindness.

"I'm sorry. I appreciate you. Really, I do. And yes, I have heard that orgasms help with period pain, but I wasn't kidding about the Red Sea. Even Moses would be intimidated."

He's quiet for a beat, his breathing suddenly louder than the ceiling fan, its pace quickening. "I bet I can make you come without even touching your pussy."

My breath catches in my throat. "What are you talking about?"

In a gravelly voice, he asks, "Have you ever had a nipple orgasm?"

I blink. I have. *Once*. But never with a partner.

When I don't reply, he continues. "You're considering it, aren't you?"

"It's not gonna work," I huff.

"Trust me, I can make it work."

Apprehension and excitement clash in my mind. "Don't be cocky."

"My cock will not be involved. Promise."

I inhale deeply, considering. Maybe this really could be the solution. I could get some relief without having to disturb the rough waters down below. Would it really hurt to try? You know, for science? Or as Joey would say, *for the plot*.

But... "Don't you think that's a little weird?"

"Why?"

"Because..." Eyes closed, I sigh. "We're not together."

"That didn't stop us before."

He's not wrong. And now that he's mentioned the possibility, I'm feeling desperate.

Rolling onto my back, I drag my fingers up my body, only stopping when I reach my nipples. Over the sheet, I unabashedly circle them once, then twice, eliciting pleasure that has me squirming for more.

"This is a ridiculous idea," I mumble.

"More ridiculous than pretending to be married?"

He's got me there.

I drag the sheet down my body before I have a chance to overthink. "Fuck it."

When Ezra's fingers dance across my stomach, I draw the fabric up, subtly signaling that I'm not at ease with being touched there. I haven't let anyone touch me intimately since my weight gain.

"Millie." He inches closer, his breath tickling the side of my neck. His birthday wish rushes back to me then. *I wished you'd feel comfortable in your body again.*

I grip the sheet beneath my navel, my elbow brushing against his bare chest.

He skates a hand over my right breast, sending chills across my entire upper body. "Breathe," he commands gently.

Oh my gosh, now I understand why romance authors write lines like *She let out a breath she didn't even know she was holding.*

On my exhale, he flicks my erect nipple with a single digit, back and forth. Then he pauses to assess my reaction.

I nod, signaling him to continue.

He pinches, and I gasp.

He tugs, and I moan.

"Can I use my mouth?" he whispers.

Heat pools in my belly in response to the question. "Mmhmm."

Raising on his forearm, Ezra hovers over me and sucks my areola into his mouth. The way he flicks and nips is pure torture. All I can think is how much I wish it was my clit he was working over instead.

"Does that feel good?"

A "fuck" escapes my lips.

"I'll take that as a yes." The cheeky bastard grins against me, his beard tingling my already sensitive skin.

He catches my other nipple between his teeth and cups the

breast he's just abandoned, rolling the bud between his fingers while he sucks hard.

Back arching off the bed, I moan.

"Straddle me."

"What?" I force my eyes open.

His dark irises are depthless as he drinks me in. "Get on top of me." He rolls onto his back. "I can play with you better that way."

I jackknife to sitting. The move causes the sheet to dip dangerously low on his hips, reminding me that he sleeps in the nude. "Pillow. Lap. Now," I command.

With a roll of his eyes, he obliges, and once the pillow is in place, I straddle him, my legs caging his hips and my hands planted on either side of his head. He wastes no time squeezing my heavy tits together in front of his face. When he buries his nose in my cleavage and inhales loudly, a bolt of desire shoots through me. God, why does that turn me on?

He jiggles them—also a huge turn-on—between kneading and gripping. In tandem, he rolls and flicks and tugs on my nipples. Finally, he opens his mouth, his tongue poised, wide and flat, and laps at me again and again. I writhe against the pillow as I hover above him, dipping my breast into his mouth. When I pull back, he catches the pebbled bud between his teeth, the unexpected move causing my body to rack with pleasure.

He releases, but only so he can capture my other nipple.

"Fuck, that feels good."

Eyes hooded, the bastard smirks up at me. With a hand grasping each breast, he rubs his beard back and forth across my skin. "You're so sexy," he says into my chest. "Fuck my mouth with your tits."

Obediently, I lower until one nipple brushes against his lips. With a groan, he opens and then sucks relentlessly, the move mimicking how he'd suck my pussy if he had the chance, I'm sure of it.

My clit swells at the sensation, and my cunt pulses.

He digs the fingers of one hand into my flesh, holding me where he wants me, and with the others, he flicks and rolls my free nipple. He moans loudly against my skin, and I nearly lose it.

"Yes, Ezra. That's it. Fuck, I'm close."

He smacks the side of my breast, and I'm a goner. My core tightens and contracts, my cunt spasming like it's been fucked.

*Slap.* My toes curl in ecstasy.

*Slap. Pinch. Tug. Pull. Suck, suck, suck.* My body coils and convulses, and I may or may not call out his name.

As I come down, he suckles my nipple tenderly, lessening the pressure and easing me back into the stratosphere. I collapse against his chest, my ear to his sternum, where his heart races just as rapidly as mine.

He trails his fingers down my back and settles his hands on my thighs, his touch soothing this time. Maybe I'm too euphoric to care that he can feel all my imperfections.

I roll off him and onto my back, not bothering to rebuild our pillow wall—or cover my tits. I'm too blissed out from my nipplegasm.

"How do you feel?" he asks against my shoulder.

"Relaxed, thank you," I mumble.

"I told you I could do it."

That cocky motherfucker. With my eyes closed, I shake my head against my pillow, too loopy to fight back.

I hate that he was right.

Although, I kind of don't.

# Chapter 18
## Ezra

When Millie's still in bed around noon, I don't think too much of it. My mom never shied away from details about how a woman's period can knock her off her feet.

I leave her with a bowl of soup and ginger ale while I catch a few waves. When I return and find the bowl untouched, a prickling feeling emerges beneath my skin. She says she's too nauseous to eat but promises she's fine.

Still uneasy, I hop in the shower, and just as I've finished and have wrapped a towel around my waist, Millie comes racing into the bathroom. She barely makes it to the toilet before she throws up.

I rush to her side and drop to my knees. "What's wrong?"

With a groan, she slumps against me.

Water from my hair soaks her bare shoulder. "Millie."

She hurls again, then collapses in my arms, her body limp.

Heart pounding, I clutch her to my chest. "Hey, come on. What's wrong?"

"Don't feel good," she moans. "Stomach hurts bad. Blood. Bleeding."

Shit. She's out of it, and fuck if it isn't really freaking me out.

"Okay, honey, I'm going to help you get dressed, and I'm taking you to the hospital."

I expect her to protest and insist she's fine, but all she does is heave over the toilet once more. When there's nothing left to vomit up, I support her weight and help her into a T-shirt and a pair of cotton shorts.

Once I'm dressed, I shove my wallet and phone into my pockets, then gather her things as well. I help her slip into her sandals on the way to the car and ease her into the passenger seat as gently as I can. She clutches her knees into her chest the whole ride, her face as white as a sheet.

Okay, I'm officially worried. Periods aren't supposed to be *this bad*, are they?

We don't have to wait long after she's checked in before a young man in blue scrubs appears from a set of double doors and calls her name.

Whispering assurances, I help her stand and lead her across the room.

"Are you family, sir?" the man asks.

I could say no. I *should* say no. But there's no way in hell I'm letting her go back there by herself. "She's my wife."

"Very well. Follow me, Mr. Greer."

A nurse takes over, checking Millie's vitals and asking a whole host of questions. "Are you on birth control?"

Millie shakes her head, and I shit you not, my dick twitches. The idea of Millie not being on birth control? Yeah, I can't deny I like it when she calls me Daddy, but clearly, she was on to something when she asked if I had a breeding kink.

"Could you be pregnant?"

"No," we answer in unison, our voices a little too loud.

Shit. Based on that response, she probably thinks we hate kids.

*For the Show*

"Well," she says, her eyes bouncing between us. "Let's take a test anyway, then we'll draw some blood." She hands Millie a plastic cup and directs her down the hall to the restrooms.

I follow, arms out cautiously in case she stumbles.

At the bathroom door, she turns and presses a hand to my chest, stopping me from following her in. "I'm fine."

"What if—"

"I'll be fine." She rolls her eyes.

"Leave the door unlocked, just in case."

She's out of breath just walking down the hall. If she passes out in there, I'm not waiting for someone to get the door open for me.

"Yes, sir." Her sarcasm could scorch a hole in the ground.

After Millie leaves a urine sample and has had her blood drawn, an ultrasound tech appears with a rolling sonogram machine. Despite the insistent questions I ask, he won't reveal anything.

Once he's gone, the nurse informs us that she'll be taken for a CT scan next. The symphony of the hospital—rhythmic beeping, overhead announcements, murmurs exchanged between members of the staff—is the soundtrack to our silence.

"What if they found something?" Millie eventually asks, her voice laced with nerves.

Clutching her hand, I rub the delicate skin between her thumb and forefinger.

"Oh my god, what if I need surgery?" A sob escapes her pale lips. "I've never even broken a bone or gotten stitches."

"You're so—"

"I know, I know." She drops her head back against the elevated hospital bed. "I'm being dramatic."

I run my fingertips through her fine hair in soothing strokes. "That's not what I was going to say."

She holds my gaze, her beautiful eyes clouded with tears.

"You're so right to feel this way, honey. It's okay. I've got you. Whatever happens, I'm not going anywhere."

Her smile is weak and tired, but it's genuine.

I drag my fingers up and down her arm, distracting myself from my own worries by focusing on the feel of her velvety skin. I'm nervous, too, but I must be brave for her.

Her eyes flutter closed, and for the next hour, she sleeps, her chest rising and falling slowly.

When a nurse noisily breezes into the room, Millie startles abruptly, confusion flashing across her face. I squeeze her hand, hoping the gesture will soothe her.

Unfortunately, they won't let me go with her for the CT, so I'm left behind in the stale triage room with no company except my obnoxious bouncing knees. I reach for my phone multiple times to call Cam or Joey, but ultimately decide I should wait for Millie's permission.

Finally, she's wheeled back in, and a few minutes later, a doctor joins us.

"Hello, Amelia, my name is Dr. Renz. I'm an ob-gyn," the woman announces as she sanitizes her hands at the door. She sits on a stool with wheels and rolls across the tile until she's at Millie's side. "Your labs came back. Negative pregnancy test. However, your hemoglobin is a little low. And since you're bleeding, it's my recommendation that you have a blood transfusion. After reviewing your labs and symptoms, I suspect endometriosis, though I can't be sure without further testing. We did find a cyst on your ovary, but—"

"What?" Millie goes rigid, her hand clenching mine. "Am I going to need surgery?"

"No, no," the doctor says with a gentle smile. "We can treat the cyst with an NSAID like ibuprofen or naproxen and birth control. That'll help with the bleeding too."

## For the Show

Rubbing circles on the top of Millie's hand, I clear my throat. "A blood transfusion? That sounds serious."

"It is," the doctor replies. "But it's common, and we'll take good care of your wife, Mr. Greer."

My stomach dips at those words. *Wife. Mr. Greer.*

"We'll monitor you overnight and likely send you home in the morning," she says. "In a couple of days, you'll feel like a new woman." With a pat to Millie's thigh, she rolls back a foot or so. "You're going to be fine. I'll send someone in to admit you, and we'll do our best to find a room with a chair big enough for your husband to sleep in." She eyes me up and down.

"It's okay," Millie says. "He's not staying."

"*Amelia.*" I loom over her. "You're my wife," I say loud enough for the entire hospital to hear. "I'm staying." With that, I kiss her on the forehead and slink back into my seat, but I keep my eyes locked firmly with hers.

"I should call my parents," she finally says, breaking the staring contest we've been engaged in.

Only then do I realize we're alone. Standing, I yank her phone from my pocket and hold it out.

As she takes it from me, she eyes me like she wants me to give her privacy. Instead of leaving, I drop back into my seat and cross my arms.

Millie doesn't beat around the bush. She quickly informs her parents that she needs a transfusion, her voice laced with fear as she speaks. "No, no. Don't fly out here. You won't make it out in time anyway. Seriously, Dad, I'm fine." She's quiet for a moment, then she huffs a sigh. "I can take care of myself."

"Gimme the phone," I whisper.

She shakes her head.

"*Now.*" I hold out my hand.

As she shakes her head again, I snag it from her grip.

"Hello, Mr. and Mrs. Greer?" I ignore Millie's giant eye roll.

If she weren't in so much pain, I'd be inclined to teach her a lesson about rolling her eyes at me. Instead, I focus on the conversation with her parents.

"Is this the doctor?" her dad asks.

"No, sir. This is Ezra, Millie's…"

Arms crossed, she shoots me a death glare.

Shit. She's terrifying when she wants to be. "Millie's friend."

"Ezra? What are *you* doing there?"

"Excuse me?" The question is probably not as polite as it should be, but right now, I'm not sure I give a fuck. What does he mean, *what am I doing here?*

"She said she was going to Hawaii with a friend."

"Yes, that's what I said." I'm confused. Did Millie not tell them who she was traveling with?

"We know all about you and what happened."

My stomach sinks. The hookup in Greece? Or the sick love triangle with Samantha?

"What we don't understand is why you're in Hawaii—and at the hospital—with our daughter."

I cover the phone with my hand. "Did you not tell them?"

Millie holds a hand out. "Give me the phone."

I put it on speaker and hold it between us.

"Mom, Dad—"

"I thought you were in Hawaii with a friend," her dad interrupts. "What's going on?"

"Ezra *is* the friend." She regards me, her lip caught between her teeth, and whispers, "Can I tell them about Kane?"

I nod, and she dives into the story of how we ended up here.

"Well," her mother says, her tone lighter. "I can't say I haven't done stupid shit in my lifetime, but I hate that you're going through this while you're so far away."

"I promise she's in good hands, Mrs. Greer."

"Is that so?" her dad pipes in.

"I can take care of myself," Millie says, arms crossed over her chest.

"No, you can't," her father and I say in unison.

The look she levels me with is enough to have my balls drawing up into my body. Shit.

I clear my throat. "What I mean is that while you *can* take care of yourself, you don't have to." I swipe a hand across her forehead. "I'm here, and I'm not leaving."

## Chapter 19

# Millie

I doze off while I wait to be transferred to a private room, and when I wake in an unfamiliar space, it's quiet and the lights are dim.

The only sound I can make out is Ezra's voice. "Yeah, man, I promise to take good care of her. Try not to worry. Do you want my number, in case your sister doesn't answer?"

*Sister?* My heart stumbles a little. Is he talking to Asher?

I inhale, working up the energy to speak, but it's no use. My eyelids are too heavy and my mouth is too dry.

The next time I wake, the room is empty. An IV has been inserted into my arm, and I'm groggy as fuck.

Where's Ezra? Did he go home?

I spot my phone on a table a few feet away and force myself to sit up.

Just as I swing my legs over the bed, a deep voice reverberates through the room. "What are you doing?"

Ezra strides around the foot of the bed and places a hand on my shoulder.

"I have to pee," I croak.

*For the Show*

"Stay still. Let me call someone."

A minute later, a nurse helps me out of bed, and when I'm mostly steady on my feet, Ezra offers to take over.

"I can do it myself," I snap. The moment the phrase is out, I regret my tone.

"I didn't say you couldn't." He wraps his arm a little too tightly around my waist as I hold the IV pole.

I'm in a hospital gown and fuzzy socks that keep the coolness of the tile from soaking into me as I pad over to the en suite restroom. Fuzzy socks that look oddly familiar, actually.

In the doorway, I stop and study my feet. "How did I get these?"

"Val dropped a bag off."

Ezra turns so his back is to me but refuses to close the door while I pee. Then he's practically carrying me back to bed.

The nurse checks my IV and the bag dangling from the pole. "We've got you hooked up to fluids for now. We're waiting on the blood bank, but we'll start the transfusion shortly. If you have questions, I'm sure your husband can answer them for you." With a chuckle, she winks at Ezra. "He's asked more questions than any patient or spouse I've ever met."

He shrugs his shoulders in return.

*Husband.* He told them we were married so he could come back with me to triage. How long is he going to keep this charade going? And why do I like it so much?

Once the nurse leaves, Ezra presents a small duffel. "I wasn't entirely sure what you'd need, but Val did a good job packing. I'm sorry I wasn't here when you woke up. I was trying to find out why it's taking so long to get the transfusion started."

"It's okay. Really. You can go home if you want." I run my fingers through my hair, noting the rat's nest of tangles at the back of my head, and for the first time in hours, I think about how truly horrendous I must look.

"You must be out of your damn mind if you think I'm going home after you lost so much blood."

The vehemence in his response makes me chuckle. "You're awfully bossy."

"What can I say? I like bossing you around."

There's no fighting my grin. "Are you flirting with me, *Mr. Greer*?"

"Lay back." He glares.

I quirk a brow.

"Not like that," he huffs, though his lips twitch in amusement. "You need to relax."

"Why does every phrase you utter sound like something you'd say in the bedroom?"

He tucks me in, then props a hip on the bed, slipping his large hands to my feet and kneading them through the sheets.

A sense of calm instantly washes over me. "Thank you." Sighing, I rest my head against the paper-thin pillow.

"For what?"

"For staying."

---

The transfusion is uneventful and over in a couple of hours, though the doctor wants to keep me overnight to make sure I don't have an adverse reaction.

Between the transfusion and delicious hospital food—no, seriously, it's amazing—I feel significantly better.

Despite the way the chair pulls out to a bed, Ezra has to twist his body unnaturally to fit. I'm tempted to once again suggest he go home, but there's no point. He won't go. Plus, I really don't want to be here alone.

His phone dings, and he smiles at the screen.

"What's with the goofy face?"

"Huh?" He peers at me over the device. "My face isn't goofy."

Grinning, I huff a laugh. *Yeah right.*

"Look." He turns his phone around, but he's too far away for me to see clearly.

I pat the bed and scoot over. He obliges without fussing, his right hip flush against my left on the single mattress.

He holds the phone out again, showing me a picture of Bea with a giant bubble of snot coming out of her nose.

Laughing, I zoom in to see her adorable little dimples. "How do you have a picture of my niece?"

"Asher sent it," he says, tapping the screen.

"My brother Asher?" Dumbfounded, I sputter, "B-but how do you have his number?"

"He called your phone when you were out of it earlier, and I gave him my number. We've been texting."

My chest tightens. Did Ezra tell him about our scheming? Shit. "*You've been texting*? What have you been chatting about?"

"I've been keeping him updated. Your parents too. We got on the topic of parenting, and I told him about Kane. Asher seems like a cool dude. I don't know how he's raising a kid all on his own. He said he's happy to give advice any time I need it."

I suck in my bottom lip. What the hell? He's asking my brother for parenting advice? We're supposed to be faking this whole marriage thing, yet suddenly, it all feels a little too real.

"I should call my parents."

"I already did. They said to call when you wake up, but it's three a.m. in New York. It's only midnight in LA, and Joey said she would wait up. Why don't we call her first?"

*We?* Before I can agree, Ezra has tapped the FaceTime icon, and the room is filled with the request tone.

Joey answers quickly, her eyes wide. "Amelia Ruth Greer, you gave me a fright."

"A fright?" I laugh weakly, ignoring the way my whole body aches. "Easy, Hallie Parker."

"Hallie? I thought Annie said it."

I smirk at my cousin. "Technically it's Annie, but she's pretending to be Hallie."

"Who's Annie? Who's Hallie?" Ezra whispers.

"The girls from *The Parent Trap*." I elbow him. "Only my favorite childhood movie."

"Hi, Ezra."

"Hey, Jo." He salutes the screen.

"How are you, boo?" she asks me.

"I'm fine."

My head and Ezra's are pushed close together so we're both in the frame, and we're sporting matching top knots.

"Feeling much better after the transfusion."

"Are you taking good care of our girl?" She wags a finger.

"He is," I answer.

At the same time, he kisses the side of my head and says, "Of course."

Fuck, he's really gotta stop with all the damn sweetness.

Or else.

No more than two seconds after hanging up with Joey, a text from Asher comes through.

"What's he doing up in the middle of the night?"

"Bea's molars are coming in, and he can't go back to sleep," Ezra informs me, like he and my brother are lifelong buddies.

What the hell is happening?

Another picture of Bea comes through. This time, she's fast asleep, snuggled in footed pajamas and cuddling my old stuffed bunny—also called Bunny. *Feel better, Lee Lee*, the text reads.

*For the Show*

As I soak in the image of my niece, my nose burns and tears well in my eyes.

"Hey, what's wrong?" Ezra pulls me tight against his side.

"What if I can't have kids?" I wipe my eyes. "I don't even know if I want them. I mean, I'm pretty sure I do, but ugh…"

"Where's this coming from?" With his lips pressed to my head, he rubs my arm, soothing me.

I let myself melt into him. He smells like hand sanitizer, but I don't care because he's so damn warm.

"The doctor said she suspects endometriosis. My aunt has it, and she was never able to get pregnant again after Joey. What if—"

"Shh. Let's not jump to conclusions. We can ask the doctor more questions in the morning."

There's that "we" again. It'll go to my head if he doesn't stop.

# Chapter 20
## Millie

"I'm not a Tamagotchi," I snap. "You don't have to feed me every five minutes to keep me alive."

He takes away the plate he's just set in front of me. "You've only been out of the hospital for two days."

"Three nights," I correct him, holding up a trio of fingers. "And you heard the doctor. She said I'd feel a thousand times better and could resume normal activities right away."

Ezra's face flashes crimson, like maybe he's replaying that conversation in his mind.

*"Having sex won't be a problem, so long as you're feeling strong enough."*

*We didn't ask, but Dr. Renz includes it in her instructions anyway. She spends a few minutes discussing methods of birth control in front of Ezra, which is awkward as hell.*

*"What do you think?" I turn to Ezra, pretending to involve my husband in this decision. You know, for the show.*

*"Your body, your choice, honey," he replies like a perfect spouse. "Whatever you're most comfortable with."*

*For the Show*

Ultimately, I decided on the pill. The thought of having a miniature pogo stick floating around my uterus sounds dreadful.

"Can we do something fun today? It's supposed to be our honeymoon, *honey*." I bounce on my toes and bat my lashes dramatically. I don't want to be laid up in bed any longer. Not unless someone is laid up on top of me. Now that my period has packed her bags and taken off, I'm hella horny, and while the man standing before me is a natural caretaker, he's not helping in the way I want him to.

I briefly think about faking my period for one extra day just to get that nipple treatment again. I've got to release this tension somehow, and it's *not* going to happen in the bedroom.

"I have some things to take care of for Kane, but after, I'm all yours." He passes a mug to me, then picks up his own. The bitter notes of coffee and Earl Grey swirl between us. He's dressed in navy shorts that hug his thick thighs at the perfect length—I secretly call this pair his *slutty shorts*—and an ivory short-sleeve button-down clings to his biceps like a koala to a tree.

"Do you need me to come with you?"

We still haven't told Kane our marriage is fake, and I can't help but worry that we're doing the wrong thing by keeping the truth from him. But that's Ezra's choice to make. His lawyer knows we're not married, at least. We have zero interest in trying to fool officials or doing anything illegal.

"That's sweet of you, but I think you should rest." The space between his brows furrows, the sight urging me to smooth the line with my thumb.

I resist and instead let out a sound of frustration. "That's sweet of you, *sweetie*, but I don't wanna fucking rest anymore." I consider stomping my foot, but I'd hate to be a cliché.

"How about this?" Ezra steps forward and takes my hand in his, his palm hot from the tea. "Do you have anything to record today?"

Lips pressed together, I nod.

"If you promise to sit your butt down when you record, I'll consider that enough rest. Then I'll take you out for dinner. Deal?"

"Deal."

Once Ezra heads out, I trade my coffee for water and do my vocal warm-ups. Narrating audiobooks and recording erotic stories for LULU has brought me so much joy and solace since I was basically forced out of my role in *Mamma Mia*. I get to perform without being judged by the way I look and without panicking because I can't wiggle into my costumes. The only thing missing is dance. Oh, how I miss dancing.

Besides the night at the karaoke bar, I haven't moved my body like that in months. Dancing makes me feel the way a good orgasm does—alive and on top of the world.

I record an hour of a paranormal why-choose romance—*that was a first*—then two scenes for LULU. I thought I'd be exhausted after faking orgasms—the only time I'll allow a fake one, *thank you very much*—but instead, I'm energized.

Screw Ezra and his bossiness. Rather than rest, I need to release this pent-up energy.

Headphones on, I scroll through my playlist until I find just what I'm looking for. Once I tap my screen and the first strain of "Unwritten" plays, my hips don't stand a chance. I can't *not* bop around when I hear this song. I turn the volume all the way up, and with Natasha Bedingfield's voice as my guide, I release all my inhibitions. When it's over, it starts from the beginning again. Huh. I must have clicked the repeat button. This time, the formally trained dancer in me can't help but choreograph to the lyrics. It comes naturally, and I'm riding a high when I spin and—

My heart lurches out of my chest when I catch sight of another person, and when I realize it's Ezra, my cheeks heat in utter mortification.

"Oh my god." Wishing the floor would open up and devour me, I whip my headphones off and throw them at him.

With one hand propped on the doorframe, he catches them, his face breaking into a wicked grin.

I slap my hands over my face and whimper. This is almost as bad as the time my roommate in college caught me masturbating. This was before I discovered vibrators, so she walked in on me full-on humping a stuffed animal. (*Not* Bunny.)

"Hey," he says, his tone concerned. "Are you—are you embarrassed?"

"Of course I'm fucking embarrassed." Hands still covering my face, I drop onto the bed.

He takes a seat to my right and forces them away. "How did you feel?"

"I told you. *Embarrassed*."

"No, I mean before I walked in."

I force my chin up, and when I look at him, his nearly black eyes scorch mine. The delicate creases on the sides contradict the heat there. Instead, they give off a mature kind of comfort.

"I felt... alive. Invigorated," I reply, embracing quiet confidence that's trickled back into me.

"You looked spectacular." He zeroes in on my mouth, and I can't help but mirror him.

I lick my lips. This feels like the moment in the movie when the heroine gets kissed.

He slips a hand across my lap to the outside of my thigh, his touch hot against my skin. Internally, I cringe at the thought that there's no cotton layer between his palm and my dimply skin. Ezra's bare hand is touching my cellulite. *I don't even touch my cellulite.*

I clutch his wrist and tug, but that only makes him cling tighter, like an anchor to the ocean floor.

"You looked so beautiful dancing." He angles in, his nose

brushing against my ear. His fingers dig into my thigh, sending shockwaves straight to my core.

I rub my legs together, desperate to stifle the ache.

*What are you doing?* The question leaps to my lips, but before I can force it out, he ghosts his mouth over my neck, and the words tiptoe off the edge. It's not a kiss; he drags his skin along mine, like an artist would with a paintbrush across canvas. Only when I swallow does he kiss my pulse point. Once, twice. Then he moves to where my ear meets my jaw.

I subtly push against my pelvis with my intertwined hands, easing the throbbing in my core. Maybe it's coincidence, or maybe Ezra notices; either way, he moves his hand from my thigh to my hands and presses, adding pressure to the desperate ache.

His lush lips rest at the side of my mouth now, and when he pushes his hand against mine again, my lips part in a silent gasp. He takes this as an invitation, and I don't turn him away. The tip of his tongue dances across my bottom lip, then slips inside.

I pull my hands from beneath his and spread my legs just enough for him to rub against my throbbing center. With a moan, I thread my fingers through the hair at his nape and brush my thumb against the soft bristles at his jaw. I'm lost in the synchronicity with which he works his tongue in my mouth and his finger at my clit. It's as if he's choreographed this duet.

The pressure against my lips has me lying on my back, legs bent and feet planted wide. Ezra folds his body over mine, his erection pressing into me. *Fuck.* I push my hips up in approval, our mouths never breaking contact, my nipples tight and sensitive and brushing against the thin fabric of my shirt.

I flick my tongue, and he groans into my mouth, and—*fuck, do we have a moaner?*

The kiss intensifies, and I rock my hips faster, dry-humping him like a feral teenager.

Between my dancing and Ezra's suffocating seal over my lips, I'm out of breath and dizzy with lust, which only intensifies the torture between my legs. I'm so close, perched on the edge of ecstasy, even though we're both still fully dressed.

As I work the first button on his shirt, a chime comes from his pants, startling me.

"Shit." He sits up, still straddling my body, and retrieves his phone from his pocket. "It's the lawyer," he says, deflating.

"Answer it." My voice is breathy, my chest heaving.

With my body still trapped beneath his, he takes the call. Dammit. I wish I could finish myself off right now. Instead, I slide up the length of the bed and slip out to the lanai to give him privacy—and beg the fresh air to slap some sense into me. I nearly got off again, and Ezra has yet to even touch my pussy.

Several minutes later, he joins me outside. In his proximity, instant goose bumps erupt on my skin despite the eighty-five-degree weather.

"Is everything okay? With the lawyer," I clarify. Asking if everything is okay between us is a loaded question.

"Yes, actually." He smiles. "Kane is mine."

My heart stutters. "What?"

"Turns out the judge is an old friend of Val's. That may have helped the paperwork process faster. I've been granted guardianship."

"Seriously?" I hug him, then quickly pull away. "What about full custody or adoption?"

"That'll take longer, unfortunately, but the lawyer thinks the odds are in my favor so long as Rob doesn't change his mind and step up."

"Do you think he will?"

"No. I don't." His arms are crossed, but his face is alight with optimism.

"I think we should tell Kane." I lean against the railing, mirroring his stance. "About us."

Lowering his head, he sighs. "You're probably right."

"Come again?"

"You're prob—" He straightens. "Oh, for fuck's sake, Millie."

With a cackle, I punch him in the bicep, then I slip back inside.

---

"Where are my bathing suits?" I call from the bedroom. We're headed out to pick up Kane for a waterfall hike with the hope that it will be the perfect setting to break it to him that we're not really married. I pray it doesn't affect their relationship.

"In your drawer." Ezra comes out of the bathroom in light purple swim trunks and a white muscle tee. There are those juicy biceps, teasing me again. Why did his brother have to live in Hawaii? Why couldn't he live in coastal Alaska, where it's sweater weather?

"I only see the white one. Where are the others?"

"I don't know what you're talking about," he says, pulling the tiny white string bikini from the drawer.

"Ezra Whatever-The-Fuck-Your-Middle-Name-Is Miller, give me my bathing suits back." I hold out my hand.

"Not a chance." He preens, his large frame towering over me.

"I'm not wearing that."

"How about this?" With the suit looped over one finger, he swings it between us. "You wear the bikini, and I'll give you another nipple orgasm."

"What?" My cheeks flush instantly. "No. That was a one-time thing."

"Pity." He shrugs. "Fine. Pick what you want."

*For the Show*

*I want the fucking nipple orgasm.*

I worry my bottom lip, assessing him. "Okay... I'll wear the damn bikini if you do karaoke."

He smirks. "Easy. Done."

I hold up a finger. "But *I* get to choose the song."

## Chapter 21

# Ezra

"How long is this hike?" Kane questions when we pile out of the car.

"Are you whining already?" Millie asks. "Don't tell me you're one of those sullen teenagers." She bumps him with her hip.

"You two are something else." Chuckling, I take the lead on the trail.

We trek in comfortable silence for several minutes, soaking in the beauty of the white butterfly ginger and birds of paradise lining the dirt path. Eventually I clear my throat and peer over my shoulder at Kane. "How's driver's ed going?"

"You're taking driver's ed?" Millie jumps in. "Gosh, I totally failed my driver's test the first time."

Kane laughs, and she playfully punches him in the arm.

"I definitely wasn't driving at fifteen or sixteen in New York City," I say.

"Me neither," Millie agrees. "Are you taking any other classes?"

"Yeah, math," Kane says. He doesn't elaborate, and we fall into silence again.

*For the Show*

Coming clean to Kane is the right thing to do, but dang if I'm not nervous about telling him that my marriage is fake. What if he's angry that we lied to him? What if he doesn't want to live with me if Millie isn't part of the package? He lost his mom, and while no one could ever replace her, would he be upset if he didn't have a female figure in his life again?

My mom has been the one constant in my life, and I can't imagine not having that relationship.

Millie comes up behind me and laces her fingers with mine, then gives them a squeeze. *It's time.* She tips her head back, locking eyes with me. Her irises are even greener against the lush, tropical backdrop.

I squeeze back and nod to a bench several yards ahead, beneath a banyan tree. We stop, the need to rehydrate the perfect excuse, and sit on either side of Kane.

"Hey, buddy." I try out the endearment Millie uses for him, but it feels foreign and forced. I clear my throat and try again. "We have something we want to tell you."

Kane rubs his palms against his thighs, swallowing audibly. "Wha—what is it? Is it something with Rob? Am I not going to live with you?"

"No, no, no, it's nothing like that," Millie chimes in, her voice sweet and reassuring.

A modicum of tension drains from his body, but his knees still bounce.

"You know how we told you we're married?"

"Yeah?" He blinks at me, his lips parted.

"We're, uh. Actually, we're not." I hold my breath, my heart hammering in my ears. *This is it.* This is where he calls me a liar and refuses to trust me ever again. I've failed him before I've even had a proper chance.

With a giant exhale, Kane takes his hat off and rakes his fingers through his messy hair. "That's it?"

"What do you mean, *that's it*?" Millie asks.

He drops his head back. "Dude, I already knew that."

Air whooshes from my lungs. "What?"

"I didn't know for sure, but I figured."

"How?" Millie shifts on the bench, her hands pressed to her knees.

"C'mon. You didn't know your own damn last name." He elbows me.

Millie peers around Kane, and when our eyes meet, we break into a fit of laughter.

"There were other things too," he continues. "You didn't know her taco order. Or that she *sorta* eats Jewish."

"Kosher," I correct.

"Yeah that." He winces. "Sorry. *Kosher*."

Millie squeezes his knee. "You're very observant for fifteen."

"Perks of being a wallflower, I guess."

My heart is still beating wildly, but now in excitement rather than panic. "So... you're not mad?"

"Nah, man. We're cool."

"*Cool*, huh? Did you hear that, Mills? *I'm cool*."

He barks out a laugh. "That's not what I said."

Millie wraps an arm around his shoulder and pulls him in for a hug, but at the concerned look on his face, my heart sinks.

"What's wrong?"

"So you guys aren't married, but are you together?"

Millie releases him and looks at me. I stare dumbfounded right back.

"Um..." *I mean, I've given her one and a half orgasms in the past week. That's gotta count for something, yeah?*

"We're not." Millie's abrupt answer is a dagger straight to my heart.

"M'kay" is all he says.

"But that doesn't mean I can't be in your life."

*For the Show*

Her words nearly bowl me over. A warmth that has nothing to do with the heat of the day blooms in my chest as I observe her while she talks to my brother.

"How about as an honorary *cool* aunt?" She nudges him.

"Yeah, sure," Kane replies, though his tone is subdued.

Millie and I look at each other helplessly, but neither of us says more.

"Let's go." I pat my brother's knee and hop up. "I'm dying to see this waterfall I've heard so much about."

As we make our way down the trail, the whooshing sound grows progressively louder. A glimmer of silver peeps through the rainforest, and as the bamboo thins out, we're met with the most gorgeous sight. The three of us stand in wonder at the majestic veil of water that plummets with relentless force into a clear, natural pool. The force of the waterfall causes the ground to vibrate beneath us, and the mist in the air creates tiny rainbows in all directions. As awe-inspiring as the view is, I can't help but stare at Millie, who's fixated on the scene in front of us, her face lit with fascination.

She kneels and dips her finger in the water just as two tiny neon green-and-yellow birds swoop by. "Did you see that?" The grin on her face is brighter than the Hawaiian sun.

The three of us stand at the water's edge, my hand brushing Millie's as I wrap an arm around my brother. "Who's ready for a swim?"

"Me." In a rush, Kane tosses his shirt aside and kicks off his shoes. "C'mon, Millie."

"Yeah, *c'mon, Millie,*" I echo, pulling my shirt over my head. "We had a deal." I waggle my brows.

"Get in the water," she commands, no doubt fighting the urge to roll her eyes.

I raise my hands in submission. If she's stripping down, I'll do whatever she wants.

*Except tear my eyes away.*

I'm waist-deep in the cool water when she finally slides her thumbs under the elastic of her athletic shorts and shimmies them down her thick thighs. Next, she grabs the hem of her tank and lifts it over her head. With her arms lifted and the shirt covering her face, she stops, her whole body tensing.

When she spins, her movements jerky, panic jolts through me. Shit. Something's wrong. I climb out of the water quickly, nearly slipping on a rock and landing on my back in the process.

"Help me," she shouts, her words muffled by the fabric of her tank. "I'm stuck. I can't—I can't breathe."

"Shh, it's okay. I've got you." Keeping my tone even and calm, I slip my fingers beneath the shirt. She's sweaty, and the stretchy fabric is plastered to her skin, but with a strong tug, I pull it over her head.

The only problem?

Her bathing suit top comes off with it.

My instinct is to cover her, so I press my body against hers to prevent passersby from getting a peep show.

"Ezra?" she pants, still worked up.

"Yes?"

"Why is your naked chest against my tits?"

# Chapter 22
## Millie

*Fuck, that feels nice.*

Ezra's wet chest is pressed against my bare tits. The contrast between his cool skin and my overheated skin is jarring. And the tight, purposeful grip he has on my waist feels too damn good.

Based on the thick, solid rod poking my belly, I'm going to go out on a (large) limb and say he shares that opinion.

I tip my head back, though all I can see is the column of his neck. "Ezra?"

His throat works in a way that nearly hypnotizes me. "Yup, I know."

"How are we going to do this?" *This*, meaning get my bathing suit top on without blinding the people nearby with a shot of my super pale breasts.

"If we shuffle that way"—he tilts a fraction in one direction—"There's a towel in my backpack."

"Yeah, okay. That could work."

Still chest to chest, we sidestep in tandem until we reach his bag.

"Now bend," he commands, and together we squat like two

idiots getting low at a middle school dance. I wobble, certain I'm about to go down, but Ezra steadies me.

"For fuck's sake," I mutter. This is absolutely ridiculous.

Once he's got the towel in hand, we carefully stand, and he wraps it around my back, creating a makeshift curtain.

"Eyes up, buddy," I quip.

The motherfucker smirks, but he obediently averts his attention to the clear skies above. With shaking hands, I straighten the white dental floss around my neck, then hold the fabric in place at my chest.

"Could you, um, help me with the back?" I ask, turning.

He tosses the towel to the side and, collecting my ponytail, lays it over my shoulder. Then with warm, gentle fingers, he ties the strings at my back. Goose bumps erupt all over my body at his touch.

After a solid thirty seconds, he still hasn't released me, so I peer over my shoulder. "Have you forgotten how to tie a bow?"

"Nope." A moment later, he pats my bottom. "Let's swim."

In the shower that afternoon, I replay my bathing suit snafu—how I went from panicky to horny in two minutes flat. With my hands, I mimic the pressure of Ezra against my bare chest, the way my nipples rubbed against his hard body, imagining the beating of his heart against mine. I lower my hand, remembering how his growing thickness felt, the way my clit pulsed in response beneath my swimsuit. Stifling a moan, I paint circles over the bundle of nerves, eliciting pleasure. And with the assistance of the detachable shower head, I find my release, with Ezra's name drowning on my lips.

*For the Show*

"Have you seen my—*whoa*." Ezra's jaw drops, and his focus gets stuck on my exposed midriff.

I'm wearing high-waisted jeans that hug every curve and, this evening, I feel really good in them. The lacy white crop top is an item Joey forced me into buying the last time we went shopping. The straps are thin, and it has a built-in underwire so I don't need a bra. Ezra took way too long in the shower, which left me no time to style my hair, so I've parted it down the middle and pulled it into a low ponytail.

"I'd say the white makes you look virginal, but..."

A laugh escapes me as I shuffle to the closet. "Please don't say *virginal*."

"You look like an angel."

Heart in my throat, I stop in my tracks. I can't tell whether he's being serious. "Are you flirting again, Mr. Miller?" I ask, keeping my tone even as I slip into my wedges.

"It's Mr. Greer." He drops to his knees in front of me and works one buckle. "And absolutely." He looks up, surveying me from beneath dark lashes. "Is it working?"

*Is what working? Seeing Ezra on his knees?* "Hmm, we'll see."

He promised me karaoke in exchange for wearing that damn bathing suit, and he's staying true to his word. To be honest, it wasn't as horrendous as I anticipated. The way he couldn't stop drooling over me made it worth it. Unless he was wrestling Kane in the water, his attention was fixed on me, drinking in every one of my curves. It was a major boost to my self-esteem. I started this trip with massive body insecurities, and I was positive Ezra would be disgusted with my new figure. But that is not the case. While I'm still not totally comfortable in my skin, it eases my mind to know that he isn't judging me in the least.

We indulge in authentic shave ice before walking to the Japanese BBQ place next door to the bar where we sang karaoke last time and both immediately drool over the menu.

"I think telling Kane the truth went well," I say, picking up my glass of water.

He's silent for a moment, eyes fixed on the menu. Finally, he cups my free hand and looks at me. "It did." He squeezes. "Thank you."

He releases me, but I grasp his wrist to stop him. "You're welcome. I meant what I said, too, about staying in his life. If that's okay with you, of course." I bite my bottom lip and inspect his expression, searching for clues about how he feels. Maybe I'm overstepping here. Kane and I don't have any type of link connecting us now that our fake marriage has been revealed. But in the short time I've known him, I've come to really like the kid. Not only that, but I understand what it's like to be a queer person in this world; it's beautiful, but it's not easy, and I feel the urge to be a safe person in his life.

Ezra pinches the bridge of his nose. "You'd do that?"

"Of course."

"You're something else, Mills. You know that?" His dark eyes bore into me, his expression so endearing I swear it causes the elastic on my panties to snap.

The blush I'm now sporting is not from the Hawaiian heat. "So, um…" I pull my hand away.

He does the same, picking up his own water. "Have you picked out a song for me yet?"

I perk up and bite back a smile. "Yup."

"And…" He raises a brow. "Are you going to tell me?"

"Nope."

Dinner was delicious, and the conversation flowed as smoothly as my mai tai, but I'm most excited about karaoke. Ezra tries to perform the second we arrive, but I make up excuses to put it off; I'm waiting till there's a full house. We pass the time by playing a stupidly competitive round of darts that nearly has me aiming for his stupidly tight ass. He's wearing his slutty shorts again, paired with a button-down. His chest is smattered with dark hair, distracting me in a way that makes it impossible to aim. I make up for the loss, though, when I beat him at foosball. All those years at theater camp have finally paid off.

Just as I'm about to win another round, Ezra is called to the stage.

"Go get 'em, big guy." I slap him on the ass.

He scowls playfully. He's only a little annoyed that I still haven't told him what song I picked.

Leaning against a tabletop to the side of the stage, I pull my phone out, ready to record.

At the podium, Ezra grips the mic but leaves it in the stand. His hair is pulled back in a low bun, and beneath the colored lights, his temples are dotted with perspiration. It's the only hint that he may be nervous. He stands tall, his shoulders back, the perfect picture of confidence. That facade slips a little, though, when the title is revealed on the screen behind him and on the smaller one in front of him.

"Man, I Feel Like a Woman!" by the one and only Shania Twain.

*This oughta be good...*

He hangs his head, and for a second, I think he's going to back out. A single curl falls from his bun, and he tucks it behind his ear without looking up. The first seven notes played by the horns come through the speakers, and on cue, he announces, "Let's go girls."

I scan the crowd, finding a mixture of secondary embarrassment and amusement plastered on each face.

His voice is quiet at first, but as soon as he pants "Uh!" and the crowd cheers, his entire demeanor changes. He sways his hips and—*no, no, no*. This is not how this was supposed to go.

He might as well be fucking Harry Styles in a sequined jumpsuit with the way he's working the crowd right now.

Annoyance licks up my spine. This was supposed to be payback for making me wear the flimsy bikini; instead, he looks like he's having the time of his life. And when the lyric about letting our hair hang down appears on the screen, Ezra pulls out his own elastic and shakes his curls free.

The women in the bar go absolutely feral in response, making it impossible to hear the next few lines.

That's it.

I concede.

There's no way I can come back from this.

He even imitates Shania's high-pitched *whoo*s at the end.

*That fucking mother-fucking-fucker.*

When he descends the stage, he's followed by a sea of women —and one man—acting like cats in heat as he strides to the high-top. I'm shoved out of the way by a cougar, but Ezra steps around her to get to me. "Sorry, ladies, but I'm here with my wife." He flashes them his wedding ring, and I swear their groans of disappointment are louder than their screams.

"Is your shirt unbuttoned?" I ask as his little fan club disperses.

"Oops, don't know how that happened." With a laugh, he does up the bottom few.

"So…" He pulls me in by my waist, holding me against him. "How was I?"

I scowl.

"That good, huh?"

*For the Show*

"I cannot believe you." With a groan, I pick up the vodka soda our server sets on the high-top. She's thin and leggy and zipped from toe to tits in tight black leather. Her hair is cropped a lot like Sam's was when we dated. She places an arm on Ezra's bicep, the move sending a zap of jealousy through me. At the same time, though, she's also ogling my boobs. That's when I notice a rainbow sticker on her name tag next to a pin that reads *she/they*. Is she flirting with us both? Would I be into that? *Would Ezra?* I've only ever had one threesome. But for years, I've had to fight like hell to convince people that not all bisexuals are nonmonogamous, despite the stereotype.

In my tipsy state, though, my judgment is a tad clouded. I can't tell whether Ezra is flirting or being friendly. Sometimes they look the same. The server writes her name and number on a cocktail napkin and winks at the both of us before turning to leave.

"Would you ever have a threesome?" I blurt over the rim of my drink.

"*Amelia.*" He takes my glass and sets it on the table. "Shh, not so loud."

"What? She seemed interested." I shrug.

He holds me hostage in his gaze, his expression unreadable. Then, before I know what's happening, he drags me by my waist and pins me between him and the high-top, pressing me in so firmly the wood digs into my spine. "I will only say this once." His breath, laced with whiskey and orange, is hot against my ear. "I do not share my women." He slides a hand under the hem of my crop top and digs his nails into the skin of my back. "If I'm with you, I'm with *only you*. Got it?"

I'm pretty sure my responding gulp can be heard all the way to Maui. Does he mean *you* as in *me*? Or *you* as in *women in general*?

Either way, I nod.

"Good." He pushes off me, but not before I feel the bulge in his shorts.

After one more drink, Ezra cuts me off. He's nursing an old-fashioned, the spicy citrus scent of which brings me back to the night we shared in Greece. I was so riled up about his surprisingly stellar karaoke performance that evening. I never expected him to win the crowd over when he sang "Under Pressure" by David Bowie and Queen. But he did. One thing led to another, and I found myself riding his hand in a storage closet, followed by a night that should have been hot but turned out to be a flop.

I was itching to try out the vibrator I'd purchased from a vending machine in Crete's city center. After stealing batteries from the hotel's TV remote, we put that bad boy to good use. But when I went to return the favor, Ezra stopped me.

"You've been drinking," he said.

"So?" I argued. "If I'm sober enough to have an orgasm, I'm sober enough to give you one."

"That's not how it works."

I guess he was right about the *not* sober part because the details are fuzzy after that. The next morning, Joey and Cam walked in on us buck naked in bed together. Ezra tried patching things up the next day, but it was too late—my ego had already been bruised, and I dismissed him.

I'd like to think I've matured since then, though. I'm done writing him off.

# Chapter 23
## Millie

"Ha." I stick my tongue out at Ezra in the bathroom mirror. "I told you I wouldn't have a hangover."

"That's because I cut you off and forced carbs and two ibuprofen down your throat before bed."

"Always looking out for me, Daddy," I tease.

He drops his deodorant in the sink, blinking rapidly.

I can't help but laugh at his dazed expression. "What are you dressed up for?" He's wearing shorts and a nice shirt rather than his usual athletic shorts or swim trunks.

"Val's daughter is visiting, so I'm meeting her for breakfast. Wanna come?"

*Val's daughter?* My stomach sinks. He made plans without discussing them with me first? Wait. I force myself to take a deep breath. Why do I care? It's not like he owes me a play-by-play.

"Uh, no. That's fine. You, um, *enjoy*." The word tastes sour on my tongue. "I had plans to head down to the beach, actually."

"I'll text you when I get back. If you're still there, I'll join you, yeah?"

With a noncommittal sound and a weak smile, I scurry into

the bedroom to change, and when the door at the bottom of the stairs closes, I let out a strangled scream.

At the beach, I spend a solid hour stewing, and eventually, I FaceTime Joey to pass the time.

"Hey, babe," she cries when she accepts the request. "How are you?"

I swallow back my frustration. "I'm fine. What are you doing? Can you talk?"

"Yup. We're in Catalina." She flips the screen, and Cam waves from a doorway, wearing a bathrobe.

"Hi, Cameron," I sing, but the screen is already back on my cousin.

"What's up?" she asks. "Are you on the beach? Is Ezra with you?"

"No. Just me. He's, uh, with Val's daughter?" My voice goes up at the end, though I don't mean for it to. "They went for breakfast or something."

Joey frowns. "Why do you seem bothered by that?"

Shoulders pulled back, I lift my chin. "I'm not bothered."

Joey's infamous brows challenge me.

"Fine. I'm a *little* bothered," I admit. "But..."

"But you don't know why?" She words it as a question, but she goes on before I can answer. "It's because someone's caught feelings for their fake husband."

"Fifty bucks," Cam shouts in the background.

"What's that about?" I tilt my head, as if doing so will allow me to peer around her and eye her fiancé.

"Oh nothing," she says with a wave of her hand. "Just that Cam bet you'd fall for Ezra before the trip was over."

"It's the Bearded Effect," he calls out.

"Anyway," Joey continues. "What's wrong with falling for him? I can't believe he's adopting Kane."

"That's the hope. As for what the issue is here, the guy is the epitome of a family man, and I never really envisioned that for myself."

She cocks her head to one side. "What happened to the Millie who planned her entire wedding on a PowerPoint instead of studying for her bat mitzvah?"

I laugh. She's got me there, but... "I always planned to marry a woman."

"So? You also made the DJ play 'The Thong Song' three times in a row. You've evolved since then. Just because your version of playing house involved two wives, that doesn't mean you can't marry a man someday. Love is love. Aren't you always getting fired up about people giving bi babes a hard time?"

"First of all, no one said anything about love. Second, yeah, you're right." There are a ridiculous number of people out there who don't understand that bisexuals aren't "switching" between straight and gay.

"What do you want?"

"She wants that pierced dick."

"Cameron No-Middle-Name Connelly," Joey shouts.

I suck in a breath, and at the same time, the breeze picks up, so I end up choking on a chunk of hair that blows across my face. "A pierced *what*?"

"I can neither confirm nor deny." Cam appears beside Joey, wearing a mischievous smirk. "Guess you'll have to find out for yourself."

He refuses to elaborate, despite my best efforts (and threats), and eventually, we move on to other topics. Joey fills me in on her latest book, but we're cut short when gray clouds move in and it begins to rain.

With my sarong wrapped around my waist, I hightail it back to the apartment. Once I've hung my wet towel in the garage and kicked off my Birks, I climb the stairs. My phone managed to stay dry, but I must have accidentally hit the *Spotify* app in my hurry to beat the storm because a Chappell Roan song is playing.

I click it off at the top of the stairs, and the music is quickly replaced by the sound of *moaning*.

I freeze at the entrance to the bedroom, blood whooshing in my ears. Ezra is moaning on the other side of the bathroom door. Then a woman joins in, and I stagger back.

*The fuck?*

I'm gone for one hour, and he has a woman in the apartment? Is it Val's daughter? We're not really married; he can hook up with whomever he wants. But this is our shared space.

Anger ignites in my chest and flares through my extremities. The audacity of this motherfucker.

"Strip for me, Daddy. I want to see all of you. Hand on your cock. *Now*," the woman commands.

*Oh.* That is *not* Val's daughter. No, I recognize that voice.

# Chapter 24
## Millie

It's my voice.

Jules, really.

Holding my breath, I creep closer to the partially open door and feast on the image spread out before me. Ezra's back is to me, but I can see the entire front side of his torso in the mirror. His shorts are pulled down just enough for his cock to be exposed, and he's got one hand splayed on the counter for support and the other wrapped around his shaft.

When he tugs along his length and stops at the tip, it's confirmed: my fake husband *does* have dick bling.

I smother my gasp with my hand and take a step back.

But it's too late. He lifts his head and locks eyes with me in the mirror. "Don't you fucking move."

Feet planted firmly on the ground, I slowly push open the door.

"Did you think I wouldn't see you, blondie?" Stroking his cock, he keeps his focus fixed on my reflection. This man sleeps nude every night; I should have known he wouldn't be shy.

A shiver rushes down my spine, and not from my wet bathing suit.

"I've been so good for you. I want a taste of you. I'm begging you, please," Jules says from Ezra's phone.

"Th-that's me. Did you know?" I ask, barely above a whisper.

His jaw goes rigid. "Of course I fucking know."

"How?"

Ezra smirks, the expression menacing. "I knew the second you called me Daddy."

My stomach flip-flops. Oh. That's what that look was about. I clutch my hands to my chest. "I knew you had a daddy kink."

When he doesn't respond, I venture a step back. "I, um, I'll leave you to it, then." I salute. Like an idiot.

"Stay." It's a command, not a request.

"What?"

He's still facing the mirror, hand locked around his length. It's taking everything in me not to stare at it.

*It's a beautiful fucking cock.*

"Now that I have the real thing in front of me, I don't want *that*." He juts his chin toward his phone. Jules—er, *me*—is moaning now. "Plus, you can't look away. You want to stay, don't you?"

"I do not—"

"Liar." His words are sharp, accusatory.

I bite my bottom lip, desperately reeling in a smirk.

"So what happens next?" He taps Pause on his phone with his free hand.

"Huh?"

"In the story," he clarifies. "She was just about to get on her knees. *You* were about to get on your knees." He quirks a brow, those dark eyes almost black.

"You want me to *act it out*?" I damn near choke.

"You said you're a good actress. Show me."

*For the Show*

Oh fuck, he's serious. Heat pools in my belly as my heart takes off at a sprint.

I'd be lying if I said I don't remember what happens in the story next; it's one of my more recent recordings, as well as a favorite. Jules is a teasing brat in this scene. Narrating it was a blast, and I got myself off in record time afterward. Perks of the job.

Ezra turns to face me, still holding his dick.

As if an invisible force is pulling me in, I step forward. A look of trepidation passes between us, but I find myself removing my sarong and kneeling on the plush bathmat before him.

I'm used to performing live in front of hundreds of people, but I've never been more nervous than I am right now, with an audience of one.

"Do you consent?" he whispers.

Without hesitation, I nod.

As he slides his shorts down his thighs and steps out of them, I clear my throat, preparing myself to step into my role as Jules. Tilting my chin up, voice lower and grittier than usual, I ask, "Do you want me to suck your cock, *Daddy*?"

Above me, Ezra's throat bobs sharply, and he juts his chin.

"Too bad," I rasp. "You'll have to wait."

His hooded eyes narrow. "You fucking brat. That's not what happens next."

I raise a brow. *Oh, he's already listened to this one, has he?* "Do you want me to do this or not?"

"Go on," he grits out.

"Stroke yourself for me."

He huffs an exasperated breath, but he obeys.

While he works himself over, I take the opportunity to study what we're working with. With my mostly dry hair gathered over one shoulder, I angle in a fraction.

Silently, he guides his cock toward his abdomen, exposing the underside of his shaft, where four small silver barbells reside.

Fuck. I've never been with a pierced man before. I'm dying to find out if it's worth the hype.

"Like what you see?"

I nod.

"I can tell. You're a fucking whore for it, aren't you?" He clutches my hair and tugs, yanking my head back so I'm forced to look at him. He studies me intently, I assume, to see if I'll change my mind. When I lift my chin higher, he says, "Now be my good little slut and tell me what happens next."

He releases his grip, and I straighten my shoulders and get back into character. "Yes, sir."

"You drive me mad, Mills."

The heat in my belly ignites when he calls me that. "Spit on your cock," I command, sticking with the original script.

Ezra obeys, catching his saliva and rubbing it along his shaft.

"Now *slowly* stroke it." I'm entranced by his every move. "That's it. Fuck that hand. Do you wish you were fucking my mouth or my pussy right now?"

Rather than answer, he grunts, his hips jerking, his length sliding through his fist.

"Or maybe you'd want to take my ass." I keep my focus fixed on the sight before me. "Is that what you want? Me on all fours, my tight hole hungry for your cock? Spit on it again. Get it real wet for me."

He does as he's told. "Fuck." His breathing is rapid, his thrusts erratic.

"Are you close?" Turning up the seduction, I steal a peek at his face. His features are pinched; he's straining to hold back. "Let me hear you."

He grunts.

## For the Show

"Louder," I urge. "That's it. Fuck your hand like you're fucking me. *Harder.* I like it rough," I rasp.

In response, his throaty groans fill the room.

I'm practically dripping at the sight. There's nothing sexier than a man moaning.

I'm still on my knees, worshipping this solo act. One flick of my tongue, and I'd be touching the tip of his dick.

"Are you ready to come for me, Daddy?"

He curls over me, a hand on the countertop once again, his sweat droplets landing on my bare shoulder. "Open your mouth," he demands.

I hold my tongue out wide, and when Ezra spits on it, my body spasms with need.

"Now suck on my dick until I come down your pretty little throat."

*With pleasure.*

My core throbs with want, but I resist the urge to touch myself. Instead, I coat his cock with the mixture of our saliva, relishing the way the cool metal of his piercings feels against my tongue and fantasizing about how they'd feel in my pussy. Or my ass.

I peer up at him.

"You're incredible," he groans, the tendons in his neck tight.

With both hands at the back of my head, he holds me still and shoves his dick deep.

Surprised by the move, I gag on him.

"That's it. Choke on my cock like the good little slut you are. You said you like it rough. Were you lying?"

I shake my head, my eyes watering.

"Good."

*Slam.*

I clutch his muscular thighs, anchoring myself against him.

"You're going to take my cum, honey."

*Slam.*
"Every."
*Slam.*
"Last."
*Slam.*
"Drop."

With one more thrust, he's pouring into my mouth, and I'm doing everything I can not to make a mess of his release. The sound of his guttural moans echoing off the tile will be the soundtrack of my dreams for years to come.

# Chapter 25
## Ezra

I should pay the LULU app double for my subscription. Hell, I'd pay triple. Because the 4D experience is life-changing.

When my breakfast with Val's daughter was cut short and I discovered I was alone in the apartment, I couldn't resist the urge to slip my hand into my pants. Existing in such close proximity to Millie has been torture. The woman may be easy to get along with and neat as a pin, but the bombshell sleeps naked, and a man only has so much willpower.

Waiting until she falls asleep every night to sneak to the bathroom to jerk off is no longer cutting it. I'm loud, and I'm not ashamed of it, but there's no way I'm waking her up with my moans.

I'm also sick and tired of being quiet.

Knowing Millie was at the beach, I saw an opportunity. And when I was literally caught with my dick in my hand, I saw yet another. I'm a smart man, after all.

I signed up for LULU a year ago, shortly after meeting Millie. I'd never heard of an erotic stories app before. I played around with the filters but could never pinpoint her voice. In my exhaustive search, I've nearly devoured all the recordings (even the ones about fairies and mythology). It wasn't until she playfully called me Daddy that it clicked.

*Millie is Jules.*

So when I found myself alone this morning, I opened the app and navigated to my favorites, then selected the first story. It's categorized under *daddy kink* and *you + her*, where a female narrator guides the listener through the scene while the listener imagines they're a part of it.

I envisioned Millie's sexy curves in that tiny bikini beneath the waterfall yesterday. That image, paired with her sultry voice on my phone, had my cock stiffening in record time. Fantasizing about Millie calling me Daddy? Hard. As. A. Rock.

But never in my wildest dreams could I have imagined the story would come to life.

When I caught her at the door, I almost let her sneak away. Call it *temporary insanity by hormones*. I don't know what I did in a former life to earn the privilege of having Millie on her knees, but I swear I'll pay it forward. She didn't even flinch when I spit on her tongue, that wet, pink flesh waiting and eager.

I'm dying to see another pink and wet part of her anatomy.

And when she let me come in her mouth? Who needs the audio when they've experienced the live performance?

Now, she's still on her knees, her eyes swimming with lust.

"Don't swallow," I quickly command, praying I'm not too late.

She seals her lips, focus fixed on my face.

"Good girl," I praise, helping her to stand. "Let me see it."

She parts her lips, showing me the cum pooled on her tongue.

My dick twitches at the sight. "Fuck," I groan. "The only place my cum would look better is dripping from your pussy."

At those words, she nearly chokes.

I wrap my hand around her throat. "You can swallow now."

*For the Show*

Her throat bobs beneath my palm. And when she licks her lips, my dick is ready for round two.

"Can I kiss you?"

She angles in, her tongue darting into my mouth.

When my own taste registers, I nearly black out with need. Hands on her ass, I tug her closer. "Jump, baby."

She pulls away, her brow knitted with apprehension. She's thinking I can't hold her weight, but I don't let her get away with brushing off the command.

"When I say jump, *you jump*," I growl. "Now go."

We bend together, and I effortlessly lift her off the floor. With her legs wrapped around my waist and my cock wedged between us, I carry her to the bedroom.

Carefully, I set her on the bed and take a step back. "On your hands and knees, honey."

# Chapter 26
# Millie

WHAT THE FUCK IS HAPPENING?

One minute I'm ready to drop-kick a bitch for hooking up with my fake husband, the next I'm falling to my knees, eager to suck the man off.

I've had some heated hookups, including one with him, but none like that. His authoritative stance and the way he told me exactly what to do had me weak in the knees.

I'll take stage direction from him anytime.

Now, standing over me, he growls, "On your hands and knees, honey."

I instantly obey.

The bed dips behind me, and then Ezra gathers my hair at my nape and brings it over my shoulder. Slowly, he trails his fingers down my spine, eliciting a shiver from me, and stops at the strings tied in the middle of my back. When he tugs and the fabric gives way, my breasts hang free and my nipples immediately harden to points. He unties the strings at my neck as well and tosses the top to the side.

In tandem, he releases the bows at my hips, and the bottoms

*For the Show*

fall to the bed, leaving my ass on display. The mattress gives, as if he's backing off.

Heart in my throat, I peek over my shoulder. Hovering beside the bed, Ezra pulls his hair back with the pink scrunchie I left on the nightstand, his biceps flexing.

When he steps forward again, he curls over me, his bare chest brushing my back, and grinds his piercings against my ass.

"When did you get those?" I ask, the question escaping with a gasp.

"Shortly after that night."

*That night.* The evening we found out we'd both been played by the same woman.

"I cut my hair really short too." He laughs against my ear.

I lock my arms, stiffening. "You did not." I cannot imagine Ezra without his signature locks.

He hums. "I did. The hair was on a whim, but I got the piercings to mark turning a page in my life. I hated what she did to me —*to us*—and I wanted a way to signify an *after*. Maybe it's silly, but—"

"No, it makes sense." Some men purchase a motorcycle during a crisis, others get a Jacob's ladder.

"Plus, I hear it's amazing for women."

My pulse picks up at the thought. "Do you not already know that?"

"Nope. Haven't been with anyone since, remember?" His lips graze the shell of my ear. "Wanna see if the rumors are true?"

Flames lick up my spine. "Fuck yes."

He sits back on his haunches behind me. "On your elbows."

Dropping to my forearms, I present my ass to him.

"Fuck, Millie. You're so sexy." He grips both globes and squeezes. *Tight.* Spreading my cheeks apart, he asks, "Can I touch it? I want it. I need to have it. Need to have *you*."

"Yes. Take all my consent and fuck me up, Daddy."

Without warning, he smacks my ass. First the right cheek, then the left, the sting causing desire to gather in my core. Then he spits.

Wetness coats my puckered hole, and when his finger makes contact, I jolt in surprise. A heartbeat later, though, I push my hips back, urging him to slip inside.

"Butt plug. There," I pant, pointing to the nightstand.

He chuckles. "Why did you bring a—*never mind.*" Carefully, he removes his finger. Then he rounds the bed and shuffles through the drawer. "I don't see it."

Huffing, I crawl across the mattress to retrieve it myself. *Why can men never find anything?*

But when I dig in the drawer, I come up empty-handed. I snag my phone off the nightstand instead and open the *Find My* app, then I click on *Items* and the eggplant emoji that reads *Toys*.

An instant later, there's a delicate chirping nearby.

Ezra guffaws. "You have an AirTag for your butt plug?"

"My sex toy bag." I grin up at him.

He scoots the nightstand out a little and checks behind it. Then he drops to all fours, pulls a satin black bag from under the bed, and holds it above his head with an *aha*. "When did you—*never mind.*" He hands over the bag.

I procure a baby pink glass plug with a matching gemstone at the end, along with a travel-size bottle of lube.

Now that we have all the necessary supplies, I return to all fours.

Once he's squirted the lube directly between my cheeks, he notches the plug at my opening.

"Ready?"

"Yes." I shift back as he pushes in carefully and grunt at the initial burn of the toy's intrusion.

He puts a hand on my hip and squeezes. "You okay?"

"Mm-hmm." Sighing, I relax my core.

"God, that's a beautiful sight." Slipping his hand to my ass, he gives it a jiggle.

The move sends a shudder of pleasure straight to my pussy. When his fingers find my opening, I tremble, and as he collects my arousal and teases my clit, playing with the pressure of his touch, that tremble turns into a tsunami.

I undulate my hips, desperate for more. As if he can read my mind, he thrusts his fingers inside me.

"*Ah*," I moan, reveling in the sparks of need arcing through me.

"Do you hear how wet your cunt is?" His breath skates across my nape.

He pumps and stretches, each move more exquisite than the last. Between the fullness of his fingers and the plug, I'm already nearing an orgasm.

"Faster," I call, lacing my fingers on the mattress and resting my forehead on my clenched hands. "More. Please."

He pistons his fingers, over and over, hitting *that spot*. The spot that'll cause me to make a mess of the duvet.

Shit, I need to warn him.

"Ezra, I—"

"That's it, baby."

"I'm gonna... St—" The word *stop* is on the tip of my tongue, but he's ramming into me so hard and so fast I can't catch my breath. And the truth is, I don't want him to stop.

Tears well in my eyes, threatening to fall with each thrust. I clamp my lids shut like a dam and suck in a breath, clutching the fabric beneath me like a life raft.

"Take it, baby. It's yours," he grunts.

"I'm—I'm—" The sensations are all too much. I reach behind me to swat his fingers away.

With one final curl of his digits, he obeys. And that's when it happens. My body convulses violently for what feels like a lifetime before I finally collapse.

"*Fuck*, Millie. Daddy's drenched."

My heart clenches. "I'm sorry. I didn't—"

He rolls my limp body to one side and lowers himself so we're eye to eye. "What are you sorry about? That was the hottest fucking thing I've ever seen. C'mere." He pulls me into his arms.

I'm shivering, my body still coming down from orgasm, as I rest my head on his shoulder and take pleasure in the way he pushes my hair off my face and strokes my arm.

"Fuck," I breathe when the wetness beneath us registers. "I should have laid a towel down, but I wasn't expecting to..."

"Squirt?"

I bury my head in his chest. "Ugh, I hate that word."

"There's nothing to be ashamed of. It was impressive." He plants a kiss on my forehead, the featherlight sensation of his beard against my skin making me shiver again.

"I'm not ashamed. I just wish there was a more attractive word for it." I chuckle, wiggling in his hold.

"Are you okay? I wasn't too rough, was I?"

Warmth spreads through my chest at the concern in his tone. "No, not at all. I still have the plug—"

"Oh." He sighs. "Do you want me to help you..."

I shake my head. "You promised me a test drive with your new pimped-out ride."

With another kiss to my forehead, he lays me on my back, avoiding the mess I've already made, and kneels between my legs, smirking and stroking his length, slowly revealing one piercing at a time. "My cock is not a pimped-out ride."

"I'll be the judge of that."

I'm laid bare and vulnerable before him, but just as my mind reverts to its evil self-conscious being, he shuts down the thoughts.

*For the Show*

"You're a vision." His dark eyes blaze a trail down my body, inch by inch. "So fucking stunning." Instinctively, I bring my hands to my abdomen, but he pins them at my sides before I can hide. "Don't. Let me worship you."

I lie still, relishing each touch. Ezra palms my breasts, bringing them together and brushing his thumbs against my sensitive peaks, then letting them fall heavy against my arms. With one hand gripped around his cock, he drags his other leisurely down my sternum, pausing at my navel. He caresses the soft flesh and grips the rolls that live there.

It takes effort to tamp down on the urge to bolt out of here. But in the end, I rein in the sensation. There's nothing but heat and desire in his expression. I never could have imagined being turned on like this. That he could trace my stretch marks and leave me panting and wanting more. He scoots down the bed and dips in low, a look of determination on his face. I'm certain he's going to devour my pussy; instead, he plants a kiss on my navel. One, two, three kisses, until he's nipping and sucking at my skin and I'm whining in response.

He peers up at me, and I snap a mental picture of him resting his chin on my belly, memorizing the crinkles at the sides of his eyes when he smiles.

"For fuck's sake," I cry when he lingers like that.

He laughs into my curves. "You're a greedy girl, aren't you? Do you want something from Daddy?"

I nod feverishly, my heart thumping against my sternum in response to his decadent tone.

"You're gonna have to ask for it."

"Give me your cock," I breathe out.

"*Nicely,*" he corrects me.

That bastard.

But I can play his game.

"May I have your cock, *please*, Daddy?"

"Lift your hips."

I obey, and he shoves a pillow beneath me. Looks like we'll be doing a lot of laundry after this.

"Do you have a condom in that Mary Poppins sex bag of yours?"

I shake my head. I haven't been with a man in I can't remember how long.

"Dammit," he hisses, hanging his head like a sad puppy.

"It's fine. I'm on birth control, remember?"

His body goes rigid above mine, and he raises his gaze. "Don't be a fucking tease."

Despite his mature language, he isn't doing a very good job of hiding his boyish anticipation. His eyes flash with excitement, like he's just been told he gets to open his presents first on Christmas morning.

"I'm not teasing you. You said you haven't been with anyone since... *her*, and neither have I. Just make sure you pull out."

Exhaling loudly, he nods.

I snag the bottle of lube from the mattress and hold it out to him.

With a *tsk*, he slides his hand over my pussy. "Darling, we won't be needing that." He's right. I'm still soaked. He pushes my legs wide, my glistening cunt at his mercy.

Notching his cock at my opening, he guides his crown in an inch, but pauses there, his brow furrowed.

"What's wrong?" My chest constricts. Is he reconsidering fucking me bare? Reconsidering fucking me at all?

"I don't want to hurt you."

"You won't."

Zeroing in on the place where our bodies meet, he hooks his arms under my thighs and slams inside.

*Shit, maybe he'll hurt me after all.*

The sudden intrusion stings, but the sensation is quickly

replaced by an acute awareness deep inside my body. *The piercings.*

With my legs wrapped around his waist, I squeeze, holding him still. Chest heaving, I focus on my breathing, willing my body to adjust to his size. After a moment, I relax my legs and give Ezra a tentative smile.

He plants his hands on either side of my head and presses his lips against mine as he slides his cock along my inner wall slowly.

The plug in my ass and the metal on his cock rub together through the thin layer of smooth muscle, sending a shudder through me. Fuck. It's a tight fit.

"That feels good," he moans into my hair. "Fuck, Millie. That pussy of yours is perfect. I need to taste it." Without a second of hesitation, he pulls out.

A cry escapes me. "No—" My protest is cut off when he licks and flicks my clit with more ferocity than a wildfire. Just when I think I can't take anymore, he runs his fingers up my body and pinches my nipples. I claw at his hands, too sensitive, but he clamps down even harder.

"Ezra. Fuck," I sob. *"Fuck, fuck, fuck... you."*

Finally, he comes up for air, a total mess, his beautiful beard sopping wet. He's never looked hotter. Pinning my shaking thighs to the mattress, he rises onto his knees and moves closer.

I grasp his cock between us and run my thumb along the underside of his shaft, delicately exploring the perfectly placed metal. "How does it feel when you're inside me?"

"Like heaven."

With a groan, I feed his cock to my pussy. I don't stop until he's seated fully. He rocks his hips in a steady rhythm as the heady smells and sounds of our union fill the room. Lost to the sensations, I arch my back. My vision blurs, and tears stream down my cheeks. Nothing has ever felt like this.

Ezra rests his forehead on mine, our sweat mixing, our breaths mingling.

Anyone in their right mind would pay good money to hear the sounds coming out of this man's mouth. He's loud, and I fucking love it.

"More," I beg, matching his rhythm, my tits bouncing.

With a grunt, he bends to catch an eager nipple in his mouth. He sucks hard, sending sparks of electricity straight to my core.

"That feels good," I praise. "So good. Don't stop."

I slip a hand between our bodies. The wet, swollen bundle of nerves is ready for its encore.

"That's it, baby. Play with that clit. Come for Daddy."

That's all it takes to send me hurtling over the edge. I'm lost in the forest of orgasms and never coming back. It was nice knowing you, world, but I'm broken. Broken by my Brooklyn Boy.

Before I've completely returned to the moment, Ezra groans, the sound pained. "Fuck, Millie. Where can I come?"

"Here." Without hesitation, I tap a finger to my navel.

He pulls out in a rush, his motions jerky, and hot bursts of cum stain my stretch marks.

I've never felt so beautiful.

He collapses onto his back beside me, running a hand along my inner thigh.

Jolting, I grasp his wrist. "Stop."

"Wh—what's wrong?" he asks, retracting his hand like I've burned him.

"Nothing. I'm just ticklish there after I come."

His body sags in relief beside me, and for several minutes, we silently stare at the ceiling. Eventually my eyes drift closed. I'm not sure whether I dozed off or zoned out, but I'm startled back to the moment by a warm, wet sensation at my belly. I blink myself back into existence and discover Ezra hovering over me with a wet washcloth, cleaning his cum from my body.

Once he's taken the washcloth back to the bathroom, he collapses onto the mattress and draws me into his side.

I resist and point to the plug still inside me. "Uh, I need to..."

He sits up, his brows lifted. "May I?"

No one has ever offered to remove my anal plug. The idea of it feels incredibly intimate.

Yet I find myself nodding and tilting my hips in his direction.

Cautiously, he removes it, then tosses the plug to the end of the mattress.

"Look at it gaping, greedy for me to fuck it."

My body shudders with need, even as I drop back to the mattress, completely spent.

He angles in and kisses the place where my neck meets my shoulder. Then, with a nip to my collarbone, he rises. "Next time."

He clamps his hands around my ankles and drags me to the edge of the bed, making me gasp, then giggle with delight, and throws me over his shoulder with ease.

Pivoting toward the bathroom, he smacks my ass. "Let me draw you a bath."

# Chapter 27
## Ezra

"You look ridiculous with my scrunchie in your hair."

"Liar." I pinch her nipple. "You're just jealous because it looks better on me."

Millie is wedged between my bent legs in the bath, her back resting against my chest and her head nestled into the crook of my neck. The tops of her breasts peek out of the suds, making my dick harden again.

"How do you feel?" I wasn't my roughest, but I wasn't gentle either.

"Like I could sleep till next Tuesday," she sighs, sinking deeper into me.

With her painted toes, she plays with the faucet. Besides the sound of water dripping, we're silent.

Just when I think she's drifted off in my arms, she speaks. "Can I tell you something?"

My stomach flips with nerves, but I ignore the sensation. "Of course."

"When I heard you in the bathroom earlier, before I realized it was *me* on the app, I thought you were with Val's daughter."

"Jade?" I reel back. "She's married with five kids."

"*Five?*" She twists in my arms, sloshing water over the side of the tub. "What kind of psychopath is she?"

I laugh. "What? You don't want children?"

"I didn't say that. Just... *five?*"

The primal urge to press her on her thoughts about children runs rampant in my veins. After coming on her stomach, I can't help but picture it swollen with my child. What the fuck is that about?

My therapist loves to say *fake it till you make it*. Have I inadvertently been doing that? Is our fake marriage starting to feel real? Does Millie want it to be?

Question after question swirls in my mind. I'm only snapped out of the spiral when she leans her head back again and lets out an exasperated noise.

"What are we doing?"

My stomach tightens with apprehension. "What do you mean?"

"That." She hikes a thumb toward the door to the bedroom. "This." Her hand hooks around the back of my neck. "We just told Kane we're not togeth—"

"I realize that." I wrap my arms around her so her teardrop breasts rest on my forearms and drop my chin to her shoulder. "What do you want?"

Silently, she pulls the scrunchie from my hair and plays with the strands at my neck for a long time.

I don't dare speak or move. Hell, I'm barely breathing as I wait for her response.

"I—I don't know. You're kind of hot, so there's that."

"*Kind of?* Jeez." I feign offense.

She's deflecting, but I won't call her on it.

"I am having a lot of fun with you. You're funny and kind, and you can sing."

"Go on..."

She chuckles. "You're a good man, Ezra. Can we see how things go when we get back to the city?"

"Sure." I kiss the top of her head as a seal of compromise. I want so much more, but for now, I'll take what I can get.

---

The next few days are filled with lots of phone calls and paperwork and waiting. Though I work hard to hide my frustration from Kane, Millie sees it.

She does her best to support me, even making matzo ball soup using my recipe. Let's just say she is talented in other areas of life. I appreciate having her here to vent to, especially when she talks me off the edge after Rob doesn't answer his phone—or door—for three days. He was supposed to turn in the final paperwork, but instead, he took a trip to the Big Island and didn't bother to tell us.

I was livid.

*I barely get the car in park before I fling the door open and dart for his front door.*

"The fuck you think you're doing?" *he yells from his recliner in front of the TV when I storm inside.*

"Me? Where the fuck have you been?"

*He sets his beer to the side, right on top of the guardianship paperwork, as if it's nothing more than a coaster.*

*I yank the papers, knocking the can over in the process.*

"Ez—"

"Sign the goddamn papers. Now."

"Relax, son." *He stands and lazily wanders to the kitchen, where he pulls a pen from a drawer.*

*Leaning over the counter, he scribbles his signature, then pops another beer from the fridge and watches as I flip through the documents, making sure he signed on each designated line.*

*Gathering the papers, I look him square in the eye.* "You will not call Kane—or me—ever again. Do you understand?"

*I turn on my heel and stomp toward the front door.*

*Behind me, he slams his can down on the counter, startling me.* "You think you have what it takes to be a father? You think you're so much better than me? Just because you've got yourself a pretty little wife—"

*I whip around and stab a finger in his direction.* "Do not bring Millie into—"

"I had a wife once."

*My gut drops. That's news to me.*

"Before your mother. Doesn't mean shit. Guys like you and me don't settle down. It's not in our genes. I was just like my father, and you're just like me."

"I'm nothing like you." *The anger that's coursed through me since I stepped into the house boils over. The man is delusional if he thinks misogyny is genetic.* "I will be faithful and loyal to my wife. And I'll never make my kids feel like they need to be anyone other than themselves. I came to Hawaii hoping to prove to you how wrong you are about me. So you'd stop holding this... this thing *over my head. I should have known you'd never change.*"

*When he doesn't respond, I step back into the room.*

"I'm done with you."

*With that, I'm striding out of the house and slamming the door behind me, stealing his chance to have the last word.*

Thank god for Millie, who has kept me distracted with another waterfall hike, plenty of walks on the beach, and even another *live* erotic story experience.

That last one helped the most.

Millie sighs, slumping against the arm of the couch. "I can't believe it's our last day on the island."

Somehow, I've found myself rubbing her feet again; she's sneaky like that. "I can't believe I'm coming home with a kid."

"Are you nervous?"

I pull her closer, keeping her legs draped over my lap. "A little. I'm not worried about whether I can handle it; I'm just worried about him. Life here and life in the city are night and day. I hope the transition isn't too hard. He's already been through so much."

She hums. "You'll make a great father figure. You're already a great *Da*—"

"*Don't* even say it." I flip her onto her back and dig my fingers into her sides, eliciting the most contagious laugh.

"Safe word! Safe word!" she calls between gasps of air.

Lowering over her, I bring my lips close to hers but don't make contact. She parts her lips for me, and I suck in the sweet citrus of her breath before finally dipping down and slipping my tongue into her mouth.

When she grinds against my growing erection, I tug on her bottom lip with my teeth, wishing I could lick between her legs right now.

"We can't," she sighs.

"Why not?" I move to her neck and suck on the soft flesh.

"Because..." She rocks her pelvis into mine. "Because we're leaving in the morning... and, um... and we have to pack."

"Leave your clothes here. I'll buy you a new wardrobe when we land." I run my tongue between her breasts, inhaling her floral perfume.

"Ezra." She grasps my hair and tugs, lifting my head. "We can't."

"*Millie*," I whine back. "Please."

*For the Show*

"Excuse me, sir, are you begging?" The smirk on her face would win a competition with the devil.

"I will only beg once." I slide down her body.

"Then you better make it worth my while."

# Chapter 28
## Ezra

"Now DO you see why we need to be at the airport two hours before?"

"Yeah, yeah, whatever." Millie waves me off, unbothered by the idea that we nearly missed our flight.

On our way, Val insisted we stop for malasadas and an authentic Hawaiian hibiscus mint ginger drink. Then Kane realized he left his phone behind, so we had to turn around. The check-in desk was understaffed, and the conveyor belt was broken, so we had to wait for maintenance. Security was a nightmare. Millie's carry-on was flagged for her Mary Poppins bag, and I was forced to watch a geriatric pervert sift through her sex toy collection in front of half of Honolulu.

"Do you have your band?" I ask as we shuffle down the jet bridge to the plane.

"Yes." She shoves a hand into the side pocket of her carry-on and pulls a silicone bracelet out. "Thank you for reminding me."

"Are you going to miss Mano?" she asks Kane once we've taken our seats.

*For the Show*

We're in the center aisle, with Kane to my left and Millie to my right. No first class for us this time.

My heart aches for the kid. They ended things amicably. It was the best choice, in my opinion. They're too young to do long-distance, but I hope they remain friends.

"Yeah. He was my first sorta-boyfriend, you know? But moving is the best option for me, and I'm kind of ready for a change. Hawaii reminds me too much of my mom. Not that I wanna forget..."

"I know what you mean, buddy." She reaches across me to squeeze his forearm. "Plus, your brother said he'd bring you back to visit, if that's what you want."

He lifts a shoulder and lets it fall. "Maybe. Would you come too?"

Lips pressed together, she surveys me, then focuses on him again. "If you want me to."

As we take off, I close my eyes and give in to the fantasy that a world exists in which the three of us return to Hawaii as a family.

---

Once we're in the city, things turn awkward. It feels wrong leaving Millie behind in the Uber; she only lives a few blocks from me. But she insists I get Kane settled and that we'll talk in a couple of days.

"Text me as soon as you get home," I say as I bend to kiss her on the lips.

She bats her lashes. "Yes, Daddy."

"Gross, I heard that," Kane calls from behind me.

"Oh, I almost forgot." She twists the rings off her finger and passes them through the window.

I'm frozen in place, my hand out, the two white-gold circles resting in my palm. This feels wrong too. But I garner my strength, force a tight smile, and tuck them into my pocket. Then I step back and watch as the car pulls back into traffic.

I introduce Kane to our doorman and request an additional key so he has access to my apartment, then we head upstairs. The flight was long, and we're both exhausted, but I want to help him unpack the things he brought with him. Though it cost a fortune, I arranged to have his and his mom's belongings shipped over. It's important to me that he makes this his home too.

Halfway through unpacking, my phone dings.

> **MILLIE**
> I'm home. Thank you for a wonderful trip

I type out *Thank you for*, but pause, because what am I thanking her for? Coming to Hawaii in the first place? Pretending to be my wife? Sticking up for Kane? Celebrating my birthday? All the amazing sex?

> **ME**
> Thank you for everything

I delete *I miss you already*. I don't want to come on too strong.

After Kane's first slice (or four) of NYC's infamous pizza and half a dozen cookies from Levain's, I consider taking out a loan for his teenage appetite. He can barely keep his eyes open on the sofa while we watch *The Office*, so as my first fatherly duty, I send him to bed. Luckily, Cam left behind all his furniture when he moved out, so a fresh set of sheets was all I needed to prep the second bedroom for him.

A long, hot shower feels good, but sliding into cool sheets naked is even better. Or it would be if there was a curvy blonde in my bed. I figured I'd pass out quickly after a full day of travel. Instead, I'm wide awake.

## For the Show

I text my mom to let her know we're home and that we'll see her tomorrow. She's itching to meet Kane. I'm eager to introduce them too. His mom is gone, but I'll happily share mine.

I haven't checked my social media since Kane found me, so in hopes that some scrolling will help my mind settle, I open Instagram. Several notifications pop up, including one from Millie.

*@amelia.r.greer tagged you in a post*

It's the picture my brother snapped of Millie and me before we left the island. We're on the beach with our backs to the camera. I'd just smacked her ass, but the photo captured my arm outstretched behind her. The caption reads *Paradise <3*

I scroll her feed, but the following pictures in her grid are from months ago, when she was touring with *Mamma Mia*.

My fingers find their way to our text convo.

> **ME**
> Are you awake?

> **MILLIE**
> Yes. Can't sleep

> **ME**
> Why can't you sleep?

Three little dots dance on the screen, then disappear. Then reappear, then disappear. Finally, a new message appears.

> **MILLIE**
> There's not a giant naked man in my bed

> **ME**
> I'd sure hope not...

> **MILLIE**
> How's Kane?

Oh, so we're changing subjects. Got it.

**ME**

Asleep

Wish you were here

*So much for trying not to come on too strong.*

**MILLIE**

Me too

What would you do if I were in your bed right now?

Heart beating faster, I prop myself up against my pillow. Is she doing what I think she's doing?

**ME**

I would strip you down

**MILLIE**

You know I'd already be naked. Try again

A heavy ache forms in my lower stomach as I consider my options.

**ME**

You're on top of me. Your pussy is soaking my cock

**MILLIE**

Oh, Daddy came to play. Go on…

**ME**

I'm slipping my fingers inside you now. Do you wish it were my dick?

**MILLIE**

Yes

**ME**

Are you touching yourself?

*For the Show*

**MILLIE**

Yes

**ME**

Where?

**MILLIE**

My pussy

**ME**

Are you wet for me?

**MILLIE**

Always

**ME**

You're so wet my cock slides in easily, filling you up

You fucking love my cock, don't you, little slut?

**MILLIE**

Yes

**ME**

Yes, what?

**MILLIE**

Yes, Daddy

**ME**

That's my girl

**MILLIE**

Are you touching yourself?

With my free hand, I reach into my nightstand and squirt a dollop of lube directly onto my shaft.

**ME**

Yes. I'm so fucking hard for you

**MILLIE**

Stroke that cock. Imagine it's me riding you

**ME**

Get that disco ball toy. Turn it to the last setting. Pretend it's me fucking you

We ran through her entire bag of toys in Hawaii, though she said it was only her travel stash.

**MILLIE**

Got it. Fuck, you feel so good

Are you moaning for me?

**ME**

Yes, baby. I'm so close. Can I come inside your pussy?

We haven't done that yet, but it's at the top of my list of fantasies. Is it for her too?

**MILLIE**

Yes, fill me up. I want it all

My balls retract, and my phone falls to the side. Pumping my cock, envisioning the way her tits would bounce in my face if she were riding me, I let go. My stomach contracts and long, narrow streaks of cum shoot onto my abs.

The second my brain comes back online, I call her.

She answers on the first ring, but rather than greeting me, she breathes heavily. Between groans, I can hear the faint whirring of her toy.

"That's it, baby." I talk her through it. "Play with that clit. Take what you need from my cock. You ready?"

"Mm-hmm. M'coming." Her euphoric cries send shivers up my spine.

*For the Show*

As I wait patiently for her breathing to even out, my cum dries on my abdomen.

"Hey," she whispers.

My chest pinches with affection. "Hey, honey. You good?"

"I'd be better if you were here, but yes. Thank you."

I want to say "Fuck it, move in with me," but resist. For now.

"You're welcome. Sleep well."

"You too," she sighs, the sound pure bliss. "Good night, Ezra."

"Night, Mills."

# Chapter 29
# Millie

The last two days have been rough. I don't know why Cam and Joey enjoy traveling so much. Jet lag is no joke. Ezra suggested I wake up at the time I typically do in hopes of acclimating quickly, but that all went to shit when I slept through my alarm and well into the early afternoon. Then, I had a terrible headache from lack of caffeine, so I compensated by drinking two cups of coffee, only to be up half the night and repeat it all the next day.

Finally, by day three post-Hawaii, I've gotten my act together. Only I don't know what I'm powering through for. What am I even doing with my life? My work for LULU and the occasional audiobook are my only sources of income, and neither job pays all that steadily. Sure, I'm smart with money and could support myself comfortably using my savings for a few months, but then what?

Hawaii was literal paradise. All expenses paid—tacos, foot rubs, and nipplegasms, included. It's hard not to wish I could be transported back.

While lazing my days away, I didn't consider what I'd do

once I returned to the city. I have a slew of messages from my agent about potential auditions; I should be grateful for the opportunities, but I let every one go unanswered. Because the truth is, I'm not sure I want to return to the theater. I love performing, but do I want to go back to touring? Packing and picking up every few nights was stressful, not to mention the havoc it wreaked on my body.

Speaking of bodies, I have a long way to go, but I haven't felt this comfortable in my skin in months, and do I really want to fuck up the progress I've made by subjecting myself to the body shaming that's deeply ingrained in the industry?

There's got to be a way I can keep the magic of performing while preserving my worth.

---

Ezra invites me over, but I tell him I'm busy. In reality, I'm not. I just don't want to be a distraction to Kane as he acclimates to his new life.

My brother and parents call, but I don't answer. Instead, I respond via text. By day five, they're no longer buying my jet lag excuse. After Asher plays dirty, sending a picture of my niece with a message bubble drawn above her head that says *Answer your phone Lee Lee*, I finally call.

"It's about damn time," he scolds.

"Hey, Ash."

"How are you?"

"I'm good."

"That's it? You escape to Hawaii *with a man*, get a freaking blood transfusion, and all I get is *I'm good*?"

"*Fine*," I sigh. "You want the truth?"

Tone sympathetic, he says, "Always, Mills. What's going on?"

"I don't know what I'm doing with my life." A sob claws its way up my throat, but I hold it back.

"Want to know a secret?" he asks softly. "None of us do."

"But you're a dad and running a whole damn camp."

"That doesn't mean shit," he laughs. "Don't get me wrong, I love Bea more than anything, but she comes with a whole host of challenges. Keeping the retreat center and camp going is stressful. And the pressure to keep Daisy's legacy alive is immense. The camp doctor, who's been here since the center opened, just told me he's retiring, so now I'll need to fill his spot before next summer. If you know any doctors looking to moonlight up this way, let me know."

"Cam's sister is a doctor. I forget which kind, but I'll find out."

"Thank you. Speaking of doctors, have you made an appointment yet?"

Dread curls in my gut, making it difficult to formulate words.

"*Amelia.*"

Oy vey, he sounds like Ezra. I chuckle to myself. "I will, I will. I promise."

"Are you coming to Mom and Dad's for brunch tomorrow? Joey and Cam will be there."

I can't deny that I'd like to continue hiding out, but if I don't show up, my entire family will be knocking down my door. Plus, I could really use a Joey hug.

"I'll be there."

---

When we moved to the city, back when I was a teenager, we lived in a tiny apartment. Asher and I were lucky to have our own rooms, even if mine was only big enough for a twin-size bed and a shoe bin. Last year, though, my parents moved into their dream home. The corner apartment has three spacious bedrooms and a gorgeous view of Central Park. The upgrade means my dad won't retire any time soon, but that's probably best for everyone's sanity—especially Mom's.

It takes a little over half an hour to reach my parents' by train, and within minutes, I regret not hopping in an Uber. It's too damn hot. At least the Spanx under my sundress are saving my thighs from chaffing.

As soon as I enter the apartment, I'm tackled by the cutest four-year-old.

"Lee Lee," she squeals.

"Hi, Dolly." I scoop her up and swing her in a circle, Disney princess style. "How's my favorite girl?"

"Hey, I thought I was your favorite girl." Joey darts around the corner and hugs me, squishing Bea between us.

My niece remains glued to my hip while I embrace Dad, Asher, and Cam. I'm hit with question after question in such quick succession I can't consider a single one, so I promise to answer them after I've had a drink.

"Mimosa or Bloody Mary?" my dad asks, taking Bea from my arms.

"Mimosa." Rather than let him wait on me, I shuffle to the bar cart and pour orange juice and champagne into a flute, drink a little, then top it off with another splash of bubbly.

"I hope you don't mind, but I brought a french toast casserole," a familiar voice calls from around the corner.

Heart in my throat, I whip around. "Ezra?"

He comes into view, and behind him, Kane appears.

"Hey, buddy." I immediately pass Ezra and wrap his brother up in a hug. "I didn't know you were going to be here."

"You what?" Ezra says.

Before I can answer, introductions are being made at the

kitchen island, where handshakes are thrown out the window and hugs reign.

When Asher and Ezra fall into conversation, I pull my mom to the side. "You invited him?"

"No, you did." She tilts her head, inspecting me like she's worried I have amnesia.

"What? No I didn't." *Who would have*—"Josefine Noa Connelly," I whisper-yell.

"Whoa, Connelly. I like the sound of that." Cam appears at the counter.

Joey playfully smacks him in the chest. "We're not married yet, silly boy."

"You might as well be," I say.

The two share a sweet, contemplative look.

In the silence of the moment, I remember why I called her over in the first place. "Did you tell my mom I invited Ezra?"

Brow furrowed, she frowns. "No."

Huh. I actually believe her. "Then who?"

"I did," my dad chimes in on my mom's other side. "I wanted to meet the man who took such good care of my little girl."

My stomach sinks. Oh, he *took care* of me, all right.

Across the kitchen, Ezra is crouched, laughing at Bea as she yammers on. The way his eye crinkles at the side is like a blow to the chest. God, he's so good-looking.

As if he can feel my gaze, he pivots on the balls of his feet, still squatting, and locks eyes with me. He shoots me a quick grin, but then he quickly focuses on Bea again, holding an arm out so she can give his fist a bump. It's then that I notice his ring finger is bare and my stomach clenches involuntarily.

He comes to stand in front of me, his bare feet bumping into mine. He's wearing dark jeans, despite the sweltering temperature, and a sage green short-sleeve button-down with palm leaves stitched into an abstract pattern. The one I bought him at a boutique on Oahu. His curls are wild and free, and his beard is perfectly trimmed.

"Hi." Though I'm hit with the urge to pet his cheek and revel in the feel of his scruff, a shyness like I've never experienced takes over. It's ridiculous, really. We sexted, and I orgasmed over the phone just a few days ago, but seeing him in my parents' kitchen is throwing me off.

He plants a chaste kiss on my cheek. The move could be considered platonic if he didn't grope my ass at the same time. No one is behind me, yet I still scan for witnesses.

"I take it you didn't know we were coming?" he asks.

"No, no. Of course I—"

He arches a brow, shutting down my denial.

"I..." I exhale, my whole being sagging. "Nope. But I am glad you're here. It's good to see you."

*It's good to see you? For fuck's sake. The man has taken you to Pound Town and back, and that's all you have to say?*

"How's Kane?"

"You can ask him yourself," he says, his voice kind and even. "But not yet. Right now, I want to know why you've been avoiding me."

"I'm not avoiding you. I'm sorry if I've made you feel that way. I just wanted to give you space and—"

"I don't want space."

My breath catches. "What?"

Tucking a strand of dark hair behind his ear, he clears his throat. "I mean, we're, uh, we're good. Kane is good. I'm good. We're good."

"That's... *good.*" I chuckle.

One side of his mouth kicks up. "He got a part-time job washing dishes at Bubbe's Nosh Pit."

"Oh yeah?" Smiling, I find Kane, who is rearranging the magnets on the refrigerator with Bea. "That's... *good.*"

With a laugh, Ezra collects my hands and angles in close. "Hey, let's not make this awkward. We said we'd see how it went when we got back to the city, right?"

"Right." I figured we'd have more time to date and fool around before he met my family. Yes, definitely more fooling around.

With his hand at my lower back, he leads me into the dining room, which was a major selling point for my parents when they were shopping for an apartment. The table they chose for the center of the space extends to fit the entire group, plus some, and the floor-to-ceiling windows bring in a ton of natural light and give us an incredible view.

My dad and Asher flank Ezra at the table, and Joey forces me to sit across from him. She guides Kane to sit on my right, then plops into the seat on his other side. Brunch is served family-style, and each time one of us takes a bite of Ezra's french toast casserole, a moan echoes off the walls.

"I hope you'll share this recipe," my mom says, holding her fork aloft.

"Of course, Mrs. Greer." He's speaking to her, but he's looking at me.

I squeeze my thighs together at the memory of being called Mr. and Mrs. Greer when I was discharged from the hospital.

When he winks, I'm certain he's thinking the same. "It's my mother's, so I can't take all the credit."

"You'll have to bring her next time. I'd love to meet her."

Heart lurching, I jerk my head toward my mom. She's never shown interest in the parents of the people I'm dating.

"So, Kane," my dad says. "What do you think about the Big Apple?"

"Dad," I laugh. "No one calls it that."

"I want an apple," Bea shouts from across the table. She migrates from my brother's lap onto Ezra's.

Asher murmurs an apology, and Ezra smiles, whispering "no worries."

"It's loud," Kane answers my dad's question. "But it's interesting. Thanks for asking, Mr. Greer."

"Please, call us Ethan and Rachel." My dad waves a hand, dismissing such formalities.

"So, Ezra, how do you like teaching middle school?" my mom calls from the head of the table.

Before I can ask how she knows he's a teacher, he says, "Love it. Middle schoolers aren't as awful as everyone makes them out to be. Hormonal, yes," he chuckles, "but they're beginning to form their own thoughts and opinions, and I like cultivating their young minds."

"He's being modest," Cam interjects. "He's in the running for an open principal position."

"What?" I home in on the man across the table. "Since when?"

He dips his chin, smiling shyly. "I had a meeting with the board yesterday. I should hear back soon."

A round of "that's wonderful" and "congrats" circulates the table, and a sense of pride swirls around my heart.

"Millie, what about you? Any new auditions?" my dad asks.

"Hey, did I tell you Dr. Parsons is retiring?" Asher jumps in, saving my ass.

*Thank you*, I mouth to him.

Ezra's questioning gaze burns against my skin, but I keep my focus averted.

"What? He's been the camp doc since the beginning."

"I know." The crease between my brother's brows has gotten deeper since I last saw him. "Oh, that reminds me." He turns to Cam. "Millie mentioned your sister is a doctor."

"She is," he replies. "A family physician, actually."

"She wouldn't want to come work for me, would she?"

"She's working for a private practice, but I guess it wouldn't hurt to ask." Cam pulls out his phone, and the two exchange numbers.

Ezra ties his hair into a bun, still balancing Bea on his lap. When she notices, she asks him to put one in her hair too.

"What's it called?"

"What do you mean?" He gives her a curious smile.

"My daddy does piggy tails and bear ears. What's your hair called?"

He grins. "I've never heard of bear ears. You'll have to teach me someday. But my hair is called a man bun, I guess."

She straightens, her face breaking out in a wide smile. "Then I want a man bun too."

As the group dissolves into laughter, the most adorable moment plays out in front of me. Ezra pulls an extra hair tie from his wrist and proceeds to collect Bea's hair into a man bun.

---

"Tell me you're not ready to have his babies," Joey chirps.

I shooed everyone else out of the kitchen so I could wash the dishes and have a moment to myself, but Joey refused.

"I—I don't." There's no use lying; she knows me too well. But I can't even think about having Ezra's giant babies with the doctor appointment I've yet to mention to anyone looming over me.

Before I left the hospital in Hawaii, I scheduled a follow-up appointment with an ob-gyn in New York. I fibbed to Ezra and Asher about it because they'd hound me for answers if they knew. If the news is not good, I want to receive it privately.

One look at my best friend, though, has me spilling my guts. I detail just how sweet—albeit possessive—Ezra was when I had my transfusion. How the doctor suspects endometriosis. And how I went down a WebMD and Google rabbit hole that led to the potential infertility.

"Oh, babe. You must be so scared." She hugs me close.

It takes all my strength to hold back the waterworks as I squeeze her in return.

"When's your appointment?" she asks, holding me at arm's length. "Do you want me to come?"

"No, no. You'll be in London."

"You know I'd stay back for you."

"I know you would, but I promise I'll be fine. I need to do this on my own."

# Chapter 30
## Ezra

I've allowed Millie to give Kane and me as much "time to adjust" as I can stand. I'm no idiot. She's using this as an excuse to avoid me.

What I can't figure out is why she's doing it. Cam gave me a little peace of mind when he reminded me that Joey grew distant and pushed back when their relationship got intense.

Is that what Millie is doing? Is she afraid of commitment?

I'm about to find out.

After Kane takes off for summer school, I walk the few blocks to Millie's. I've never been inside, but I finagled her apartment number out of Joey by telling her it was the least she could do after she used me to make Cam jealous the night we met.

I slip in behind a resident, bypassing the call box outside her building. As I knock on her door, two elderly women pop their heads out from the apartment next door.

"May we help you?"

I look over my shoulder to confirm they're talking to me. "I don't think so, but thank you."

"Are you here to see our Millie?"

*Their* Millie?

"Yes," I respond as a wave of trepidation rolls through me.

The smaller woman scans me from head to toe. The intensity in her demeanor instantly tells me I should be scared of her, even though she's half my height.

"What are your intentions with our girl?" She asks the question at the same time the door in front of me flies open.

"Ezra." Millie's wearing an emerald satin robe, her exquisite cleavage on full display.

I'm pretty sure my tongue lolls out of my mouth at the view.

With a scowl, she pulls the robe around her tighter, hiding all that gorgeous skin. "What are you doing here?"

"Apparently getting the third degree." I nod to my right.

"Peg, Fran," Millie scolds. "What are you up to?"

"Don't mind us. We're just checking out the new guy."

The new guy, huh? Stepping forward, I extend my arm and turn on the charm. "I'm Ezra. It's a pleasure to meet you."

The smaller one shakes my hand first. "I'm Peg, and this here's my wife, Fran."

"Do you plan to be around long?" Fran asks, eyes narrowed.

"For as long as she'll have me." I don't know whether she wants to know how long I'm staying *today*, or how long *in general*, but either way, the answer is the same.

The women's faces light up with glee, so I must have passed some sort of test.

"We good here?" Millie asks, leaning against the doorframe.

"We just need samples. Urine and blood will do. Then you two can be on your way," Peg says.

"What?" I choke on a gasp.

"Ignore her." Fran cackles. "Let's leave these two very attractive young folks alone. It was nice meeting you, Ezra. It's been a while since someone's knocked on that door."

Millie lowers her head and picks at her nails.

"It was nice meeting you too," I reply.

Fran is already shoving her wife through the door, saying something about a cockblock, I swear.

Millie welcomes me into her apartment, and I lead her to the sofa by her wrist and pull her onto my lap before she can speak. Her robe separates when she straddles my hips, revealing nothing but luscious skin underneath. The golden wisps of hair that have grown between her legs since I last saw her have my cock aching within my shorts.

I grip her thick thighs, but when my fingers slip against the satin, I grasp her ass and pull her in until her bare belly is flush against my shirt.

"I missed you." Angling in, I capture her lips. My tongue requests entrance, and she opens, welcoming me with a tender urgency.

All too soon, she pulls back, leaving my cock protesting. Her fingers are linked at my neck when she says, "Should I call you *Principal* now?"

With a swat to the side of her thigh, I growl. "I haven't gotten the job yet."

"You will." Her eyes shine with adoration and confidence.

"Speaking of jobs…"

"Ugh." She releases her hold on me and drops her hands to her sides. "Can we not?"

"Why?"

Slumping onto the cushion next to me, she covers her body with her robe.

Dammit. Why did I have to go and open my big mouth?

Her arms are crossed, her body language closed off, but she remains angled toward me. "My agent's been after me about auditions."

My first instinct is to say "that's great," but her expression makes it clear that would be the wrong response.

## For the Show

A heavy sigh escapes her. "I don't think I want to perform anymore."

With my thumb and forefinger at her chin, I guide her head up so she's forced to look at me. Her eyes swim with hurt.

"But you love performing." I wipe at the tears that crest over her lashes. "I've seen you. Watching you on stage is… is magical." It's the truth. Each time I recall watching her shine, I break out in goose bumps.

"I love the theater," she admits. "But I need to rethink what that looks like. Maybe there's a way to keep it in my life without bending and breaking and starving myself for it. I just don't know what that is yet."

"What if you coached? Or taught theater at Asher's camp? Oh, there's that dance studio between my apartment and yours. You could teach there." I'm practically bouncing off the sofa with ideas now.

"Ezra." She puts a hand on my thigh, her expression serious. "Can you not do the typical man thing?"

"What?"

"Don't try to fix it," she says, eyes pleading.

Shit. Like an idiot, I jumped straight to Mr. Fix-It mode.

"I'm sorry." Heart pinching, I gather her by her nape and kiss her forehead. "Do you want to be helped, hugged, or heard?"

"Huh?"

"It's what my mom used to say to me when I was young. So, do you want to be helped, hugged, or heard?"

"Hugged." She throws a leg over my lap, resting her chest against mine.

With one arm around her waist, I tangle the other in her hair and comb through the strands with my fingers. After a few minutes, she relaxes into me like I knew she would.

"Thank you." The words are whispered into my neck. She

follows up the sentiment with a kiss to the edge of my beard. Her next kiss is in the same place, but this time, it lingers.

With a slow exhale, I drag my hands down her back. In response, she rocks into my hips and follows up the move with a lick to the skin below my ear. When she rocks a second time, I get the hint.

I thread a hand between us and untie her robe, and while she sucks and nips at my neck, I slide the silky fabric down her arms, caressing the soft, warm skin there. I sink my teeth into the soft flesh at her shoulder, eliciting a moan from her. Then she's rocking her hips against my growing erection with more intensity.

"Hey, Millie?"

"Mmm?"

"Do you want to be helped, hugged... or fucked?"

# Chapter 31
## Ezra

"I want to be fucked."

Grasping Millie's juicy thighs, I stand and flip her onto her back on the sofa. She yelps in surprise, but I stifle the sound by sealing my lips over hers. My tongue demands entrance, and she welcomes me in with enthusiasm, gripping the hair at my neck. She tugs hard, and I growl into her mouth. As I forge a trail down the delicate skin along her throat with my tongue, she circles her legs around my waist, pulling me flush against her, her hips rocking and my erection swelling against my zipper.

I let her indulge in the friction, cursing the barrier between us, and rub and thrust against her like a horny teenager.

Arching back, she cries, "Take these off."

*Oh, thank god.*

Scrambling off her, I kick off my shoes, then I shed my pants.

"Those too." She points to my boxer briefs.

I peel them down my legs without hesitation, then drop to my knees on the plush rug while tugging my shirt over my head. I push the coffee table back to give myself more space.

If I were an artist, I'd revel in the privilege of painting her naked body, curating every ample detail of her lush curves and flushed skin. Instead, I use my fingers like a paintbrush, worshipping every inch of her delicious figure.

"Spread those legs for me, sweetheart," I request, playing with the fine hair curtaining her clit.

With her right knee bent and flush against the back of the sofa, she slides her left foot to the floor. I caress her thigh, gentle at first, then greedily grabbing for purchase when the sparkle of her arousal grabs my attention. Dipping a fingertip into the tender place between her legs, I gather her wetness, then I treat her clit with the respect it deserves.

Moaning, she guides my fingers to her entrance. "Again."

I oblige again and again until her perfect pussy is glistening.

I bend forward, perpendicular to her pussy, and when my tongue makes contact, she sighs.

"Fuck." She brushes my hair out of my face and hums as she watches me work. The woman does love a good show.

"That's it," she praises. "You eat my pussy so good."

I slide my index and middle fingers into her channel and rest my pinkie at her ass, then tip my head, silently asking for permission.

When she nods and angles her hips up, I spit at her entrance and slide my pinkie inside her tight hole. Two fingers in her pussy, one in her ass, and my mouth on her clit: *the sex trifecta*.

"More," she encourages, bucking against my mouth and writhing, her tits bouncing with every thrust.

"Make a mess, Millie," I order, pumping my fingers with so much ferocity her head is nearly hanging off the arm of the sofa.

"Towel," she gasps.

There's no time, so I swipe my shirt off the floor.

Then she lets go.

I catch her release in my shirt, but mostly with my mouth.

"It's too much," she whines, though she doesn't squirm away.

*For the Show*

Still inside her, I'm greedy for every quake and pulse of her orgasm. I remain there, gently massaging her G-spot until the last flutters cease.

She flinches at the loss of my fingers when I finally extricate them. I rest my wet face against her ribs, her rapid heartbeat like a personal sound machine, and watch as she pants, her beautiful breasts taunting me with each rise and fall.

I wait for her heart rate to settle, then I ask, "When are you going to let me fuck those gorgeous tits?"

Head tilted up, she hits me with a devious smirk. "Go for it, big guy. They're all yours."

*Mine.*

I wipe my face with my shirt, then slide it under her and help her sit up. When I rest my knees at the edge of the sofa and grasp the back for support, precum leaks from my tip and onto her chest.

Millie captures my cock between her tits and spits, allowing me to slide between the soft skin with ease.

"Tighter."

With a hum, she pushes her breasts closer together, trapping me. "Fuck, that feels good," I groan as I grind my hips into her cleavage, savoring the warm, slippery sensation.

The seductive look she gives me has my balls clenching. She releases her hold, and just as I'm about to protest, she grabs my shaft and takes me into her mouth, simultaneously stroking and sucking, coating my cock until it's slick enough that she tucks me back between her tits.

As we work in tandem, she whispers words of encouragement, sexy little phrases that have me nearly slipping off the sofa with every thrust of my hips.

"I'm close," I warn her.

"Are you imagining it's my pussy? Do you wish you could come inside me?"

*"Fuck."* That does it. Those words and the image of unleashing inside her bare send me over the edge. Hot ribbons of cum brand her throat like a pearl necklace.

When I'm spent, I slump onto the cushion to her left, my chest heaving and my cock still leaking.

Millie pulls my shirt out from under her and wipes my release from her neck, then passes it to me.

It's sopping wet. "Shit," I laugh.

"I'll wash it for you," she says, angling forward like she's going to stand.

Before she can, I pull her into me and cocoon her in place. When I kiss the top of her head, she relaxes against me. Fuck, my chest aches with so much admiration for this woman. For a long while, she plays with the dark hair at my navel while I feather my fingers against her hip. My eyes are closed, my mind wandering, when she brushes my inner thigh, startling me.

She kneads the muscle there, her knuckles brushing against my balls. "How much time do you need?"

I open my eyes to meet hers. "Huh?"

She grabs my balls and tugs. "How much time do you need before you're ready to go again?"

# Chapter 32
## Millie

Joey is still the only person who knows about my appointment with Dr. Thomas. My mom would have dropped everything to come with me, but sometimes she acts a bit too much like a stereotypical Jewish mother. The woman can be downright suffocating. If she catches wind that I have a headache or sniffle, she's at my doorstep with a noodle kugel. I don't even like noodle kugel.

I have another ultrasound in order to determine whether the cyst has gotten bigger since my hospital stay in Hawaii. Waiting on the results is excruciating, like standing at the edge of a cliff, teetering between hope and despair.

Dr. Thomas drops into his stool and rolls closer. "Good news, Ms. Greer. The cyst has not grown, so you won't need surgery anytime soon."

My shoulders deflate with relief. "Does that mean I don't have endometriosis?"

"*Well.*" He stretches out the vowel. And just like that, the balloon of fear is inflated again. "Maybe you do, maybe you don't."

A frustrated scream gets stuck in my throat. "What do you mean, *maybe?*" Aren't you a fucking doctor?

He explains that a laparoscopic procedure would determine whether I have endometriosis, but that the cyst isn't big enough to warrant the procedure.

"Make that make sense."

Bless him, this man is patient. "It's okay to feel frustrated. I wish I could give you a more concrete answer. For now, if your symptoms get better while you're on birth control, then it's possible this is endometriosis."

My heart aches with longing for my mom. I should have called her.

"What about having kids?" I ask, biting at my thumbnail. "My aunt wasn't able to have any more after my cousin was born."

With a sigh, the doctor adjusts his glasses. "There's always a possibility, but we'll cross that bridge if and when we need to."

Annoyance flares, like sparks in my veins. I'm so sick of ambiguous answers.

I leave his office with a refill of my birth control and a zillion more questions.

After a quick trip to the pharmacy, I pop into a café, and while I'm waiting for my coffee, a familiar voice calls from a table behind me. "Millie?"

Turning, I search for the source, and when I find her, my stomach twists painfully. Sam is quite literally the last person I expected to run into. But that's New York, I suppose. Millions of people, and yet we're always bound to run into someone we know. Her hair has grown to just above her shoulders, with streaks of strawberry in it now. When she gives me a once-over, I'm instantly reminded of my weight gain. While my body dysmorphia will always be a back-seat driver, I haven't let her control the radio in a while. Not since Ezra's been worshipping me. But Sam hasn't seen me since last November, and her face is etched with genuine shock.

"You look—"

"Yup, different. I know."

The barista calls my name, so I turn to pick up my to-go cup from the counter. When I spin again, Sam is still inspecting me.

"You look really pretty."

With my heart in my throat, I study her face, looking for a lie, but I come up empty. "Oh. Thanks."

"How are you?"

The café is busy, and when the barista calls another name, I'm forced to step closer. "I'm fine. You?" That may not be the total truth, but I'm not getting into anything deeper than surface level with this woman.

"I've been meaning to call you."

The knot in my stomach tightens. "Oh?"

"Do you have a minute?" She motions at the open chair.

For a heartbeat, I waffle in indecision. She doesn't deserve my time, but curiosity gets the best of me, and I take a seat across from her, deciding I'll give her until I finish this coffee to say her piece.

She scans my body again, and I inwardly cringe at the scrutiny.

"You look tan. Have you been traveling?"

"Hawaii."

"Oh, wow. I've always wanted to go there. How was it?"

"It was great, but there were lots of fucking chickens and roosters." I can't help but chuckle at the memory of the shock I felt when I saw so many. They're nearly as rampant as pigeons here in the city.

"Did you go with anyone?"

My heart stutters. Do I tell her?

Fuck it. Why not?

Eyes locked with hers, I lean forward. "Actually, yes. Ezra."

She chokes on her iced latte. Setting it down quickly, she wipes her mouth with a napkin. "Really? Are you two together now?"

I nod.

"I did not see that coming," she mumbles.

"Why's that?" My question is laced with a bit of snark. *Okay, a lot of snark.*

Sam runs her fingers through her hair, the move revealing a new tattoo on the inside of her toned bicep. It's a bird, similar in style to the three I have on the back of my tricep. "I'm just surprised. He was always talking about wanting a wife and kids, and you were always..."

"Always what?"

"Always... *not.*"

Blood rushes in my ears as I fight to keep my tone even. "What's that supposed to mean?"

"C'mon, Mills."

I shudder at the sound of my nickname on her lips.

"I'm surprised you're with a guy." She shrugs. "It's not bad. It's just, when you and I were together, you told me probably a dozen times that you'd never marry a man."

"Who said anything about getting married?" *Legally, at least.*

Her eyes metaphorically stab mine. "*Millie.* This is Ezra we're talking about. That man oozes marriage material. He probably has paternity leave paperwork on standby."

Normally I'd laugh at that joke, but it hits a little too painfully. She's not wrong.

I clear my throat. "What is it you wanted to talk about?"

With a deep inhale, she fiddles with her plastic cup. "I wanted to apologize."

Elbows on the table, I study her, picking up on the way her eyes dart to my cleavage. My breasts have been upgraded a bit since she last saw me, and I don't feel the least bit bad about flaunting what she'll never get to have.

"For what?"

"For the way things went down between the three of us. I was really confused, but that's no excuse. I should never have been dishonest with you."

"Thank you for the apology." I take a sip of my drink, and when the taste registers, I'm tempted to spit it back out. This is *not* my order. How people can consume black coffee is beyond me.

"Are you in a show? I haven't seen you at FrenchSHEs."

I shake my head and swallow back the pain that hits every time I think about the theater. "I'm taking some time off."

"Is everything okay?"

No, *Samantha*, everything is not okay. I may or may not have a disease that could prevent me from having kids, and the guy I was fake married to, who I'm currently fucking, is the legal guardian of a fifteen-year-old and wants nothing more than to be married with babies.

"Yup. Everything's good." While I once would have spilled my guts to the girl in front of me, she no longer has that privilege. "It was nice running into you"—*it was not*—"but I've got to run."

I rise, and she follows. Her arms flinch at her sides, like maybe she's considering reaching out for a hug. Before she can, I toss the liquid dirt—*and her*—into the trash, then dart out of the café.

---

I pop into Bubbe's Nosh Pit for a quart of chicken noodle soup on the way home. With a wink, Mark throws in extra black-

and-white cookies and tells me to share with Ezra. It was only a matter of time before he found out about us.

If there is an us.

I need to think long and hard about what I'm doing with my life. Who am I if I'm not performing? I'm finding the idea of saying goodbye to the theater difficult. But if I'm always on the road, could our relationship survive? Does he really want a partner who's never home? He wants a wife and 2.5 kids and a picket fence. And a dog. Or maybe he's a cat person?

As I head toward my building, my phone rings, dousing the fears pummeling me from all sides. I dig in my purse and blindly answer the phone. "Sorry I forgot to call you back, Jo. I—"

"Millie?"

I frown in response to the unexpected masculine voice. "Ezra, hi. What's up?"

"It's about Kane," he says, his tone dripping with concern.

"What's wrong?"

"He didn't come home from summer school."

"Have you checked the location of his phone?"

"Shit. I didn't think about setting that up. And I teach middle school. Dammit." Poor guy, he's beating himself up.

"Hey, it's okay." I work to maintain a soothing tone. "Just stay home. I'm sure he'll show up. I'm walking into my building now. Do you want me to come over?"

"No, it's okay. Maybe?" He groans. "Fuck, I don't know what to do. How long do I wait before I call the police?"

"I think it's at least a few hours." As I turn down my hall, I come to an abrupt stop. "Ezra?"

"Yeah?"

"He's here."

"What?"

"Kane's here. At my apartment. I'll call you back." I hang up and squat beside Kane, who's sitting on the floor with his knees tucked into his chest.

"What's wrong?"

He pulls his hands away from his face, revealing blotchy skin, but he keeps his head lowered.

I rest a hand on his arm and give it a gentle squeeze. "Did something happen at school today?"

He nods, sucking in air on a sob, and slumps against me.

"Whatever it is, you can tell me." I wrap an arm around him and rest my chin on his head. "Wait. How do you know where I live?"

"Ezra put everyone's contact info in my phone just in case." He sniffles before he continues. "I thought New York would be better. More inclusive. It was just Pride Month."

My body tenses. Dammit. I see exactly where this is going.

"Oh, love, what happened?"

He shakes his head like the words are too painful to say aloud, but when he finally looks up at me, I gasp. One eye is nearly swollen shut, and his cheekbone is already dark purple and angry crimson. He lets me examine it, yet he flinches at my delicate touch.

"C'mon." I stand.

He follows obediently. I swear he's grown since I met him; he's nearly as tall as his brother.

"Let's get some ice on that."

At the small table off my kitchen, I hand him an ice pack and a can of sparkling water.

"Do you want to tell me what happened? It's okay if you're not ready."

He takes a sip, sets the can down, and spins it on the tabletop. "I thought he was into me. Maybe I misread the signals. I thought he was trying to hold my hand, so I..." A hiccup escapes him, his chest heaving. "I grabbed it back." He wipes his nose on his shirt.

"Then he called me... he called me a f-fag, just like Rob did. Then he punched me."

Angling in close, I collect his hands in mine. "I'm so sorry that happened to you. That was *not* okay. Did you tell a teacher?"

"No. We were halfway home. So I came here."

"How long did you sit outside my door?"

He shrugs, his head lowered again. "Two hours, maybe."

"Ezra's freaking out, you know."

He sighs, peering up at me through his lashes. "I just—I wasn't ready to tell him. He's done so much for me, and I didn't want him to think moving me here was a mistake."

"Do you?" I search his hazel eyes. "Think it's a mistake?"

"No," he says, though his shoulders sink. "My mom's death was the mistake. Why did she have to die?"

My heart plummets into my stomach. No, it falls right out of my body with a splat. Damn. This kid has been through so much in such a short amount of time. I don't know loss like he does. I'm the girl who makes people laugh when they drink too much tequila and accidentally like their partner's ex's Instagram post from five years ago. I'm the girl who hypes up others and plans surprise parties for their successes.

When my brother's wife died, I was barely an adult. No one expected me to say the "right thing." My parents filled that role. But now? Kane's watching me, his eyes mournful, like I'm the closest thing he has to a parent, and I'm frozen with dread. Dread that I'll say the wrong thing and royally fuck it up.

Then, like a love tap on my shoulder from a higher power, a memory of the rabbi from my Uncle Noah's funeral many years ago surfaces.

Maybe the story won't resonate with a fifteen-year-old boy, but then again, maybe it will. "Someone once told me that, instead of asking 'why did this terrible thing happen?' we should be asking, 'what do I do now that it *has* happened?'"

*For the Show*

He lowers the ice to the table and throws his arms around me. I hold him while his body releases wave after wave of gut-wrenching sobs, unable to hold back my own tears. My shoulder goes numb, but I don't dare disrupt him. After a good fifteen minutes, the door flies open, startling us both.

"What the fuck happened?" Ezra booms.

I stand to meet him, but he bypasses me and hovers over Kane, chest heaving and face slicked with sweat. "I was worried sick. What the fuck were you thinking? I—"

Kane looks up at him, giving him a clear view of his red, swollen face, and Ezra drops to his knees, his expression turning to fright. "What happened?" he asks, his tone much softer this time.

Rather than answer, Kane looks at me, his eyes silently pleading for me to tell the story. So I place a hand on Ezra's shoulder and rub soothing circles and relay the details to him. With each one, I swear smoke steams from every crevice of his body.

When I'm finished, he hauls himself up. "I will fucking kill him."

My heart lurches in response to the pure fury radiating from him. "*Ezra.*"

"This is exactly why I didn't want to tell you," Kane says.

"It's my job to protect you."

"Listen." I grasp Ezra's arm. "I want to rip that kid a new one, too, but that's not going to solve anything."

His chest is puffed like a gorilla gearing up to fight for dominance in his troop. "Then what do you suggest we do?"

"We?"

"Yeah, Kane and me. What should we do?"

Oh, *that* we. Without my permission, disappointment needles its way into my heart.

"Kane?" I step forward. "Would you like to be helped, hugged, or heard?"

Ezra deflates, still crouched on the floor. Wrapping his arm around my waist, he buries his face in my abdomen.

"Millie already listened to me," Kane answers.

"Would you rather have a dog or a cat?"

"Cat," Kane answers at the same time Ezra says, "Dog."

"Uh-oh," I laugh, going in for another taco.

Ezra put in an order and picked them up, and while Kane and I waited, I forced him to eat my soup. That hasn't stopped him from polishing off two of his own tacos, though.

"We're not getting a fucking cat."

"I'll help you get the fucking cat," I whisper loud enough for Ezra to hear.

"You're in trouble, you know that?" He winks.

If a minor was not present, I'd have a good comeback for that.

"Would you rather be able to fly or breathe underwater?" Kane asks.

"That's a good one," I say. "I think I'd rather fly."

"Me too," Ezra agrees, wiping his mouth with a napkin. "My turn. Would you rather be a millionaire or find true love?"

"Millionaire," Kane replies instantly.

With a roll of my eyes, I ruffle his floppy hair. It's overdue for a cut. Or maybe he's growing it out like his brother's.

I think for a long moment, acutely aware of Ezra's intimidating gaze. "True love," I decide, then quickly steamroll to the next question. "Would you rather everyone you know read your thoughts all the time or for everyone you know to see your emotional support screenshots?"

"Your what?" Ezra sits back, crossing his arms. "That's not a thing."

"Of course it is. They're the screenshots you take of things that make you happy or things you don't want to forget—which is ironic because you'll probably forget you screenshotted them in the first place."

He throws his head back and guffaws. "Let me see your emotional support screenshots."

"Absolutely not."

"Why not? What do you have hidden?"

With a shimmy of my shoulders, I shoot him a wink. "Oh, I have a separate hidden folder."

"Gross. I'm sitting right here." Kane groans, slumping low in his chair.

By the time we've demolished the last of the tacos, Kane looks like he's about to fall asleep at the table.

"You ready to go home?" Ezra asks, standing and collecting trash from the table.

"Yeah," he answers, stumbling to his feet. "Millie?"

"Hmm?"

"You coming?" he asks.

I collect our glasses and tuck them against my chest with one arm. "Coming where?"

"Coming home with us?"

I freeze in place, my heart stuttering and my mind going blank. "No, I, uh, I have to record something," I finally stammer. Without my permission, my eyes flick to Ezra.

By the frown he's wearing, it's obvious he knows I'm fibbing.

He goes for the assist, nonetheless. "Why don't you come over later, then? We'll pop popcorn and the three of us can watch a movie."

Lips pressed into a line, I nod. "Sure. I'll bring candy."

Kane gives me a long hug, his lanky frame arcing awkwardly

over me. I revel in the affection. I love that he's so open, both physically and emotionally. As he releases me, I silently praise his mother for raising such a fine young man.

Ezra envelops me in a hug next and kisses the top of my head. "Thank you," he whispers. "You're amazing."

Once the door closes behind them, I lock up and slump against it, pressing a hand to my heart.

He asked if I was *coming home* with them. Shit. I told him I'd be the cool, fun aunt, but there was absolutely nothing fun about today. Today was hard. And Kane is growing attached to me quickly. I want to be there for him, but I don't know if I'm cut out for this.

*Fuck, what have I gotten myself into?*

## Chapter 33

# Ezra

TODAY WAS HARD.

Millie was magnificent.

*What have I gotten myself into?*

Fear swamped me when my brother didn't come home or answer his phone, clouding all rational thought.

The first thing I do when we get back to the apartment is call my mom and apologize for the time Cam and I said we were at a buddy's in Hoboken when we were really getting drunk. That night, I broke my wrist, and the hospital *in Atlantic City* called her. I'd never seen my mom that angry.

"Oh, sweetheart. It's okay," she assures me over the phone. "That's part of being a parent. The good, the bad, the ugly. You get it all. Parenting is mostly just worrying about your kid. Even thirty-six years later, I still worry about you. You know that."

I huff. Yeah, I sure do.

"What if I'm fu—screwing this whole thing up? What if I'm not a good guardian?"

She's silent a moment, her rhythmic breathing the only sound. "I'm going to let you in on a little parenting secret."

I hold the phone closer to my ear so I don't miss a thing.

"None of us know what the fuck we're doing."

The laugh that explodes from me can probably be heard in Hawaii. Tears of relief spring to my eyes with my mother's validation.

"You're doing a good job. I've seen you with that boy. If you feel like you're screwing up, you're doing it right."

My chest aches with affection for her and for my brother. "Thanks, Mom."

"Of course. That's what I'm here for. So." She changes the subject. "What's going on with you and Millie? Has she gotten over her *jet lag*?" She emphasizes the last part. My mom was sorely disappointed about Millie's absence when we stopped by shortly after we returned.

"She's coming over later. She was remarkable with Kane this afternoon."

"They seem like they have a special bond."

Pride and gratitude flood my veins. "They do."

"Just be careful."

"What's that supposed to mean?"

"I don't want to see you hurt again," she says in her most motherly of voices.

It takes effort not to sigh in response to her overprotectiveness. "I'm fine, Mom."

"Didn't I just tell you it's my job to worry?"

"Millie's different."

*Isn't she?*

---

Though she's thirty minutes late, Millie arrives with an overflowing bag of candy. "I didn't know what you two like."

She kicks off her shoes with gusto and hangs her purse by the door.

Kane holds the bag hostage, immediately ripping into the Sour Patch Kids and Swedish Fish. With a "Thanks, Mills" tossed over his shoulder, he settles back into his corner of the sofa.

"Mills, huh?" She hands me a bag of dark chocolate M&M's—good guess.

"You two have really hit it off."

She nods in response to my comment, but her eyes swim with an emotion I can't read. Before I can give it any more thought, she's pouring herself a glass of wine and telling me all about Cam and Joey's latest travels to London. I listen intently while I pop popcorn, pretending it's new and exciting information, even though I just got off the phone with Cam.

"What are we watching?" she asks as she pulls a pair of fuzzy socks from her purse.

Once she settles next to Kane, I set the large bowl of popcorn on the table in front of us and take a seat on her other side.

Her feet have crept their way into my lap before Ferris Bueller has even said, "Life moves pretty fast. If you don't stop and look around once in a while, you could miss it."

At one point, Millie and Kane get into a debate about which Sour Patch Kid flavor is the best, so I pause the movie and bask in the moment. Damn, life really is great.

Unsurprisingly, my brother passes out before the credits roll. While Millie collects candy wrappers, I pull his long legs onto the sofa and cover him with a blanket. As I back away, an image of scooping up a younger version of Kane flashes through my mind: blond hair like his, curly like mine, and green eyes like Millie's.

"I guess I'll head out."

"Stay." I mean for it to be a demand, but it comes out more like a plea.

She lowers her focus to a spot on my shirt. "But I don't have any of my things."

I narrow my eyes. "You don't wear pajamas. And I have an extra toothbrush. What more do you need?"

When she doesn't have a comeback, I drag her by the hand into my bedroom and set a new toothbrush on the counter by the sink. We brush side by side, then she watches me in the mirror as I peel off my clothes.

In the bedroom she removes her shirt, revealing a pale blue bra. The dusty pink of her nipples peeks through the lace. "Why do you have sheets on top of your sheets? And are these waterproof?" she asks, poking the heap of linens on my mattress.

"Dammit. I changed and washed them but forgot to put them away. And of course they're waterproof." I wink. I fluff out the fitted sheet, then haphazardly fold it, though it looks more like a soft rock by the time I'm done with it.

"Whoa, whoa, whoa," she gasps. "What are you doing?" Her expression is much like the one I give my students when they use the newest slang: confused and repulsed.

"Think you can fold a fitted sheet better than this? I'd like to see you try." I throw the bunched-up fabric at her.

She meticulously yet effortlessly folds it, giving Martha Stewart a run for her money.

Strangely, my heart rate kicks up at the sight of her. Am I in love?

She looks up. "What?"

"I don't know anyone else who can fold a fitted sheet."

"It's a good party trick."

"What kind of parties are you going to?" I laugh.

"The kind that needs new sheets." She gives me a saucy wink.

Tackling her onto the bed, I tickle her sides until she's yelling "safe word."

"Shh," I mumble against her lips. "You'll wake Kane."

That quiets her quickly.

With a deep breath in, I savor her scent, then nibble on her earlobe. "You're so talented."

"Why? Because I can fold a fitted sheet?"

"Among other things." I kiss a path down her neck, capturing the strap of her bra between my teeth as I go. As I drag it down her shoulder, her breast breaks free, and I suck her nipple into my mouth, reliving the moment she let me come all over them the other day.

"Wait."

I immediately stop, rolling onto my side to give her space.

Her breasts hang heavy over her high-waisted leggings when she sits up. "We should talk."

Dragging myself and my half-hard dick under the covers, I hold them aloft and invite her in too. "What's up?"

She slips in beside me and rests her back against the pillow. "I went to the doctor this morning."

"Why didn't you tell me?" My chest tightens with trepidation. "I would have gone with you." I'm acting like we're still fake married, but I'm too invested in her health, with her life in general, to stop now.

"I was going to call you after, but then all that stuff with Kane happened."

I nod. "What did they say?"

She bows her head and picks at her fingernails. "Ezra, what are we doing here?"

My heart thumps painfully against my sternum. "What do you mean?"

"What if I can't have children?" She still won't look at me, though from here, I can tell her eyes are glossy.

"Where is this coming from? What did the doctor say?"

"He says I might have endometriosis. My Aunt Elin has it,

and she's lucky she even has Joey. What if that happens to me?" She runs the back of her wrist over her cheek. "What if this thing between us gets serious and you want kids, but I can't give them to you? Maybe we should end this before we get in too deep."

"Hey." I stop her from tearing up her nails by placing my hand on top of hers. "Look at me."

This is *not* how I saw this night going. One minute I've got her tit halfway down my throat, the next she's talking about calling it quits. How did we get here?

"What if I can't have kids?" she repeats. "You want to be a dad so badly. And I want that for you. But what if I can't give that to you? I don't want to take that dream away from you. Sam said—"

"Sam?" My heart drops to my stomach. "Samantha? When did you talk to her?"

Millie finally looks at me, her eyes wide. "I, uh, I saw her after my doctor's appointment. I ran into her, and she asked to have coffee together."

"You went on a date with her?"

"Relax. It wasn't a date."

My hackles rise. "Don't tell me to relax."

"I didn't mean it like that." She shifts beneath the sheet so she's facing me. "I bumped into her randomly. She wanted to apologize. That's all. Nothing happened. I swear."

I want to believe her, I do. But my past is creeping up and tightening around my lungs like a thorny vine. "Did she hit on you?"

"No? I don't think so. She told me I looked pretty, I guess, but—"

"Fuck." I grip my hair with both hands and tug. "I can't believe this."

"Ezra, what the hell? I'm telling you nothing happened. I

wouldn't lie to you. I know you've been burned badly in the past, but I'm not like those women."

"I want to believe you, I do. It's just..." I drop my head and focus on my breathing.

"I think I should go," she whispers, shuffling toward the side of the bed.

"No." I clamp down on her arm. "Why would you go?"

"Because. We're fighting and—"

"So what? That's what couples do. But don't you dare walk out on me. I can't—I can't have another woman walk out on me," I croak, vulnerability lodged in my throat like a rock.

Our eyes lock and hold in a standoff.

*Please.*

"You're right. I'm sorry. But it's awkward now. Am I just supposed to lay next to you while we're in the middle of an argument?"

"Yes." I stroke a thumb over the back of her hand. "Listen. It's been a long day. The stuff with Kane was a lot. We're both emotional, so why don't we table this discussion until we've had a good night's sleep and some strong coffee and tea in the morning? I'd rather go to bed awkward and upset than say stupid shit we might regret."

With an audible exhale, she nods.

"And let's face it, it'll be more awkward if you leave. Please stay. I'll even build you a pillow fort if that makes you feel better."

"It's a pillow wall." She giggles. "I didn't think couples were supposed to go to bed angry."

"Oh, are you confirming we're a couple, then?"

She rolls her eyes, but rather than answer that question, she says, "Fine. I'll stay." After she's stripped out of her leggings and thong, she dips back beneath the sheets.

It's silent between us, just the sounds of the city seeping in through the windows, and it doesn't take long before her skin brushes against mine and her arm is draped over my chest.

"Earlier, you said *before we get in too deep*." I rub the soft skin of her bum. "It's too late, Mills. I'm already in too deep."

"That's what she said." She cackles.

"Oh my god." I pinch her side. *I love you* nearly slips out, but I lock that shit up tight. "Let's fight in the morning, and you can tell me all about your doctor's appointment, yeah?"

"Sounds good. Good night, Ezra."

---

In the morning, I wake to Millie snuggled in close and a slick layer of sweat between my hip and where her thigh wraps around it. Her breath is warm against my neck, and she's rubbing her finger against my beard in soothing motions.

"What are you doing?" I ask, my voice rough with sleep.

"It's like ASMR. It's satisfying."

I squeeze her thigh. "If you're trying to be cute to get out of our talk, it won't work."

"How about a blow job?" she asks, her tone full of mirth. "All right, fine." Sitting up, she swings her legs over the bed, giving me the perfect view of her naked back. I want nothing more than to drag her over me and impale her with my cock, but we need to work through some things first.

"Where are you going?" I ask.

"To brush my teeth, dumbass." She stands and saunters toward the bathroom, leaving me gawking at her sinful body. "I'm not arguing with morning breath. Plus, you promised me coffee."

I check on Kane, who made his way to his room sometime during the night, and leave two pain relievers, a banana, and a glass of water on his nightstand for when he wakes up. When I return to the bedroom with two mugs, I nearly spill the hot liquid at the sight before me. She's scrolling through her phone, wearing *my* shirt in *my* bed. For several heartbeats, I linger in the doorway and commit the image of her to memory.

After a minute, she looks up and makes grabby hands for the coffee, and I obediently deliver it to her.

"Mmm," she sighs as she swallows. "This tastes like the macadamia nut coffee I had in Hawaii." She tilts her head, scrutinizing me. "But you don't drink coffee."

I take a sip of my black tea before setting it on the nightstand. "The coffee is from my mom's stash, but Kane thought we should buy this creamer for you."

A weak smile comes to play across her face. "That was sweet of him. He's a good kid. Is he awake?"

With a shake of my head, I pop open my prescription bottle. "Forgot to take my Viagra."

The joke garners a bigger grin from Millie. God, I need more mornings like this.

Though I'm desperate to know if she put on panties, I focus on the tough conversation looming over us instead. Flipping through my mental catalog of therapy lessons, I begin. "I felt..." I take a deep breath, "shocked and hurt when you said you met Samantha for coffee. It felt like you went behind my back. In the future," *Lord, I hope there's a future,* "I would appreciate it if you communicated with me right away if something like this comes up."

She could catch flies with the way her jaw hangs open.

"What?" I ask.

Stuttering, she blinks rapidly. "I just... you're just... I didn't expect you to be so direct yet kind. My last boyfriend yelled at me and flipped over a vase during our last argument, and we never talked again."

I bristle and silently beat up the asshole in my mind. "I would never yell at you. I've done enough therapy and I've done the work. I can communicate my feelings. I may not always get it right, like last night, but I try my best."

"That's refreshing," she says. Her lips are turned down, though she looks impressed rather than upset. "I really am sorry about yesterday. She caught me off guard. I swear to you nothing happened. She apologized, and then I hightailed it out of there before I could even finish my coffee. I truly never care to see her again."

"I believe you."

Her expression goes soft for a moment, but then her lips twitch. "I think she might have been pissed when I told her we went to Hawaii together."

"Good. Serves her right." I laugh. "Now, can we talk about your doctor's appointment?"

Her eyes drop to her coffee, like she's found an interesting specimen floating in her mug.

"Look at me, honey."

Chin lifted, she worries her bottom lip.

"I realize we haven't had the most traditional start to our relationship." I cock a brow. "Lord knows you gave me a run for my money in Greece. I wasn't looking for anything serious..."

She lets out a breathy scoff.

"Okay, fine." I chuckle. "But I never imagined the girl who blew me away singing karaoke, then presented me with her vending machine dildo would make such a lasting impression on me."

Her cheeks flush and her eyes glimmer at that.

"I like you. A lot." *I might even be in love with you.* "I want to be with you. But I'd be lying if I said I'd be okay with you taking too much time to figure things out. I have Kane to think about now, and he's already made you a part of his life. Plus, I'm old."

She giggles, though she lifts her mug to hide the way her lips quirk up.

I love that I can make her laugh in the middle of a serious conversation. "So please. Talk to me."

With one more sip, she sets her coffee on the nightstand. Then she curls her legs under her body and faces me. *Yeah, definitely no panties.*

"Okay," she breathes. "I've never imagined a guy being my endgame—not that I'm saying *you're* my endgame." A flush creeps into her cheeks as she peers at me. Fuck, it's the most adorable thing I've ever seen.

With a nod, I go easy on her. "I know what you mean."

"Any time I've thought about marriage, I've pictured marrying a woman. I don't know why." She shrugs. "For years, I haven't let myself stray from that vision. Being bi can be so complex. And I guess I thought that if I married a man, then I'd be betraying the part of me who fights so hard to convince people that the B in LGBT is real. I am the B, you know?"

I nod. I can't pretend to understand what it's like to be queer, but I want her to know that her feelings are worth listening to.

"There's so much stigma, even in the queer community, surrounding bisexuality. It's hard not to worry that if I marry a man—*one day*, of course—I'll be erased from the community."

As much as I want to tell her that she shouldn't have to prove her sexuality to anyone, I remain silent.

"Logically I know that's not true. It's just taking me time to rethink my future."

"And what do you see in your future now?" I grab her hands and rub my thumbs over her smooth skin.

*Please say me.*

She pulls them away, and my heart sinks. "There's more." She sighs. "When I think about your future, I see you as a father.

You're practically one to Kane now. It's only a matter of time before you get full custody, right?"

Teeth pressed into my bottom lip, I nod. "That's the plan."

"The desire to have kids of your own is written all over your stupidly handsome face." She waves a hand in front of me. "And… and I'm afraid I won't be able to give that to you. I can't be certain, of course, but between what the doctor has told me and what I've googled"—she says that last part under her breath—"it's a possibility. It's wild to talk about having children together when we've only started dating, but I'd hate for things to get too serious and for hearts to get broken." Her eyes go misty, her focus set on my face.

Fuck, I yearn to wipe her tears away. "Millie…"

"Wait." She holds out a hand, fingers splayed. "You're going to say none of that matters, but stop and think. *Doesn't it?* Doesn't it matter to you that you one day have kids?"

With a deep inhale and exhale, I study her face, waiting to see whether she's got more to say. "Is it my turn?"

She nods.

"Fine." I gather her hands in mine, and this time, she doesn't pull away. "I can't sit here and tell you it wouldn't be a disappointment if I didn't get to see your beautiful body round with my child." My eyes dip to her stomach. "And I'd be lying if I said it doesn't turn me on just thinking about it. But there are other ways to have a family. People do it all the time. Take Cam's parents, for example."

The confused frown that mars her face tells me she doesn't know what I'm talking about.

"He's an IVF baby."

Her eyes widen, and her breath catches.

"So it's not impossible. Plus, I'd be open to adoption. But Millie, even if none of those work out, it will be okay."

*For the Show*

A single tear rolls down her cheek, and this time I do wipe it away.

"But how do you know?" she asks.

"Because I'll have you."

# Chapter 34
## Millie

Ezra and Kane don't let me go back to my apartment the next night. Or the night after that. But by the third night, I'm officially behind in recording for LULU, and if I don't get started on the audiobook for an indie romance I was hired to narrate, I'll hate myself later. Ezra begs me to stay, which is tempting, especially when I envision him getting on his knees. Even so, I force myself to leave so I can tend to my responsibilities.

When I return to my apartment, Peg and Fran bring over a fresh plate of chocolate chip scones and their opinions. They gush about how much they enjoyed meeting Ezra and hope to see more of him, and they don't hold back.

"Will he be moving in here, or will we have to say goodbye to another one of our girls?" They're still upset with Joey for moving out, and I'm the one who has to suffer with the guilt trips.

"No one said anything about moving in." Though the image of Ezra and I sharing a bed permanently has crossed my mind.

My plants are completely dead. All I can do is laugh about it. That's one stereotype about being bisexual that stands true for me.

*For the Show*

I record two erotic stories and an hour's worth of the audiobook before my vocal cords raise a white flag. Just as I've settled into bed with a mug of lemon and honey tea and have cued up an episode of *New Girl*, my phone buzzes with a text from Stevie.

**STEVIE**
Get your saucy ass back to the club

**ME**
Hi to you too

**STEVIE**
I don't have time for that shit. Sam is gone, and the girls want you back

**ME**
What? Gone?

**STEVIE**
She moved back home. We miss you. Please say you'll come back

I set my phone down. Sam wasn't the only reason I avoided going back to FrenchSHEs. I was ashamed of my weight. When I worked behind the bar or hosted drag queen brunches on Sundays or sang karaoke, I wore tiny outfits that complemented my tight figure.

Apprehension swirls in my stomach, but there's a hint of excitement there too. I pick my phone up again and tap out a response.

**ME**
I'll think about it

**STEVIE**
I put you on the schedule for this weekend. See you then, bitch

All night, I toss and turn, unable to put thoughts of my body and how different I look out of my mind. Eventually my thoughts wander to Ezra and how incredible he makes me feel. Logically I believe beauty comes from within, but when a person suffers from body dysmorphia, that cliché is a load of horseshit. One day I'm disgusted with my body, and the next I feel like a total bombshell. Sometimes the roller-coaster ride of confidence and impostor syndrome is too much to bear. But when I'm with Ezra, the ride is less roller coaster and more like riding It's a Small World at Disney—slightly annoying, but steady and smooth, so I don't feel like I'm going to throw up. He worships my body in ways I never imagined anyone could. And when I don't love my body, he loves it enough for me.

The day before I return to FrenchSHEs, Claire joins me for a shopping spree. When she arrives, she's flustered, and her wet hair is pulled into a topknot. We met through Joey and became fast friends, but between her schedule and mine, we rarely see one another.

"Sorry I'm late. I had a last-minute patient thrown in my schedule," she huffs when she hugs me.

"That reminds me," I say after she's updated me on what's going on at work. "Did you ever talk to my brother?"

"I did." She pulls a bobby pin from the pocket of her overalls and uses it to secure the bangs that keep falling over the gold frames of her glasses.

"And? Are you considering the position?"

She lifts one shoulder. "The offer was very kind. But I haven't been working for Dr. Edwards very long. I can't quit on him."

We fall into a rhythm where I hold up an outfit and Claire either nods in approval or scrunches up her nose.

"Oh my god," she shrieks one aisle over. "This one. *This one.*"

She pulls a silver sequined catsuit from the rack and drags me by the arm to the dressing room.

"It's never going to fit," I whine when I catch sight of the size.

With a lip stuck out, she pouts, much like my niece does when she's trying to get her way.

"Fine." I close the curtain, being sure to throw extra angst into the move.

While I stand in the middle of the small fitting room, hands on my hips, the spectacular jumpsuit taunts me from the hanger. *You know you want me.*

I do. I really, really do. But I cannot get stuck in my clothing in a dressing room again.

*Do it for me, honey,* Ezra's voice sings in my head.

That's enough to bolster my courage. So I take a deep breath and peel off my clothes.

When the stretchy material slides over my butt and hips with surprising ease, I gasp. And when I slip my arms through the holes and the fabric hugs my tits like a fitted sheet, I yelp.

"You okay in there?" Claire asks. "Let me see."

Inspecting myself in the mirror, I can't help the smile that spreads across my face.

Call the fire department; I'm fucking *hot*.

When I drag the curtain open, I find Claire standing so close I nearly knock her over.

"Holy shit." Her squeal causes every person in the dressing room to stick their head out to gawk. "I'm sending a picture to Ezra," she says, retrieving her phone from her pocket.

"Wait. I want him to see it in person."

Her eyes dance as she holds the device up to her face to unlock it. "Great idea. I'll send it to Joey instead."

I give her my best *Mamma Mia* poses for a solid five minutes before trying on a few more casual yet sexy outfits. After I've dropped nearly half my paycheck on a new wardrobe (that I'm praying I'll make up for in tips this weekend), we head to a café nearby.

"Thanks for shopping with me," I say as we take a seat side by side at a high-top by the window.

"Of course." She drizzles dressing from a packet onto her salad. "I wish I could pop in and see you at the club, but I'm swamped with work."

"Do you ever get a break? What's your dating life like these days?"

With a huff, she stabs at a tomato. "Nonexistent."

"So it's not like *Grey's Anatomy*? No one is hooking up in the call room?"

Laughing, she shakes her head. "Sorry to disappoint."

"I have a question. It's been on my mind for some time, but I've been too afraid to ask."

"*Okay.*" She swivels in her seat to face me. "You're making me nervous, but go for it."

"Have you and Ezra ever—"

She lets out an unladylike snort and slaps a hand over her nose and mouth. "Absolutely not. He's much too old for me."

"Hey, we're the same age." I jab her arm playfully.

"So you like older men. I'm not judging." She grins. "I was a kid when I met Ezra and he was already a *man*, you know?"

I conjure an image of an eighteen-year-old Ezra. Yeah, he was probably one of those boys to hit puberty at ten.

"He's my brother's best friend—and not in the cool, sexy romance books way. He was always like another big brother. Still is."

The anxiety knotting my stomach eases. "That's fair. Even if you had a history with him, I would have been okay with it." It wouldn't have been nearly as awkward as the weird love triangle we found ourselves in with Sam. Still, I'm relieved they've never had a romantic connection.

*For the Show*

Claire has barely finished her salad when the alarm on her Apple Watch goes off. She attends an art class any time she can, so we share an Uber back to Washington Heights.

After she's stepped out onto the sidewalk, she pokes her head back in and gives me a soft smile. "I haven't seen you and Ezra together yet, but I've known him for over half my life and have never seen him this happy. Something tells me you have a lot to do with that."

✦

Between the time I get dressed and the time I step into FrenchSHEs, I collect enough boob sweat to fill a small fish tank, but it's like I never left. The entire crew smothers me with hugs, including two new performers I've never met. Autopilot kicks in, and I quickly fall into the groove of things, blessedly and effortlessly feeling like myself again.

A little before midnight, Stevie's voice comes through my earpiece. "Millie. You're neglecting a customer."

My stomach plummets. *What?* I scan the length of the bar. No one is leaning over the countertop, trying to get my attention, and every glass looks at least partially full.

"The high-top on your far right," they say, voice tinny through my earpiece.

Huh? I'm behind the bar tonight. That's not my jurisdiction. I crane my neck, scoping out the scene, then bark out a laugh.

"You bitch," I tease.

The customer sitting on the stool is certainly not neglected.

Even so, I saunter that way, beaming. "What are you doing here?"

Stevie is suddenly at my side, shooing me out from behind the bar with a wink.

Like a magnet, my body is drawn to Ezra's. I settle between his legs, and he engulfs me in his strong arms.

"I missed you," he says into my sweaty neck.

I pull back, soaking him in. His curly hair is down and styled, smelling like eucalyptus, but his beard is slightly overgrown. His light purple shirt hugs his biceps, while his jeans are doing something pornographic to his thighs.

Heat gathers in my core as I pan the club to see if anyone else is observing how goddamn good he looks.

With his hands at my waist, he asks, "Should I have not come?"

"No, no, it's not that." I knead his shoulders and reassure him with a smile. "I just didn't expect to see you tonight."

"What happened to that disco ball catsuit I heard so much about?"

"Oh, so you talked to Claire?" I laugh. "That's for special occasions. Tonight, I'm just working behind the bar."

Nevertheless, he gives me a thorough once-over, his eyes shining with so much lust I'm nearly blinded. My brand-new black leather mini skirt hits my waist in the perfect place, and I've paired it with a shimmery gold crop top. Ezra plucks at the strings in the back like he's playing a guitar, his fingertips against my bare skin soothing me.

"You'll have to give me a private fashion show when we get home, then." He smirks.

"Home?"

He drags a hand around to my ass and squeezes. "Kane's at a friend's tonight. I'm all yours."

My insides vibrate, and I bounce on my toes. He hasn't spent the night at my place yet.

"If you don't like that idea, I can see if Peg and Fran want a sleepover instead."

"You're not their type." I chuckle.

He rears back, feigning offense, but the look is quickly replaced by one dripping with need. Angling in, he sinks his teeth into my neck. "There better be coffee behind that bar because you're going to be up all night for what I have planned for you."

# Chapter 35
# Millie

"I'm going to have to start calling you Eager Ezra." I laugh as he kicks off his shoes and sprints to my room.

"You can call me a lot of things, honey. Just don't call me that." He gives me a quick spank, then tosses his phone onto my bed and heads to the en suite bathroom. From the other side of the cracked door, he says, "Can you look at my phone and tell me Kane's location? I want to make sure he's nothing like me at his age and is where he says he's going to be."

When I pick up his phone, I'm met with his lock screen. "Uh, it's locked."

"It's 242424."

"Whoa, whoa, whoa. Giving me your passcode is the modern-day equivalent of giving me a key to your apartment," I joke. "I'm not sure we're there yet."

"I have nothing to hide, Mills."

I open the tracking app and give him the location, which is met with a sigh and a "thank god."

We trade places in the bathroom, and when I'm finished, I find him already in my bed. He looks right at home against my mountain of decorative pillows, with his hands behind his head and his elbows out. A wicked grin peeks out from beneath his almost unruly beard, making my skin tingle with anticipation.

"Strip, baby," he commands.

My heart trips over itself. "Where are your manners, Mr. Miller?" I tease, loving this tug-of-war game we often play. "Or should I call you *Principal* Miller?"

"Don't brat me unless you're serious, sweetheart," he warns.

I cross my arms, standing my ground. For now.

All the wind is knocked out of me, though, when he hoists me up and tosses me onto the bed. A giggle bursts out of me, but he smothers the sound with his mouth. But not with a kiss. No. He bites my bottom lip before licking the sting away.

I lightly push back on his chest. "I'm so proud of you."

"I know, baby."

I've only told him a million times since he was offered the principal position two days ago. "Will you let me throw you a party?"

"Absolutely not. You know I don't like celebrating myself."

With a harrumph, I push my lower lip out. "How can I show you how proud I am, then?"

"I can think of a few ways…" He drags his fingers down my silhouette and stops at the hem of my skirt. "Do you know what these fucking boots do to me?"

Excitement flashes through me. I thought he might like my thigh-high black leather boots.

"These stay." He smirks.

He fumbles at my waist to pull down my skirt without success, so I reach behind my back and undo the zipper for him.

"Thanks," he mumbles.

"Oh, so he *does* have manners."

That earns me a pinch to the nipple through my top.

He slides my skirt down my thighs, groaning when my lacy black G-string is revealed. "Fuck, Mills, are these new too?"

Biting my bottom lip, I nod. "Do you like?"

The noise he makes at the back of his throat rumbles through me, followed by a wave of heat.

"Sit up," he demands.

I oblige, letting my legs hang off the bed.

With his breath tickling the shell of my ear, he unties my top. As the fabric gives, I raise my arms. Painstakingly, Ezra guides the material up my body until my breasts fall, heavy in their escape.

He takes a step back, wiping a hand down his face, his brows pinched in concentration.

"Your turn," I urge, my breaths coming quicker.

He shakes his head. "I'm just getting started. Lay back and spread those legs for me. And if you sass me, Amelia, I won't let you come."

"Yes, sir." I scramble back to the top of the mattress. As much as I love being bossed around in the bedroom, I really don't want to be edged right now.

Ezra runs a single digit from the top of my underwear, down to where it disappears between my thighs, eliciting a full-body shiver.

"What are your limits?" he asks. "Anything you don't want me to do tonight?"

I shake my head. I can't think of anything but how pained Ezra must be with his erection trapped within the confines of his jeans and how long he'll make me wait for it.

As if he can read my mind, he straightens and yanks off his shirt, then unbuttons and unzips his pants. Though he doesn't remove them, he sighs in relief.

The gleam in his dark eyes tells me he knows exactly what he's doing to me. *That fucker.*

He hooks his fingers under the strap of my underwear, then

releases with a loud *thwack*. Before the sting registers, he does it again. And again.

When I drop my head back and groan, he soothes my skin with a chaste kiss. His facial hair tickles the sensitive area, making me squirm, but he keeps his lips at my core, pushing the barely there fabric to the side and resting his finger against my cunt. I spread my legs wider, making room for him. Regardless of what he does next, I'm desperate for it.

He continues kissing the perimeter of my panties, teasing me with nips and quick kisses. All the while, his finger remains torturously still at my opening.

Then, in one fluid motion, he sinks in deep.

"Yes," I sigh. *About damn time.* "More," I beg without shame. "More."

He slips a second finger inside and curls them, hitting the perfect spot in repetitive movements. It's a surefire way to get me to come quickly, and he knows it.

I pull the fabric farther to the side to give him better access, and he instantly laps at me.

"Fuck." I arch my back. "That feels nice."

He blows against my clit. "Make that pussy purr for me."

My toes curl as much as they can in my boots, and as euphoria builds inside me, I dig the stilettos into the bed. The ecstasy gathers at my core, coiling tight and teasing me with the promise of its inevitable release.

"So close," I whisper. With my hands in his hair, I hold him exactly where I want him, grinding my pussy against his mouth, smothering him. "There. *Theretherethere.*"

On cue, he does that thing with his tongue I love so much, the one he usually saves for the finale.

"Fuck," I scream.

He rides out my orgasm with me, his fingers still buried inside me and his tongue on my clit, and he doesn't let up until the last waves and flutters of my orgasm settle.

I'm spent, but by the way he's stroking himself, it's clear he's not done with me. Moving with confidence, he shucks his pants and tosses them to the side. Then he removes my boots one at a time. He hovers over me, his body radiating heat, as I fist his cock and guide his length between my thighs, using him as a personal dildo.

"Stop," he croaks, his eyes squeezed shut.

Holding my breath, I freeze and peer down between us, discovering that one of his piercings has snagged on the lace of my G-string.

"Oh, shit. Don't move."

His arms tremble on either side of me as he holds himself up, his breaths becoming choppy.

It's too dim to make out the details of the situation. I worry that without light, I'll make it worse. "Can you reach your phone? I need the flashlight."

Sighing, he turns his head only. "It's a little out of reach." He lowers himself gently, trapping his tangled cock between us. "Scoot with me. On three. One, two..."

On three, I lift my hips to stay flush with him. I don't even want to consider the worst-case scenario. But he's taken me to the emergency room, so I suppose I'll return the favor if I must. At the thought, I can't help but imagine rolling up to the front desk and reporting the incident.

Despite my best efforts to rein it in, a giggle slips free. It's a small nasally noise at first, but if I'm not careful, it could easily turn into a full-on belly laugh.

"Amelia," Ezra reprimands, his brows furrowed and his expression stern. "It's not funny."

"It's kind of funny." Another giggle escapes me, so I bite my tongue and force myself to breathe evenly.

*For the Show*

Balancing on his left arm, he reaches for his phone with his free hand and passes it to me.

I shine the light between our bodies and tuck my chin to assess the situation. "Can you hold it up a bit?"

When he pulls his crown back a fraction, I can make out the place where the lace has snagged. As Ezra breathes heavily above me, I pray to the sex gods that I don't mess this up. Very gently, I pinch the thread and unwrap it from the metal. His dick bobs, and after he's confirmed it's free, he collapses to the bed beside me.

"Oh, thank fuck," he exhales, his hand resting over his half-hard cock and his eyes closed.

I take a moment to study every peak and valley of his chest and abdomen, paying close attention to the swirling patterns of the hair on his thighs.

When I rest a hand on his chest, his body vibrates with laughter.

"Oh, so you can laugh, but I can't?" I pinch his nipple.

"It wasn't *your* dick that was literally hanging on by a thread."

And now we're both flat on our backs, cackling up at the ceiling.

I shed the villainous undies and fling them across the room dramatically. "There. Who knew lace could be so evil."

Eventually our laughter tapers off to a comfortable silence, and we migrate to our sides so we're facing one another.

"Did we totally kill the mood?"

Propping his head up with his hand, he swirls his fingers around my nipple, leaving goose bumps in his wake. Then he drags them down my body, pausing at the crease at my thigh. "I'm always in the mood when it comes to you."

# Chapter 36
## Ezra

I was true to my word and kept Millie up all night long. The sun was awake before we were asleep, and I kept her snug (and naked) in my arms until Kane called, wondering where I was. Apparently he didn't realize the tracking app goes both ways. When I woke Millie, she whispered "five more minutes," then sat on my face before I was allowed to go home.

Home.

"*Let's go home,*" I'd said to her last night. Technically it was *her home*, but that phrase feels inclusive somehow, like it's *our home*.

While I didn't grow up with a sibling and have never shared a bedroom, I love having Millie in my space and I love being in hers. It isn't the least bit awkward. When she's not in my bed, I crave her like a drug. I'm consumed by thoughts of when I'll get my next hit.

The remainder of my weekend is spent hanging out with my brother, reading over endless documents, and watching videos in preparation for my new position as principal. On Sunday evening, when I settle into bed, I pull up the picture Millie texted

*For the Show*

earlier. Suited from head to toe in silver sequins, she looks like a walking disco ball. She's posed with her hip cocked to the side and one hand thrown in the air. The grin she's sporting is bright, much like the one she wore a couple of days ago when she modeled the outfit for me in her bedroom. It was nearly four a.m. and we were both exhausted, but I pouted and threatened to throw her toys away unless she showed me.

I'm still drooling over the photo when a text notification appears at the top of the screen.

> MILLIE
> What are you doing next weekend?

> ME
> That depends
> Will you be naked?

> MILLIE
> Not at my brother's house

I laugh out loud as another text comes through.

> MILLIE
> Asher invited us to his camp. Kane too

> ME
> For the day?

> MILLIE
> Friday to Sunday, if you want. There are spare cabins

I toggle to my calendar app, where I've input Kane's schedule along with mine.

> ME
> Kane works until two on Friday. We could leave after?

**MILLIE**

Sounds good

Good night 💋

**ME**

One nude before you go? Maybe something from that "hidden" folder?

A photo appears right away, making my breath hitch. But when the image registers, I deflate.

**ME**

That's a closeup of your elbow, you brat

**MILLIE**

No it's not

**ME**

You're not fooling me. I know what your body looks like. It's ingrained in my brain

When she doesn't respond right away, I fire off another text.

**ME**

You better not be ghosting me. I know where you live

Three little dots appear and disappear a handful of times before she finally replies.

**MILLIE**

I don't have any recent pics

**ME**

Then we'll have to change that

*For the Show*

Kane rambles on and on during the drive to Daisy Lake Retreat & Camp, clearly ecstatic about the break from city life. While he's allowed to roam around the city within safe parameters, it's got to be stifling in comparison to the free rein he had in Hawaii.

According to Rachel and Ethan, the camp in upstate New York, which Asher and his late wife, Daisy, ran alongside her parents, was originally used for team-building activities for corporate organizations. Several years ago, Daisy and Asher expanded and began hosting family reunions and yoga and wellness retreats. But it was Daisy's dream to create a family summer camp, so that's what Asher did to honor her after she passed away.

The dry earth and gravel crunch beneath the soles of my sneakers as I step out and turn to help Millie out of her parents' SUV. Her father surreptitiously eyes our clasped hands and scrutinizes me when I plant a kiss on the side of her head. If he thinks I won't be showing his daughter affection in front of him, he's got another thing coming. I'm a grown man, and I will kiss my woman whenever I damn well please. With her consent, of course.

"Uncle Ezra," a tiny voice squeals from the door of the cabin.

Heart stuttering, I turn to Millie. *Uncle?*

"Looks like you're not just *Daddy* anymore," she whispers.

Without bothering to hide from Ethan, I swat her on the behind.

I've barely turned toward the house again when a little body crashes into my thighs, halting me in place. With her head tipped back, Bea holds her arms up. Unable to resist, I awkwardly scoop her up, realizing in this moment that I can't remember ever picking up a small human like this.

The second she's situated on my hip, she buries her hands in my hair, wiping a sticky substance on my neck in the process. She smells like jam and peanut butter, so I hope that's all it is.

"Where's your man bun?" She pouts, pulling the flat bill from my head and dropping it onto the ground. "I asked Daddy for a man bun so we could match, but..." She taps her head, gesturing to the lopsided pigtails Asher must have insisted on instead.

I barely know her, but my chest warms with affection for the precocious girl.

"Maybe *Uncle Ezra* can do your hair later, Dolly."

With a blinding smile, Bea throws herself into Millie's arms, practically giving me a heart attack at the sudden move.

"Sorry about that." Asher appears, picking up my hat on the way to greet us. "I hope you don't mind the uncle thing. She learned about family trees this week and assumed that since Millie is her aunt, that you must be her uncle."

"Totally fine," I assure him, secretly honored by the distinction.

Rachel and Ethan make their way to one of the cabins lining the gravel drive while Asher leads us to ours. The structure is small but airy, with an open-concept kitchen and main living space flanked by a bedroom on each side. Duffel bags in tow, Millie and I claim the larger one with the en suite bathroom, and Kane retreats to the other.

Once we've abandoned our things, Bea drags me to the sliding glass door, and I follow her out onto the deck.

"This is my mommy's lake," she says, lifting her arms up again.

Holding her in the crook of my arm, I follow her petite finger to the calm water about fifty yards away.

Confused, I frown at Millie and Asher.

"Daisy Lake," Asher says. "It's the lake my wife was named after."

"It's very pretty," I tell Bea, and she beams with pride.

"Okay." Asher claps. "Let's go see what Mimi and Papa are up to next door." He scoops his daughter from my arms despite her protests and takes the path in the back. "Dinner's at six," he calls over his shoulder.

---

"Last night was fun." Yawning, Millie wraps an arm around me.

Eyes closed, I soak in her warmth. Waking up to a naked Millie will always be my favorite way to start the day.

"I think I still have marshmallows in my hair." I pull on the strands stuck together on one side of my face.

Unsurprisingly, Bea was glued to my lap while we sat around the bonfire last night.

"She's really claimed ownership of you, hasn't she? Should I be worried?" she teases.

I roll and pin her onto her back. Sucking on her neck, I inhale the scent of her coconut shampoo mixed with a hint of sweat and a touch of campfire smoke. "The only one who can claim me is you, honey." With a grunt, I grind my hard cock against her thigh.

Just as she digs her nails into my ass, there's a knock at the door.

"Are you guys coming to breakfast?" Kane calls from the other side.

"Coming," Millie shouts.

"Not yet, you're not," I growl against the shell of her ear. "But it won't take me long."

"Ezra," she whisper-yells. "Your brother is on the other side of the door, you horndog." She tries to push me off, but I've unleashed my dead weight, and she's struggling. "Knock it off," she laughs beneath me.

I tickle her until she cries "safe word."

"Fine." I hop off the bed, my cock still eager.

Millie takes notice of my length and breaks out in a wicked smirk. "Later, okay? Promise."

A cold shower and a quick hair wash to get rid of leftover marshmallows is all I need to sober up. Fifteen minutes later, the three of us take a golf cart to the cafeteria, where breakfast is being served. Bea is seated between her grandparents, and Ethan is cutting up her Belgian waffle. When Bea spots us, she stands, unintentionally dipping her little fingers in syrup in the process. Asher intercepts like a ninja with a wet wipe seconds before she reaches us.

Damn. Kids are sticky. I didn't get the privilege of knowing Kane when he was little, but even at fifteen, things are still… *sticky*. At least when it comes to laundry.

Over breakfast, I sit back and listen as Bea and Kane plot our day. Since we couldn't possibly fit all their plans into a twenty-four-hour period, we help them narrow down the activities, paddle boarding being first on the agenda. An activity where Millie must wear a bathing suit? Sign me up.

---

"Can you swim?" I ask Bea once she has her life jacket on.

Asher got called into the office, so he left his daughter with us.

"Uh, can fish swim?" She puts her hands on her hips and cocks her head to the side.

"Yes? But you're not a—"

"I'm a fish." With that, she skips off to the end of the dock where Kane is waiting. Asher wouldn't leave his daughter if she didn't know how to swim, right?

*For the Show*

Bea insists on riding on my board, and I nearly have a heart attack when, about halfway across the lake, she screams "cannon ball" and jumps off. I leap in after her, but it's unnecessary. Bea may actually be a fish after all. That kid is fearless.

Millie is cackling on her board nearby, clearly already aware that her niece can swim. With Bea safely bobbing above the surface in her extra-small life jacket, I sink into the water. I count to thirty, then push the bottom of Millie's board up and knock her into the water.

She surfaces quickly, sputtering and with her hair stuck to her face. "You mother—"

"Ah-ah." I cock a brow and nod at the four-year-old.

She splashes me instead of cussing me out. Bea finds this hilarious and mimics the move. Pretty soon, Kane jumps into the lake and joins us in our shenanigans. After we're all thoroughly waterlogged, we paddle back to shore and engage in a mud castle–building contest.

In the stables after lunch, I hand Millie a helmet.

Rather than take it, she crosses her arms and steps back. "No thanks. Horses freak me out." She wanders to the other side of the fence and props herself up on one of the posts as Rachel helps Bea onto a pony.

"Seriously? But don't you read all those country cowboy rodeo books?" I specifically remember her going into detail about a very steamy stable scene recently.

Nose scrunched, she huffs. "There's a reason it's called *fiction*."

Damn, she's cute when she's riled up.

Straightening, she peers over her shoulder. "Where's Kane?"

"He went on the trail with your dad."

She smiles at that, the expression soft.

Fuck, is she thinking what I'm thinking? Our families mesh so well.

I join her on her side of the fence and pull her in by her hip so she's flush against me, and every time Bea rides by, we wave and snap pictures.

Not only are kids sticky, but they also don't come with off buttons. Kane and Ethan are gone for quite a while, and during that time, we've taken Bea to pottery and swimming in the lake again.

At dinner, Bea ends up wearing more spaghetti than she consumes, and when she can't eat her ice cream without yawning, Millie's parents offer to put her to bed.

Rather than go quietly like I expect, she throws a fit and begs to stay up with us.

"What if Uncle Ezra puts you to bed?" Millie suggests.

*Me?*

"Yay!" Bea catapults out of Ethan's arms.

I catch her at the last second, then wander to the cabins. Rachel, thankfully, accompanies us and directs me to pick out a book while she helps Bea change into her pajamas and brush her teeth.

Once she's in bed, she pats the mattress. "Sit."

Beside her, I stretch out my legs on top of her pastel rainbow comforter and begin reading.

"No, no, no," she says two sentences into the story. "You have to do the funny voices."

My chest tightens. "I don't—"

"You heard her." Millie stands in the doorway, as if she's appeared out of nowhere.

I raise a brow, silently conveying that I know what she's doing and that she'll pay for it later.

After a full day with the little girl, I understand why Asher is the way he is. It's impossible to say no to that puppy dog face.

Bolstering my nerve, I clear my throat and attempt my best toad voice.

Immediately, the girls fall into a fit of giggles.

"Why do you sound like an Irish Jamaican?" Millie gasps.

Rachel sidles up next to her daughter, her hands on her hips. "What's going on here?"

"Uncle Ezra is funny." Bea climbs to her knees and wraps her arms around my neck.

I return the embrace, realizing that the room has fallen silent. Still in the doorway, Millie leans into Rachel, and the two of them share a sentimental look.

"Okay," Bea says far too loudly when she's so close to my ear. She flops back onto the bed and burrows under the covers. "I need my booty sleep now. Good night."

I chuckle. "*Booty* sleep? I think you mean *beauty* sleep."

She tilts her head, her messy hair dragging across her pillow. "Then what's *booty*?"

Across the room, Millie gives me a soft smile and nods in approval.

"Uh, well"—I scratch at the back of my neck, suddenly worried Asher may murder me—"your booty is your butt."

Her eyes widen, then she breaks into another fit of laughter, kicking her feet under the covers.

"All right, you two." Rachel flips the light off and steps into the room. "It's time for bed, little one. You'll see Ezra in the morning."

"Uncle Ezra," she corrects her grandmother.

I ruffle her hair. "Good night, Bea."

"Night, Dolly." Millie blows her a kiss from the door.

"Hey, Uncle Ezra?"

"Yes?"

"Are you going to marry Lee Lee?"

I choke on my saliva in response to her unexpected question. Millie and her mother watch me, their eyes scorching me.

Once I've collected my wits, I lean in and whisper in Bea's

ear. When I pull away, she grins and presses her pointer finger to her lips in silent confirmation that she'll keep my surprise.

On the short walk over to our cabin, Millie asks, "What did you tell her?"

I drape an arm over her shoulders and tug her into my side. "Guess you'll just have to wait and see."

---

We find Kane passed out face-first in his bed, still fully dressed. Once I've plugged in his phone on his nightstand, I close his door and head to the bathroom, where Millie is brushing her teeth, her brow furrowed and her shoulders sagging.

My chest pinches at the sight of her. "What's wrong?"

"I'm way too tired to have sex," she mumbles around her toothbrush.

The tension behind my rib cage eases as I step up beside her. "Oh, okay."

"Sorry." She spits into the sink, then wipes her mouth, keeping her gaze averted. "I feel bad. I promised you earlier, but—"

"Amelia." I lift her chin with my thumb and forefinger, forcing her to look at me. "Don't ever feel bad about listening to your body. It's really okay." I rub her arms. "We can be intimate in other ways. Why don't I draw you a bath?"

She leans in for a hug. "I'd like that," she says into my chest.

We soak without saying a word for the first several minutes, the spa music playing from my phone the only sound.

"Can I wash your hair?" Millie asks, turning to face me. The move causes bubbles to slide down her flushed chest, drawing my attention to her half-hidden nipples.

"But I washed it before dinner."

"Please?"

Damn. It looks like the puppy dog face Bea is so good at wielding is hereditary. That look is all it takes to convince me to pass over the shampoo bottle.

While she squirts a dollop into her pruny palm, I wet my hair. With my legs spread wide and my knees bent, I make room for her to kneel between them. Her face is inches from mine. I can practically taste the mint on her breath as her fingers make contact with my scalp and goose bumps erupt along my arms.

I sigh into her touch and close my eyes, breathing in the scent of eucalyptus and tea tree oil while she lathers my curls.

"How long have you had a beard?" she asks.

"Most of my adult life, why? Do you want me to shave it?"

"No." She rubs at my jaw, a lazy smile pulling at her lips. "I like the feel of it between my legs too much."

My cock twitches at the image her words create in my mind. "I thought you said you were tired."

"Doesn't mean I can't flirt."

"*Hmph.*" I shut my eyes again and savor the sensations as she massages behind my ears and at my nape.

"I love when you moan," she whispers.

I crack an eye open. "I didn't realize I did."

The soft sparkle in her eyes has me curious about where this is going.

"Again, I thought you said you were tired."

"I am," she yawns. "Sorry."

Grasping her wrists, I pull her hands into my chest. "What did I tell you? Don't apologize." I hold her attention until she nods, then kiss her chastely on the lips. While I have her this close, my stomach clenches with the need to tell her more. "I love…" Her hands go rigid beneath my touch, and all my courage flees. "I loved spending time with your family today."

"Uh, yeah." She reaches around me to grab the shower hose.

"It was fun watching Bea on those evil giant dogs." Chuckling, she guides my head back and rinses my hair. "And Kane looked like he had a good time with my dad."

"Yeah. He invited us to go golfing with him."

She replaces the hose and sits back. "You golf?"

"No. But how hard could it be?"

A too-loud laugh escapes her, and without another word, she kisses me on the nose and rises from the tub.

With my hands behind my head, I enjoy the view. The bubbles have mostly dissolved, but a few cling to her hips and ass for dear life. Damn, I now identify as soap bubbles.

After we've rinsed off, I wrap Millie in a towel, then grab one for myself. When I join her in the bedroom a few minutes later, the lamp on my side of the bed is lit, casting just enough light to reveal that her eyes are closed. I stand in the doorway, watching her breathe for a moment, then climb under the covers, turn off the lamp, and pull her in close.

With her back securely against my front, she doesn't stir, clearly as exhausted as she said she was.

The pillows aren't as comfortable as the ones at Millie's, so it takes a bit to get settled. When I do, I realize how quiet it is outside the city. For a second, I contemplate pulling up a New York City Soundscapes playlist on my phone in hopes that it will help me fall asleep. Instead, I focus on her breathing, letting the rhythmic pattern lull me into a relaxed state.

Just as I'm about to slip into a slumber, I whisper, "I love you."

## Chapter 37
## Ezra

"Your phone is ringing, Mills."

"Who is it?" she calls from the bathroom.

While she dresses, I'm stripping the sheets. Asher said we could leave them, but I'm doing him a courtesy. Millie was anything but tired this morning when she woke me up with the best blow job of my life.

"Kris." *Who the fuck is Kris?*

"Just ignore it. I'll call back later."

I hit the button on the side to send *fucking Kris* to voicemail. "Who's Kris?"

"She's my agent."

A text preview appears on her lock screen. *I need an answer. Call me back ASAP. Rehearsals start...*

What the—

Millie steps into the bedroom in her bra and underwear, eyes on her phone, which is still in my hand. "What?"

I toss it to her.

"Oh," she sighs when she opens the notification.

"When were you going to tell me?" I don't mean for my tone to sound accusatory, but there's no quelling the hurt working its way through me.

"Never? I'm not taking the job."

My spine snaps straight. "What do you mean?"

"I'm not taking—"

"I heard you. Why not?"

She lifts one shoulder and lets it fall. "Maybe because during the last show I was in, the director practically forced me to quit because I was fat."

My heart pangs. Dammit, I hate that this conversation is bringing up bad memories for her. "Don't let one asshole ruin your career, Mills."

"It's a little too late for that. But I'll find a new career," she says nonchalantly as she pulls a pillow from its case. "Between LULU, narrating audiobooks, and FrenchSHEs, I make pretty good money."

"But this is—"

"Drop it," she scolds.

Damn, I've never heard her voice laced with so much venom. Raising my hands, I back out of the bedroom. "I'll be next door while you finish getting ready."

When I walk into Asher's cabin, Kane is working on a puzzle with Bea on the floor. I don't know who is more frustrated—Bea, who keeps forcing half of the kitten's eye to fit with half of the puppy's eye, or Kane, who can't convince her to lay out the corner pieces first. When Kane spots me, I offer him a sympathetic look.

"Good morning," Rachel says when I enter the kitchen.

I return her smile. "Good morning. Something smells good."

"Thank you, though it's no french toast casserole," she says as she flips a pancake on the griddle.

"I'm sure it's just as delicious."

"Where's Millie?"

I plaster on a smile, hoping it looks natural. "She was still getting ready but should be over shortly."

Ethan and Asher enter through the door to the back deck, Ethan's arm slung over Asher's shoulders. The sight tugs at my heartstrings unexpectedly. The only time Rob ever wrapped an arm around me was when he was dragging me from one bar to another when I was a teen, wearing a drunken smile, not the genuine grin that's painted on Ethan's.

A question hits me then. Will I ever get that opportunity? Not as the son, of course, but as the father to my own child. I shrug off the thought, determined to enjoy my last bit of time here.

Millie joins us just as I finish preparing her coffee.

"Thank you." She kisses me on the cheek and steps back.

I scan her face, hoping her expression will reveal her true feelings, but it doesn't.

"Who wants pancakes?" Rachel calls. "We've got plain, blueberry, and chocolate chip."

"Oh, me. Me. Me. Chocolate!" Bea erupts, nearly knocking over a glass of orange juice in her excitement.

"Anyone?" Rachel asks, pretending not to hear her.

"Me," Bea shouts louder.

"Oh, darn. Guess I'll have to eat them all myself." Sighing, she forks a pancake and drops it onto her plate, then does the same with a second and a third.

"*Mimi*," Bea scolds, her cute little hands on her hips.

"Oh, I'm sorry," her grandmother says as she places the giant stack of pancakes in front of her.

Asher quietly reprimands his mom for offering his daughter so much chocolate for breakfast, but Ethan waves him off.

"That's what grandparents are for. We do all the dirty work raising kids, then get to enjoy our grandbabies."

Grandbabies. Does Asher plan on having more children one day? Or is he referring to the possibility that Millie might?

Though I try to focus on the discussions taking place, the image of children with my hair and Millie's eyes around this table in the future creeps its way in, nonetheless.

I eventually force myself to tune into the conversation, and breakfast goes smoothly until Bea finally does knock over the glass of orange juice. Right onto her chocolate pancakes. She immediately bursts into pitiful tears, but thankfully, Kane saves the day when he sacrifices his meal.

"Amelia," Ethan says once the pancake drama has dissolved, "heard anything from your agent lately?"

"Dad," Asher says, his voice low, just as Millie says "no" and I say "yes."

Millie whips her head in my direction, her eyes narrowed to slits.

*If looks could kill.*

Shit.

Both her parents' eyes widen with excitement. Dammit, it's too late to backtrack now.

"Millie?" Her mom sets her fork down, waiting for her to answer.

She stabs at a blueberry pancake, probably visualizing my face.

"Mills," I murmur, nudging her beneath the table.

Eyes narrowed, she shoots daggers my way. "Kris sent in an audition tape, and I got the role of Ms. Honey in *Matilda*." Her tone is flat as she speaks, belying the magnitude of the admission.

After a heartbeat of silence, the table breaks into roars of excitement, and I join in with pride. *Matilda* has been Claire's favorite movie for as long as I can remember; she will flip when she finds out.

"I'm not going to take it."

*For the Show*

The group abruptly falls silent, all eyes on her. Even Bea can read the room and watches with wonderment.

"Excuse me?" her father asks.

Millie rolls her eyes, no doubt because this is the second time she's been asked that question this morning.

"Why wouldn't you take it?" her brother pushes. "I thought you were just on a break."

"I was, but..." She huffs a breath, her jaw rigid. "I don't think I want to put myself through that anymore."

"But you love the theater. And this could be one step closer to Broadway." Asher sounds more disgruntled than I feel. I like this guy.

I tilt closer and wrap a comforting arm around her shoulder, but she shrugs me off. Heart sinking, I lean back and cross my arms, waiting for her to justify her reasoning.

"Yes, I've dreamed of Broadway my entire life," she says. "But things change, okay? Maybe I'm just not cut out for it."

I turn to face her. "Honey—"

She rises from her seat, cutting me off, and exits the room.

"Where'd Lee Lee go?" Bea asks, syrup dripping down her chin.

Rachel stands, but I politely hold up a hand, stopping her. "I'll go."

I find Millie on the front porch swing of our cabin, and the second she notices my presence, she rounds on me. "You had no right to tell them my business. Not cool."

Tears well in her eyes, and for a split second, I contemplate keeping my mouth shut, but... *here goes nothing*.

"No." My tone brooks no argument, the harshness causing her to startle. "You know what's *not cool*, Amelia? Giving up on your dreams."

"I told you—"

"I know what you told me. But I won't sit back and let you

throw it all away because of one fucking prick. If I did, I wouldn't be a supportive partner. You know if the roles were reversed, you'd do the same thing for me."

She opens her mouth, then shuts it just as quickly.

Satisfied that she's actually heard me, I fling the screen door open and let it slam behind me with a *thwack*.

# Chapter 38
## Millie

"He's right, you know."

I jump at Asher's intrusion, but before I can protest, he takes a seat on the swing.

"What's going on?" He nudges me with his elbow.

Dammit. My big brother is the kind of person who never gives up. And he's annoying as fuck. When I had my first big breakup in high school, he dragged me to every social event happening over the next few months. It was a kind gesture, but he also told every person we met that I was newly single and ready to mingle like I was a fifty-year-old divorcée, not a high school sophomore.

As stubborn as I can be, he's worse. So I relent and spill my guts. He listens intently as I divulge the details about the body-shaming director from hell, and he never once interrupts.

"So that's my story." I exhale, feeling lighter after getting it all off my chest.

"Yes, and—"

"Asher, this isn't improv."

"Yes, but you get to rewrite the ending of this story." He taps me on the leg for emphasis.

The creaking of the swing and the steady buzz of cicadas and crickets are the soundtrack to our silence.

"You've got a good man in there, Mills." He juts his chin in the direction of the door.

A storm of emotions brews inside me as I think about Ezra.

"You're scared, but don't push him away. Dolly will never forgive you," he adds, bringing a little levity to the moment.

With an embrace, he leaves me to stew by myself. After I've had a long while to think, I go in search of Ezra. He's settled on the back porch, a cup of coffee resting on the railing and his attention fixed on the lake.

"Hey," I say, my tone full of caution.

"C'mere." He offers an outstretched arm, and I bury my face in his chest.

His shirt absorbs my tears, and when I sniffle, he hugs me a little harder.

"Thank you."

"For what?" he asks.

"For not giving up on me."

*Six weeks later*

"Are you sure about this?" I ask over takeout.

Smiling softly, Ezra eases onto the cushion beside me. "Absolutely, baby."

"But what if the long-distance thing is too hard? What if—"

"Hey, hey, hey. One thing at a time." He rubs calming circles on my wrist. "Yes, long-distance sounds hard, but I listened to that podcast you sent me. You were right. They have a lot of great ideas about how to stay patient and connected. And I'm not just talking about video sex." He smirks.

"But what if—"

He stops me with a kiss. "We'll figure it out," he says as he pulls away. "I already told you—I'm not going anywhere."

It's a relief, knowing that soon, Ezra will be busy transitioning to his new position as school principal and helping Kane adjust to a new school. The podcast claims it's important for both partners to be close to equally active and occupied, or else one partner may grow bored or resentful.

"Do you promise to tell me if it's too much?"

If absence makes the heart grow fonder, then what does *out of sight, out of mind* imply?

"I promise." With a smirk, he holds a piece of sushi to my mouth, effectively shutting me up.

Rehearsals began immediately after I booked the job. It turns out that I wasn't the first choice for Ms. Honey, but the other actress injured her vocal cords and had to back out. Fortunately for me, rehearsals took place at a studio in the city, so I had time to find someone to sublease my apartment before I head out on tour.

"Did your friend move in today?"

"They did."

One of the bartenders at FrenchSHEs recently broke up with their partner and needs a place to stay until they can find a more permanent solution.

"It was nice of your mom to keep Kane tonight."

"It was Kane's idea, actually." Ezra picks up another piece of sushi with his chopsticks. "Said he didn't want to be around for *all the sex.*"

I nearly spit out my wine. "Will I get to see him before I fly out tomorrow?" My heart pangs as I regard my suitcase and carry-on by the door.

"Yes, my mom too. They'll be back in the morning."

"How early?"

"Knowing Mom, probably nine, if not earlier."

"In that case…"

I take his wineglass from his hand and set it on the table next to mine, then lead him into the bedroom.

Standing at the side of the bed, I silently examine his face, memorizing every detail. "I'm going to miss you."

Ezra lightly drags his fingers down my arms and spins me. When he pulls me flush to him, his erection presses into my lower back, and I rub against him like a bear against a tree.

"I'll miss you so much." His lips ghost the sensitive spot behind my ear. "I'm going to take my time with you," he whispers, which is code for *I'm going to edge the shit out of you.*

"How about we make a bet?"

"What did you have in mind?" He wraps his arms around my midsection, teasing the place where my shirt meets my shorts.

I cover his hands with my own and drag them to cup my pussy. "Wanna see who can make the other come first?"

"Oh, my competitive girl." He *tsk*s. "That doesn't seem very fair."

"And why not?"

"Because…" He slides a finger beneath the hem of my shorts and teases my entrance. "You'll lose."

I scoff, but his arrogance fans the flames of my desire, nonetheless.

"But I'll play your little game." He dips a fingertip inside me. "What are we playing for?"

I've already thought this through. "Winner gets to do butt stuff to the other person."

His breath hitches. "Hmm," he rumbles behind me. "If you

win, I'm good with that. My ass is all yours. But if I win, I want something else."

"What do you want?"

He's silent a moment, toying with my cunt—in and out, in and out—stoking the fire in my belly into an inferno. "I want nudes for my hidden album."

I go rigid, trapping his fingers between my legs.

With a growl, he removes them, then spins me so I'm forced to face him.

"I, uh…"

"I know you haven't taken any in a long time." He ducks his head, his expression full of understanding. "And I understand you still have insecurities about your body. But baby…" He runs his hands along my silhouette and squeezes my hips. "I fucking love this body."

God, he's so good to me.

I don't realize I'm biting my lip until he forces it free with his thumb.

"Please." It's a demand, not a request.

When I nod, he unleashes a wicked grin. "Good. Now prepare to lose, *honey*."

# Chapter 39

# Ezra

We undress each other rapidly. The hell with taking our time. That was Ezra of the past. Ezra of the future claims naked real estate, fighting Millie's hands for purchase until her face lands between my legs, and mine between hers. Lying on my side, with determination in my veins, I yank her by the thighs and glue my mouth to her pussy. When she grasps the base of my shaft and rests my crown on her wet lips, I'm not so confident I'll win this bet.

She licks teasingly first, then slides me in and hollows her cheeks, gripping me so tight, my balls retract. When she hums around my cock, I try to pull back, but she smacks the side of my ass as punishment and draws me in tighter.

I have to win this silly fucking competition. I need those nudes.

With two fingers shoved deep inside her, I do that thing she loves so much with my tongue, the thing I usually save for the finale.

"Not fair," she yells when she pops off my cock with a slobbery *smack*. "You play dirty." Whimpering, she doubles down on her efforts to suck me off. She rubs my taint, but by the way her movements slow, then pick up, then slow again, I can tell I've got this in the bag.

*That's it, Millie. Come for Daddy.*

"Fuck, fine." Her body goes limp, and she concedes.

*Good girl.* I want to praise her out loud, but my mouth is otherwise occupied.

My cock rests against her lips, her hot breath teasing the tip and her tongue occasionally darting out as if she needs a taste.

"Right there, *right there*," she cries.

After two more pumps of my fingers and quick flicks to her clit with my tongue, she's screaming. Her pulsing pussy is confirmation of her climax. I peer up, unwilling to miss witnessing the way her body convulses with every quiver. With the flat of my tongue pressed to her, I let her ride out the last of her orgasm against me.

"*Fuck.*" She giggles in euphoria. "*Feels… so… good.*"

Once she's hoisted herself up on her elbows, I give her my prize-winning grin.

"Asshole," she laughs.

"*Now* can I take my time?" I lower my hand to her thigh, but before making contact, I pull away, careful to avoid the sensitive area.

"Sure thing, big guy." She smirks. "Just give me a minute."

I patiently—*okay, not so patiently*—wait for her to return from the bathroom.

Though Millie's contract is set for three months, there is a good chance it'll be extended. And why wouldn't it be? She's spectacularly talented. She has a weekend off in about a month, so I plan to fly in a day early to watch her perform, then spend the rest of the time worshipping her. Until then, I'll do everything in my power to make her feel loved.

*Love.*

I haven't told her. Not while she was conscious, at least. If I told her now, right before she's set to leave, would it freak her out? What if she thinks it's too soon and doesn't say it back, then leaves behind a huge sack of awkwardness on her way out the door? Could I survive the heartache if she doesn't return the sentiment?

I'm a grown-ass man. Why is this so scary?

"C'mere, baby." I lift the sheets and welcome her beside me, soaking in the heat of her body and hanging on to the moment for as long as I can. "How do you feel?"

I love asking her this question after I make her come. I can almost guarantee she'll curl up against me and purr, totally blissed out.

"Amazing."

Gently, I roll her onto her back, resting my body on top of hers. I caress her lips with mine, and when she parts in invitation, a pit forms in my stomach. It's painful, knowing this will be the last time we're physically intimate for a while. But it's a delicious sensation, her tongue against mine.

*I love you* is at the edge of a cliff, ready to take flight. If I say it, will it sink or will it soar?

"I need you, Ezra."

"Anything for you." My lips burn a path down her neck, and I pay extra attention to the place where her pulse beats rapidly. The coconut scent on her breasts reminds me of Hawaii and the time I got her off just by sucking on her nipples.

So much has happened since then.

She lets me suck and nip and play for a bit. Eventually, though, she reaches into my side drawer and pulls out a bottle of lube. I rock back onto my heels and squirt the liquid directly onto my cock. Once I've stroked my length, certain I'm coated in it, I slide my slick fingers inside Millie, savoring her heat and the smooth gliding motion, anxious to feel the sensation elsewhere.

Green eyes sparkle with salaciousness as she notches my cock at her entrance.

Tentatively, I slip inside her a couple of inches, watching her expression for cues.

Back arched, she moans. "More. Keep going."

Ever so slowly—*I told her I was going to take my time*—I sink in to the hilt. She wraps her arms around me and pulls me so I'm flush against her chest. We stay like that for a long time, with my cock buried deep inside her and our hearts beating in harmony while I whisper sweet words against her skin.

*You're so beautiful.*

*I'll miss you.*

*You make me feel so good.*

Then I move. In and out, over and over, at a steady pace.

"I can feel every inch of you." Her voice catches on my next slow thrust.

"You're so tight, baby." This isn't enough. I want to crawl inside her skin and stay there so I'm a part of her forever. But I'm on the precipice, my spine tingling.

"Don't come yet," she says, clearly picking up on the signs that I'm about to hurtle over the edge. "I want to ride you."

What my girl wants, my girl gets.

Carefully, I slide out of her and lie on my back. She straddles my hips, spits on my cock for good measure, and lowers her gorgeous body.

"*Thatta girl*," I praise. "That's my perfect fucking girl."

I meet her thrust for thrust, watching the way her tits bounce, tucking away the image for a lonely day. Seeing her like this, in control of her body—and mine—is a colossal turn-on. Her confidence has grown in leaps and bounds since we reunited months ago. And since she's been dancing again, she's unstoppable in the bedroom.

But... "Shit. If you don't get off me, I'm going to come inside you."

Rather than slow, she doubles down in her efforts. "Do it."

As an electric surge courses through my veins, I dig my fingers into her skin to still her, my grip so tight I'm sure I'll leave marks.

*Good.* Think of it as a going-away gift.

"W-wha—are you serious?" My cock is the hardest it's ever been. It takes all the strength I have, and then some, to hold back my release. "Don't fuck with me, Amelia."

With a mischievous smirk, she splays her hands over my chest and grinds against me.

"Amelia."

"Ezra." She pouts. She fucking pouts.

Eyes drilling into her, I buck up into her once. "I need to hear you."

She doesn't hesitate. "I want you to come inside me."

"Say it again."

"I want you to come inside me, Ezra."

"*Fuck.*" I lick my thumb and rub her clit. "Can you get there with me, baby?"

"Mm-hmm."

"Are you sure? Have you done this before?" I've never come inside a woman bare, and the thrill of it has me teetering on the edge of my release.

She shakes her head.

"No, what?" I grit out, pausing my movement on her clit. *No, she isn't sure,* or *no, she hasn't done this before?* Shit, I'm barely holding myself together.

"Yes, I'm sure," she pants. "No, I haven't done this before."

Knowing I'll be the first man to come inside her has me ready to explode.

She slowly works herself up and down my shaft while I continue to roll my thumb over her clit, holding back my own release while I work to get her caught up.

"That's it. Yes. Don't stop. Just a little... *harder, faster.*"

Finally exhaling, I zero in on her face. "Ready?"

She gives me a sharp nod, and I drive up into her hard and deep, once, twice, before arching my back and unleashing the loudest moan in the history of ecstasy.

She pulses first, but then I join in, and I can't separate one from the other—mixing and tangling, our releases lost to the crashing waves.

"*Fuckshitdammitiloveyou.*"

Fuck. Shit. Dammit. My lower body stills, but my breathing is ragged.

Did I just say that aloud?

"Millie, I..." Stunned by my slipup, I keep her pinned on top of me, nervous that she'll bail.

"I love you too," she replies in the most gentle, out-of-breath voice.

Tears pool in her eyes, but she's laughing too.

And because she's giggling, her body relaxes, and my cock slips out. She lowers her focus to the intimate place between us, and I follow her gaze, finding my cum leaking out of her and onto my piercings.

"Holy shit. That's fucking hot." I spread her open for a better look, then dip my fingers into her cunt and hold them to her parted lips. "Tell me you love me again."

"I love you." The words have barely left her lips before I slide my fingers, coated with our climax, into her mouth.

As I draw them out again, my cock twitches beneath her.

She leans down, hovering her plump lips above mine. "Your turn."

"I love you," I whisper.

Then the taste of us is on my tongue.

A groan rumbles out of me. "Fuck, baby, that's hot."

She attempts to roll off me, but before she can, I loop my arms around her waist and force her to sink into me. *Just a little longer.*

Only when our combined climax is dry and sticky between us do we stumble our way to the shower, where she lets me fuck her—and come inside her—again.

The thrill of seeing my cum run down her leg is addicting. Fuck. I don't know how I'll ever give it up.

What's even more addictive is being on the receiving end of her declaration of love. Now that we've unleashed those words, neither of us can stop vocalizing it.

"You sure I didn't freak you out?" I plug my phone into its charger, then climb into bed.

Millie is on her back, so I lay my head on her chest, nuzzling into her breast like I would a pillow.

"You didn't freak me out." She runs her fingers through my damp hair. "Maybe a little cliché in delivery…"

"*Hey.*" I sink my teeth into her tit as punishment for that sass, and she pulls my hair in return. "I'm glad you said it back. I don't know what I would have done if you left me hanging."

"Thank you for being brave enough to say it first." She kisses the top of my head.

Warmth blooms in my chest. "Looks like you're rubbing off on me."

"What do you mean?"

"Aside from my mom, you're the most courageous woman I know."

"First of all, please do not mention your mother while we're naked in bed."

I snicker at that.

*For the Show*

"Second..." She trails off for a beat, her fingers running listlessly at my roots. "You helped me get that piece of myself back. So, thank you."

With a kiss to the hollow of her neck, I settle back down and let the delicate rhythm of her heartbeat lull me to sleep.

# Chapter 40
## Millie

By the sound of the heavy machinery outside, I know it's morning before I even open my eyes. Keeping them closed, I flip through memories of last night. Our time together was a dream, and I'm not ready to wake up.

Ezra told me he loves me. And I let him come inside me. I opened the floodgates—pun intended—by taking that next step in our relationship, and I'm certain that he won't want to stop.

I can't blame him. It was unbelievable, having all of him inside me. I don't know what kind of magic his seed is laced with, but just the memory of that moment has me needy and squirming under the sheets.

He stirs beside me and lazily drags a hand up my thigh. "Mmm," he groans in that morning voice I want to record and play every day while I'm away. "What did you dream about that's got you so wet?" He whips back the sheets, and the cool air of the bedroom instantly assaults me. He parks himself between my legs and rests his chin on my belly. "Morning, gorgeous."

Suddenly, being awake has its perks.

*For the Show*

The person who said exercise was the best way to start the day was sorely mistaken. I'd kill to be woken up like this for the rest of my life.

And my heart rate is definitely up. Surely that counts as exercise.

"Now sit on my cock and tell me you love me."

---

I turn off the shower, instantly registering the sound of Ezra's voice. That means his mom and brother have arrived. Releasing my dry hair from a claw clip, I give it a shake. Quickly, I run my fingers through it, then apply a little bronzer and mascara. My cheeks are still flushed from my wake-up call, so I skip the blush.

"Millie, my love," Dawn calls when I emerge from the bedroom. "How are you?"

I eagerly accept her embrace, letting her powdery rose scent soothe me.

We spoke two nights ago, yet I find myself filling her in on the everyday occurrences since then. Somewhere along the way, we bonded over unlikely animal friend videos. I send her one of a duck and a fox, and she sends me one of a squirrel and a deer. It's our love language.

Over breakfast, she pummels me with questions about the show. Her enthusiasm is so contagious and intoxicating that I'm suddenly wildly invigorated to be back on stage, performing in front of a live audience.

"Oh, Kane. Go get that thing for Millie," she instructs, abandoning the dishes at the sink.

When he returns, he places a small black velvet box in my palm.

"Bro, you better not be proposing to my girlfriend." Ezra shoves him with brotherly affection.

"Dude." He pushes back. "I'm gay, remember?"

We're all still chuckling as I open the box and discover a necklace with a gold star pendant nestled between two small diamonds. "It's beautiful," I gasp.

"Tell her what it means," Dawn stage-whispers to Kane.

He clears his throat. "Oh, uh, sure. The star is you—"

"Because you're a star." Dawn clasps her hands over her chest, her face alive with delight.

"And the diamonds on the side represent me and Ezra."

My breath hitches and my heart pangs in the sweetest way. Despite my best efforts to remain stoic, tears prick the corners of my eyes.

"It's perfect. Thank you. I love it." Stepping forward, I tug Kane down for a hug. "I love you," I tell him, tossing a wink to Ezra over his brother's shoulder.

He squeezes me in return. "I love you too, Mills."

Ezra rubs at his beard, the crease between his eyebrows deepening, making me wonder if he's heard those words from him yet.

I hug Dawn next, and she's all too eager to latch the necklace.

"Way to make me look bad," Ezra teases, clasping Kane's shoulders from behind.

"You've gotta up your game, old man," he volleys back.

"Old man, huh?" Ezra quirks a brow. "You better sleep with one eye open, punk."

"Enough, you two," Dawn scolds, her face still lit with joy. "Will you kids be fine if I head out, or do you need supervision?"

I frown at her. "You're leaving?"

"Yes, sweetheart. I'll say my 'see you later' now and give you all some privacy."

Tearful hugs are exchanged—*again*—and then Dawn is off, headed for the train back to Brooklyn.

We're so lost in soaking in our time together that when I look at the clock, my heart lurches. "Shit. I've gotta go."

Kane wanders into the kitchen while Ezra watches me frantically throw toiletries into my bag. When I'm done, he hands me a motion sickness band and an external charger wrapped in a bow. "It's not diamonds." He gives me a tentative smile. "But at least you won't throw up and your phone will stay charged."

"*Ha ha.*" I give him a mock glare. He'll never let me forget the time I showed up at JFK with a dead phone battery. "I love it. You're so thoughtful." Chest aching, I pinch the star at my collarbone. "Your family is lovely."

"They're your family, too, you know. You told me you love me, so now you're stuck with me." He kisses me on the lips.

"I knew you were a stalker," I tease.

He clears his throat, his expression going serious. "I've never told a woman I love her before."

Breath catching, I blink up at him. "Never?"

He hums. "I told plenty of girls in high school, but I didn't mean it."

"Ezra Theo Miller," I scoff, desperate for a little levity. "You call those women up right now and apologize."

He tugs me into his chest. "I don't have their phone numbers. That was back in the olden days before everyone walked around with cell phones."

"How old *are* you?"

With a chuckle, he smacks me on the ass. "None of those counted. I didn't know what love was until you."

My heart thumps against my sternum as his words register. Lord, this man knows how to make me swoon. "And now that you know?"

"I'm never letting you go."

"See? *Stalker*," I deadpan. If I don't mess with him, I'll crumple into a blubbering mess. I'm going to miss this.

"Shut your mouth and kiss me."

"How can I shut my mouth *and* ki—"

He cuts me off with his tongue shoved down my throat and only pulls away to call me a "little shit" before devouring me again.

## Chapter 41
## Ezra

THE FIRST WEEK Millie is gone flies by. If I'm not consumed by trainings at work, then I'm busy with cramming tutoring sessions in with Kane. If I'm not occupied by Kane's tutoring, then I'm consumed with guilt over whether he's making friends. If I'm not consumed with guilt, then I'm hung up on how to expedite permanent guardianship. These days, my life feels like the fucked-up adult version of the children's book *If You Give a Mouse a Cookie*.

The second week Millie is gone is a whole heck of a lot harder. It's strikingly obvious she's not around; my sheets don't need to be changed as often now that we're not up to our usual activities. The only thing that helps the ache in my heart is the joy in her voice when we talk. Even through text, her glee is evident.

> **ME**
> How's your roommate?

**MILLIE**

Sasha is great!

She's quiet and keeps to herself, which is way better than last time. I don't think I'll have to worry about her partying and staying up late

> **ME**
> What about the rest of the cast and crew?

**MILLIE**

So far so good. No one is obviously toxic. And the kids are so cute!! They make me miss Bea, though

The actors are all different shapes and sizes. Lots of kids in this cast, and the director was adamant about hiring a children's psychologist. Rumor is he's paying for it himself. The psychologist is passionate about the kids' mental health and has already reprimanded one adult for criticizing her body in front of the kids

> **ME**
> That sounds amazing 🙌

**MILLIE**

It is

I've gotta go but I miss you

> **ME**
> I miss you too. And I love you

**MILLIE**

I love you too 🤍

*For the Show*

Though I encouraged her to take the role of Ms. Honey and follow her dreams, a secret part of me hoped it would fall through. Maybe I'm an asshole, but mostly, I was worried she'd have to deal with another jackass like her last director.

> **ME**
> Is the cast still behaving? Do I need to fly down to Florida and have a word with any of them?

> **MILLIE**
> Easy there, killer

She doesn't need my protection, but the Neanderthal in me cannot be convinced otherwise; I'd quit my job and protect her twenty-four seven if I could. But every text and phone call I receive is like a salve to a wound, making this long-distance situation a little less painful.

> **MILLIE**
> Two weeks down

> **ME**
> Feels like a million more to go…

> **MILLIE**
> 😟
> But I'll see you in two weeks!!

> **ME**
> Can't wait 🖤

At first, I figured spending time with Millie's family without her would be awkward or that it would make her absence even harder to bear, but it's been nothing but natural.

When we're out and about one day, I send her a selfie of Asher, Bea, Kane, and me.

> **MILLIE**
> OMG! So jealous. Where are you?

> **ME**
> The slime museum

> **MILLIE**
> Lol. You at the slime museum? Was it a sensory nightmare?

> **ME**
> Quite the opposite, actually. Though I thought I might throw up when Bea dragged us to the exhibit where you can take your shoes off and walk through the slime. 🫣 The things I do for that girl...
>
> I don't know who had more fun—your niece or my brother
>
> We're about to meet Cam and Joey for dinner in Little Italy. Want us to FaceTime you?

> **MILLIE**
> I wish 🥲 I have to get ready for a show, but send my love xx

---

No matter how hard we try, communication is a struggle, and I can't imagine it ever being enough to sate me. Though I love the hit of dopamine when my phone chimes as much as the next guy, nothing beats conversing back and forth in real time.

> **ME**
> Video sex?

*For the Show*

> **MILLIE**
> New phone who dis?

> **ME**
> HA HA

> **MILLIE**
> No hello first? Lol

> **ME**
> I'm impatient

> **MILLIE**
> Ugh... I wish I could, but Sasha is here. She never leaves the room

I'd hate Sasha if she hadn't become a safe space for Millie. Not only that, but she's a good influence, preparing smoothies and keeping her active with YouTube Pilates workouts.

> **MILLIE**
> I accidentally went running with her today

> **ME**
> How do you *accidentally* go running?

> **MILLIE**
> 🌿 A bunch of us walked to the botanical gardens, but we got turned around. It was a freaking maze in there
>
> Then we got a text that our call time had been moved up an hour, so we were forced to run back

> **ME**
> Does this mean you'll go running with me when you're home?

> **MILLIE**
> Ezra, I love you, but that's a big fat NOPE

> **ME**
> Fine...

> I can think of other ways we can work up a sweat together

> **MILLIE**
> You horndog

> **ME**
> I love you too

---

Even when our schedules match up and we get to FaceTime, our conversations remain brief so she can rest her voice. She's loving her role as Ms. Honey, though, and I cannot wait to see her in action.

> **MILLIE**
> Two more days, and I get to kiss your stupid face

> **ME**
> Stupid, huh? You'll pay for that...

> **MILLIE**
> Don't tempt me with a good time, Daddy

> **ME**
> AMELIA

> **MILLIE**
> EZRA
>
> OMG please don't tell me you've shaved your beard or cut your hair

*For the Show*

ME
I may have a stupid face, but I'm no dummy

MILLIE
Good ☺

ME
I have a meeting at the school, but I emailed you the Airbnb reservation for this weekend in case you get there before me

MILLIE
I can't wait

# Chapter 42

## Ezra

"What do you think?" I ask Kane.

Before he can respond, Ethan slaps him on the back. "Not too bad, son."

We enter the dining hall at the golf and country club, and before my brother removes his flat bill hat, I catch a glimpse of a grin. I can't help but smile too. Ethan has been more of a father in the last two hours than Rob ever was to either of us.

"I won't be a pro any time soon, but I guess it was all right."

Ethan winks at me like *teens, eh?*

"I had a blast," I chime in. "Thank you."

"You sure you don't want to go for a full eighteen?"

Kane scoffs. "There are *nine* more holes?"

He downs an entire glass of water at the table before our food arrives, and while Ethan and I get into a friendly debate about the New York City public school system, I notice Kane picking at his food. The kid is like a garbage disposal, so this raises a red flag. "Is your steak okay?"

"Yeah." He swirls his fork over his potatoes. "My stomach doesn't feel great. Must be something I ate earlier."

*For the Show*

His cheeks are flushed, and his hairline is sweaty, but it's a million degrees on Long Island today, so that isn't unexpected.

When Kane excuses himself to use the restroom, Ethan leans in across the table. "You're a good man to that boy."

I straighten, caught off guard by the compliment. "Oh, I don't know—"

"Ah-ah." He points at me with his fork. "Don't do that. My son does that too. Deflects compliments on his parenting ability."

"I just..." Lips pressed together, I take a moment to gather my thoughts. "I just want to make him happy."

"I may not be your father," Ethan says, "but can I offer you a piece of parenting advice?"

"By all means, please."

"It's not our job to make our kids happy."

"But—"

"No." His voice is stern but benevolent. "It's our job to keep them safe and fed and *mostly* clean and to love them unconditionally. But it's not our job to make them happy. Nor is it their job to make *us* happy."

I shift in my seat as I let his words sink in. "How do I know if I'm doing a good job, though? It's not like he's passing out gold stars."

"Our children are not going to praise us. Sure, when they're young, they tell us we're the greatest dad in the world. But then, for many years, that stops, and we're forced to put up with their shit." He laughs.

I huff in return, wondering if one day I'll understand that firsthand.

"I'll have to share those stories another day. The point is that though they may not tell us we're doing a great job in the obvious sense, they tell us in other ways."

"How so?"

"Does Kane come to you if he has a problem? Does he tell you about his day?"

When I don't answer right away, Ethan takes a sip from his IPA and regards me. "Did Millie ever tell you about the day she came out to us as queer?"

With a quick look toward the restroom, I shake my head.

"My older brother is queer, and we did our best to raise Millie and Asher as allies, so when they were in elementary school, my wife and I sat them down and told them that regardless of their sexual orientation, they'd have our full support. That we'd love them no matter what."

Damn, I want to be Ethan when I grow up. I don't know what that says about my daddy kink, but I'll worry about that another day.

"How did they respond?"

"Asher asked if he could have ice cream, and Millie wanted to know if she could go back to playing with her Barbies." He chuckles. "They were kids. I didn't expect them to say 'gee, thanks, Dad; you're so cool,' but when the time finally came for Millie to come out—which, to be honest, *was no surprise*—she told us during family dinner. The whole spiel was matter-of-fact, like she was telling us about her favorite television show."

Imagining such a safe space for Millie warms my heart just as much as it pains me that Kane wasn't afforded that same experience by his own father.

"She didn't open up about how confusing that time was for her until later," he says. "But she did eventually. I'll take it as a win."

That kid tells me every nutty detail about working at Bubbe's. That's a good sign, right? "I think he's more comfortable around Millie than he is with me."

"That's understandable. My daughter's a gem."

"The brightest." I beam. She's been a safety net for my

brother in so many ways. No one could ever replace his mother, but Millie has been the next best thing.

"From what I've seen, you're doing an incredible job. Try not to be so hard on yourself."

Kane returns then, walking stiffly and with a hand on his abdomen.

"You okay?"

Clutching the back of his chair, he doubles over. "I don't feel well. Can we leave?"

"Of course."

We say a rushed goodbye to Ethan, then we catch a train back into the city. Kane is somber, resting his head on my shoulder the whole way home. When we return to the apartment, he refuses to eat, though I do coerce him into taking a pain reliever before he lies down.

When dinner time rolls around and he's still sleeping, unease washes over me. But when I wake him, he swears he's just tired. He reluctantly drinks water and eats a few crackers, then goes back to bed.

I fall asleep watching reruns of *The Office* but am startled awake at dawn by a noise in Kane's room. For a moment, I experience déjà vu. Someone I love is kneeling in front of the toilet.

"Hey, hey, hey." I approach him, keeping my tone calm. "What's going on?"

He chokes and sputters, saliva sliding down his chin. I snag a washcloth from under the sink and wipe at his mouth. His arms are wrapped around his stomach, his shoulders are curled in, and his face is pinched.

I sit with him until he's heaved up the meager contents of his stomach, then help him to the sofa. One touch to his forehead confirms that he's got a fever.

Heart racing and worry whirling in my brain, I reach for my phone. "Mom?"

"Ezra," she asks, her tone almost as panicked as mine. "What's wrong?"

"How fast can you get here?"

"Why? What's going on?"

"Kane is sick."

My brother lets out an agonized groan from the sofa.

"Shit. Actually, can you meet us at the hospital?"

"You're scaring me. What's—"

"I don't know. Yesterday he said his stomach hurt, but I assumed it was something he ate. The pain is much worse this morning. He won't eat and—"

"Where's the pain?"

Raking a hand through my hair, I dart over to Kane, who is in a fetal position on the sofa with a trash can by his side, and relay the question.

"Just below the belly button."

"I bet it's his appendix," Mom says.

"*Fuck.*"

"What? What is it?" Kane's voice is weak and strained.

"She thinks it's your appendix, buddy." Sitting next to him, I rub his back.

His pale, sweaty face scrunches in pain.

"Do you think you can stand?"

"Hurts... so... bad," he cries.

"Ezra, hang up. Text me which hospital. It's going to be okay."

We nearly miss the Uber I order because it takes so long to get downstairs and out of the building. Once we arrive in the emergency room, everything moves quickly. Kane's blood-curdling scream when the physician presses on his abdomen pierces my heart. Blood and urine tests rule out infections, and a CT confirms the appendix has not yet ruptured.

After he's wheeled back for surgery, my mom rubs a hand on

*For the Show*

my nervously bouncing knee. "He's going to be fine. It's laparoscopic. Recovery won't be bad."

I hyperfixate on the cacophony of noises in the waiting room. The rerun of *CSI* playing too loudly, the rustling of cough drop wrappers, and whispered conversations all make me want to crawl out of my fucking skin.

I'm so dysregulated that when my mom speaks again, I flinch. "Is Millie okay? She was looking forward to this weekend."

My heart plummets. "Shit." I startle the middle-aged couple in the corner. "I forgot to call her."

Ignoring the sign that reads *No Cell Phones*, I dig the device out of my pocket.

She answers on the first ring. "Hi. I just checked into the Airbnb. I had no idea it was on the water."

Fuck if this isn't going to make it that much harder.

"Hey, honey..." The words come out in my middle school teacher voice. Dammit.

Mom pats me again on the knee.

"Listen. There's been an emergency."

"*What?*" Distress wraps around her voice like a vine.

"Kane had to have an appendectomy. I'm so sorry, baby, but I can't make it out this weekend." My voice hitches and my heart constricts at the thought of her precious but disappointed face.

She gasps, the line between us crackling. "Is he okay?"

"He's in surgery now, but he should be. I'm so sorry, Mills."

"Why are you apologizing?"

My throat goes tight. "Because I—"

"No," she stops me. "I'm fine. The most important thing is Kane. Yeah, sure, it sucks that I won't see you, but you need to be there."

The way she's putting Kane's needs above her own makes me fall in love with her even more.

"What about next weekend?" I ask.

"Can't. We'll be flying. I think I'm free the weekend after that. Could you come to New Orleans?"

"I have that thing for work."

"Hmm. We'll figure it out."

---

We don't figure it out. Kane recovers well, consuming more homemade matzo ball soup than I've eaten in a lifetime, but weeks go by without any concrete plans to visit Millie.

*What about this day?*

*Tickets are nine hundred dollars.*

*Don't you dare spend that much money.*

*I have back-to-back shows, and I'm on vocal rest that weekend. It won't be any fun.*

"This fucking sucks," I finally admit to her one evening.

"It does. I'm sorry."

I breathe deeply, willing the ache in my chest to abate. "I thought it would be easier."

She exhales. "I did warn you."

"That's not helpful." My tone comes out much harsher than intended. I'm so tired and I miss her.

"That's not what—I'm just trying to—"

"I'll call you later."

"Ezra..."

"It's been a long day, and this isn't working."

"What?" she gasps. "*This isn't working*? Are you breaking up with me?"

My lungs seize, and it takes me a handful of heartbeats to remember how to breathe. "Shit. No. I meant *this conversation*. Just... It's been a long day, and I need to get some rest."

"But you promised that if things got tough, we'd talk to each other about it." The pain behind her voice is unmistakable.

"I know. But it's really late, and I'm tired. I don't want to say anything I'll regret."

"Like what?"

"Millie. *Please.*" The tag on my shirt brushes across my back like eighty-grit sandpaper. Without thinking, I rip it from the seam. *Dammit, that's another hole.*

"Fine."

"I love you," I tell her, just as she says "bye" and hangs up.

*Fucking great.*

## Chapter 43
# Millie

My performance tonight was shit. Sasha swears it wasn't, but she's too nice to tell me the truth. When I wake up, I have zero text messages from Ezra, and when I call him, he doesn't answer. I text Kane, who informs me his brother went for a run. Nausea consumes me as I waste the entire day waiting for his call. After the matinee performance, I'm greeted with a missed call notification, but the theater is forcing us to clear out of the dressing rooms, so I'll have to call him later.

It's a rush to the airport and through security, so when I finally get the opportunity to sit down, I pull out my phone, only to find that it's dead.

Digging into the side pocket of my carry-on, I locate the external charger Ezra gifted me. I smile to myself, considering whether to actually admit to him just how many times I've had to use it.

As I'm waiting for it to charge, Sasha passes me her phone. "Did you see this?"

The headline reads *The Final Curtain Call*.

At the sight of the man in the photo at the top of the article, a giant pit forms in my stomach, but I power through the text.

*Renowned Broadway director Taron West was abruptly dismissed from the popular traveling production of* Mamma Mia *after multiple allegations of bullying and harassment.*

*Several present and past cast and crew members have come forward, claiming that West made demeaning comments about actors' weights and appearances, pressuring them to meet unrealistic standards.*

*A current cast member who wished to remain anonymous said, "[Taron] would scream at women in front of the entire cast and say they weren't 'cut out for Broadway if [they] couldn't lose the weight.'"*

*West has yet to comment publicly on the allegations. His wife, Diane, did not wish to comment on his behalf.*

"Wasn't he the director you told me about?" Sasha asks.

"Mm-hmm."

She slumps in her seat next to me.

When my phone powers on again, a voicemail notification from an *Unknown Caller* pops up.

"Ms. Greer, this is Diane West. I think you know my husband. I'd like a word with you. It's time sensitive, so please call me back immediately."

## Chapter 44

# Ezra

"Dude, I haven't heard from her, and every time I call, it goes straight to voicemail. She never charges her fucking phone. I'm kinda freaking out."

It's been hours since Millie's show ended, and I can't get a hold of her. Would it be overbearing to ask her to share her location so I can track her like I do Kane? Probably.

"I'm sure she's fine," Cam says. "Hold on. Joey just walked in. Let me see if she knows anything."

Pacing my apartment, I hold the phone to my ear and wait for his response. "Jo says she's on a flight."

I exhale loudly. "Fuck, I forgot. I can't keep up with her schedule."

"I'm sure she'll call you when she lands."

"Yeah, you're probably right." Despite my words, I can't help but feel like that might not be the case. We left things on a sour note, and it's killing me that I haven't had the chance to explain my reaction yesterday. Between my exhaustion and the way she was pushing me, I was concerned I'd stick my foot in my mouth and make matters worse. This long-distance thing is wearing on me. I miss my girl.

The phone vibrates at my ear, and I pull it back to look at the screen. "Finally. It's her."

Cam wishes me luck, and with a quick thank-you, I tap the screen and accept the call.

"Millie?"

"Hey." She sounds out of breath.

"Listen, I'm—"

She cuts me off with her own "I'm sorry."

"No, *I'm* sorry, honey. I feel awful for making you think I was breaking up with you. I would never—"

"I know. I know. And I'm sorry for pushing you. You told me you were tired and wanted to table the conversation, and I should have listened."

My heart hammers as I soak in her words and her gentle tone. "I miss you."

"I miss you so fucking much, Ezra." The authenticity in her tone makes my chest squeeze.

"Where are you?"

"I... I'm just getting off the plane. I sent over Levain cookies for you and Kane. Did you get them yet?"

"No? I haven't heard the buzzer, and Kane didn't say anything when he left for work. I'll go check."

If I don't get them now, he'll eat them all. Phone still pressed to my ear, I yank the door open, my attention homed in on the welcome mat. Where I expect to find a box of cookies from my favorite bakery, I find a pair of white sneakers.

I drag my gaze up the legs and torso in front of me until I'm face-to-face with the most beautiful woman in the world. "Millie? What are you doing here?"

"Surprise," she sings.

The echo of her squeal through the phone causes me to

wince, then instantly fall into laughter. I disconnect the call and tentatively reach out, convinced she's a hologram. Thankfully, rather than pass through a 3D image, my fingers make contact with soft skin, confirming she's not a vision I conjured up.

"What are you doing here?" I can't take my eyes off her red-stained lips. She's wearing fake lashes and her hair is in a topknot.

"Aren't you going to invite me in?" She giggles.

"Shit, of course." I take her suitcase from her and step back.

In the entryway, she drops her carry-on and purse and flings herself into my arms.

We sway in exuberance. When she finally pulls away, I keep my arms looped around her and kiss the top of her head. She smells like a bouquet of flowers covered in aerosol hairspray.

"What are you doing here?" Third time's the charm, right? Or is something wrong? Shit. My heart plummets as I hold her at arm's length and inspect her. "Are you okay?"

"I'm fine," she promises, breaking into a wide grin. "I actually have some news."

"Should we sit down?" I lead her into the living room. "Do you want something to drink?"

With a shake of her head, she drops onto the sofa and tucks her legs beneath her. She's wearing the leggings I love so much, paired with a tight cream-colored tank top that pushes her breasts up. Thank god for the hidden folder on my phone, otherwise I'd be ripping that damn tank in two right now.

"So?" I scoot in close, my knee bumping hers, and rest my arm along the back of the sofa.

"Remember the jerk of a director I dealt with when I was in *Mamma Mia*? Taron?"

My blood heats at just the name. "Mm-hmm."

"His wife called me."

My eyes nearly leap out of their sockets in response to that revelation. Before I can ask an entire host of questions, she grasps my hand.

"Ex-wife, I should say." She tells me about an article published about West and how his ex-wife called, first to apologize for the man's behavior, then... "She offered me a job."

I'm hit with a jolt of excitement, though it quickly mixes with confusion. "What do you—"

"It's here. The job. It's in the city." She's bouncing so animatedly she's practically in my lap now. "She's been workshopping a brand-new top-secret musical and wants me to star in it. On Broadway."

My heart stutters at the pure elation on her face and in her tone. Tugging her the rest of the way onto my lap, I smother her with a kiss. "That's wonderful news. Congratulations." I stamp her entire face with kisses until she's giggling and squirming against me.

Having her in my arms again is incredible. My dick would agree. It's pretty damn sick of my fist these days.

I lean back. "But what about *Matilda* and your contract?" I don't know how the theater world works. Could she really just up and leave?

"It turns out Diane has a lot of connections in the industry. She got me out of my contract in record time. We were already at the airport, so I switched my flight and came here. My understudy is amazing and was thrilled to step up." She shrugs. "Everyone wins."

A sense of peace washes over me. She's back in the city. For now, at least.

"What's this new production?"

She twines her fingers into the hair at my nape, sending a shiver down my spine. With a lustful grin and a twinkle in her green eyes, she says, "*The Proposal.*"

For the next several minutes, she remains exactly where she

belongs—on my lap—and gushes about the musical rendition of the early 2000s rom-com.

"But what about your apartment?" She sublet her place and can't just kick the person out.

"The sublease is up in a month and a half." She twists her fingers in her lap. "It's not a *legal* contract, but…"

"You'll move in with me."

"Okay, big guy. No one said anything about moving in." Cheeks flushed, she peers up at me from beneath her fake lashes. "But maybe I could stay here for a bit?"

"No."

"Oh…" Lowering her chin, she slumps.

I tilt her face so she's forced to meet my gaze. "You'll move in with me."

She makes a choked sound. "You're serious?"

Collecting her hands in mine, I nod. "There's no reason for you to live four blocks away when I want you in my bed every single night."

"But what about Kane?"

"I've already cleared it with him."

Brows lowered, she frowns. "What? When?"

"One night when we were playing would you rather. At first it was hypothetical, but then we got to talking about it more seriously."

"So this has been on your mind?"

"Mm-hmm."

Her cheeks pinken further. "You promise he's okay with it? He's had to adjust to so many things recently—"

"I wouldn't put him in an uncomfortable position. You know that." And I love the way she always puts his needs above her own.

"Of course. Okay, wow. Um, can I think about it?"

My stomach tightens uncomfortably. "Oh, uh, sure." I was

confident she'd accept my proposition. Shit. How can I convince her? Joey would know. Maybe I should text her—

"Can I take a shower?" she asks, cutting off my spiraling thoughts. "I came straight from the theater."

"Absolutely." As I'm setting her on her feet, the alarm on my phone goes off. "I have a virtual with my therapist anyway."

"Do you need me to leave to give you some privacy?"

"No, no. Just take a long shower." With a wink, I snag her suitcase. Then I roll it into my bedroom. "Kane's working for a few more hours, so I'll use his room."

"You doing okay?" She scrutinizes me, searching for hidden answers.

"Yeah, baby. Promise. I'm doing even better now that you're here."

# Chapter 45
## Millie

HE ASKED me to move in with him. Scratch that. He *told* me I'm moving in. Honestly, my hangup has nothing to do with how we'd get along. The man picks up after himself and cooks. And he never complains about hair in the shower. Plus, we already have great bed chem. Did I mention *he cooks*? He doesn't drink coffee, but no one is perfect. At least he keeps the fridge stocked with my favorite creamer.

I welcome the hot water as it rinses away the hearty smells of the theater. Can I move into *this shower*—with the fresh eucalyptus leaves hanging from the rainfall shower head? That's easy to imagine.

After brushing my hair, I throw on one of Ezra's shirts rather than digging through my suitcase for clean clothes. Something tells me he won't mind.

His bed is made, but there's a pile of sheets in a basket on the floor. One sniff confirms they're freshly laundered, so I fold them while I wait for his therapy session to end. It's a turn-on, how proactive he is about his mental health. The world would be a much better place if more men thought the way he does. He's concerned about screwing things up with Kane, but he's a sensational father figure. Every time I think about the way he stepped up immediately, I swear I ovulate. Not many women get to preview how their partner will be as a parent, but seeing Ezra with Kane reassures me that if we ever have kids together, he'll be the world's best dad.

Exhausted from my travels but too antsy to rest, I lie on the bed and read through the contract and rehearsal schedule Diane has already sent. She was kind enough to give me a few days to get situated before diving in. Though she warned it will be a lot of work, the vibe she gave off during our call set me at ease. I fire off a few texts—one to let my parents know I'm back in the city and I'll explain later, one to Joey to thank her for not spoiling the surprise for Ezra, and another to my understudy, telling her to break a leg tonight.

I remove the lid from the container of slime on Ezra's bedside table and mindlessly play with it while I wait for his appointment to end, and when he appears in the doorway, I give him a smirk. "If I didn't know better, I'd think this was some kind of new sex toy."

"Honey, I don't wanna know where you think that might go." With a laugh, he closes the door behind him.

The gooey texture mixed with tiny pieces of foam is satisfying between my fingers. "What scent is this?"

He lies next to me, his athletic shorts bunching. His thighs look more muscular than when I saw him last; I can't wait to find out whether it feels different when he holds me down with them.

"Blue Hawaiian," he answers.

I scrunch my face. "But it's orange."

"Orange is my favorite color."

I turn on my side and study him. "I didn't know that. Do you know my favorite color?"

"Mmm..." He feigns contemplation. "Pink?"

"Okay, fine. But there are other things you don't know about me."

His face is so close to mine I can almost taste the chai on his breath. "I want to learn new things about you every day for the rest of my life."

"Are you proposing, Mr. Miller?"

With the most stoic of expressions, he says, "Not today, baby."

*Not today?*

I clear my throat, ignoring the way the air between us has thickened. "You know what we haven't done in a while?"

"Fucked."

I cackle. "Okay, *that*. But also… would you rather walk on slime or walk on marshmallows, barefoot, for the rest of your life?" I hold the slippery substance up between us.

His face contorts in disgust. "Ugh, neither."

"C'mon." I play punch him. "You have to answer."

He takes the slime from me and squishes it between his fingers a few times before returning it to the container. "Slime, I guess. I still have nightmares from Bea and those marshmallows," he teases, pulling at the ends of his hair. "Okay, my turn. Would you rather keep playing this game or let me eat you out?"

Stunned by his provocative question, though I really shouldn't be, I gasp. "You don't have any patience, do you?"

He trails a finger up my leg. "You're wearing my fucking shirt, Mills, and I haven't seen you in forever," he says, his voice pure grit. "What do you expect?"

Throat tightening and core heating, I snuggle close, my hard nipples pressed to his chest. "Last one," I breathe. "Would you rather wash the dishes or take out the trash when I move in?"

"Wash the—*What?*" His smile shines brighter than spotlights on a stage. "You're moving in?"

Biting back a grin, I nod, barely able to contain my excitement. In the time we've spent apart, I've realized that I'm ready for more.

He brushes his lips against my ear, eliciting a trail of goose bumps down my arm. "Would you rather have my cum all over your tits or my cum in your pussy?"

"P-pussy. Definitely."

"I wanna hear you beg for it." He tucks my damp hair behind my ear and rests his hand at my throat.

"Please, Ezra. Make love to me and come inside me."

With a guttural growl, he pins me on my back. "Take off this fucking—" He claws at my shirt, and when he sees I'm wearing nothing underneath, he groans. "You naughty girl. You've been laying on my bed with no panties this whole time?"

I capture my bottom lip between my teeth. "When does Kane get back?"

"Not for a few hours."

While he clumsily sheds his shorts, I whip the T-shirt over my head. Once we're both naked and his hard cock is on display, he gives it a stroke, then uses it to slap my pussy.

My core contracts, and my arousal soaks my inner thighs.

"Spread 'em. Show Daddy his pussy."

With one hand, I spread my lips, presenting the main event.

Swiping a hand down his beard, he studies me with an intense adoration. "You're perfect." This sentiment is whispered to my pussy. Then, with his eyes locked on mine, his jaw ticking, he says, "*You're* perfect."

He slaps my pussy with his cock again, sending electricity sparking through me. "You like that?" The smile in his eyes contains a sensuous flame.

Warm pleasure rushes through my veins. I have to touch him. *Now.*

I reach for him, but he grasps my wrist before I can wrap my fingers around his length.

"I want it." I tug, but he doesn't release me. "Give me your cock, please."

He arches a thick brow. "Now who's the impatient one?"

"Ezra. So help me god," I grit out. I'm writhing beneath him like a pathetic kitten. "If you don't fuck me right n—"

He slams into me, and I cry out. Holy fuck. I'll feel him inside me until New Year's.

Above me, he trembles, a whimper escaping him. *A fucking whimper*. It's single-handedly the sexiest sound I've ever heard. And I work for an erotic stories app—I know sexy.

"Fuck, I missed you." His dick twitches inside me and my pussy clamps around him in response. *We missed you too.*

"Move, baby. I need you to move," I gasp. My heart is fighting to leap out of my chest.

An agonized expression floods his face. "I can't fucking move, or I'll explode."

He's defenseless, exposed, and so fucking handsome right now.

I reach between us, holding the base of his shaft, my pussy clenching around him.

"Not helping," he grouses.

With my free hand, I trace the edge of his beard near his ear, and he turns his head to delicately kiss my palm. I slip my fingers behind his neck and pull him in until his forehead rests against mine.

Though I long to keep touching him, I release his length and rub circles over my clit. Ezra pants against my lips, sucking in gasps of air like his life depends on it.

The familiar feeling of ecstasy swirls deep in my core, and in response, a knowing smile spreads across his face.

"You gonna come with me, baby?"

An incoherent noise escapes my lips. With both hands, I tug

him flush against me by his ass, his muscles clenching in restraint beneath my grip.

Focus fixed on his face, I undulate my hips. "I love you."

He draws back *slowly, slowly,* before sliding in to the hilt again. "I love you too."

With precision, he glides back, then thrusts into me, over and over, his lips still pressed to mine.

I swallow his cries of pleasure and relinquish mine to him. Warmth floods my channel, and my orgasm sucks in every last drop of his release.

Still inside me, he nuzzles into my neck, kissing my pulse point. We stay there for I don't know how long before our muscles finally relax and he's forced to slip out of me.

He kneels between my legs, sweat glistening at his hairline and across his chest. "Let me see it."

Clenching my core, I obey.

In wonderment, he watches his cum leak from my pussy. He gathers it with his fingertips and shoves it back into my cunt, and now *I'm* the one whimpering. "There you go, honey. Save that for round two."

# Chapter 46
## Millie
### Ten Months Later

Months ago, I overheard Ezra talking to Cam about wanting to wait until the show got off the ground and the dust settled before he proposed. But *The Proposal* was practically an overnight sensation, and life has yet to slow down. In fact, between Ezra's new role as principal, the unexpected success of the show, and Kane's school and work schedule, we've been going a mile a minute. I was even nominated for a Tony for best performance by an actress in a leading role in a musical. I didn't win, but the show did bring home an award for best original score. Ezra looked so breathtaking in his tux on the red carpet, I considered flushing my birth control that night.

    I was convinced he'd propose while we were in the Hamptons after the Tony's last week. Joey and Cam met us there, which felt like a dead giveaway, but when I came home without a ring on my finger, I did my best not to be salty.

    Turning onto my side, I tap my phone screen. Two a.m. Ugh.

There's no use lying here when I can't sleep, so I slip on a pair of comfy cotton shorts and one of Ezra's shirts, then pad my way into the kitchen for a cup of chamomile tea.

Just as I sit on the couch with my mug, Ezra appears. With one eye still glued shut, he tucks his messy curls behind his ears. The plaid pajama pants hanging from his hips reveal the panty-dropping, delicious lines pointing straight to his—

"Everything okay?" He props himself against the doorway with his arms crossed.

"Can't sleep," I say over my steaming mug.

"Do you feel okay?"

"I'm fine."

His brows pinch together in uncertainty, but he doesn't continue to dig.

Uneasy under his scrutiny, I blurt out, "Why haven't you proposed?"

Something like shock spreads across his face.

Before he can answer, I go on. "Do you not want to marry me?"

He immediately rounds the sofa and sits beside me. "What would ever give you that idea?"

"Nothing, actually." I shrug, setting the mug on the table. "I just—we've been living together for nearly a year."

"Mills." He rests a hand on my thigh. "We've been so busy. I didn't want to add any more busyness to your life."

I keep my attention downcast, but his gaze burns my cheek.

"Wait right here," he finally says.

When he returns, he drops to his haunches, his knees hitting the floor between my feet. Then he grips me by the hips to pull me closer to the edge of the sofa. A hard object digs into my hipbone, but before I can see what it is, he's presenting me with a dark red velvet box.

"Millie." He clears his throat. "Amelia, you captivated me

from the moment I met you in Greece. You sparkled and shone like a diamond. Maybe it's corny, but it's the damn truth. I couldn't take my eyes off you. While we may have had an unconventional reunion"—we both chuckle at that—"we were given a second chance." He quickly wipes at his eyes. "You make everything in my life brighter. Being with you is entertaining and exciting. It's a privilege. And I promise I won't ever let you feel otherwise. I loved pretending to be married to you. I want to do it for real." He takes a deep breath. "So, I have a question…"

My heart races, and my stomach is twisted into knots. My hands are trapped in his. Otherwise I'd wipe the dampness from my face.

"Would you rather…"

I toss my head back and roar with laughter.

When I've mostly calmed myself, he starts again. "Would you rather drink black coffee every day for the rest of your life or… be my wife?"

"Hmm." I tug my hand free and tap a finger on my chin. "That's a tough one."

His dark eyes are soft and spectacular, full of patience. But I can't make him wait a second longer.

"Wife! I pick wife." I fling my arms around his neck with so much force I nearly knock him over.

Settling next to me, he slips the ring onto my finger. I hold up my hand, my breath catching, and the two of us admire it like a painting in a museum.

"Is this the same ring?" I bring it closer to examine it in the dim light. It's a circular diamond with smaller diamonds surrounding it set on a white-gold band, just like the one he gave me at the airport last summer. "It looks more sparkly."

"That's because it is." He kisses my knuckle right above the ring. "I exchanged it for a moissanite diamond. It's the brightest gem there is."

"Ezra, it's stunning." I preen. "I love it. I love *you*."

"I love you so much, baby. I'm sorry for making you question whether I wanted to marry you. Of course I want to marry you. I've wanted to marry you since the moment I called you my wife at the hospital in Hawaii."

"Really?"

With a nod, he licks his lips. "The thought of calling you that every day for the rest of my life felt so fucking good."

Folding into his tight embrace, I study the stone, unable to get enough of it.

We stay like that for so long that I startle when he finally speaks. "I think we should get married tomorrow."

"What?" I turn in his arms and blink up at him. "Tomorrow?"

"Yeah. Kane is leaving for camp in a couple of weeks, and I can't do it without him. Plus, there's something I've been meaning to talk to you about."

My heart tightens in apprehension. "Okay?"

"Since we haven't heard from Rob since I took guardianship of Kane, I can officially adopt him now."

"That's great." I bounce on the cushion, my heart leaping. "Have you told him yet?"

"No. I wanted to talk to you about it first."

Head tilted, I frown in confusion. "Oh?"

"I want your name on the adoption papers too."

My heart just about launches itself out of my chest. "Me?"

"I realize it's a little unconventional, and I completely understand if it's too much, but—"

"I'm in." I squeal, then quickly cover my mouth because Kane is sleeping in the other room.

Wetness spills down my fiancé's face, triggering the waterworks from me too. Then we're giggling and caressing each other, salty tears mixing on our tongues as we kiss.

"Can we wake him?" I squirm, excitement vibrating through my veins.

"Soon, baby." He kisses my forehead. "Let's go back to bed, and if he's not awake when we get up, then we'll wake him."

I frown. "I'm too buzzed to sleep."

"Who said anything about sleep?"

---

"Mmm, this is nice," Ezra hums in my ear, waking me from a relaxing slumber.

"What is?"

He finds my left hand beneath the sheets and brings it to his lips. "Waking up to a naked fiancée."

"Best feeling in the world," I agree.

We cradle and massage every inch of each other's skin with fondness. I never want to forget this moment. The moment where only the two of us know we're engaged.

But before long, I'm restless with impatience again. "Can we tell him now?"

Once we're decent, Ezra knocks on Kane's door. The second he calls out, I dart in and launch myself onto the edge of his bed.

"Hey, buddy. Wake up. Wake up! Remember when you asked me if I was going to adopt you?"

"Okay, we're jumping right in," Ezra chuckles behind me. "*Good morning*," he says, modeling an appropriate introduction.

Sitting up, Kane rubs his eyes. "Huh? What are you talking about?"

"Do you remember the time you asked if I was going to adopt you?"

He nods, his brow knitted and his lips tugged into an apprehensive frown.

"Is that something you still want?" My heart dangles from the edge of a cliff while I wait for his response.

"What?" he asks again, clearly not awake enough to process well.

Raising my hand, I flash him my engagement ring. "Your brother and I are getting married. For real this time. Tomorrow, actually."

"And we have the green light on an official adoption," Ezra says, sounding as elated as I feel.

"So is that—"

"Yes." Kane rockets off the bed and engulfs me in the biggest hug. Then he rises to meet his brother for a long and tearful embrace. When he steps back, he pokes Ezra in the shoulder. "I'm not calling you Dad, though."

"That's okay. I already call him Da—"

Ezra clamps a hand over my mouth and brings his lips close to my ear. "Do *not* finish that sentence."

"Or what?" I mumble against his hand.

His dark eyes flash. "You don't wanna know."

I lick his palm. "I think I do."

"Oh my god." Kane slaps a hand to his face. "Is it too soon to move out?"

Laughing, we head toward his door, but he calls out, stopping us.

He looks to me, then to his brother. "I... thank you." His lips are pulled in tight, but then they loosen. "I love you."

Ezra's throat bobs as he stares unabashedly.

Fuck, the sight makes my heart race.

When he stands taller, pride seeps out of his pores. "I love you too."

If he could have traded sexual favors for the ability to bypass the twenty-four hours we had to wait after applying for our marriage license, I think Ezra would have done it. At least it bought us time to move my clothes and a few of my belongings over.

Standing in my underwear in our closet, I huff. "I have nothing white."

"You do have that bikini..."

"Ezra, I am not marrying you in a fucking bikini." Normally I'd find his joke adorable, but not when I have nothing to wear to my own wedding.

"Okay, okay." He holds up his hands. "Don't you still have those white sundresses from Hawaii?"

"They don't fit anymore."

Working with such a body-positive cast and crew was one of the greatest experiences of my life. Show business has a long way to go in this department, but I'm optimistic the rising generation will continue to drive the industry in a more supportive and inclusive direction.

"You don't have to wear white. What about that pink dress?" He sidles up next to me—naked, having abandoned his own efforts—and nods to the back of our closet. "The tags are still on. That could be your something new."

"I guess that will work." I ease it off the hanger and turn to him. "Will you help me zip up the back, please?"

I make him stand with his back to me while I slip on my Spanx. While I love my body, there are some things a fiancé doesn't need to see.

When the magenta dress with flowy chiffon sleeves easily glides over my hips, I let out a relieved sigh.

With deft fingers, Ezra drags the zipper up my back, the move causing goose bumps to blossom across my chest where the pendant from Kane lies.

*For the Show*

Wrapping his arms around my waist, he tugs me against his naked body and kisses my temple. "Today, you become my wife."

I hum. "I like the sound of that. It's a shame I only get to call you my fiancé for a few more hours. But I guess 'my husband' has a nice ring to it."

His dick twitches against my back. I think he likes it too.

"Does it bother you that we aren't being married by a rabbi?" he asks.

"A little," I admit. "It's important to my parents. They've always assumed I would. But they're okay with having a ceremony in a synagogue later. I can't wait to start planning."

"Thank goodness you have your PowerPoint."

I tip my head back, glaring at him. "How do you know about that?"

He chuckles against my ear, still holding me tight in his arms. "Asher emailed me a copy."

"That little turd," I laugh. "I think my vision has changed a bit since."

"I'd say, since your partner has a penis and not a vulva."

"You're hilarious," I deadpan. "Ugh, can you imagine how adorable Bea will look in a flower girl dress? Oh, that reminds me." I rotate my head to look at him again. "Remember when you put her to bed that first time? With those awful animal impressions? What did you whisper to her?"

He gives me a squeeze. "That I was going to make you my wife."

"Cocky, were you?"

"Always. I can't wait to marry you." He sucks at my neck, making my knees buckle.

We sway together, my head resting against him and his lips moving along the sensitive skin of my jaw.

While I love the way his hard cock presses into my ass, that will have to wait until later. "Put some pants on. You better not get precum on my dress," I scold playfully as I pull away.

"Or you could…" A mischievous look washes over him.

"Get changed, big guy." I tap his dick, and he contracts in surprise. "Let's go get married."

⬤

"We have a surprise for you tonight," Stevie announces from the stage. "Please welcome, and give a great big mazel tov to our very own queen, Millie, and her *very average-looking new husband*"—they give an exaggerated wink—"Ezra."

The crowd at FrenchSHEs goes wild as a spotlight shines on us.

My parents, Dawn, and Kane were our four witnesses at our perfect little courthouse wedding. It was logical for us to end up at FrenchSHEs on karaoke night, doing what we did the night we met.

"What are you going to sing?" Joey asks as Cam passes around glasses of champagne. Asher got a babysitter, and Claire is here too.

"I haven't thought about it, actually," I admit. "Ezra says he's got it covered."

She quirks a brow, surprised that I'd relinquish control like that, I guess.

"Look." I point to where Stevie, Kane, and Dawn are dressing my dad in a Dolly Parton wig. "I think he's having more fun than anyone."

Once it's in place, he can barely keep his head up. My mom snaps pictures from all angles, probably to ensure she has the best shot to put on this year's Chanukkah card.

*For the Show*

"Hey." Ezra appears next to me and squeezes my ass. "It's time."

"For what?"

Without responding, he drags me up the stairs, and instead of standing center stage, he leads me to a chair slightly off to the side.

He gently forces me to sit with my back to the audience so all I can see is my husband, who now has full control of the mic.

When a loud whistle rings out, the crowd quiets. I whip my head around to find the source and catch Asher tossing up a very dorky-dad thumbs-up.

"Good evening," Ezra announces.

He's removed his suit jacket, and though his white shirt is still tucked into his hunter green slacks, he's undone the top few buttons, showcasing a smattering of dark hair, and he's rolled his sleeves. His pants taper above a pair of brown loafers that complete the outfit. Who knew a man's naked ankle could be so sexy?

"Many of you know my wife, Millie."

Everyone cheers and I toss a reluctant wave, still at a loss for what the fuck is happening.

"What some of you may not know is that we met at a karaoke night. And let's just say, things got very heated… in more ways than one."

The room fills with hoots and hollers, and my dad yells, "That's enough, son."

Ezra chuckles. "Millie and I don't shy away from friendly competition, but I thought I'd do things a little differently tonight." He turns to me. "You're always the one performing. Now it's time for you to sit back and enjoy the show, *honey.*"

He winks, and the familiar chords of an iconic Shania Twain song play as the house band's guitarist walks on stage.

My heart tightens in my chest, and tears push their way to the surface as Ezra serenades me with an acoustic version of "You're Still the One."

As he sings, I can't help but think about just how far we've come and all that we've been through: The closet in Crete. Discovering we were dating the same woman. The moment he told me his ridiculous plan. Meeting Kane. My stay at the hospital, where Ezra never left my side. So much matzo ball soup. Making a long-distance relationship not only work but thrive. And now this—marriage.

He's better than any man I could have ever dreamed of.

Any *person* I could have dreamed of.

Our love is so strong.

And our love will go so far.

*This is only the beginning.*

Ezra's voice cracks at the end, and when I leap into his arms, the audience breaks into applause. The microphone digs into my back as he clutches me to his chest, but I don't care; I'm too busy laughing and crying into my husband's neck.

"I love you," I promise him.

His eyes shine with his own tears. "I love you too."

We're separated in the crowd for a bit, passed around like a bottle of champagne until we finally reunite at the back of the club.

"You know," I say over my glass of bubbly, "I never commended you for your acting skills back when we pretended to be married."

"Honey, none of that was pretend."

A surprising ache clings to my ribs as an overwhelming sensation of warmth zips through my body.

We dance for what feels like hours, never once letting go of one another, despite being sweaty messes.

"Tonight was perfect," I affirm in the middle of the dance floor, dazedly soaking in my husband's handsome features.

My *husband*. My new favorite word.

"It's not over yet."

Turning in his arms, I play with the damp hair at his nape and bring my lips to his. "Take me home, Mr. Greer."

# Epilogue

## One Year Later

### *Ezra*

"Congratulations, buddy. You did it." Millie ruffles Kane's hair.

With an ear-piercing screech, Bea tackles him. "I wore a dress like this for my kindergarten graduation." She pulls a lollipop from her mouth and tugs on his cobalt blue gown with her sticky fingers.

He hits me with a pleading expression. "Can I take this thing off yet?"

"After we get a few family pictures," I promise.

Cam sets up his tripod and positions everyone. At the last second, Millie and I present Kane with a white-and-purple lei. Locating one in Manhattan was like finding a needle in a haystack, but my wife insisted the Hawaiian tradition was important, and by the look on Kane's face, I'd say she was right. *She usually is.*

"Everyone say 'family,'" Cam announces.

"Ohana!" we all shout.

Though our apartment is small, we host a gathering to celebrate Kane. He's evolving into a remarkable young man. The lanky kid we brought to the city two years ago is as tall as me now. Though I still outweigh him, he's looking more like me every day, save for the blond hair.

When the last of the guests leave and it's just the three of us, we present him with an envelope.

"We hope you're proud of yourself," I tell him.

He tears open the manilla envelope and pulls out three plane tickets. "We're going to Maui?" He rubs at his breastbone, then flips over the papers, his mouth agape and his eyes wide.

"I can't tell if you're excited or..." Millie frowns, studying him.

With a shaky voice, he thanks us. "This is really cool."

"*Cool?* Folks, we've got a 'cool.' Did you hear that, Mills?" I throw my hands in the air for flair.

"You dork." She giggles.

"But I'm supposed to work for Uncle Asher."

"You will. We cleared it with him. You'll head over there when we get back."

"Happy graduation, buddy." Millie kisses him on the cheek. "We love you."

---

"Would Mr. Greer please come to gate twenty-two?" The announcement is so garbled I'm not sure they're actually calling us, but we head that way regardless.

"I still can't believe you took my last name." Millie squeezes my hand.

"Did you really think I'd let you be Millie *Miller*?"

Sure, we could have kept our own last names, but with our unique love story, it felt right to take hers.

"Good morning." The man fights back a yawn as he greets us. "It looks like you've been upgraded to first class both from here to San Francisco and then on to Maui."

"Oh? That's wonderful, but we're traveling with—"

"Kane Adams? Yes. It looks like he's been upgraded as well."

Millie reaches into her back pocket for her phone.

"The Connellys again?" I presume.

With a smile, she nods at her device. "Those two really need to get a dog or something. They can't keep spoiling us like this."

We're ushered onto the plane first. Millie sits in the aisle, of course, and Kane sits across from her, next to a man who I'm fairly certain is a professional surfer. My brother's cheeks flush, and he adjusts his pants when the objectively good-looking guy has to shuffle in front of him to take the window seat.

Millie notices, too, and lays a hand on my thigh, her silent signal to leave it.

He's eighteen now, but damn if my mom wasn't right. I'll always worry about him.

"Thank you for being on time this morning," I tell her as I pull out an advanced copy of Joey's new book.

According to Cam, this one's spicy. Apparently there's a pegging scene at the end, and I'm worried I won't be able to look him in the eye after I read it.

"Like I had a choice. Starbucks wasn't even open yet. Thank you for packing my charger, by the way." She rifles through her bag. "Shit," she cries. "Have you seen my motion sickness wristband?"

I shake my head.

"Dammit. I think I left it at home." She drops her head forward. "Please don't say 'I told you to pack it.'"

"Wasn't gonna." *I thought about it, but I quite like the balls between my legs.* Instead, I rub soothing circles on her back. "That really sucks, baby. I'm sorry. We'll order a glass of ginger ale."

It does little good. I lose count of how many times Millie has to rush to the restroom, though she only throws up once. During our layover, we purchase a motion sickness wristband. It doesn't rid her of all the symptoms, but it gives her enough relief to allow her to sleep for the last few hours of the second flight.

It's early afternoon when we land in Maui, and the second we drop our bags in our hotel room, Kane is itching for adventure. Millie, on the other hand, drops right onto the bed.

"You okay, baby? Still nauseous from the flight?"

"A little. Once I sleep it off, I'll be fine. I drank too much ginger ale, though. Now I can't stop peeing." She laughs pitifully. "You two go do whatever it is you're going to do, and I'll catch up with you for dinner."

I leave her with a forehead kiss and a promise to return with a macadamia nut iced coffee.

## Millie

Last night's luau dinner was much more fun than our meal two nights ago when I practically fell asleep at the table. Even after a long nap, I couldn't keep my eyes open. It seems the older I get, the harder it is for me to recover from traveling.

On our second full day in Hawaii, I wake up feeling nauseous again, this time with pressure in my lower abdomen, and I can't stop peeing. Ezra wants to take me to urgent care, but I insist that he go surfing with Kane. I need to get him out of here so I can make arrangements with the resort for his birthday tonight.

The clinic is only a ten-minute walk, so I call Joey on my way.

"Is everything okay?" she asks when I tell her where I'm headed.

"Totally. Just a little UTI situation." A passerby gawks at me. Clearly, I've forgotten I'm not in NYC, where people don't bat an eye at TMI cell phone conversations on the street.

"Millie. Didn't your mother ever tell you to pee after sex?" Her voice is so loud I have to adjust my phone's volume.

"I know, I know. I never fall asleep after sex. It's just that—"

"He fucked you six ways till Sunday with that bedazzled monster cock?"

"Something like that. Where are you? I wasn't sure you'd answer."

"We're in LA."

"Fun. Tell Aunt Elin I say hi."

"Actually," she says. "We're not here to see my mom."

"Oh?"

"Do you remember my very first writing friend, Brooks?" She doesn't wait for me to answer, though I remember him well. "He works for a production company now and got me a meeting to discuss turning my book into... *I don't know...* something," she squeals. "A series or a film, I don't know yet."

"Shut the fuck up." My heart floats in my chest. "That's amazing. I'm so happy for you."

"Thanks. I don't want to get my hopes up, but we'll see."

"They're gonna love you," I say as I approach the urgent care building.

Thankfully, I'm seen right away, and the physician's assistant checks my vitals while waiting for my urinalysis. "What's the date of your last menstrual period?" she asks.

"Oh, um..." I rack my brain for a date. While performing in *The Proposal*, I skipped the sugar pills in the birth control packets so I wouldn't have to deal with my period while on tour, meaning it started when I finished my last pack around the time of my last performance. "It would have been"—I pull up my calendar app and scroll back to check the date of the party we attended to celebrate the end of the run—"two months ago?"

"You haven't had a period since?" she asks.

My chest tightens as I try to decipher her masked expression. "No."

She looks at me, then at a piece of paper and back again, her eyes widening for an instant before she gains control again.

"So do I have a UTI?" I ask, the hair on my arms standing.

"Nope."

## Ezra

"If you make a *Forgetting Sarah Marshall* reference, I will ditch you out here," Kane calls from his surfboard.

"What do you know about *Forgetting Sarah Marshall*? You're too young to know that movie."

"I don't really believe in age or numbers..." he says, quoting Paul Rudd's character.

"You little shit," I laugh. All it takes is one knowing look between the two of us, and we both sing, "Oh, the weather outside is weather."

I sweep my foot through the water and splash him in the face.

"My mom's out here," he says quietly. "Her ashes, I mean."

"Oh yeah?" He rarely talks about his mom's death, and I haven't pushed him on it; that's what his therapist is for.

"Yeah. We had a whole traditional paddling out ceremony, where everyone gets on surfboards and tosses flowers and leis, but I snuck my board out the night before and scattered them. I wanted her all to myself for a little longer. It was selfish of me, but—"

"Not selfish," I interrupt, the salt from my tears mixing with the salt of the ocean. "You were a kid, and you'd just lost your mom."

"You're right." He sighs, swirling his fingertips along the surface of the water. "I hate that she's gone, but if she weren't, then I might never have met you."

My heart clenches. "Life's weird like that, isn't it?"

"How so?" Turning to me, he holds a hand up to shield his eyes.

"Sometimes tragedy leads us to people and places we never imagined. If I'd never met you, I might not have had the courage to cut ties with Rob."

"Do you ever regret it?"

"Not one bit." The only time I think about Rob is when I silently thank him for giving me Kane. "All right, enough of this sappy shit," I clear my throat. "Millie will be mad she missed it."

---

When Kane and I return to our adjoining rooms, my wife is wrapped in a bathrobe, her makeup freshly done, blow drying her hair. When I ask her to join me in the shower, she turns me down, but she keeps me company in the bathroom.

"Did your trip to urgent care go okay? I'm sorry I wasn't there." I'm met with silence, so I pop my head out of the shower, wiping the water from my eyes. "You still there?"

"Yeah, sorry," she says, applying mascara. "No wait time. Are you excited for your birthday dinner?"

I blow a raspberry under the water. "You know how I get about celebrating my birthday."

"Yeah," she says, her voice all tease. "But that was before you met me."

The restaurant at the resort is modest, exactly as I hoped it would be. As much as Millie would like to spoil me, I'm damn grateful she respected my wishes for a low-key night. I'm with my two favorite people on this beautiful island; what more could I ask for?

Millie elbows Kane. "Isn't that the guy from the plane?"

In unison, we scan the restaurant, and sure enough, Maybe Pro-Surfer Dude is leaning against the bar.

"Did you see that?" Kane asks, his hazel eyes swimming with anticipation.

"What?"

Millie grins. "Oh, I saw it, all right."

"What?" I huff. "Will one of you please tell me what's going on?"

"He gave him *the look*." Millie waggles her brows.

"What look?"

"Dude, you've only been married for a year. You shouldn't be that clueless," Kane goads.

"You should go over there," Millie encourages, pushing his arm lightly. "He's hot."

"Amelia," I scold. "Do not encourage him."

She waves me off, and Kane doesn't bother looking at me before he strides over and rests an elbow on the wooden surface. I do not approve of this situation, but I must admit I'm proud of his confident stance.

Maybe Pro-Surfer Dude drops a napkin, and Kane bends to pick it up.

"Did you see that?" I scoff as the guy checks out my little brother as he straightens. "I don't like the way he's ogling him." I squint. "He's gotta be ten years older than Kane."

"Hmm. Really? I can think of another couple with a similar age gap," Millie murmurs.

My stomach sinks. "That's different."

My wife quirks a brow.

"Fine." I sigh, picking up my drink. "If he wants a vacation fling, fine. I just—"

"Know what you were like when you were eighteen?"

"*Hmph.*" Fuck yeah, I do. I take a long sip of my mai tai to calm my worries.

In true Millie fashion, she makes a big spectacle out of singing "Happy Birthday," encouraging the entire restaurant to join in. But I love her for it.

Rather than return to our rooms with us, Kane takes off with *actual* pro surfer Drew Durham. On the walk back, I follow him on social media from my wife's phone, just in case I need to keep tabs on him.

We brush our teeth in tandem, then Millie asks for privacy in the bathroom.

While waiting for her on the bed, I reply to a few text messages from my colleagues and shoot off a couple of pictures from dinner to Cam, Joey, and my mom, all of whom I FaceTimed earlier. Asher sent a video of Bea singing to me that pulls at my heartstrings. As a wedding gift last year, Asher asked Millie and me to be her guardians should anything happen to him. I don't know who cried more, Millie or me.

All thoughts of my niece quickly fly out the window when my drop-dead gorgeous wife appears in the doorway.

Dressed in a pale blue satin bra and panty set, she's a vision.

"Get in your birthday suit," she commands, her voice dripping with seduction.

"How long have you been waiting to say that?"

"Three hundred sixty-five days." She giggles as she struts to the side of the bed.

*For the Show*

I stroke her leg, toying with the elastic at her hipbone, but when she yawns, I pause.

"Sorry." She covers her mouth. "I'm still a little jet-lagged."

"It's okay, baby," I soothe, sitting up against the pillows. "If you're too tired—"

"No." She cuts me off. "Undress. I need to feel you."

I hesitate for a moment, but my apprehension flees quickly when she starts tugging at my clothes. When she straddles my lap, my hands immediately gravitate to her thick thighs. I squeeze them tight, knowing how much she likes the bite of pain, and she rocks her hips against me in return, seeking friction.

The smooth satin of her panties feels like heaven against my growing cock. "Fuck, Millie. You're soaked. Is that for me?"

Catching her lip between her teeth, she nods, eyes hooded. "Wanna see?"

"God yes," I pant, impatiently tugging at the elastic and tearing the panties off her body.

Gasping, she greedily rubs her clit over my cock. With a teasing smirk, she unhooks her bra and tosses it off to the side—probably worried that if she doesn't get rid of it, I'll ruin it too—leaving her breasts hanging heavy above me.

"I want you so fucking bad right now, wife." I take one perfectly peaked nipple into my mouth. "But fuck..." It pains me to still her hips. "Should we? You're not supposed to have sex if you have a UTI, right?" Please, *please* tell me I'm sorely mistaken.

I like to think I know my wife better than anyone, but the unreadable expression she dons is baffling.

"About that..." she says, voice quivering. "Do you want the good news or the bad news?"

Still pinned beneath her, I break out into a cold sweat.

"The good news," she says, putting me out of my misery, "is

that I don't have a UTI. So yes, we can have sex. The bad news? I don't think I can call you Daddy anymore."

I frown. "What are you talking about?" If she's no longer into my kink, I'll understand, even if I don't like it. I'd never want to make her feel uncomfortable.

Avoiding eye contact, she mindlessly runs her finger through the hair at my navel. After what feels like an eternity, she fixes her attention on me. "If I call you Daddy, what will the baby call you?"

All the oxygen is purged from my lungs, and my soul hovers above my body as my dreams come to life.

"What? There's a baby... in there? Right now?" Blinking rapidly, I survey her midsection. "Fuck, Millie. *Fuck*. Why does that turn me on so much? Can I?" I hold a hand up, hovering an inch from her belly. I have to touch her. Hold her. Tell her how magnificent she is.

When she nods, her eyes brimming with tears, I roll her gently onto her back and rest my head on her stomach.

"I'm sorry." She sniffs.

"What for?" I prop myself up, giving her my full attention, caressing the skin of her abdomen with my thumb.

"Between *The Proposal*, the Tony's, my transition to full-time narrator, and Kane's graduation, life has been hectic. I haven't been very consistent with my birth control."

"I wasn't exactly doing my part in preventing things, was I?" And I sure as shit shoved my cum back inside her many times, secretly praying for a baby.

"You're happy?" She runs her fingers through my hair and tucks the strands behind my ear.

"The happiest." *I'm finally going to be a father.* "What about you?" I brush the tears from her cheek. "Are you happy?"

"Yes," she sobs. "It's a surprise, but the best one yet."

*For the Show*

"I love you." I kiss her, silently making a million promises, then I lie back down to kiss her belly.

Her breathing evens out, and her body relaxes. So much so that I think she might have drifted off to sleep.

"Hey, Millie?"

To my surprise, she responds right away. "Yes?"

"I love celebrating my birthday now."

# Bonus (Spicy) Scene

## Ezra

### The Wedding Night

"It was nice of Cam's parents to put us up at their hotel." I pull the key card from my back pocket and slip it between my teeth, then hoist Millie off the ground.

"What are you doing?" she shrieks, clinging to me.

"Carrying my wife over the threshold. It's tradition," I say, key card still clenched between my teeth.

"Easy, Tevye," she says, taking the card from me. "I don't think we're the traditional type."

I grin. "Maybe not, but let me have this one, wife."

Holding the plastic card up to the sensor, she uses the heel of her shoe to turn the handle. Once it's unlatched, I kick the door open wide, then quickly step through and let it slam behind us.

"Oh no," she says, peering around the gigantic suite. "One bed. Whatever shall we do?"

"You brat." I tickle her side, and she wiggles out of my arms.

As I bring my lips to hers, she stiffens and jumps back. "Who did this?" She cackles and points to a gold banner tacked above the bed that reads *Last wiener to go between her.*

Bright pink balloon penises hang from the ceiling fan, rotating like a merry-go-round.

The floor is covered in multicolored disco balls and penis confetti. Damn, I am not looking forward to discovering what crevices those will get stuck in.

"Do you have your phone? I want to take a picture," she says.

I slip the device from my pocket and hand it over.

"Those bitches." Giggling, she shows me the screen.

There's a text from Joey pulled up. It's a picture of her and Claire posing provocatively in the bathtub with two blow-up dolls. Snort-laughing, Millie runs into the bathroom and returns with a new friend in each arm.

"What the hell are we supposed to do with those?" I laugh, batting them out of her hands.

"I don't know, but I found our stuff. It was nice of them to drop our bags off, along with all... *this*." She holds out an arm in a sweeping motion.

And that's when I spy the frosted sugar cookies on the table.

"Amelia Ruth Greer," I scold. "Why do these penis cookies have *piercings* painted on them?"

Her eyes bulge out of their sockets.

"Did you tell—"

She makes a run for it, but I take off after her and scoop her up quickly, then toss her onto the California king bed. Pinning her between my thighs, I tickle her until she's crying "Safe word. Safe word."

Finally, she catches her breath and tugs me down by my collar. "Kiss me, Mr. Greer."

I plant a chaste kiss to her lips, then stand. "I've got a better idea." I work a button free, then another. "Use your AirTag to find that Mary Poppins bag and meet me in the shower."

My eyes are closed when Millie joins me under the showerhead, wrapping her arms around my waist and gluing her body to mine.

*We're married.*

Millie is my wife, and tomorrow, Kane will officially be ours.

Life is funny like that. One never knows how it will turn out.

We sway together under the hot water for a long while, her gently scraping her nails along my back, me playing with the ends of her hair. When I adjust the temperature to cool the water a bit, I spy a neon orange dildo suctioned to the wall and nearly choke as I inhale a mouthful of water.

"Where did that come from?" I sputter.

"It's new. Do you like it? It's your favorite color." She flicks the tip with one finger, letting it reverberate like a door stopper. *Damn, the hold that thing has on the tile is impressive.*

"Is this what you had in mind when you mentioned my Mary Poppins bag?" she asks with a mischievous grin.

"Depends on what you plan on doing with it."

She squirts a dollop of soap from the container attached to the wall and lathers her chest, the suds immediately sluicing down her teardrop breasts. "I'm going to fuck it while I suck your cock. Is that okay?"

Her eyes dart to my hardening dick, where she gets her answer.

After we've soaped up and rinsed off, I spin her and instruct her to place her hands on the tile. Then I push on her lower back. Obediently, she bends over, her perfect ass on display.

Lowering to my knees, I spread her cheeks and swirl my tongue against the pleated aperture.

## For the Show

She bucks her hips in response, her audible pleasure echoing off the tiles. "Fuck, that feels good, baby."

I smack her ass, then knead her flesh, my fingers struggling for purchase against her slick skin.

Upright again, I turn her to face me and drink her in. She's already removed her makeup, and her flushed face has never looked prettier.

She grips my cock, lazily stroking it between us, my piercings rubbing against her beautiful belly. Fuck, I have to rest my hands against the wall behind her to keep my knees from buckling.

Just when I think I may come from this hand job alone, she pushes me back. She leans out of the shower stall and returns with a travel-size bottle of lube. Once she's coated the orange dildo with a liberal amount, she rubs the remainder onto herself. She gives my chest another gentle push, and I willingly take a step back, giving her room to bend over. Before I have a chance to see the dildo slide inside her, she's gripping my hips and sucking my cock between her lips.

"*Fuck*, Millie," I groan. I gather her wet hair into a ponytail and hang on for dear life. "That's it, little wife. You suck my cock so good."

I thrust, and she gags. But when I pull back, she digs her nails into my skin and suctions harder. She may not cook, but she sure can suck a cock.

Every time I buck my hips, it forces the dildo deeper inside her. God, spit-roasting her like this has tingles shooting up my spine. "Mmm, baby. You look so gorgeous taking a dick in your pussy and a dick in your mouth at the same time."

She pulls off me with a loud *pop*. "Who said it was in my pussy?"

Body going rigid, I release her hair. *The fuck?*

Still bent over, she gazes up at me with enough fire in her eyes to burn down an entire city.

"You mean it's in your—"

She nods.

I glide a hand down her back and slip one finger between her cheeks until I bump into the silicone dick where it's lodged in her ass.

With a primal growl, I lift her up by the shoulders. She rises on her toes, adjusting to this new position with a moan.

"Who said you could do that? That ass is mine. *Mine.*"

The heat in her eyes only blazes brighter. She knew this would rile me up.

"The only cock fucking that ass tonight is mine. Got it?"

Her eyes flit to my mouth then back to my eyes. "Yes."

"Yes, what?"

"Yes, Daddy."

"That's my perfect girl." I pinch her nipple, earning a sharp gasp.

I turn the water off, then step out of the shower first and wait with an open towel as she carefully removes the silicone toy. We're only partially dry when I grab the bottle of lube and the bag of fun.

With the duvet pulled back and a towel covering the sheet, Millie lies on her back and rests her head on the pillows, waiting patiently, like the good girl she is.

"Lift up your hips," I instruct.

When she does, I prop a pillow under the towel, angling her for better access to her ass.

But first, I must please my wife.

I lie on my stomach, thankful for the pressure the mattress puts on my dick, then force her legs open so her glistening pussy is at my mercy. When I trail kisses along her inner thigh, she shivers. Once I reach the delicate crease of her groin, I move to her other thigh and start over. She's bucking her hips, fucking at nothing but air, keen for contact.

"What a greedy wife," I whisper across her core.

She thrusts her hips again, this time grazing my lips with her cunt.

She gets a slap to the clit for that one. But by the wild way she bucks in response, she loves it.

Finally, I put my mouth on her, sucking that bud between my lips and tugging.

Her body spasms, and my ego grows. As does my dick. My wife's not the only one who's desperate.

I lick and suck the delicate skin of her labia, alternating sides, then suction her clit and plunge two fingers inside. As she writhes, I flatten my tongue and let her undulate her hips the way she loves, never slowing my thrusting motion.

"That's it," she praises. "So close. Don't you dare fucking stop."

She clutches my hair, causing water droplets to drip down the side of my face.

Millie's movements grow erratic, and her climactic scream has me worried someone will call to check on us.

Once her legs have relaxed, I slide my fingers out and sit up on my haunches, stroking my length, coating myself in her juices, and watching the rise and fall of her flushed chest.

Hooking her feet behind me, she reels me in by my ass. I kiss her lips, then snag the lube and drip a generous amount between her legs and on my cock.

"Wait." She grasps my thigh, stilling me, then digs in the satin bag beside her. With a flourish, she presents me with a silicone cock. It's realistic, with veins and all, though it's smaller than mine.

I growl. "I told you, this ass is mine."

A wicked grin spreads across her face. "It's not for my ass."

My wife is full of surprises.

"Do you want what I think you want?" *Please say yes.* While we've agreed we're not interested in a real-life threesome, it doesn't mean we can't add a little extra fun.

We are good at pretending, after all.

Her nod alone may have me prematurely blowing a load all over her beautiful body.

Though the toy in the shower helped prepare her, I slowly feed my fat cock head inside her hole, careful not to go too hard too fast, especially with my piercings.

My dick whines in protest. *Lube and patience, my friend. Lube and patience.*

When her ass naturally sucks me inside, she hisses.

"Tell me if it's too much." Though she's never had to use our real safe word, I still check in.

"That hole opened up for you, didn't it?" She spreads her legs wider and teases her swollen clit with the dildo.

I settle in to the hilt, waiting for her to adjust to my size. Beneath me, she squirms, as impatient as my dick, but I hold steady, ensuring she's absolutely ready. "You look so pretty when you're aching for my cock."

"God dammit," she cries. "Fuck me already."

Easing over her gently, I nip at a spot on her neck near the star necklace she almost never takes off. "That's odd," I say against the shell of her ear, "I didn't hear 'please.'"

"Please, Husband. Please fuck my ass."

With precision, I slide out of the tight ring of muscle before dipping back in. Slow at first, then picking up speed once she's bearing down on me, desperate for more.

"Oh my god, oh my god," she pants.

The dildo is resting at the entrance to her pussy, just begging to be included. So I take it from her and rub it back and forth against her clit, then give it several rapid taps, followed by a strategic swirl.

"You're going to make me come again," she whines, her head tipped back.

"That's the point, honey. Let go."

Her breathing quickens as I continue to slap her clit with the dildo, and her ass grips my cock like a vise. It takes everything I have not to spill inside her as she rides out her short release.

*Fuck, she's stunning when she comes.*

She's barely come down from the high when I squirt another dollop of lube between us and onto the toy. I notch it at her opening, then slowly dip the tip into her pussy.

We both gasp at the intrusion.

"You sure you can take it?"

Her face is pinched in pleasure. "I can take it."

As I slide the dildo deeper, I feel every inch of it through the thin layer of muscle separating it from my cock. Both holes are stretched open wide, and fuck if it isn't the most provocative sight.

I pump the toy in and out, pleasuring us both at the same time, gritting my teeth in an effort not to rut into her.

After a moment, Millie takes over, holding the dildo in place and rotating and thrusting her hips between the two dicks.

"Fuck, honey. That feels good. Does it feel good for you too?"

She nods quickly, her movements jerky.

Sweat from my temple drops onto her chest as I hover over her, watching her every expression. When I weave my fingers through her free hand, anchoring myself to her forever, I moan.

"Louder," she commands.

"Mmm. You like when I moan for you, don't you, baby?"

"Best... sound... ever," she says between erratic thrusts.

Her grip on the dildo slackens a bit, signaling that she's close.

"C'mon, Wife." I'm barely holding on.

"I don't think I can," she cries. "I'm s-so sensitive."

"You've got this, Mills. One more. C'mon. Give it to Daddy."

She eases the dildo from her pussy and grabs me by the back of the neck, pulling me in until we're skin to skin. Mouth to mouth. With the absence of the toy, I sink farther inside her ass. The sensations amplify, sending me hurtling off the edge and unleashing the most intense orgasm of my life.

Millie groans and grunts as she grinds her clit up against my abdomen. I swallow every sound, tasting copper when she bites my bottom lip and rides out the waves of ecstasy.

I stay inside her for the span of several breaths, inhaling her plumeria perfume mixed with sweat, then very carefully slide out. My cum creaming out of her ass knocks the air from my lungs before I roll onto my back beside her.

She drapes a leg across my thighs and splays her hand over my blissfully beating heart.

"Thank you, honey." I flick a confetti penis off the back of her hand, then cover it with mine.

"What for?"

"For agreeing to be my wife." I kiss the top of her head. "For real this time."

"I'd say yes to you every day, for the rest of my life."

**One Last Thing**

Want to read the full LULU script that Ezra was listening to? Scan the QR code to find out. (It's spicy!)

Come hang out in Katie's Chaos Crew on Facebook and interact with Katie. Early announcements, exclusive content, bonus giveaways, and so much more!
*Come for the chaos. Stay for the happy ending.*

Be sure to sign up for Katie's newsletter on her website so you never miss a thing about Ezra, Millie, and the upcoming All for Love series.

Did you love the book? Please consider leaving a review and telling a friend. This is super helpful to indie authors.

# Also by Katie Van Brunt

### *For the Plot*

*Cam and Joey's story is available in paperback, on Kindle Unlimited, and performed in duet narration on Audible.*

In a story of serendipity and personal growth, two individuals' lives will intersect in the most unexpected way.

Joey Beckham exudes creativity and independence. She's about to embark on a once-in-a-lifetime vacation, fulfilling her late father's dream of visiting the Greek island of Crete. But Joey's world is flipped upside down when she discovers a heart-wrenching betrayal.

Cam Connelly is accustomed to taking care of others, but he desperately yearns to break away from his family's expectations and nurture desires of his own. Will he choose the life they set out for him or the path that fuels the spark in his soul?

Fate weaves its intricate web when Joey and Cam find themselves stranded on a picturesque Greek island. They must join forces to navigate their way home.

There's just one problem: The bed-and-breakfast has only one vacant room.

With one bed.

But it's fine. They'll never see each other again, right?

**Packed with laugh-out-loud humor, witty banter, and a whole lot of spice, *For the Plot* proves second chances are possible and that a person can pursue their dreams while sharing them with the people they love most.**

# Acknowledgements

Thank you, amazing reader. Whether you read For the Plot first, or this is your first taste of me (*smirks*), thank you for taking a chance. Whether you're here because you saw "double penetration with a toy" or "found family" or something in between on social media, or picked up this book because of the stunning cover, I appreciate you. I hope you stick around for more happily-ever-afters.

Alyx Levesque. Thank you for being an important person in my life. Should I tell everyone you're the inspiration for the disco ball vibrator? Also. I'm still waiting on that "fuck a chair" video. I love you.

Hannah Brixton. Thank you for subscribing to my one-woman podcast... aka voice memos. I've learned so much about myself through your empathy and commiseration. Thank you for making me feel seen when balancing writing and motherhood seems impossible. Here's to many more years of the raunchiest and most random convos that light up my life. (P.S. You're still funny.)

Ronnie Mathews. I truly don't know what I'd do without you. Thank you for always knowing the right thing to say at the right time. You keep me grounded and sane, and do it in the most gentlest of ways. I'm never letting you go! Talk to you in five minutes after writing this...

Lauren Gnapi. Thank you for putting up with me! For your

patience when I want to change a design—yet again. Thank you for driving to my first ever book signing. I'll never stop holding that memory as one of my favorites. I love sharing all my "firsts" with you.

Beth. Please never leave me, m'kay? Thank you for polishing my writing without smearing my voice, for taking the time to educate me, and for never making me feel bad about overusing my emotional support exclamation points!!!

Brooklyn. I'm so glad I got to work with you. I'm grateful for your expertise, attention to details, and your willingness to walk me through last-minute details.

My alphas, betas, and sensitivity readers: Albany, Bee, Cata, Chase, Jenn, Jenny, Jordan, Kayla P., Kayla R., Lauren, Lottie, Malia, Nik, Nora, Riya, Ronnie, and Stacey. This book would be nothing without you. Or rather, it would be good but it wouldn't be GREAT. I'm forever appreciative of your time and attention... and every unhinged comment!

The Smuttering. Hands-down the best group chat. I literally don't know what I would do without your support, girl-butt pics, and "why is this five hours long" reels. You give me life and I love you all.

Good Girls Write Lots of Words writing sprint accountability group. Thank you for every gold star and "good girl" meme. You helped me finish writing For the Show earlier than I planned.

KVB's Street Peen (like a Street Team, but spicer). MY PRETTY PEENS! I don't deserve you. Thank you for every like, comment, share, edit, reel, and feral reaction. I'll never be able to repay you for your generosity. I'm the luckiest girl to have you all by my side.

ARC Readers. Thank you for taking a chance on me. I screenshot every kind word/review for when imposter syndrome strikes. Thank you for your thoughtful praise and support.

Alex Taylor. Thank you for helping your elder millennial with all the technology. You helped streamline so many things for me. I love that you never gatekeep. (FYI: Alex is the only reason you're able to sign up for the bonus content, because I couldn't figure it out!)

Jordana Blake. Thank you for the personalized spreadsheets that keep me organized. I would be so overwhelmed without your generosity.

Tisa Matthews. For encouraging and convincing me that making time for my physical health would actually boost my creativity and help me write more words. I didn't want to believe you but you were right.

Morgan @what.she.shelved. Thank you for the gorgeous edits! You've taken a huge weight off my shoulders and I'm so grateful.

To every independent bookstore who took a chance on me. You've made my dream of seeing my books on shelves come true.

Hailey Dickert and Scribbles Bookshop. For being the first person to sell my books. I don't know what I'd do without your voice memos filled with validation, support, encouragement, and "what the actual fuck?" Love you, twinsie.

Alexis Paige and JF Harding, and Gin Hannon at PinUp Audio. You brought Joey and Cam to life in For the Plot and couldn't have been more perfect. (If you haven't listened yet... run!)

Mom. Thank you for reminding me that I can get through hard things because I've done it before. I love you.

Dad. *May your memory be a blessing.* I miss you.

Kids. Sorry, but you still can't read Mama's books. Thank you for your patience with me, and for being my mini marketing crew when we're in public. Also, I appreciate you for always being on "cock patrol" and protecting me when there are too many damn roosters in Hawaii.

Blake. My real life Dr. Book Daddy Husband. Thank you for keeping me fed and alive. Quite literally couldn't do this without you. Thank you for all the times you said "yes" when I asked, "Can I use that for the book?" Maybe I should have made you co-author. You are my Everything and I love you.

## About the Author

Katie Van Brunt writes steamy rom-com stories with banter and lots of texts on page. She's a total mood reader, has a love-hate relationship with spin class, and is working on being more spontaneous.

Before writing romance, she was a dance and yoga instructor. Originally from Florida, she has also lived in California, North Carolina, Virginia, and the island of Crete in Greece, but she currently resides in O'ahu, Hawai'i with her husband and three children—until their next adventure.

www.katievanbrunt.com

Printed in Great Britain
by Amazon